PRAISE FOR JEMIAH JEFFERSON AND *VOICE OF THE BLOOD*!

"Die-hard vampire fans are going to love it!"
—*Hellnotes*

"Jemiah Jefferson has proven herself as an
author to watch with this novel. If you let *Voice of
the Blood* get under your skin, you'll be hooked."
—*Horror World*

"Jemiah Jefferson [is] a welcome voice
in character-driven horror fiction."
—*Gothic.net*

"Jemiah Jefferson draws us into an erotic,
violent and tragic world of vampires.... *Voice of
the Blood* delivers all the bittersweet irony and
tragedy requisite of modern Gothic horror."
—*Dark Realms*

THE MOMENT OF HIS CREATION

She pressed her lips against the side of my neck, and I felt a minute pinch as her teeth nipped me. I stroked the bones of her spine with my fingertips for a moment before I lost all will and ability to move, unable to do more than emit a deep sigh. I heard nothing but the sweet low throbbing of blood against my eardrums.

"What have you done," I whispered, my voice too slight to make a question.

"I saved you," she said. She kissed me, pushing the taste of my own blood into my mouth. How delicious it was, ripe with cognac. "You will never again be alone, my sweet boy," she whispered with a kiss.

Of course I believed her. And she spoke truth indeed. But I did not yet know the face of the murderous desire that would become my constant companion, did not feel the velvet noose that would strangle me, nor hear the lover's whisper of the guillotine that would sever me from my soul.

And the darkness consumed me.

Other books by Jemiah Jefferson:

WOUNDS
VOICE OF THE BLOOD

FIEND

JEMIAH JEFFERSON

LEISURE BOOKS NEW YORK CITY

To my dead homies:
Julia Margaret Harrison
Rich Will Powers
Rocio Q. Kosok
You made me greater than I ever imagined possible.

A LEISURE BOOK®

April 2005

Published by

Dorchester Publishing Co., Inc.
200 Madison Avenue
New York, NY 10016

ISBN 0-8439-5364-0

The name "Leisure Books" and the stylized "L" with design are trademarks of Dorchester Publishing Co., Inc.

Printed in the United States of America.

Visit us on the web at www.dorchesterpub.com.

ACKNOWLEDGMENTS

Enormous thanks to the people without whom I could not have completed this book: my benefactor, Jon Lasser; my beloved readers, Cecilia, Myrlin, Blossom, and Sedona; Dr. Carol Timpone and the interns at the Pacific University Vision Center, for taking care of my eye; my editor, Don D'Auria, and the cool folks working at Leisure; Mom and Dad and Terry and Gary and Joey, for being proud to be related to me; and to all my friends and fans—thank you for sticking with me.

Ho con me l'inferno mio.
I have my own hell inside me.
—*Ranieri di Calzabigi*, Orfeo e Euridice

PROLOGUE
The Coffin

My God—give me light!

The coffin is smaller than I had imagined it would be. The silence screams in my ears, and only a faint whisper of air leaks through a hairline fissure in the unvarnished wood. My heart has not beat in so long, I can no longer remember how that feels. And yet I lie awake, staring at nothing. No light can reach my eyes here in the crypt; and yet I see. I do not breathe, and yet I breathe. I am neither asleep nor awake.

I am certainly not dead.

It has been a long time since I heard the faint scraping sounds of Father Christopher cleaning mortar from the last sepulchral brick, his whisper of the Final Rites, and his quiet, vanishing footsteps away. I do not hear him anymore. I do not miss him. But I could smell the track the tear made, cleansing a path down a dusty, unshaven cheek, and felt my own eyes ache in sympathy.

I was his friend, as much as he is mine.

And yet I smelled his tears, and my stomach clenched with hunger for his blood.

I imagined springing onto his neck, where the red furze of his beard grew sporadically, and before he could draw another mournful breath, ripping into his throat, spilling his life into my mouth. The taste of the sea, the scent of human terror, just barely thicker than water, indelible, infinite, the taste of God Himself—

No! No more of these thoughts! I will end this!

I am a murderer, demon-possessed, a monster, an unnatural, accursed fiend. I know that with the same certainty that I know that I am a man. But, indeed, am I even still a man? I am no longer human. My humanity was taken from me.

No, I gave it willingly. God forgive me. I remember.

That is why I am here, now, in this narrow pine box on a shelf, in the catacombs below an English cathedral. I seek to protect humanity, to protect the Father Christophers, to defend the lamb against the leopard, the vicious slinking predator inside me. I will suffocate this beast. I shall die at last.

Time for my rest, Lord. Please allow me to close my eyes and not open them again, even if it is only to be cast immediately into Hell. I have sinned too often, and too wickedly, for me to expect otherwise. But have I not made penance enough? Am I not allowed, even so, to seek forgiveness? Do mankind's rules even still apply to me?

I am tired. I am one hundred forty years old, and I am tired. Please, Lord, I am tired; I humbly beg you to let me sleep, to know a final oblivion.

I wished that everyone I loved would live forever and never be taken from me. Please forgive me.

I wished for extraordinary mysteries to be revealed. I wanted to know everything. I wanted to be everything. Please forgive me.

I wished the devil's inexorable powers of temptation. Please.

I wanted to be a god.

No. No longer. I want nothing, except an ending. The ultimate denial. I am finished. I am ready to leave the party; I am weary and I want to go home. I want to return to the earth from whence I came, pull up a coverlet of earth and stone, and know no more of myself or anything else.

Please, let me die.

I don't even know if that's possible.

My eyes remain open.

Recommendation of a Departing Soul

What is this, this disease, this mutation, this deformity, this insanity, this vampirism? What is it, truly, that has refused, for twice the age of a man, to release me? What kind of monster have I become, that my prayers to the Mother of Mercy go ignored?

I was not born this way. I was created. I was given this warped form, these desires, as an act of love, of hunger, and of power over the weak-minded. For (it is true) all mortals are weak-minded to the vampire. I offered no resistance—no, not at all! I leapt into the arms of perdition with an exceptional zeal. But I was heading there, even before. I have never been virtuous. Compassionate, perhaps. Generous, absolutely. And I have continued to observe my sacred duty, even broken and bloodstained. I take Communion, I ask liturgical counsel, I seek absolution. My beads are even now wrapped around my hands, my index finger resting on the yellowed ivory crucified body of Our Lord.

Credo in Deum Patrem omnipotentem. Amen.

But there has not ever been a catechism written for

my kind. I may well be the only blood-drinker who has ever had the Rites performed for him; the rest simply perish, undoubtedly horribly, in fire and misery. Or perhaps they do not perish at all, and go on living, trapped in a cage of rotting meat and silk, as I do, praying for my thoughts to cease.

There are so many more things, now that it's too late, that I would like to ask Father Christopher about. . . .

I felt him anointing my eyelids with oil as I lay paralyzed in the coffin, and I know by his thoughts (wavering like words written in mist on a mirror) that he wondered if the consecrated oil would burn or blister my skin. Father Christopher had to see for himself if I was the kind of monster I confessed to him that I was. (Foolish man; did he not recall seeing me take the Body and Blood every Saturday night for the last five years? Surely he could not be deceived by penny-dreadfuls and picture shows? I have a higher opinion of him than that!) When nothing happened, his relief was so palpable that I let out a faint wheeze of a sigh. And then, if I am not mistaken, Father Christopher jumped back two feet and wet his pants.

Earlier, he had pushed back my lips for a closer look at my four sharp fang teeth, no longer subtle, easily concealed points, but grown long and savage with age. He wondered how he had never noticed this unmistakable sign of my true nature before. He lifted my hand and squeezed my wrist in vain, searching for a discernible pulse. He pushed back my eyelids to look closely into my unfocused eyes. I perceived a dull glow, nothing more, but I sent my thoughts into his mind, requesting that he stop. I am not certain that he knew that it was my ethereal interjection, but he let my eyelids relax, and then began daubing oil on my bare chest, over my motionless heart.

That was not the first time I frightened him, but he

never pissed himself like that before. Perhaps my true nature didn't seem real until he thought I was dead—that he had performed the Unction and offered me indulgences and prayers as I breathed my last. I had looked dead for two days—and then I moved, and showed him that I somehow still live.

He did finish the Rites, finally, though it took him almost an hour to grasp the courage to return. Good lad. Seal the box, lay the bricks. Walk away. Say nothing to anyone about the fate of that strange, sick young man who lurked around the rectory, or the new wall of fresh bricks.

I am sorry, Father Christopher, that you had to do this. But I am grateful that you did.

But perhaps you ought to have given in to that impulse that flickered across your mind, and burned me alive. . . .

Descendit ad inferna.

The Lord descended into Hell.

I don't know how long ago I stopped having any sense of my legs, or the ability to turn my head or flex my wrists. It could be days or weeks or years. The animation has gone from me, but my thoughts race more vividly than ever. I am powerless to stop it. Once, I could have distracted myself with the concerns of the concrete; but deprived of sense and action, the mind endlessly reflects itself to itself.

How is it that, the weaker my body grows, the recollections of my past strengthen and dominate? Have I made the transition from grave to cradle? How is it that the oppressive blackness of the crypt fills my sight-starved mind with brilliant, buttery sunshine, my isolation gives birth to visions of rosy-cheeked and vexatious sisters, the priests and peasants of the village of Piedmonte, my father with a face like carved stone, my mother's calm smile? Are my eyes truly open? Where I should see the void, I see the farm, a patchwork of olive groves, vineyards, and silky rolling hills.

How could I have forgotten what was in my blood?

I did have a childhood, once upon a time, and a happy, warm, and fortunate one, at that. Indeed, I was spoiled and insulated, and inevitably, ferociously dissatisfied! I was sick of the blanketing scent of sheep shit, yeast, and grapes, the humble limestone village church, the sun-roasted skin of the villagers employed by my father, the skim-milk complexions of my sisters. I longed, desperately, for a different life—a life of adventure, poetry, sailing on the *Argo* in the guise of my namesake, battling at Jason's side. My brilliant music and angelic voice would charm the very stones themselves. Instead, I was just an ordinary boy with an unremarkable treble and clumsy fingers. As far as I am able to determine, I was not extraordinary in my level of youthful folly, yet how depraved it seems, seen through the lens of age and care.

Why do we long for that which we can never have? Had I remained a human, the one thing assured me was my death. Now? I don't know. Perhaps this is my penitence—an eternity of remembrance, the golden thoughts of Campania just out of reach, my Tantalus heart thirsting for that sunlight, that stability, and those troublesome girls.

Four sisters had preceded me into the world: Maria Elena, Anna, Venetia, and Mirabella. My childhood was crowded with girls, and all their vexing habits and mysterious scents, their hysterias, and their inabilities. And they were all bigger than I was, as though my father's virility had been used up by the time I was conceived!

There had once been a brother, firstborn, even before my sisters, named Vittorio, after my father. He died in infancy, before any of us were born, but he would never be forgotten; my mother and father spoke of him frequently, and made it plain that they considered Vittorio to have been the best of us. "If Vito was here, he would be grateful to his father for the opportunity to study the piano," my father said. "He would fight to defend the honor of his family! He would have grown up to be a strong fellow, not a sissy!" To my mother, Vittorio was more precious than diamonds and as virtuous as a saint. "He was such a wonderful child, he was a pink-edged rose—eyes like the sea—as good as gold." My sisters and I had no choice but to believe every word our parents said, as they seemed mouthpieces of God himself. We knew no other truth. Vittorio had been called back by the angels before sin could mar his perfection.

Not so, the subsequent son.

Oh, but my mother, the former second-string contralto at the Venetian Opera, possessed the same romantic temperament as myself, presented with a beautiful turn of phrase and a rich imagination. She had given me a demigod's name and a fool's capacity for fantasy. Her stories of "Vito," describing him in vivid detail, adventures that he would have, things that he would say, thrilled me as I sat at her knee. Her tales recreated my lost brother so beautifully that I could see him before me as though he had never died, and an eldest brother lived among us. I wanted to see him so badly, I willed him into being. But only I could really see him. Mama spoke of him, but she did not allow herself to truly believe. I became obsessed with proving his existence to her. But how could I make him appear?

He would be tall, with dark hair, and luminous eyes the blue color of my mother's Roman glass perfume bottle. He would be slim but vigorous, rakish and gallant: a gifted horseman, a brilliant conversationalist, skilled with the rapier, and as agile as a monkey. He loved me completely, and I him. We were inseparable companions. I cut my hands and licked at the resulting blood, shuddering with nauseous joy at the flavor, knowing that it was my brother's blood I tasted. While at play, I lowered my voice to a manly growl when I wanted him to answer; he would always say what I most wanted to hear. How I despise the moment when we were interrupted in the middle of an adventure in the undercupboards, and the glorious Vittorio dissipated back into nothingness and idle fancy!

"Talking to yourself, rabbit? Only lunatics and idiots do that," Mirabella said, and Anna and Venetia echoed her, their giggles rising in pitch, until I ran away, determined not to show them my frustrated, shameful tears. I knew I could never explain to those three . . . *If only Vito would come and teach them a stern lesson . . . But he won't.*

He is dead and he will never grow up. But I must.

But when I grow up, no one I love will ever die. I'll make sure of it.

Yes, I remember.

And then Elena came and met me on my miserable way back to the nursery, and gave me the bowl of goat's milk and honey I had desired, without my ever having to speak it aloud to her, or even think of it in detail myself. Elena just knew. She kissed me on the mouth, tousled my hair, and went away. I sighed for her. Was that the moment when I began to recognize my desire for her, when we had been at innocent play for years previous?

Elena—milk and honey remade in human form! Her abundant, curling, carnelian-red hair always strayed free from any constraints, and loosed from its pins, caught and caressed the air as she departed. I ached to run after her and cling to her legs, but I turned away, my ears burning, knowing that I was too old to hide in her skirts, that I must stand on my own. But oh, I wanted to pursue. I wanted to lose myself in her.

Rather, I simply lost myself. And I lost her as well.

My Elena! What I have given to see you again, even in my memories!

If only she had been a man—as the eldest, the farm would have been hers . . . but had she been a brother, and not Elena, would she have taught me, shared with me, what she had? Would I have loved her so completely, without thought of taboo? Would I have loved Vittorio the same way?

Can I undo the memories of such passion, such splendid pleasure? If I do, will my soul be saved?

. . . I have nothing left but the last fragment of hope. I am where I am now because of it.

Heavenly Father, give me the strength to detest this sin, for I have lacked it thus far. Father Christopher told me that it is not too late. I must share his faith. I shall not sin again. I will slip away in a state closer to Grace.

Why do I not slip away?

Olive Oil

I feel the darkness choking me, but I cannot move. I cannot fight it. I am lost to the world of men and beasts. I just wish I were unaware.

This is the true face of Purgatory, this utter solitude, longing to touch, feel, breathe, love again, strangled in these memories, terrifying in their vivid clarity. I have thought on my birthplace, but without such crystalline recall of every molecule, every thought, every motivation. I did not see it in its fullness before. I am blessed with hindsight, and perhaps only true repentance standing between me and Heaven? Wash away my sins, as I see them so clearly.

Grant me the strength to despise them.

But oh, sometimes I still miss him, even after every crime he committed against me and against God.

How can I still want to feel love when it brought me to this? My God. My God. I cannot bear more. Help me. Let me feel that Heaven is near.

Light a candle for me, Father Christopher.

* * *

I have been trying to resist recalling Lorenzo, but I must follow where God leads me, through the tangled thicket of my past. Lorenzo, of whom I never wanted to think again. But there he is, as clear as if I had seen him yesterday—those eyes, that Giaconda smile, the sculpted valley between nose and lips, the outsized hands resting folded on the pommel of the saddle, or jerking Metafora's reins so cruelly that I prayed for the lean gray mare to throw him. Poor Metafora, as trapped in the servitude of love as myself.

A love misplaced, for all the ages!

If blame can be assigned beyond myself for my current state, it rests on his shoulders. But is it worthwhile to blame one, undoubtedly, so long dead? I only wish I had killed him myself.

No, I mustn't think that way.

I was young, vulnerable, and impressionable. That, I will allow.

I was fourteen years old, my voice beginning to break, freshly confirmed. (Adding to my middle name of Giuseppe, I took the name Vittorio, so as to keep my brother with me. Till my own death do us part.) Father decided that I ought to be educated beyond what the nuns at the village school could provide; I would learn languages and literature and manners. However, my father liked to do things on the cheap, so the formal education of my sisters was halted to further my own. I was to have a young Socrates all to myself.

I could hardly eat or sleep while waiting for him to arrive. My own tutor! Fencing, Juventius, and English! And best of all, I would not be separated from Elena, my lioness. She was eighteen years old, taller even than Father, possessed of a splendid womanly form, with an air of impatient toughness that I found utterly captivating. Elena had not married, though she had refused suitor after suitor. "I shall marry for love," she declared. "And

I love no one as I love my family and the farm," she added, kissing my father. Father shrugged, his cheeks pinkening with pleasure, his arm passing around her soft shoulders for a brief embrace. "Therefore, I shall never leave—and do not ever send Orfeo away, either."

"He shall have to go sometime," my father said, his eyes piercing me. "He'll want to."

Yes, I thought, *I shall. But not yet.*

I would remain Elena's skinny little hare, her baby brother plaything, for as long as I could.

He arrived, at last, in midmorning, in the brilliant, hot, early autumn, during the olive harvest.

My father clearly resented having to take the time to meet my tutor, in the middle of the morning during one of the busiest times of the year, when there was so much money to be made, and such important management in progress. But the crop was of an unprecedented abundance; my father was, despite himself, almost relaxed. "Orfeo, you will not ruin this," he said, straightening the lapels of my stiff new wool jacket. "You are a good scholar; I can see that. But I have seen you take your studies far too lightly, and you seem to have a hard time concentrating and staying out of trouble. You care more about your paints than you do about arithmetic, but paintings and poems will not keep this farm prosperous. Do you understand me? You will respect this instructor. He comes highly recommended by the tutors at the royal court. You will do as he says, or face very grave consequences."

"Yes, Father, I understand," I said humbly. The smell of the wool, dampened with my own sweat, made me dizzy, itchy, and hungry. I suddenly did not want to see this teacher; I wanted dinner, with long cool drafts of village barley-ale.

"Send him in," said my father to the housemaid.

A very young man—barely older than myself—strode in, smartly dressed, slightly strutting, his hat held firmly under his left arm. He stopped and clicked his heels with military precision, and saluted my father. "Captain Ricari. It is an honor to meet you at last. I look forward to the benefits of being in your employ." My father appeared bemused but unmoved. Then the young fellow turned to me and hinted at a bow. A dimple as deep as an arrow's wound creased his left cheek. He said:

"My name is Lorenzo Mercetti d'Aragón. I am your instructor."

How instantaneously I fall in love, and how ignorant I am of having done so!

His greatest knowledge lay in both classical and contemporary literature, and he read, wrote, and spoke Latin, Greek, French, and English as well as the Italian vernacular. Though he was well-versed in strategy, mathematics, and the concrete sciences, he strove to turn my mind to philosophy, sensing fertile ground in my introspection.

Lorenzo had developed, he said, his own academics.

"An emphasis on Plato," he said, smiling at me. "The Greeks. There is more sense, and beauty, there, that (I know well) you cannot imagine yet."

After a few days under his mannered yet deft tutelage, I was thoroughly dazzled by him. What an incredible example of young manhood! So intellectually superior, so well-traveled, so well-spoken, so unbelievably handsome! Lorenzo was a highly educated prodigy, having studied in Vienna and Geneva as well as Naples. Orphaned in infancy, a squandered family fortune had ended in bankruptcy, and he was raised as a ward of the court of Queen Caroline. When Napoleon handed Joachim Murat the throne of Naples, the young Mercetti found himself cast off. Rather than assume the training of a military officer, he now employed himself as a tutor for wealthy and noble families. Or that was his plan, at any rate; the Ricari heir was his very first assignment. "But I shall have more appointments, so, Master Orfeo, you must study well to secure my reputation."

Cocksure. That is the word to describe it. His overwhelming egotism was exhilarating. Every word seemed like a slap in my father's stoic face, and I loved it. Yet I saw my father charmed, despite himself, by Lorenzo as well. And of course, Mamma and the sisters fawned over him. He was a magnet for women. He was tall, sky-eyed, with thick waves of jet-black hair and eyebrows heavy on sculpted bones, and a low, purring voice with a faint laugh in it at all times.

But when I thought of Elena's inevitable attraction to him, and her nubile status, I felt a sense of crushing panic. How could she resist this exceptional young man? She could not, any more than he could resist that beautiful, passionate, yet sensible girl. And over dinner, they talked and laughed freely, her eyes aglow as she gazed at him across the table. She would marry him, and they would both desert me! I could barely wet my lips with the soup, when I usually devoured as much as I could get.

I lay awake that night less than a week after Lorenzo's arrival, scrambling my bedclothes; too hot to sleep, my mind in turmoil. Whenever I closed my eyes, I saw Elena lying beneath the handsome tutor, her columnar white legs gripping him about the waist, and his big lips devouring the flesh of her neck. Part of me wanted to scream, and part of me wanted this event to happen so I could see it in reality.

At last I threw the sheets away from me, and dashed to the girls' room in my nightshirt and bare feet. I tiptoed to Elena's bedside, careful to avoid the creaky spots on the floor, and shook her shoulder until she opened her eyes.

She followed me downstairs and outside the house. A glinting eyeball of full moon stared from a cloudless sky, so bright that the stars hung back. Elena gazed at the moon for a moment, then turned to me. "What is it, Feo?" Her voice was husky with sleep.

The pleas dried on my lips, and I suddenly felt very foolish. "I just don't want to lose you, that's all."

"You won't," she said. She put her arms round me. "Don't let Father scare you. He's just blowing hot air."

"No, no, it's not that. Uh . . . I mean . . . Lorenzo," I stammered, my voice squeaking like a rusty third wheel.

She poked me gently in the chest. "What's that, rabbit? Sometimes you make no sense at all when you talk, Feo! No wonder everyone thinks you're a fool! What in the world do you mean? Lorenzo? You mean the tutor?" She stood back and gave me a dubious, crooked smile. "What of him? That overdressed pretender.—Oh! Oh. Now I see. Oh, Orfeo. You really *are* a fool." And she threw her head back and laughed, but then fell silent and embraced me. "Orfeo . . . love me, but do not desire me. I am already yours. And you know you cannot have me. Not truly."

And she did not resist me when I caressed her, but at once led me back into the house, and back into my own room. I climbed into bed and gazed at her, resplendent, moonlight bleaching her freckles as they had intimidated the stars, and for a moment she was Venus, come to bestow passionate love upon me. But she bade me lie down, and drew the sheets over me. "Go to sleep," she said. "And put that nonsense out of your head. The idea that I could love a beggarly sophist is ridiculous. He may have fooled Father, but you cannot deceive a woman in such a way."

"I wish you would get into bed with me," I murmured. My voice came out as the clear baritone where it would eventually settle.

"And sometimes you say exactly what you mean in the clearest possible terms." She smiled at me. "Not tonight. Go to sleep. Now. And I'll see you in the morning."

We never touched again after that night.

And, miraculously, I hardly ever consciously thought of her in that carnal fashion after I fell asleep that night. She became just another sister, albeit a superior one; and no longer did I long, night and day, for her touch, or the sight of her bare skin. I knew that I would never experience it again. And yet I would, in my mind and heart, again and again, like an old wound that aches though not even a scar remains visible.

Lorenzo looms up in my recollection, overwhelming the memory of Elena, like the dark cloud of coal smoke that obscures the sun over factory villages, until no one living there remembers the days when the skies were clear. Lorenzo consumes me now as he did then.

As soon as my father was satisfied that Lorenzo D'Aragón was capable of teaching me the calculus of Archimedes and the levels of Dante's *Inferno*, he left us unsupervised in the garret on the top floor of the house, facing toward the vineyards. Immediately, Lorenzo's demeanor changed; he flung his coat across the table and loosened his shirt collar. "Enough of parabolas and vertices. Let's go outside," he said to me with a wink, and I happily leapt from my chair, hastening to gather my books and pens. He stopped me with a pressure of his hand on my wrist. "No, no, leave that. We won't need those. Have you a horse?"

I did: a stocky, brown gelding named Prego who had seen some years beyond my own. When I was a child, I fantasized that Prego was a winged creature, or a gryphon, or at least of a hue that could be romantically described as "chestnut"; but alas, Prego was nothing more than a brown, fat old eunuch of a horse. Of course, the young Mercetti was superior in this area as well. "This is Metafora," Lorenzo boasted, currying the sides of a sleek young mare the color of polished lead. "She does as I say, as all ladies should do."

I thought that was the cleverest thing I had ever heard.

We rode far that day, all around the boundaries of the family farm, from orchard to vineyard to sheepfold, he reciting English poetry, I mesmerized by the clipped, yet flowing, sound of his voice. "That is Lord Byron," he told me. "Someday, you will learn to understand and love him as I do. He is a great hero of our times."

I devoured every word and nourished my young soul with it, though I had no real idea what Lorenzo was talking about.

"Have you visited the olive press?" I said. He admitted that he had not, and I quivered with happiness for being able to show him something he had not yet seen.

The Fattorio di Ricari was primarily known for providing the olive oil that was used in Holy Rites. The Archbishop of Naples used our oil, as did nearly every other holy man in south-coastal Italy. At the far edge of the farm, past the orchards, olives were pressed, and the resulting oil which was carted to Naples and then exchanged for quantities of gold and political power. The oil had made my father wealthy, and his connection with former Navy sailors created an entire network of influence up and down the coast and in Sicily. The barn that housed the olive press had been off-limits to me during my early childhood; I should not have been going there even at fourteen, but I had to show off something.

Lorenzo was enchanted with this little olive-oil factory, intoxicated with the stench of fresh olive pulp. He loved to stand on the upper floor of the building, bellowing Greek oratories on the benevolent nature of olive oil at the dozen bemused villagers laboring below, while I sat patient and awestruck, drinking in his every word and gesture. Even in winter, when there were no olives to press, Lorenzo and I ate, drank wine, talked, and practiced fencing there. Many of our lessons were held there, far away from the oppressive and familiar atmosphere of the house. He taught me all sorts of things: how to smoke tobacco from a pipe, how to play cards, how to cheat. All sorts of things.

In the spring of my sixteenth year, when the olive blossoms sprayed thickly upon the branches—

Oh God, I still feel it. I still feel it even in my grave. Pray for us sinners, now, and at the hour of our death.

Father Christopher insists. Confess. But are they my sins? Is it my duty to confess the sins of others?

But they are my sins, as well.

"Recall your studies," Lorenzo said to me. "And trust that I know best for you."

He faced me toward the rough stucco wall of the oil press. "Drop your trousers, please," he said mildly.

I was shocked and startled, but merely bit my lip and waited. I imagined that I was in for a beating, though there was no reason for it. I had well finished my assignments for the week. Still, sometimes I incurred a thrashing from Father for no other reason than my existence. "He does it because he loves you and wants you to be good," Mamma explained. I thought that an encouraging word would have done just as well, and taken less exercise besides.

I stood and waited for the blow from Lorenzo, but it never came.

Instead it was a cool, oily caress.

I jumped. "Sir—" I said apprehensively.

He held me fast, to keep me from turning around and looking at him. "You will not call me 'sir'—what, don't you trust me anymore? I'm Lorenzo. Your father is 'sir,' and I am definitely not your father." The restraining hand brushed against my right nipple, which bloomed into an almost painful sensitivity. No accident, this; his fingers found the left one, and twisted it through the linen of my blouse, much more roughly than Elena had ever done with her lovely feminine fingers.

Oh, Mother of God, forgive me. No coffin or crypt is cold enough. But oh—I do not want to think about it but I cannot stop it—

"Have you not recognized a part of yourself in Plato?" He squeezed me, and I gasped. "I have recognized it in *you*. Do I speak falsely?"

"No," I whispered.

"Now. Recall your studies. 'Phaedrus.' The speech of Lysias." Lorenzo's greasy, slippery fingers parted my backside with the gentle surety of pulling apart a loaf of soft bread, and poked a tender, sensitive place that I had never consciously known as a locus of pleasure. There is nothing that God has not made; all things are good in the sight of God; it is only in action, in intention, where God is displeased . . . but how could it not be constructed as a bundle of overwhelming sensations if that was not God's will? My breath came out shuddering with panic.

His fingers continued inside me, his warm breath, smelling of pipe smoke, against my nape.

No grave is deep enough.

" 'And I claim that I ought not to be refused what I ask because I am not your lover,' " Lorenzo whispered in my ear. "And next?"

He progressed. I did not know whether to throw him off, or beg him, for I knew not what.

" ' . . . For lovers repent of the kindnesses they have

21

done when their passion ceases; but there is no time when nonlovers naturally repent.'" My response came husky and halting.

Lorenzo pulled me sharply to him, and I felt the fullness, the rigidity, of another erect phallus, for the first time in my life. There is a vast difference in degree between my own hardness and that of someone else; when it is mine, my thoughts cloud, I have intentions, but I am in control of them and they can be cast away; when it is without, I have no control; I am seized with a giddy wildness, a recklessness. I want. I want so badly. And I did not even know that which I wanted until then.

Deliver us from evil: Amen.

Oh, but those hands, the scent of his breath, of his sweat!

"Recall your studies," came his whisper against the back of my ear. "Recite. And calm yourself. I don't want to hurt you." Rubbing himself, greased and urgent, between my buttocks, the fingers of one hand insisting farther inside me while the others clutched at my own sex, not agitating it, but simply grasping, pressing, cupping.

I could not recite the next lines. I felt a violent spasm take place inside me, a vague burst of fireworks against the black backdrop of my closed eyelids. His hands immediately left my sticky genitals and pushed me down onto my face into the sawdust. "Your lesson is over," he snapped at me. "Tomorrow, we will see if you can recall anything that I have taught you, including self-restraint."

Oh, Lorenzo.

I learned from you.

Not every day, as much as I wanted to increase my knowledge, to please him more and more, every day. Some days he was a dry, imperious instructor who rapped my palms with a ruler when my handwriting was sloppy or I yawned, and he seemed hardly the same person as the young rake who, drunk on the season's first wine, climbed trees and flashed his bare buttocks at the shepherdesses driving the Merino flocks back from the fields. I never knew which Lorenzo would present himself, and I prayed on bent knees every night that it could be my friend, my partner in crime, my playmate.

Yet our couplings were never playful. When he wanted me, Lorenzo was more the stern tutor than the rascal. He would slide his rigid member slowly— excruciatingly slowly—inside me, while I recited from the Dialogues (in Greek), Byron (in English), Tacitus (in Latin). He would not thrust, but remain as still as he could, sometimes gently coaching me if I forgot a word, softly nibbling the back of my neck and my shoulders. When I arched my back, begging him with my body, he would hold me still. He would force himself into me until I screamed from the pressure, the erotic agony; and my scream, always, would trigger his own climax.

After a season, we merely clutched each other close, nearly immobile, as joined as we could be, whispering the Dialogues to each other, pressed tight on a heap of coats in a small corner of the pressing barn, out of sight. There was no way we were out of hearing, though; although I no longer screamed, for I was no longer in any painful discomfort, our combined moans, though muted, must have been plainly audible to anyone in the vicinity. Yet we were never bothered. This is the advantage of privilege, the advantage of Italy, the advantage of the teacher-pupil relationship, with its very roots in the material of our studies.

I was not Lorenzo's "skinny little jackrabbit." I was his Phaedrus, his Ganymede, his wide-eyed boy. And he was my hero, my teacher, my lost brother, my lover, less impossible than Elena, more tangible than Christ.

I confessed it. I confessed it every single week to a

heavy sigh and a giant litany of penance. I must have lit ten thousand candles in three years, and though I prayed sincerely for the reformation of souls, I found that I simply could not find the Lord's disapproval of what I had with Lorenzo.

If I did not scream, he would not climax, and I kept the cries bottled in my throat for ages to keep him from ending it. Because when he was done, it was done, no matter what my state.

It was not as though I learned only the carnal arts from him (and those "arts," in hindsight, were minimal). By the time I was seventeen, I was fluent in English, Latin, and Greek, had committed to memory the complete published works of Byron, most of the *Iliad*, and several plays of Aristophanes; I had at last become a good horseman, and I had gained enough skill with a light sword to best my own father. But the passion was what I lived for. As the lover of his pupil, Lorenzo Mercetti had become a brilliant instructor. But I also know that our moments of carnality gave him a great deal of pleasure and satisfaction; I do not think he could have deceived me on that account.

On others . . .

I should have killed him.

No, I will no longer think that way.

Litany

In the unusually cold spring, the early months of 1816, Mamma had fallen gravely ill. First doctors were sent for, then priests.

Tensions ran high. I fought constantly with Father, both on my own behalf and that of Elena. Still unmarried, and the only daughter still at home, she desired my father's consent to manage the business while he better spent his time and energy maintaining his financial contacts in Naples and ensuring adequate care for my dying mother. Father refused to yield; the Fattorio would go to me, as the eldest surviving son, as much as he saw that I was unworthy. I wanted nothing to do with any business of any kind; I did not want to buy, or sell, or produce anything. I wanted only to think, read, paint, dream, make love. Father found this intolerable.

Lorenzo found Father's perspective intolerable. "Let Signorella Elena have the farm and free your son to have his heart's desire," he scoffed. "You'll only ruin him if you imprison him here."

Father swiftly found Lorenzo's presence intolerable.

"When you have a son, you'll understand," he replied. "But I do not imagine that you will have an heir to carry on the legacy of D'Aragón, will you? That is the problem with all overeducated men; their selfishness knows no bounds. But Orfeo is mine, and he will do as I wish him to; and the sooner you assist me, as you have been handsomely paid to do, in ridding him of these useless notions, the sooner you can move along and further your own career."

On a Thursday, I waited in the garret room for Lorenzo all morning, and when the clock struck noon, I went down to Mamma's bedroom to bring her a bowl of broth and a piece of bread. She lay supine on the great bed, her eyes focused on the ceiling, a ghastly grayish cast to her olive skin. Cancer of the womb had swiftly consumed her flesh and her strength. The parish priest, a sallow old man, did not look up from the translucent pages of his catechism when I came in. I knelt down and kissed her, holding my breath against the smell of her dying mouth.

"Dearest Mamma, did Father speak to you about Lorenzo? He did not arrive for our lesson today."

The priest glanced at me, then back at the Scripture. Doubtless my confessions regarding Lorenzo had amused him.

"He has been dismissed," Mamma said, looking at me with tear-filled, laudanum-glazed eyes. She was up to two hundred drops a day, which was clearly inadequate to relieve her pain. Her grip on my hand was like an iron manacle. "I am sorry, Feo; I know that you are very fond of your tutor, but your father has decided that you have learned enough from him." She paused to take a weak, painful cough, which dried the angry protests on my lips. "Your father has ridden to Naples to consult with Bishop Giambalvo; please do not tax his temper overmuch when he comes back. He would like for you to begin on the accounting tomorrow, before shearing time arrives."

I was filled with a rage I could not display. I kissed Mamma once more, raced downstairs, and found that Lorenzo had, after receiving my father's dismissal at the break of day, ridden to the village with all of his belongings. I saddled Prego and pursed.

I found Lorenzo in the southern of the two taverns, half through a jug of wine and a meal of anchovies, mutton, olives, and flatbread. I had anticipated that he would have a gloomy countenance, having just lost his employment; but rather the converse was true. He held court with several appealing, if slatternly, young women and a handful of soldiers, proudly bearing scars and tatters of skirmishes with Napoleon's forces. "Master Ricari!" he greeted me. "Join us in a drink to the Two Sicilies!"

"I will do no such thing," I responded. "That was artificially imposed; Naples is not part of Sicily and never will be." Everyone guffawed at my refusal to take a joke, and Lorenzo scooped his arms around my shoulders and made me sit next to him.

He had not been infuriated or saddened by his dismissal; he spoke frankly of his feelings toward my father, whom he saw as inflexible and backward-thinking, "unenlightened" as it were. "Besides, I am through with country living. I am returning to the beautiful city of Geneva," he declared. "I still have friends there who can offer me lodgings and entertainment. Do you want to come?"

It was as simple as that. He asked me, and I accepted without a second thought. I was eager to see the world, and even more eager to leave behind my mother's sickbed, my father's disapproval, and the only woman I had ever loved, who was forbidden by natural law to return my love. Here was an opportunity to escape. And I imagined that Lorenzo would never request my company if he did not love me as I did him.

Following Lorenzo's detailed instructions, I rode home, entered the house without undue notice, and packed a bundle of necessities—mostly money, some linens, and food. I also took one of Father's ornamental swords that I had always jealously longed for as a child, and which he would only rarely let me touch. The dirty excitement of my crime overwhelmed my senses, and I fled from the house without kissing my mother good-bye.

I do not think I really thought I was leaving for good. I was running away the way a petulant child runs away; nineteen years old, and sneaking out of the house with a vagrant's knapsack full of sweets, cheese, and a Ricari wine of Lorenzo's favorite vintage.

But as I prepared to mount Prego again, Elena appeared down the hill coming from the grape presses, a vision of amber and ivory with her coiffure frizzing undone, and a ledger book clutched under one arm. She saw me leaning against Prego's saddle with my bundle and my criminal's guilty slouch, and she froze and stared at me with an expression of alarm.

We did not speak. I all but heard her voice in my head: *How could you desert our mother? Our father? This place?* I almost broke then—almost dropped the bag and crawled under her skirt and cried—but I did not. Instead, I lifted my chin and set my face into what I felt a man's should look like. She offered half a smile but shook her head a little, her eyes limpid with tears.

I swung onto the gelding and kicked his flanks with all the viciousness of my guilt. I was oddly consumed with a desire to drink a cup of milk.

How I loved milk.

And how I longed for it after that day. Milk and

honey, pouring down my throat and pooling in my belly, spilling over my warm, sticky fingers.

After that day, I would never taste it again.

My lioness, I would never now leave you. My sunlight, I would give anything to blind myself with your glory. My mamma—

Mother of God, pray for us sinners, now and at the hour of our—

I should be so lucky.

At the beginning, my travels with Lorenzo were a delightful adventure; dashing by horseback through the waters of the Volturno, singing bawdy songs, eating and drinking heartily in an inn until I lost my senses. By the second night, when nausea sharply curbed my intake of wine and pipe tobacco, I found that Lorenzo did not bed with me, but instead disappeared at dinner with a serving girl. I lay awake and alone in a strange room full of the scent of old straw and tallow, awaiting his return, longing for his touch, for his gaze, for the laughing purr of his voice. I even prayed to St. Valentine, but Lorenzo did not return until dawn. I pretended to be asleep.

At Naples, I sold Prego (poor old lad; he was too old for decent work and probably became dog meat), and with the money paid our passage to Genoa. On the ship, Lorenzo played at dice and amused the sailors with tales of Odysseus at sea. When we disembarked, I refused to cover Lorenzo's gambling debts to the ship's captain, standing up boldly and defending my honor with long, Latinate words, until that excellent seafaring gentleman knocked me senseless and recovered his money by force.

Lorenzo had not lost heart, however, and soon soothed me with caresses and poetry. "We still have Geneva," he said. "And we shall arrive, and bathe our feet where the Arve and the Rhône come together. Wait until you witness this beautiful sight—the green river and the blue, becoming one! And we still have Metafora. Don't spoil her; it will be tempting because she's so pretty, but don't do it." I nursed my bruised temple and leaned into his back, embracing him, rocking loosely behind him in Metafora's saddle. My mouth formed the words *I love you* but I could not give them breath.

Between Torino and Geneva lie some of the highest and starkest of the Alpine mountains, and the climate this early summer was brutal. We made very slow going, particularly because the delicate Metafora could not carry us both all the time, and so one of us (usually me) would walk. My feet were a mass of blood blisters, and there was no alternative but to walk on them until my boots were swamps of blood and leather. I did not complain; I did not feel I had the right to raise my voice. It was my decision to come along. I would be a man, and suffer in the name of love and the quest.

It was that wretched, exhausted night at the inn between Torino and the French border that my nightmares began. I saw my mother's death and burial; I heard the terrible wails of my sisters and the thud of earth falling onto her coffin. I woke choking on a scream, my swollen bloody feet in agony, shaking in terror and loathing, wanting nothing more than a warm shoulder to cling to. But, of course, I was alone: Lorenzo had once again found warmer, plumper, feminine company.

The next morning, my father's sword was gone, stolen in the night by that same feminine company. I gave voice to every complaint I'd repressed over the previous month, including sleeping alone. Lorenzo did not meet my eyes, instead staring impatiently at the ceiling. "Are you finished talking about the Passion?" he snapped. "We mustn't waste time. I have it on good faith that the Lord Byron himself is in Geneva as we speak."

He could not have found a more effective way of silencing me, or of driving my list of woes from my mind. "Byron himself!" His very name was a prayer to me!

Lorenzo smirked and tousled my hair. "While you sleep, my boy, I gather intelligence. Let us away; I don't know how long he will remain. And you may ride, since your tender feet are so bruised. Here—have a drink. It will ease the pain."

I see the mountains now: crag after brutal crag, peak after frigid peak, cresting and falling like waves of stone. Summer does not reach that part of the earth; snow falls on ice and becomes ice, embalming all things unlucky enough to be trapped and helpless in the cold. Once I saw a wild rabbit, its innards shredded by a long-departed eagle, preserved six inches deep in red-stained translucent ice.

Delirious with fatigue, I saw taunting faces everywhere in the rocks, and I was never warm or free of pain. My only dreams were nightmares. I lay frozen alongside Mamma in her coffin, sucking a spadeful of dirt that my mouth could never moisten, the weight of six feet of earth breaking my back. At first I was afraid to tell Lorenzo of my nightmares, but after some months, I clung to my memories jealously; he did not deserve to know more of my inner mind, when he refused to kiss me upon the mouth and mocked nearly everything I said. Still, I did not refuse him when he wanted me, grateful for any intimacy, with the cold faces of the mountains casting their silent judgment on every step.

Metafora brought her silent, exhausted burden to the edges of Geneva on October first. The city was beautiful on that autumn day, the sun glowing warm, the sky achingly clear, doubly so as reflected on the surface of the lake. Fecund roses burst into bloom, the tidy handiwork of their roots and branches belied by the sloppy fullness of their blossoms. I breathed deeply of this ambrosial air, and said aloud, "Geneva, held in the arms of France!"

Lorenzo chuckled. "How thoroughly you have renounced your father!"

"Let us find an Englishman and make it complete," I said.

We hailed a carriage passing on the road, and Lorenzo asked the coachman in French, "Pardon me, sir. Where does the Lord Byron reside?"

That coachman's mustache twisted into a smile as he looked at us. We were a ragged twosome, and had obviously been traveling roughly for quite some time. "Lord Byron?" he repeated. His Swiss-French accent could not be more different than my companion's, and I had to struggle to understand him. "The Lord Byron has departed Geneva, my good fellow."

Or perhaps I did not wish to understand him.

"What?" shouted Lorenzo, his face growing even redder than his Alpine sunburn.

"His Lordship departed for Italy not three days past," said the coachman, plainly amused.

Lorenzo stood paralyzed with shock, so I quavered out a "thank you" and led Metafora away from the road. I shook Lorenzo by his lapels. "What are we going to do?" I begged.

"Italy," said Lorenzo, as if speaking to a dream. "He left for Italy."

Je veux aller à Paris.

This refrain of my nightmares, this phrase whose rhythms I internalized so completely that I set it to music and sang it to myself. I want to go to Paris. A thousand, ten thousand times, my prayer, my plea, my madness.

Je veux aller à Paris.

The friends and lodgings that Lorenzo had assumed would still be in place were no longer in existence; his old schoolmasters had been victims of the civil unrest caused by Napoleon's defeat, and their whereabouts unknown. The new masters of the school shooed us away with obvious distaste, caring for neither our education nor our indigence. As an Italian, this callousness struck me to the quick, and I hurled a few choice words behind me. I had barely enough money left to acquire a room for the night in an overpriced hostel outside Cologny, where, a week previous, Lord Byron himself had trodden the very same soil. After a brief, rushed, joyless meal, Lorenzo and I collapsed immediately onto the bed and fell unconscious, our first night spent in a bed in over a month.

When I awoke to the bright beam of a lantern in my eyes and the Swiss shouts of our country host, Lorenzo was gone. I had slept (dreamlessly, for once) for almost twenty-four hours straight, and the host wanted money for an extra night. I searched through my bundle for my purse and found only my notebook and pencil, the tattered copy of *The Thousand Nights and a Night* that I had used to entertain us by the fire, and a small twist of poor-quality pipe tobacco. He had not even deigned to leave me a note. I knew he would not be back and was likely already halfway to Lausanne.

I wanted to explain, to use my hard-learned powers of oratorical persuasion, but I was too agitated to remember any French except a single phrase, which I babbled over and over again like an idiot. The hosteler retorted in a strange dialect that I did not well understand, but I did gather that he did not care where I wanted to go, as I was a thief and my companion was a thief. I was thrown, with my books and empty bundle, out onto the road.

October nights in Geneva can get very cold, but I could not return home in disgrace; death was preferable. And I thought: *Keep going. Keep going. Do not let this stop you; do not let him win.*

I did what I had to do.

Je veux aller à Paris.

The gaunt faces in mountains and snowpacks, mocking and disapproving. The hateful sneers of refusal of my attempts at well-bred beggary. The jostle of mail carriages and sheep carts shuddering through the night. The chlorine taste of a stranger's semen exploding into my mouth, the following burn of bile in my throat as I spit it out against his trouser leg, and the tricolor explosion of pain as his fist struck the side of my head. Incomprehensible French obscenities. The moon reduced to a pale smudge beneath a smothering shroud. I knew no one. I had nothing to sell except myself. I accepted this fact as my private penitence.

Je veux aller à Paris. S'il vous plait. Monsieur. Je veux aller à Paris. Je n'ai pas d'argent, mais je veux aller à Paris. I have no money, but I will do what it takes, if you can take me closer. I will ride, I will stow away, I will trade the favor of my mouth and my hands and my bottom, if you, Monsieur, can get me to Paris.

By Chalon, I hardly ever thought of home; my heart had preceded me to Paris and left my breast empty. The next man whose member found its way into my mouth was stripped of his six francs and knocked unconscious with an iron horseshoe. I could still taste him in my mouth as I swung onto the back of a farmer's cart, laden with pumpkins, on its way up the river to Monteceaules-Mines, and I laughed until the farmer surely, and not inaccurately, assumed me mad.

I had tasted the ineffable flavor of violence. I was a harlot, a sodomite, and a thief. And I was good at it. I would survive, and get to Paris, with only my wits and determination. Father, the crafty captain and brash businessman, would have been proud of me.

But the nightmares did not stop. Every night I lay with Mamma in her grave, sometimes filled in and smothering, sometimes open to the air and the rain; but I could never move. And yet in my dreams of the grave, I had not the privilege of being dead. Brigands tore my lifeless body from my mother's side and tossed me into the grass, where I lay as helpless as a rag doll, listening to their foul, porcine noises of plunder. At first the pirates wanted her jewelry, her crystal rosary, the thin hoop of Egyptian gold on her ring finger. Then, tiring of these meaningless baubles, they plundered her lifeless body: her eyes, her organs, her sex.

Thankfully, Lorenzo had not stolen my rosary beads, for I performed a decade of prayer each day. I went to Mass twice a week when I could. I prayed for the nightmares to leave me, to forget Lorenzo, to forget my family, and to get to Paris and become a different person entirely.

God does indeed grant the prayers of the truly devoted. I did not ever doubt that I would get to that city eventually, even when I lost ground, and made mistakes because I was afraid to sleep. The Lord was my shield, even as I stole, deceived, and took a perverse pleasure in my degradation. And autumn gave way to winter along the banks of the Loire.

Paris, the city of light, stretched out before me like an ocean of dirty ink, beached with mud, excrement, raw and bitter stone. The snows had not yet come, but the sky threatened, and the wind was damp and cool. Despite my stolen coat, I could not stop shaking with the cold that soaked into my bones, whispering to me that my time to die had come at last.

With my last ounce of strength, I found an open café and dragged myself out of the cold, into what felt, in comparison, like an inferno. Inside it, I caught only a glimpse of firelight and red-glowing, bearded faces turning toward me, before the room rippled like a curtain and then collapsed into a tiny blank point at the very center of my consciousness. I found it all very interesting, the shouting, the cooking and alcohol smells, watching myself fall into a heap, like a sack of corn, onto the sawdust floor.

I had caught lung fever, somewhere on the plain between Nemours and Paris, and spent the next several days out of my mind. The younger brother of the café proprietor was a physician of sorts—a barber, dentist, bonesetter, and horse doctor. I was bled, and given horrible tinctures of strong laudanum and herbs to drink, and at night when all else was quiet, watched the same crack in the plaster of the ceiling flow like a river and writhe like a snake. The thunder and crash of the noisy café outside tore at my senses. I laughed and sobbed and lay insensible and shivering, wondering when death would come. I was ready for it; I welcomed death. I was finished. I had made it to Paris.

Perversely, my young life was spared for the time being; the fever broke, and I recovered my health within twenty days. Dazed and weakened, but unable to shed my well-bred manners, I vowed in my clumsy French to repay my benefactors. When I discovered exactly how much they desired in repayment, I wished I had died instead. One hundred gold louis! From a beggar like me!

God protects, only to challenge anew.

The café owner's eldest brother, a blind man with a face as pocked as a honeycomb, had a solution for me. "I overheard you talking while in your fever," he said, speaking slowly so that I could understand. "You are obviously an educated young man, for you spoke Latin like a priest. You may find a position as a secretary or a translator; there is some demand for such knowledge, especially at a low wage."

"I will do so gladly," I replied, "for the chance to remain in Paris. Many thanks, monsieur."

His clouded eyes seemed to sharpen at the desperate note in my voice. "I know of a position available now, in fact. A household where my sister-in-law works as a cook has need of a secretary; I have heard mention of some documents, written in Greek, that urgently require translation."

"A thousand thanks, monsieur! A thousand thanks!"

"Be aware that this is no ordinary position. You must make an impression. You must be bold and yet discreet; and, young man, you *will* have to improve your French," he pointed out with a grin.

I squared my shoulders and held up my head. "I shall learn by doing," I said proudly.

"And by doing, you shall learn."

Inside

I arrived at half past six, as instructed.

The house on the corner of Rue du F— did not appear opulent from outside, aside from its size and single entrance, in a city already crammed with narrow, vertical buildings. The brief front garden stood enclosed by a pale-brick wall and tall iron gates capped with pointed spikes. In the afternoon dusk, ancient cobwebs and fragments of dead leaves fluttered in the spaces between the bars of the gates and damply latticed the grass. This was a house where the world existed only within the walls.

Shivering in the clammy wind that blew from the surface of the Seine, I pulled the heavy lead pendulum weighting the bellpull but heard no answering tone from inside. At once the door opened and I beheld a slim young housemaid, in black dress, white apron, and wooden clogs, with her hair hidden completely under a conical lace bonnet of the sort worn by country shepherdesses. She did not look at me or speak; she merely stood aside, allowing me to enter, closed the door, and walked with silent footfalls ahead of me into the foyer.

I wondered idly at this, but my mind was elsewhere, tangled in its web of questions and self-consciousness. What would be my secretarial duties in this place, large enough to house ten families? Would I be merely a translator, or was there anything else I could offer? How much would I be paid? My employers were undoubtedly aristocratic, as evidenced by the splendid narrow carpet in the hall and the skillfully painted oil landscapes upon the walls, and I had been assured by Claude-Pierre, the blind brother, that they were wealthy. Where would I live? In this building, on an uppermost floor? Richly or poorly? Did I look presentable? I had shaved that morning, even though there was really no need; my beard, at the age of nineteen, remained only a downy whisper on my upper lip and cheeks, and a great deal of examining before the glass.

Yet as I followed the white-aproned maid along the long, dark hall that stretched before us, I perceived a subtle change in the air—or perhaps not the air, but properly, the atmosphere. The air remained the same, but the feel of it against my face, the press and rustle of my clothes against my body, and the tread of my feet along the heavy carpet had changed. I felt *more* (and yet was aware of less). My sense of touch had come alive with an acuity that was almost uncomfortable. The seams of my borrowed clothes scraped against me until it burned like fire.

Ahead of me, the maid opened the sixth door on the left and slipped inside, propping the door open with her thin, muslin-clad wrist. I paused once more on the threshold, tugging at my high stiff collar, before I entered. Beautiful or not, those hateful collars were a torture device.

"Madame," I heard the housemaid murmur, "Monsieur Ricari."

And then she was gone, and the door shut sharply behind me.

The room was dark but for the light of two candles at the far end of the room, some dozen meters away, and even their light was half swallowed by the heavy draperies of black velvet curtains. I perceived no one, no movement. The crackling vibration of the atmosphere heightened to an unbearable degree and I let out my breath with an involuntarily curt sigh. "Good evening?" I called out.

And, as mundanely miraculous as a sunrise, I saw myself. Allow me to clarify. It was as if I stood several meters away from myself, watching myself creep and fidget and rub my cheek with the shoulder of my coat. It was a clearer view than anything seen in a mirror; instead of a reversed reflection, I saw myself quite truly, an emaciated youth in dire need of a haircut, dressed in an ill-fitting green coat and baggy trousers, and huge eyes that flitted anxiously along the walls. And yet I was not distasteful to myself in this view; I felt a great warmth and charm, a sense of wonder that my face, despite my obvious privation, was so keenly drawn and handsomely proportioned. I had never seen myself in this way before, and I found myself beautiful.

This is why I did not stop to consider the fact that, perhaps, something was amiss.

Ego is a powerful anesthetic.

At once, a woman appeared out of the shadows, coalescing from the glow of the candles and casting her own subtle incandescence, as though she were composed of moonlight. In her cupped hands, she held a speckled dove that sat and cooed as calmly as if it were in its nest. I gathered all of the woman in a single astonished glance—wavy masses of beaten-gold hair gathered around a heart-shaped face, round blue eyes with thick chestnut eyelashes, a suggestion of maturity on the corners of the eyelids and mouth, but skin as unmarked and silken as a petal, a broad proud bosom rising from a curved neckline of sea-blue satin, diminishing to a firm corseted waist, and flaring again into generous hips and ripples of glistening blue-and-white fabric. I had never seen anything so beautiful in my life; even the crystalline waters of Lake Geneva seemed, in comparison, a muddy gutter on a dull day. In my memory, she evokes nothing so much as the cunning spherical cakes, rolled in powdered sugar and served stacked in pyramids, made by the pastry chefs at Dumarchand's restaurant, which lay still some years in my future. She was dainty and modest, yet succulent and worldly.

"Madame," I said, astonished, falling to my knee before her. She obliged by languidly holding out one gloved hand at arm's length, while she held the dove, still calm and sleepy, on the palm of the other hand. I was seized with the desire to kiss the toes of her dark leather shoes, peeking out from under her hem. "I am your servant!"

"Yes," she replied calmly, her voice a low sonorous music like oboes and cellos. She lifted her hand, and the dove obligingly fluttered away. "Yes, you are."

She pulled off one glove, then the other, and laid one bare hand upon my bent head. I felt a surge of joy and—and forgiveness; there is no other way to describe it. She forgave all my shortcomings, past and future, with a single touch of her hand on my rumpled hair. And, as one might expect, I burst into tears of relief. I had been suppressing my feelings of guilt and terror and shame for so long that, when those feelings were drawn out of me, they overwhelmed my heart, even as they were washed away. It was a sick but glorious relief, like the lancing of an abscess.

"I am Maria," she said, and that only made me cry harder, even as I supplicated myself.

Sancta Maria! Blessed art thou among women! How I have longed for your touch! My mother—

She is in Heaven now.

My tutor—

He can never harm you again, my young one. It is so. You are under my protection now.

How glorious, how glorious. Forgive me, Heavenly Father. The flesh is weak, but the spirit, battered by circumstance, is often weaker still. Her voice in my head soothed me like opium smoke.

She let me sob for a minute but then began to shush me, and drew me to my feet by a gentle pressure of her fingertips on my wrist. "Are you now recovered, young man?"

"Yes—yes, I'm fine," I said. I dried my face upon my handkerchief, and it was as though nothing had ever happened; we stood, two reasonable adults, in a huge drawing room lit only by two candles, at dinnertime.

I looked round me for another soul but saw no one. "Where is your husband?" I asked. "I am here to— assume the position of . . . of secretary . . ."

Maria rolled back her head and chuckled faintly. "I have no husband," she replied, as if deeply amused by the question. "You work for me."

"Oh," I said. "I work for you." Yes, foolish me. Of course I did. "Are you *truly* Maria?" I asked, suddenly unsure. My pleasure, my answered prayers, had been too acute, and I had become an enlightened skeptic. "And you called for me?"

"Quite so" was the response. She turned away from me, her skirts faintly ruffling against the floor. She began to glide toward the candles, and I followed her, not daring to take my eyes away for fear that this lovely apparition would diffuse into the candlelight that it per-

fectly complemented. "You require employment to repay a debt to the ones who saved your life by caring for
you when you were ill. They have been paid in full this
very evening." She reached the candles and turned to
me with the blue center of the flame burning steadily in
her gaze. "That they would ask you to repay them with
so much money is very typical, I am afraid. But you
need not worry about them anymore. They have been
dealt with."

"Thank you," I replied breathlessly. The staggeringly
large compensation requested by the café owner and his
brothers, the doctor and the old blind informer, had
been more money than that with which I had started out
my journey from Fattorio di Ricari. But as they might as
well have thrown me out into the street to my inevitable
death, but chose not to, I felt inclined to "square it up,"
as Father Christopher would say. "And what do I do?" I
left unspoken: *Here, in your house, with you, after the skies
have already gone dark, and you with no husband.*

She laughed, and her fierce, calm eyes sparkled.
"You will perform all things I ask of you. I bought your
life from those men, and now it belongs to me. Do you
understand?"

I nodded, shrugging at the obviousness of what she'd
said. Would I disobey the Queen of the Sky? What was
my life worth in louis? I had already spent it, whatever
the amount. "Yes, madame," I said, then added, with an
attempt at evoking Lorenzo's appealingly prurient wit,
"but do I have to do *only* those things asked of me?"

She lowered her eyes to the floor, though not out of
shame; her expression was thoughtful. "We shall see,"
she replied. "We shall see." Then she smiled up at me.
"You are a spirited young man for a fellow so recently
snatched from the claws of Death."

"I was not in danger," I said with a hint of boastful-
ness.

"Not from the fever, no." She seated herself at a little table, spread with a white cloth and bathed in candlelight. She was, at once, as eerily immobile, and as yet ravishingly lifelike, as a wax carving. I began to pace, attempting to shake off the shifting waves of uneasiness and desire, and the candle flames reflected in her eyes followed me.

As my eyes adjusted to the dark, I made out the threadbare but gorgeous tapestries hung along the wall that ran parallel to the long hallway. A dragon with golden scales stood rampant against a trio of knights armed with lances; on another, a line of pilgrims faced a pale, winding road that led to a rainbow-crowned oasis. The weaving was fine, the fibers glossy at the centers of the tapestries where they had not been worn. "These are very beautiful. They look ancient," I said.

I felt an sudden urge to sit down, as if I had been gently pushed, and I took the chair opposite her. Immediately, I felt fervent relief, and I almost said "thank you." Being nearer to her calmed my anxiety.

"Do have some cognac." She poured liquor from a porcelain bottle. "They are indeed ancient. They were woven in Bayonne in the thirteenth century. They are some of my most prized possessions."

"Only some? They must have been worth millions of francs to the Emperor!"

"The Emperor," she repeated, smiling at the floor again. "You shouldn't say things like that in Paris right now."

"I would not know. I am not from here," I said. I glanced at the glassful of cognac, which I thought I had drained, but it glistened invitingly, seemingly untouched. I raised it to my lips and swallowed in one mouthful, opening my mouth to catch the burning-velvet breath of the liquor. I felt I was being smothered in hot sunshine, in Eden's vineyard of ambrosial grapes.

"Yes, I know. But I *am* from here, and honoring the titles of conquered kings has never been a prudent thing."

My glass was full to brimming, and neither of us had moved. In fact, I had not even seen her set glasses on the table to begin with. How lovely she was! "Drink," she said, and I obeyed.

"Come with me now," Maria said, rising and taking up one of the candles, "and I shall display to you the duties for which your debts were paid." Her voice contained a tang of sarcasm, and I felt the unease returning, briefly, a mere tingle along my spine. As soon as I tried to stand, that sensation was swamped under a woozy, giddy dizziness. I nearly fell over onto the table. But my drunkenness did not garner a reaction from Maria, passing soundlessly across the floor back to the door through which I had, an eternity past, entered. How had I lived without her, before? What was my life like? I could no longer imagine. Clumsily, a besotted puppy, I took the other candle and followed.

The inky darkness of the hall led to a steep and narrow staircase that spiraled up to a first floor and continued on, spinning up into murky obscurity. The flutter and pipe of other doves floated through the air to my ears, but I could see none of the birds anywhere. Maria turned at the first landing and walked into a brighter hallway, nearly the twin of the one below it, but much shorter, and hung with gauze drapes, the air sweetened with bunches of roses suspended from strings on the moldings. Most of the roses were wilted, and many of them were reduced to dried brown tissue crisps. The edges of the carpet were piled high with fallen petals. "Ah, this is the floor with the balcony which I saw from the street," I recalled, feeling that I should make conversation. "These must be handsome rooms."

"Quite" was her only response. She opened the first door on the right.

How dark the room was, and yet how perfectly I could see.

She was not as lovely as Maria, but—oh! Can one compare the wind-torn clouds of the night sky with the sea?

Stretched out on a low couch thickly clustered with embroidered pillows, an extraordinary young woman, as long and slim as a willow twig, stroked her loose black waves of hair with one hand, while the other caressed her inner thigh, edging up the hem of her ivory lace gown. I had hardly ever seen so much bare female leg in my life, and my eyes all but started out of my head. Indeed, the only thighs I had ever beheld were my sister's, and I immediately recalled the sound of Elena's voice, huskily whispering against my ear—

"Mie lepri magre piccole . . ." I tasted once more that sweet pang of my first orgasm, pressed between Elena's thighs.

"This is the Lady Georgina," Maria said, her words seeming to emanate from the room itself. Vaguely, I perceived faint moans coming from my throat. "You are hers for the night. Obey her; she is nobility, and my *very* most prized possession." I spun on my heel to look askance at Maria, but I caught only the tail of her smile as she disappeared, as silent as vapor, through the closing door.

Semen seeped into my borrowed trousers, but I was too transfixed even to feel embarrassment. My attention snapped back to the woman touching herself on the sofa.

"Don't be afraid," said the Lady Georgina. She drew herself into a sitting position, flinging her hair over one shoulder so that it flowed down her back. "Come and sit by me."

I approached, as surely as if I were drawn on a leash. I thought to myself that Maria had taken leave of her senses; no one could possess such a creature, with such smoldering eyes, tender lips, and fierce, knowing expression. Georgina belonged only to herself. "I am called Orfeo," I said.

"Yes," she said, "Orfeo Giuseppe Vittorio Ricari." Her pronunciation of my name was eroticized by her odd accent, though it brutalized the mellow Neapolitan vowels.

"How did you know that?" I sat beside her on the couch, sinking into her eyes, deeper and deeper, drowning in them. I struggled for one last moment to breathe the air, then let myself be overwhelmed.

"Don't ask questions, Orfeo. We have so little time. Do as you most want to do. Let go. No one is looking, and I won't mind."

My exalted heart leaping with joy, I bent over her and laid my head on her bare inner thigh, tilting my nose toward her body and drinking in the air near her sex. I smelled only the essence of roses that perfumed the room. Too eager to be disappointed at being robbed of one of my favorite sensual experiences, I touched her flesh with my bare hand; her skin felt champagne-effervescent, vibrating on the same frequency as the air in the room, cool, and softer than velvet. Her eyes and lips glistened in the firelight, and I sat up to take a closer, deeper look, cupping her long, slender neck with my hand. "I do speak Greek," I said. In French, literally, *I have the Greek tongue*. I found myself blushing, even as her smile widened with delight.

She laughed, a real laugh, in opposition to Maria's tightly restrained amusement. "You shall speak Polish by daybreak," she declared, moving my hand to her breast, and kissed me, devouringly, on the mouth. I pulled her into my lap, opened her legs across my loins, and tore open my damp trousers. She laughed again, coquettishly this time; she wore nothing under the dress but her God-given ruff of black lace-fleece. She was ready, wet and yielding, as though she'd been waiting all day. More swiftly than I thought possible, we were joined, and moving in a perfectly coordinated series of waves, like a matched pair of horses on a carousel. I had never been inside a woman—inside anyone—before; it was everything that I had imagined, everything that I had desired, and more.

I had almost forgotten what is entailed in making love—not just making love to a woman, but making love at all. I realized, my face buried in Georgina's breasts while she arched her body over mine, purring and cooing wordlessly, that I had never *made love* with Lorenzo; that he only took advantage of my childish attachment to him, and satisfied himself without a thought to my own pleasure. He lured me, held me down, and took me, and my ecstasy was purely incidental to him. If I was transported with joy, so much the better to keep me affixed to his side, a happy slave.

With Georgina, bucking my hips from the couch to lend emphasis to her thrusting, I felt every longing satisfied, every hour of erotically charged solitude fulfilled, every sting of guilt from every stolen orgasm cleansed from me like a stain from a bedsheet. For the second time since I had crossed the threshold of this house, I wept tears of bliss.

When we paused, Georgina, her temples damp from exertion, traced the contour of my ear with her wickedly long, polished fingernail. Her eyes examined my face. "You will be no one's slave here," she said to me.

"And yet my life was purchased," I replied. "Am I not to be your servant? I would gladly be your servant. I would gladly be the Lady Maria's servant as well. I will do anything you ask."

The corner of her mouth quirked. "Yes? Well, lie still."

She pressed her lips against the side of my neck, and I felt a minute pinch as her teeth nipped me. I stroked the bones of her spine with my fingertips for a moment before I lost all will and ability to move, unable to do more than emit a deep sigh. I hovered at the edge of orgasm, though my sex was spent; this orgasm swept my entire body, from the follicles of my hair to the innermost organs of my belly, my bones wrapped in a lattice of shimmering gold filament. I must have cried out; I could not have contained myself, but this is one thing that I do not remember. I heard nothing but the sweet low throbbing of blood against my eardrums.

"What have you done," I whispered, my voice too slight to make a question.

"I saved you," she said. She kissed me, pushing the taste of my own blood into my mouth. How delicious it was, ripe with cognac and the mild, milky taste of her genitals! "You will never again be alone, my sweet boy," she whispered with a kiss.

Of course, I believed her. And she spoke truth indeed. But I did not yet know the face of the murderous desire that would become my constant companion, did not feel the velvet noose that would strangle me, nor hear the lover's whisper of the guillotine that would sever me from my soul.

And the darkness consumed me.

I did not leave that night, or the next, or the next. I did not even leave Georgina's bedchamber for that time. It seemed to me that Georgina never left, either, but that each time I fell asleep, she would be there next to me when I awoke, wearing a different dressing gown, or holding a cup of jellied ox-broth or wine, tickling me with stray feathers we had pounded out of the pillows.

I accepted instantly the fact that this supernatural being could read my mind, and that I could communicate to her without speaking. She was an angel, or a succubus; I cared not which. We still spoke aloud, though, both of us enchanted with the sounds of our own voices and those of each other. I accepted the fact that I translated nothing, and performed no more gainful action than giving in to my most lustful desires. I did ask her, though, about her teeth.

"Why have you got fangs, like a tiger?"

"The better to seize you with, my tasty little rabbit. The better to devour you with!"

This is how she was.

"You bleed me too much; I have no strength left," I complained.

She massaged my penis, which, despite its previous exertions, eagerly swelled back to life. I could not suppress a groan. "At least this has strength," she mused, flipping her hair across my thighs. "You may rest; I will do the work. And there is much work to be done."

We poured truth into one another, by osmosis, through the skin, through my blood, through her honey, my seed passing into her body and spreading back to me.

She was Jadzia Vilma Kopernik. Maria did not like the Polish name—to the Frenchwoman, it lacked femininity—so she became Georgina. She was, or had been, and thus remained, twenty-two years old. She came from Cracow, where her father was a professor of mathematics. She was not royalty, despite what Maria would gladly claim; she was just a teacher's daughter, unmarried, and had come to Paris, to the Sorbonne, ten years ago, to find a suitable husband. She had found Maria instead.

She was no longer human; indeed, she was closer to the angel or demon I imagined, and yet neither of these.

"Now I live on blood. Maria and I. She made me. I gave my life to her. And I would do it all again in a heartbeat. She transformed me, molding my human flesh as though it were raw clay. And indeed it *was* as dull as clay, compared to the light that animates me now! The blood gives me life; it gives me power beyond your capacity to imagine. It brought you to me. I wanted you, and you appeared. Our kind is sometimes known as *wampir*. I think that is a dreadful name for something so beautiful."

This fact did not alarm me in the slightest. I had heard the legends of damned creatures who rose from the dead and stole children to drink their blood, but she bore no resemblance to the image of the pasty half-skeletons of my imaginations, their shredded winding cloths dripping with mud and their eyes full of light-ning and damnation. Georgina was a living, breathing, lusty girl; if she bit me and sucked at the blood, it only served to send me into the greatest of ecstasies.

Georgina's kisses were more intoxicating than the strongest liquor, and her only apparent savagery lay in her ravenous sexual appetite and her steadfast refusal to be too serious. If I was not exhausted from lovemaking, my sides ached from laughter.

I was more at ease than I had ever been. We made love as though we were created for each other, comfort-ably and joyously, giggling like mad children, or curling up to rest like puppies in a basket. I did not tell her about my past, about Lorenzo; she already knew all she needed to know, gently caressing my bottom with the side of her hand, tutting softly to herself. "He was cruel to you," she murmured. "Your sweet mouth deserves a gentler lover; but perhaps that is not what you want?"

"What I want is more of you. Always—more of you, my lovely."

The entry points to my bloodstream made by her teeth were deliciously sensitive but gave me no pain. "Now you know how it feels for me," she said. By morning of the third day, I was covered in pockmarks of love, set in rosettes of bruising. I offered all to her—prick, neck, thighs, wrists—and she would accept, enclosing me with her mouth and lapping gently at the welling dots of blood raised by the keen points of her teeth.

Each bite washed my memories away. I remembered my previous life only dimly, like recalling a fable read in childhood; I would not clearly recall it again for a hundred years. Good-bye, Mamma, Father, Mira, Veni; good-bye, Anna and Elena, good-bye to the slaughterhouse and the olive press. Good-bye to the vicious Alps and the cold, rushing Volturno. I had made it to Paris and the arms of a beautiful woman. I did not know that I was being made to forget; or perhaps I did understand, secretly. The memories were too painful. They still are, though I have been given the Final Rites and laid in my grave.

"You are so beautiful," she told me. "You have such sadness in your eyes—and yet such defiance."

"I am Orfeo Ricari," I maintained, though it came out slurred through numb lips. I had not recovered absolutely from the lung fever, and I had been worn out with the kind of sexual congress usually reserved for gods. "That can't be taken from me, or beaten out of me, or starved out of me. I am Orfeo Ricari."

"What are you going to do about him?"

I opened my eyes reluctantly and beheld Maria standing over the couch, her round, firm body encased in a pale gray dress with a bodice embroidered in blue thread, and her hair undressed. She was so stunning that I did not realize for some time that her expression was very displeased. She held a speckled dove—perhaps the same one, perhaps not—against her thigh, in a pocket made of her gathered skirts.

Georgina, naked beside me, frowned impatiently. "What do you mean?"

"You know what I mean. Are you finished with him? You've had plenty of time to amuse yourself," Maria claimed starkly.

I tried, in vain, to clear my head. The light that emanated from Maria blinded me.

Georgina stood up. "What of it? Can you not leave us alone for a moment more?"

She towered over Maria by at least six inches, probably more. The contrast could hardly have been more stark; my eyes roved wonderingly between the wild-haired, naked Amazon and the modest, elegant lady. "Not for a moment more" was Maria's crisp reply. Then her eyes bore down on me, and my mind cleared very suddenly, but very specifically. I could not look away, and I could not generate any thoughts besides those necessary to answer her. I lay paralyzed, vulnerable, and half naked among the pillows. "Do you know where you have come?" she demanded. "Do you understand what we are?"

"Yes," I said.

"Do you understand that this woman is mine, and that you are a stranger here?"

"Yes."

"Do you understand that you are in grave danger?"

All my muscles tensed, gathering to spring into action. And yet I did not feel any fear, only intense fascination. I felt that I could gaze at the still, porcelain curves of her face forever, that she could eviscerate me, slap me, imprison me, and that I could nourish myself for eternity on the memory of her face.

"Leave now, boy," said Maria.

At once the paralysis ended, and I jerked violently as sensation returned to my limbs. I tumbled off the couch and picked myself up from the floor. "Yes, madame," I said.

"Stay," said Georgina, her eyes still on Maria.

I sat back on the edge of the couch and ran my fingers through my hair. I felt very sick suddenly, and I wondered if I had genuinely lost too much blood, and I wanted nothing more than to crawl back into Georgina's arms.

The two women stared at each other, neither moving a muscle, while I crouched on the edge of the couch, clutching my churning belly and shutting my eyes against a kaleidoscope of broken images and dark blots of unconsciousness. I was able to gasp out, "Stop it . . . please . . . whatever you are doing . . ."

Their concentration broke, and they both stared at me. Relief came so abruptly, it almost brought on nausea by itself, and, with effort, I raised my head. "I know," I said. "I know about both of you. I know of your love for one another, and I do not wish to change or disrupt that. Now, I do not know everything, but I do not really *need* to know everything. You must understand—my life as I knew it is over." I looked from one to the other, watching their expressions soften. "I wish to stay. I gave my word; I will do as I am asked. And yet I am no one's possession. I belong only to the Heavenly Father, and it is to Him that I answer. I am not afraid. Show me a new life, or put me to death, whatever you ask. A life in your service is not something I fear. It is better than living as a vagabond—as a piece of drifting trash."

Maria and Georgina looked at each other, then Georgina looked away and closed her eyes. A concession. Then Maria brought out the dove from within her skirts, murmuring while she stared at it, "Your French has certainly improved, young monsieur. The Lady Georgina is a fine instructor." Her white fingers sunk deeply into the speckled feathers, and I heard the sounds of hollow little bones crunching.

She brought the hapless creature to her mouth and bit into its breast, piercing it. Her fangs were longer and more pointed than Georgina's, glistening in the faint light from the candle. Blood ran out of the struggling bird and over her chin, but not very much blood. Most of it was absorbed into her sucking, savage mouth.

Georgina put her arm around my shoulders, took my hand, and held me tightly, and her warm touch dissipated my shudderings of horror and shock.

"Is it indeed nothing to fear?" Maria asked, dove's down mixed with gore befouling her chin and her breast.

But I had seen the slaughter of the most helpless and adorable of lambs for the succulence in their hindquarters; this was not so bad in comparison, though unseemly for such a beautiful woman in such a delicate gown. "It is no more than I have witnessed," I said.

"We love him, Maria," said Georgina earnestly. "We must retain him." She kissed our joined hands.

Maria gave me a good look then, seemed to come to a decision, and relaxed. She dropped the dead dove on the floor, and her face assumed a thoughtful expression as she wiped blood from the corner of her mouth with her pinky finger. "You are welcome to stay," she acquiesced, "under the terms of our original agreement."

"I will do so gladly," I said, lifting my chin. "My French has indeed improved remarkably in the last few days, and I shall be happy to perform any and all secretarial duties."

Georgina kissed the side of my face. "Isn't he the very sweetest boy?" she said.

Maria's eyes, immaculately sharp razors, cut me, painlessly and swiftly. Only later came the sting. "He needs a bath," she replied. "And *you* need to get dressed."

* * *

Maria presented the house while the housemaid, Liliane, drew a bath. Georgina followed at a slight distance behind, singing softly to herself and occasionally giving a happy skip, kicking out the full skirt of her unfastened dress. I felt entirely at my ease, despite the discomfort of the borrowed clothes ravaging skin that had not, for days, touched anything coarser than velvet, or silken flesh.

"That is Georgina's bedchamber. I do not share it; you will find that she usually sleeps with me, in my room. This can be your room." We had gone up the stairs to an upper floor, and Maria flung open the doors to a dark, musty-smelling chamber that had obviously not been entered for some time. Under a layer of dust, furnishings slumbered under white shrouds. I was childishly happy to note the presence of what could only be several bookshelves, and a window facing southeast, perfect for catching the painterly early rays of the sun.

Down the hall. "This is my own bedchamber. Do not enter uninvited." She did not have to say aloud what the consequences would be; I felt something like hands gently wrapping around my neck.

I swallowed, to reassure myself that I still could. "I would never dare to presume."

"Of course you wouldn't. You're a very well brought up and intelligent young man. Most of the rest of the space on this floor is reserved for our wardrobe; I enjoy finely made gowns and shoes, and believe in giving them adequate space."

"Do not wear Maria's gowns uninvited," Georgina put in, pinching my buttocks and kissing the top of my head, which, standing, perfectly met her lips. "You might, I'm afraid, be unable to give them . . ." She ran her fingers along my chest. "Adequate space."

Down the stairs. In the little courtyard at the center of the house, wire cages housed pigeons and doves, half a dozen laying hens, and seven or eight small, plump rabbits. "Maignot looks after these; you do not have to concern yourself with them."

"We get new ones all the time, so don't get sentimental."

"I understand," I said.

"This is the upstairs parlor," said Maria, throwing open the doors to a space almost wide enough to be a ballroom, hung with blue damask and dominated by a vast, heavy glass chandelier that hung so low I could almost touch the bottom-most ornament. "Occasionally, we entertain; in those situations, I expect perfect manners, or I shall be unpleasantly stern." Georgina ruined the effect of this warning by breaking into giggles again and pretending to strangle herself. Maria strode up to her with a suddenness that led me to believe that a blow was at the end of her progress, but to my surprise, instead caressed and pulled at Georgina's hair. "Can you not be serious for a moment? Will you spoil the boy?"

"What does it matter?" Georgina retorted. "He will obey. Look at him. Look at those beautiful innocent eyes. He is ideal."

Maria looked. "No one is ideal," she said, "especially not a man. Particularly a *young* man."

"Oh, don't be bitter, my diamond."

Their lips touched. I looked away, struggling to contain my instinctive shock. I had seen glimpses of their closeness through Georgina's thoughts, but to witness this with my own eyes—two women, kissing as tenderly as comfortable spouses—mingled horror and excitement. I was a fool, of course; had I not committed such unnatural acts, and much more so, myself? But this was different, exotic, strangely stirring.

The tour continued. "This is the kitchen. This is the

downstairs parlor. This is the pantry." The pantry was bare but for several stone, glass, and porcelain bottles. Maria noted my expression of dismay. "We have little need for food in the house. Two doors down, you will find an exceptional little restaurant that should satisfy whatever needs you have. Give them my name; there is no better credit in all of Paris." Maria turned to me with a gracious smile. "I will take you there once you have some clothing that is not a disgrace."

"You are too kind, madame."

"Too kind to allow anyone to imagine that, the way you look now, you could have anything to do with me."

I had not had a bath, if one did not count ten-second-long frigid dips into the river, in over a year. I thought my skin was going to simply crumble and flake off entirely, particularly with the vigor with which Georgina scrubbed me. Maria stood a safe distance away from the splashing, watching with amusement that did not show on her face, but tickled my mind until I howled with laughter. "Poor Orfeo," Georgina purred, polishing my naked skin with a handful of twine, wound around her hand and saturated with tallow soap. "I fear that you may dissolve. There's been nothing holding you together but dirt."

Liliane returned with bread, bacon, and cheese from the restaurant, laid it all out with a bottle of wine and a glass, and curtsied to Maria and Georgina. "Monsieur Flay will be around tomorrow to outfit young Monsieur, and Monsieur Vieux-Ypres to fit young Monsieur for boots. Madame Eurite thanks you for the gratuity. May I be released?" Liliane asked in her timorous voice.

"Wait!" I said. "Before you go—isn't there a cook here? A woman named Jeanne, married to a man named Herbert?"

Liliane's face was even paler than the starched cotton of her bonnet. "Madame Jeanne is dead," she whispered.

"You may go," said Georgina. Liliane hitched her skirts and galloped for the door.

Maria looked annoyed. "Why did you have to ask that, boy?" she demanded.

"I—I wanted to thank her, that is, Madame Jeanne, for it was her who . . . she was the one who mentioned . . ."

"Has Liliane any family?" Maria asked Georgina, ignoring me.

Georgina shook her head no, idly wringing soapy water from the hem of her dress.

"Good. Would you mind taking care of her?"

"Not at all, my diamond," Georgina said, kissing Maria on the lips again and, still with a skip in her step, disappearing from the room.

I sat, suddenly very cold though I sat near the fire, swaddled in a long sacking-towel like a deposed Roman in his toga. "You're going to kill her, aren't you?" It wasn't really a question.

Maria gently laid one gloved finger against my lips, and the chill passed from my body, leaving me feeling cozy and sleepy. "Ssh," she said. "Eat your supper and thank Providence."

I wondered, for a moment, why I felt less horror at the thought of that young woman being killed than I had at the death of a thoughtless, soulless dove. But all too swiftly, that moment passed.

Intoxication

Was I not happy for a time? Blissfully happy, where each day was such a joy that I sprang out of bed with a laugh? Love and security are illusion, but the most tangible illusions known to man, more absolute, more concrete than the air we breathe or the ground we tread.

Hardly ever did pasha or princess receive such lavish treatment as I did at the hands of Maria and Georgina. I had sleek, simple, unostentatious clothing tailored in imitation of London's Mr. Brummel, with whom Georgina had developed an infatuation upon his arrival in France the previous year. The women took great joy in selecting my clothing and accessories, and dressing my hair, as little girls concentrate on the toilette of their dolls. Georgina bought me all the books and periodicals I desired from the booksellers near the Sorbonne, and I read Byron's *Childe Harolde* with a melancholy sigh for the beauty of Geneva, and a cynical smirk, regularly cursing the poet as though he were an old friend. I had expensive paints, acres of paper, and camel-hair brushes. I dined daily on the exquisite fare served at the restaurant around the corner—meats, cheeses, and, the restaurant's signature dish, a potato soup so subtle and rich that men came from the far-flung edges of the city to eat it. By the end of the first month, my favorite table, the one with the view of the kitchen as well as the street, was set aside as soon as I approached. "It's the young Macaroni!" they called me. They loved me all the more for their general resentment of Italians, since none of them had ever met an Italian before, and thus I was the exception that proved the rule. I felt that I had become a tremendous success in the world at an age befitting my precociousness. Why should I not live in luxury, the companion of sublime women, celebrated for my wit (which was mostly just stupidity), artistic, intellectual, and nearly completely idle?

I did actually perform in my role as secretary. Maria was adamant about managing anything to do with money, but she did make me address all her envelopes and correspondence, as my practiced and artistic handwriting was much better than her awkward, impatient scribble.

Georgina had sustained a relationship through the mail with her brother Jozef, but needed assistance in creating the outlandish lies that she wrote about herself, both to entertain him and to keep from revealing the actual details of her life. So far, she had told him she had been married to an Indian prince who beat her, and then she fled from him, only to fall in love with a Gypsy adventurer, who happened to come into an enormous inheritance from a past lover, and now they had settled in a secret château carved from the side of Mont Blanc. "Jozef either believes what I have written to him, or he doesn't really care, as long as he gets his monthly installment of romance," Georgie sighed. "But I'm starting to run out of ideas. You've read a lot; help me make something up. Remember, it cannot be too fantastical, and I can never be in danger by the end of the letter; we don't want him coming to Paris to try to rescue me. Jozef is pretty stupid, but he really does love me, and at least he can appreciate a good story! He is the finest brother a girl could have. Oh, Orfeo, don't cry. Here, let me comfort you."

While Georgina and I satisfied each other's sensual desires, she would not fall into slumber with me, though we lay in her room. I never saw her leave, but each evening I saw her emerge with Maria from Maria's locked bedchamber, both of them as alert as though sleep never touched their brows. A flicker of jealousy rose within me and was as swiftly smothered, as Georgina flew at me, took me in her arms, and slipped her tongue into my mouth. "Oh, my precious, are you ready?" she whispered in my ear, and immediately I was.

But she never *slept* with me. Each afternoon I would wake alone. I could not help thinking of Lorenzo, and without the direct interference of Maria or Georgie to distract me, I could. It was agony. Why did no one sleep with me? What was wrong with me that I had to be left to wake alone in a strange bed? The house was cavernous and silent without the sounds of their voices; the servants remained in their rooms until called for, and then kept their interactions to a minimum. I tried to counter the silence by walking noisily and talking to myself, but it only made the smothering quiet press inward, and increased my feelings of isolation.

There was no solution but to leave the house until they had risen. I dressed myself in my handsome, hollow clothes, left an unnecessary note, and went to the restaurant to drink coffee-and-brandy and read the newspaper, underlining the words I did not know. Despite my black broadcloth coat and immaculate short hair, despite the friendly shouts of the waiters and the appreciative smiles of the ladies, without Georgie's bawdy jests, without Maria's stern nobility, I felt un-kempt, empty, and aimless.

After some hours, I raised my head and took a deep breath of air suddenly rich with information and sweet with promise. My tense shoulders unknit themselves. I stood up, left my cup and newspaper, and rushed home to fall into Georgina's arms, to feel the sweet prick of her teeth on my skin, the warm waves of pleasure and approval washing in a tide from Maria.

I greatly preferred going about in the company of the ladies, with their exceptional beauty and grace, fiery in-telligence, and bold tongues. I learned not to laugh too loudly when they told me the thoughts of the people seated across the room from us, and listening to their well-nuanced bickering and love talk filled me with ado-ration. They were openly affectionate with one another, and delicately, sometimes playfully, condescending to me. I would respond with a quote from Swift or Lucian about the empty prattling of women, and they would pet me and call me their little Diderot. We all played our roles.

When we went out together, they would allow me to have my male prerogative in setting a pace or ordering supper, but they would silently send me hints and steer me toward one choice or another. I did not mind defer-ring to them; they knew this city, they understood fash-ion in a way still unknown to a Piedimontese farm boy, and Georgina didn't care what wine I chose. Maria did not drink wine or consume food. She merely watched us as impassively as though we were animals chewing cud. "The smell is enough to satisfy me. I live on blood, and blood alone."

Georgina did not eat anything but oysters, escargots, and soup, and those things only occasionally; but she understood the importance of dining with company. "One digests better with conversation," she said. "And we must, we simply must, fatten you up, little hare. You're so skinny, you're nearly transparent!"

"He is no hare," Maria interjected. "He is a little dog. An Italian greyhound, sharp-eyed and ready to kill on your command."

"Or sit on my lap and behave," said Georgina with a laugh.

I laughed too. "Let it be so," I said, raising my glass. "The time of the skinny little hare comes to an end; introduce the era of the greyhound."

I thought to myself: *Good-bye, Elena. Good-bye forever.*

I first tasted absinthe on the night of February eleventh, 1817. I saw the date on a calendar at the tavern on the Rue du C—, and on the newspaper spread across the top of the absurdly small café table, and in every way, it was February eleventh. Outside the wind whistled and dashed tiny particles of frozen snow against the window and underneath the door, where it melted before the fireplace, then evaporated into steam. That night, I went out with Maria, without Georgina. Georgie had been gone before either of us awoke for the "day" at half past five in the evening; by Maria's tensely calm expression, I knew she was unhappy. Still, she joined me when I said I wanted to go out, leading me to this strange café, with its doll-sized tables and the steamy reek of smoke.

We sat for a long time without speaking, I with my ale, an empty glass before her. She wore indigo that night, with a violet cloak, trimmed with black fox. The cloak's hood had disordered the careful curls, done in a classical style, around her face, and they hung as loosening coils of gold natural silk. I felt like a child, helpless before an adult displeasure I could not understand, only feel.

I sniffed at a wisp of smoke curling from a table farther back. "I know this smell," I said to Maria, attempting to distract her.

"Do you? A whelp like you, familiar with the scent of hashish?" Her lips moved, but I heard her voice in my head, unhindered by the raised voices of the café patrons.

"Is that what it's called?" I mused. "Lorenzo—"

"Do not speak his name," said Maria. "You are here now."

"Yes," I said. I saw, in my mind, the letters of his name, evaporating one by one, like sublimating ice.

"Do you have desire for hashish?" she asked. "We can easily procure some."

I shook myself. "No, I want to drink. I want to get drunk. And this ale is leaving me unsatisfied."

"Allow me, young man." She rose with a conspiratorial smile, and I watched her float through the room away from me, swallowed in the shadows and smoke. I traced my fingernail over the newspaper, rippled and rumpled, having been wet by the freezing rain. February eleven. I had been in the possession of the vampires for eight weeks, and somehow I was still alive, and better off than I had ever been before. I could not hate my tutor for delivering me from Campania; I was seized with a sudden urge to run to the church of St. Sulpice and offer a prayer in thanks to him. But before I could act on this, Maria returned with a waiter. The waiter bore a bottle, a glass, and a fork. I stared at him, then at Maria. "What is this?"

"You have drunk enough wine; you should try absinthe. I think you will like it."

My first taste was horrid enough to make me fear the second. Maria almost laughed at me, and she and the waiter shared a knowing smile. "Be steadfast, little greyhound," she said, "be steadfast. The reward will come."

"How do you know?" I grimaced. I did not know how

I would ever cleanse the harsh, medicine-sweet taste from my mouth; perhaps with a slice of blue cheese?

"I have drunk much wormwood liquor in my time," she replied. "It is an aid to childbearing."

Hurriedly, I tossed down the rest of the glass, and the waiter obligingly prepared another, this time with a larger lump of sugar. I stared at the bubbling sugar, melting under a blue flame, until the waiter extinguished this little torch with his water pitcher. How wonderful is the smell of roasted sugar! The first taste from this glass was so far removed from the previous unpleasantness that I barely conjoined the two experiences in my mind.

"Childbearing?" I asked.

"I bore seven children," Maria said. "I lost four of them in infancy."

My eyes grew wide. Seven! "And what of the survivors?"

She shrugged. "They are long dead now," she said with a tinge of regret.

"So once upon a time, you did have a husband."

Her mouth shifted gently, as though she savored the anise poison sugar along with me. "We were never married," she said. "I was a mere consort. More than anything, I was owned; I was a possession of that man. He, too, is long dead, and I regret it not. He was a stranger but for those times where he lay upon me. He was a soldier, and more often went to command battles. It was a blessing when he went away, and a struggle when he returned. He was nobility. He needed sons; I bore him sons. The arrangement was mutually advantageous."

"But there was no love," I said.

She smiled. "Ah, that is where you are wrong, little greyhound. There was love. I cannot live without love, and I never have. There was not love between the man and me, no. Of course not. That has nothing to do with begetting children; not now, not then. You well know this." She stroked the edge of her furled fan. "And I loved my sons—my strong, handsome, warlike sons. But their affection was reserved for their father and for the country; it is not manly to dote upon one's mother, only to defend her home and her virtue. That is a form of love. But I cannot live on filial duty. I need a love of my own. And I found it. Again and again. Through all the changes, all the battles, all the shifts in power, I found love."

I gazed at her. In the shifting golden firelight, my eyes misted from drink, she appeared more human than I had ever witnessed, and she took my hand. In my mind I saw glimpses of her sons in their armor, of the château where she bore them, of the fresh faces of the women who cradled her lonely head upon their breasts—and realized with a start that their clothes and hair were completely unfamiliar to me, that the language they spoke was not the French I knew but something called Lorrain, which I understood without understanding. And then the English came in a great confusion, and through the confusion slipped Maria, free.

Maria released my hand. I blinked, and I was in the café, on February eleventh, 1817. In the dim light, all surfaces glistened as though rimed with an infinitesimal layer of ice; all colors saturated, all details wavering and then leaping into sharp focus. Maria wore a pleased smile.

"How old are you? Truly?" I asked.

"Only the wormwood knows," she said. "Listen closely, and it may tell you." She took my hand, raised it to her mouth, and her fang teeth pricked through the skin of my wrist. I looked around me with alarm, to see if we held anyone's attention, but the café continued with its business, heedless to the tiny act of lust and violence occurring within its midst. And then the inevitable shock of the pleasure jolted me, curving my spine and drawing a low moan from my throat.

As unconsciously as a baby seeking its primary pleasure, my other hand slid up her arm and cupped Maria's breast. She struck me (but gently) in the face, severing the bond between us, the blood dribbling from the corner of her mouth.

"You will not touch me in that manner," she said, the tone of her words chilling me to the bone. "No man is allowed to touch me thus. Do you understand?"

Desire made me desperate, and alcohol made me bold and foolish. I knew she could kill me where I sat, but it did not seem to matter. "But I must touch—I must be close to you, my Maria, I need you!"

"You do not need me," she said, more gently, and from that very moment, like an electric current being broken, I did not. My lust for her feminine body vanished, leaving only devotion, admiration, respect—a filial love. I was now her child. Tears streamed over my cheeks.

She enfolded me in her arms then, and kissed me on the crown of my head; I felt the wet press of her lips on my scalp, stamping a rosette in blood. "Don't cry, child. Don't cry."

"Mamma," I said.

"She is dead, little one, she is dead."

I do remember the waiter returning with the bottle and the spoon. I do remember dancing, in the café and in the blowing snow. But if the wormwood shared its knowledge of Maria's true age, I have forgotten it.

One warm, cozy, quiet winter evening at home, I sketched Georgina sprawled on the rug before the fire, while Maria sat crocheting in her favorite chair. Georgina refused to sit still, and I had to keep starting over, much to her amusement. "Can't you just remember how I was? My leg fell asleep!"

"No, no, I need more detail. Please. Put your foot flat on the floor again; I was drawing the tent of your skirt. Like a Bedouin residence."

"That's an idea," Georgina said, sitting up entirely. "We should write to Jozef that I have been seized by an Arab prince—the prince of a haughty Bedouin tribe! He'll love that."

"My love, please."

"I will sit for you," said Maria.

I looked over at her; she had been so nearly silent, all through the night, that I had not expected her ever to move again. "Really?" I asked.

"I will sit for you," she repeated, "and you will paint my portrait."

"Oh, my lady! Oh! Oh, what an honor! What a delight!" I crawled to Maria and put my head on the heap of crocheted lace in her lap. She shooed me away with the gentle, nonverbal grumbles commonly used to address small, troublesome house pets.

"What about me?" Georgina pouted.

"You won't sit still," Maria said. "And I will. For as long as he likes."

"I *may* be able to paint you from memory," I said to Georgina guiltily. "It was quite a memorable pose."

"Yes, and a view right up to her bush, no doubt. Simply tasteless." Maria took up her needles again, humming to herself and smiling.

Georgina stood up and walked right over me, trapping me in the Bedouin tent between her legs, and ground her pelvis against Maria's skirted thigh. "Right up to my bush," she said mischievously. "Weren't you looking?"

"I've seen it before," Maria said, eyes on her knitting.

"Want to see it again?" Georgina offered, and grasped the trailing edge of her skirt. She flashed herself with a sharp, randy whistle at Maria, who still did not look up, and then let the skirt drop, with me inside, between her long, lean legs. I raised my eyes to Heaven.

"Georgina, I will deal with you later. Let Orfeo go."

I crawled backward out of the skirts, and Georgina tossed the crochetwork aside and dropped herself onto Maria's lap. At once they began kissing with abandon. I slid back on the rug, turned a page in my sketchbook, and drew a general outline of their bodies and their entwined mouths.

I felt Maria's thoughts directing me to go to my room and read Voltaire. I shrugged and brought my pencil and paper, and instead of reading, added details to my sketch of Georgina. But my drawing of the two of them together was an incoherent blob that suggested nothing, and I threw it away.

Maria sat for me the next night, and many of the nights that followed. Depicting her was easy; my pencil flew as through it were directed by the hand of Apollo, and the paints drenched the paper exactly as I wanted them, to display the luminosity of her beauty. Her face, lit by firelight, had just enough color to add to the whiteness of the paper.

When Maria saw the finished painting, at first her expression did not change as her eyes scanned the image. "This is what you see?" she asked me.

I nodded.

"This is what I looked like . . . before," she said, her voice breaking and her face at once wet with streaming tears. "You have seen it. You have seen me—not as I am, but as I once was."

Maria handed the paper back to me and turned away, sinking into a chair, her heart in a turmoil of memories and emotions too rapid and complex for me to follow.

Georgina immediately snatched the portrait and examined it closely. "You must paint me next," she said decisively. "I promise I will sit still."

My portrait of Georgina gave her as much astonishment, but rather than being devastated by it, it only made her laugh and smile to herself, unwilling to be parted from the painting even long enough for me to sign it. "He can do it," she said. "This is a portrait of Jadzia Kopernik. Not of the Lady Georgina. Do you see, Maria? He painted me."

"He painted Jadzia, not you," Maria pointed out.

"I *am*—"

"My dears," I said, "I feel like I'm about to be sick."

"Go vomit outside," said Maria.

"No, Maria. I don't want to fight about this. This is a beautiful painting, Orfeo. Thank you." Georgina kissed me and, giving Maria a significant look, she took the painting into her room and shut the door.

Maria and I followed suit without another word.

We Began at Midnight

"I want to keep him forever," Georgina said.

Maria got very cross whenever Georgie said that. "Why can't you leave your toys alone? Why must you always cut your dolls' hair and dress them as Red Indians? Why must you write in the margins of your books, as though you could add anything to the text already there? What makes you think that your ideas are better? Why can't you just be content?"

"Because I am young!" Georgina's rallying cry. When she said this, it hurt Maria so much that it would make me physically sick with the force of her pain. It was the same when Maria accused Georgie of slothfulness or stupidity. When they argued, I would lie down in bed, or wherever I could, and writhe in an attempt to loosen the aching muscles.

I did everything I could to keep them happy. When they were both happy, I felt invincible; when their moods were violent, I paid for it with the agony of my senses, as though their words were blows; when either of them was melancholy, or worse, both of them, I could do nothing but weep alone in my darkened room. Nothing gave me comfort until one of them felt better, then I was up and about, like a jolly marionette, sliding down the polished floor of the sitting room in my stocking feet, dancing naked with my face painted up like a palsied whore until they shook with laughter.

Each evening I drank absinthe, for which I had developed an appreciation, and the women then drank of my blood, and became as drunk and dreamy as I was. Spring brought nights at the opera; summer, midnight walks in the Tuileries, and along the Seine, arm in arm, three abreast, with me in the center, my body acting as a conduit for their silent conversations.

I want to keep him forever, Maria, my love, Georgina expressed.

Are you certain that you know that which you ask?

I am certain that I want to keep him forever.

Forever is a horribly long time, Georgina, my love.

Why should I be bound to a future I cannot see? I only know about now. And now, I want Orfeo to be our equal, not our plaything. He deserves that, don't you think?

"I desire only for your wishes to come true," I said aloud.

"We aren't talking to you," said Maria. My mouth closed as though a hand had shut it.

"That's exactly what I mean," Georgina broke in impatiently. "When you want him to shut up, he shuts up. When you wanted me to shut up, I shut up. It is better now that I am in control of myself."

Better for you, *perhaps.* "Are you in control of yourself? I see very little self-control in you, my love."

Bitch. "You are bourgeois!"

"Darling, I am *aristocracy*."

"That is worse!"

I felt as though I was being stretched on the rack, my arms being slowly pulled from their sockets. "Please don't fight," I murmured. "I . . . only want . . . to make you happy."

"Poor puppy," said Maria softly, and the pain ceased. "I'm sorry; I don't want to hurt you. I forget."

"Please let's bring him with us," came Georgina's plea. "No puppy! No plaything! Orfeo is a man. Let us make him a thousand times more even than that."

"It is a terrible thing to ask! It is a terrible fate to have!" Maria, as passionate, clenched and shook her little fist. "To become like us, you have to die! You have to die a terrible death! Do you want this?" Maria asked, staring into my eyes. The world dropped away, leaving only her face, her pursuit of my honesty. "Don't you want to father children?"

"I have never," I said, powerless to veil the ignoble truth. I had never had to face this knowledge myself; I kept it, hidden, in a back pocket, aware of it, but delaying the confrontation. Now I beheld it, as surely as I saw my appearance through Maria's eyes, too true and basic even to feel shame. "To me, it seems a prison, and the world is already a prison. The last thing I want to do is to create more inmates."

Maria scoffed at my arch nihilism. "Inmates! You know nothing of prison, child. You will change your mind, I promise you. You have experienced nothing yet of prison."

"My life is gone! I have lost everything. There is nothing left for me to want, but that I want to make her happy. I love her. I will do as she desires."

"She will never be yours, Orphée. Never."

As Maria said this, I was gazing into Georgie's eyes, my mind generating music set to the jagged tune of her voice. *I have ensnared you, Orfeo. But oh, how I love you, and I want you to stay just this way. I am yours. I shall always be yours.*

Georgina's pleasure suffused me with a gentle

warmth more profound than any sunbeam or firelight. "You have seen to the bottom of his heart," she murmured. "There is no going back for him. There never was. I have chosen him."

Maria gazed at Georgina then; and I did not perceive what passed between them, but tears wet their pale cheeks, and they embraced for a long time while I stood aside, unable to take my eyes from them.

At last they came to me, and both embraced me at once. "Please forgive me; please forgive the Lady Georgina," Maria whispered into my ear, "for what we are about to do. For it is an act of love, that which guides us all, for good or ill."

Have I forgiven? It seems so gentle now in my recollection, and yet I recollect in a wooden box underneath a thousand tons of cathedral, dead and yet unable to die, for their act of love, for my act of devotion. Was it my own decision? I shall never know where my will ended and their stronger ones began.

At the end of a week of actual work—I could have hardly written more correspondence had I been employed as secretary to the King—I requested that we attend evening Mass together. Neither of them objected; both of them had accompanied me on previous visits, and I suspected Maria attended even more frequently than I. Maria and Georgina did not make confessions that night, but I resolutely walked into the confessional and took a seat on the hard, narrow bench that seemed to enact penance just in sitting down.

"Bless me, Father, for I have sinned . . ." I found myself at a loss. Was it my duty to confess to sins I had planned for the future?

"Speak, my son."

I said all the usual things. But I did not feel complete when I had confessed everything that I had already done. "Father, I—This is my last night on this earth as a human creature," I said all in a rush.

"What do you mean?"

"I mean . . . I . . . uh, never mind."

"I don't understand. Do you mean to take your own life? Please do not attempt this!"

"No, no, I'm not," I said. "But I don't think that I shall see another morning." I was wrong about this, thank God. "I shall be transformed into something else, to sacrifice all that I am, to become something more rare and beautiful. And I do this for love. I want to stay, for eternity, with my love."

There was silence from the other side, then the priest, in a dull and distracted voice, listed some fairly minor forms of penance. "And be sure that you do them as soon as you are able," he added, "if you are correct about not seeing tomorrow."

"Oh, I shall see tomorrow," I replied. "Just not the morning. Thank you, Father. Thank you, Lord."

I received the communion with a light, clear heart, lit candles for those martyred for love, and raced through a single recitation of the rosary. I would have all week to make up the rest, I thought.

With the women, I headed to the restaurant for a final late supper of rack of lamb, fresh bread, Camembert, turnips, and the infamous potato soup. The women watched me impassively, knowing what was to come but unwilling to spoil my supper by telling me of it.

Those solid hands tore the bread.

Blunt teeth chewed it.

That solid throat swallowed it.

The solid mind had no idea.

We began after midnight.

I stood on the stone floor in the empty courtyard of the house, alone, naked, and shivering in candlelight.

The animal cages had been cleared away, and an empty bathtub stood a few feet away. I thought to myself: *Tonight I shall die.* I grasped for a sense of peace, but it slipped through my fingers, as nimble as mist. My heavy meal had made me dizzy and sleepy, and I wanted to crawl into a warm bed and doze off.

And then they came, bearing great buckets of busily steaming water, which they poured into the tub. They made several trips. I asked, after the third, "Why don't you get Yves and Maignot to help you?"

"They are helping us," said Georgina to me, as Maria returned silently to the kitchen. Maria had no expression whatsoever, her eyes like mirrors. "From inside."

"Do you love me?" I begged. "I'm afraid. I need to feel that you love me."

She gave me a small, sad smile, and I found that I no longer minded the cold. "It won't be long," she said.

When the tub was half full, they stood, one at each side of me. They kissed each other, and then each of them kissed me. I was overwhelmed by the ceremony; Maria had never kissed my mouth before, and I, of course, had never dared. Their mouths tasted of the night sky: dark, rich, mysterious, sensual. *From inside.* The servants were dead, drained, sucked into them, and it was their blood that I tasted. The animals had all disappeared that week, as well. Why had I not noticed? Too busy recopying Maria's terrible handwriting? But surely I'd notice the din of screaming rabbits?

I had less than a second to consider this.

I do not know which of them slit my throat; I felt only an immediate panic, clutching at my bubbling, gushing neck with fingers already too slippery to do much good. Georgina slid her arms around me from behind, and she laid me down against the stones, adding the pressure of her hand against mine. "Stay awake," she said to me, "stay awake," insisting, even in my mind, in my body, my veins; and I did not lose consciousness. Oh, but the pain became a dimension in itself! I could barely see anything.

Maria tore at her forearm with her teeth and held the ragged wound to my mouth. Her blood was thick and alive, vibrating faintly against my tongue. With the first mouthful, I vomited, splashing our bodies with my last supper, but she did not remove her arm. "Drink *now*," she hissed. "Swallow it! Hold it down!"

I struggled to command my throat muscles, but they were paralyzed with fright and revulsion. Some of her blood trickled down my gullet somehow, and immediately I regained the ability to swallow.

Maria's thoughts created a dim echo in my mind. *That's one.*

Georgina now held her wrist against my mouth, and I swallowed again. *It wanted me to drink it;* the blood itself possessed will! My belly clenched hard with the desire to retch, but something else prevented it.

"Georgina, now," came Maria's voice, sounding very tiny against the roaring in my ears. "That's four; enough, or you'll ruin him." Georgina's wrist pulled away from my mouth. I saw the marks of my teeth in bloody, blunt bruises; I had bitten hard into her flesh. I dropped onto the flagstones, gasping for breath, shivering again as the commingled gore on my arms and chest cooled in the dampish evening air. My jaws ached, as though I had clenched them for hours.

"That's it?" I said, with a weary attempt at arrogance. "That wasn't so bad . . ." I had a terrible headache. My leaking, slit throat ached and pounded and stung. And it itched. I scratched it before I remembered, and cried out with the pain. And yet the itching satisfied it in some way, demanding more.

Maria and Georgina stood, covered in vomit and dark blood, near the tub, staring at me with horror. I felt a prickle of unease at the base of my spine, which transformed almost immediately to the most profound, sense-stripping nausea.

"It's begun; did you see it?" Maria whispered to Georgie.

"Yes . . ." Georgie replied. Her eyes were wide with amazement. "Oh . . . Oh, Orfeo, I'm so sorry . . ."

"What? What is it?" I sat up, then stood up, and immediately doubled over, retching violently. Blood spattered the stone. *Mother of Christ!*

My throat itched, so I scratched it. I could not help it; my fingers slipped into the incision, rolled their tips over my trachea while I made a humming noise, fascinated by the feel of the vibration, the sticky slickness of tissue.

I stared up at the women. "It's begun?" I asked helplessly. In moonlight they appeared as ghosts, the stain of rot upon their clothes, wild-haired, terrified, remorseful. Maria slowly, almost imperceptibly, nodded.

Then I saw nothing.

Like a hangman's hood dropping over my eyes, everything went dark. I shouted, flailing around with my arms outstretched, but I felt nothing—the walls too far away, everything in the world except the stone under my feet, gone. "Help! I am blind!" I blundered a step or two in darkness until I barked my shins against the edge of the bathtub and felt the wood cut deeply into my flesh.

I slipped in spilled liquid and fell sickeningly sideways.

The impact of the floor broke my collarbone where I struck the stone with my shoulder, and closed my jaw with a snap. I rolled onto my side and spat out the explosion of blood that happened inside my mouth. I filled and released my lungs in what should have been a mighty shriek, but heard nothing from without—only an infinite noise from within. My blood was boiling, my tissues breaking apart like chicken meat in a cook pot, stripped of all sensations but pain. And when even pain is gone, how it is missed!

My death—so endless, so brief.

Halo

My rebirth came about much like the original: naked, shivering, howling, while softly cooing women washed my body with soft cloths.

"Look," came a voice as soft as fog. "Here he is."

I opened my eyes to stabbing daggers of light (from a single candle) and sneezed violently, producing a disgusting bolus of bloody mucus that I tried, in vain, to shake off my hand. The women laughed.

I rubbed my hand on the bottom of the tub, passed wet fingers over my eyes, and looked around me. I was bathing in blood.

"Orfeo? You're here."

I looked up at the women, crouched naked over the tub with their red-soaked cloths, anointing me in bloody water. My skin drank it in, absorbing it, tingling, growing itself. Deliriously, I thought to myself: *I have turned the water into wine. My glory is revealed.* The courtyard was painted in a single shade of rusty crimson. And those pale shreds and lumps in the corner—were they bones or scraped fat or wool? From me? For a panicked moment, I thought I had ripped off my own head.

I suddenly realized that that was a possibility.

I touched my chin, where a soft layer of wet beard lay atop warm, solid skin, and gingerly stroked my throat. It was whole. There was no scar, no pain. Now that my eyes had adjusted to light, I could see miraculously well; every focused detail sharpened itself to a keen edge. The pale shreds were the remains of muslin dresses Maria and Georgina wore previously, soaked through with our blood and my retchings, and discarded in a drying, reeking heap.

I realized that I had been sucking on my bloody, wet fingers without realizing it, and the traces of my own blood evoked, but did not satisfy, a hunger as intimately connected as my own soul.

The hunger itself was my soul.

I stood up and arched my shoulders back. "I have to get out of here," I said calmly. Dripping, I stepped out of the tub and walked into the house. At a respectful distance, Maria and Georgina, silent, as naked as myself, followed me.

I walked out of the house, onto the street. The night air felt very peculiar on my skin; I walked the few blocks to the banks of the Seine, and dove into the frigid, brackish water.

There were many corpses in the river: plant, fish, dog, cat, vermin, human, mountain. I noted them all with a cold delight. And yet I did not feel that I was among the dead. I felt only the purpose, the instinct. *Find someone.*

I surfaced on the other bank after several long, refreshing strokes, and easily pulled myself up the brick-walled banks. In the indigo peace before dawn, I saw no one. But I knew I had to find someone and instinct would do the rest; I wouldn't even have to think about it. I felt people alive and awake in this city, but I did not know where they were. I followed my senses—not the senses of smell, vision, or sight, but something similar to them that I had never had before.

I walked, nude and barefoot, not impaired by the cold. I had become an animal, with an animal's calm acceptance of discomfort. I felt invisible and luminescent at once, and did not wonder at this; I knew only my goal. The buildings contained hundreds of sleepers, their breath misting the air with waste gases and the unique perfumes of their scents. I spied an open window and made for it, climbing ironwork and brick to seize the fluttering fabric of a curtain and pull myself inside.

Three little girls and their nursemaid. How wonderful. Their dreams were full of ribbons and fairy tales.

Do we consider it murder when the tiger attacks the Malay and eats him? Do we consider it murder when an elephant tramples a Hindu who only wants to worship the great beast? Do we consider it murder when we wring the necks of geese for Christmas dinner?

None of them ever woke up; none of them ever felt pain. I would have been able to taste it.

Afterward, I sat on the floor of the little nursery, sighing, relaxing. I tested my shattered shoulder, my jaw, even thrust out my tongue; all were restored, even more handsomely than before. The skin on my legs, previously resembling that of a plucked cockfight champion, was now a gloriously smooth ivory whiteness, the brown hairs glistening thick and fine. As far as I could tell by looking down at myself, I was not merely restored but improved in every way, and yet still recognizably Orfeo Ricari.

I bent over and gazed at the now-dead little girls. Rose, Elise, and Jeanette lay with their still profiles against the glossy, yellowed bedding, still tucked in next to one another. Jeanette's mouth was open. Her sister Elise had fallen asleep with her thumb in her mouth; she was a timid thing. Rose was a cousin; she was the same age, exactly, as Elise. The nurse, Yvette, was hardly more than a child herself.

I had not spilled a drop.

I let myself out the window where I had entered, let myself drop to the street four floors below. Wondering, I gazed up and realized that I had climbed up a brick wall as skillfully as a spider, without sparing a thought.

My return swim, free of the thirst, was even more exquisite than my first.

On the left bank, Maria and Georgina sat, wearing clean gauze dressing-gowns that billowed in the cooling autumn wind, glowing in the azures and purples cast by the approach of the goddess Aurora. I could see them shining. I had always wanted to see a halo; I did not realize, as trapped in traditional iconography as I was, that a halo does not merely surround the head but suffuses the entire body; and it does not extend brightly outward very far, but clings to the contours of the form, more strongly at the head and hands and sex. It was the most beautiful sight I had ever witnessed.

"It is your first day," said Georgina, rising, and holding out her arms to me. "You have risen. You are with us now."

I went to her and allowed her embrace, and that of Maria also; and their joy touched and fortified me, but the reassurance, the thoughtlessness that I had enjoyed, was at an end. I was now their equal.

And I had murdered innocents painlessly.

I sat and watched the dawning of the day from my little room. The light was overwhelming, and I turned away before the sun had appeared at the horizon, my eyes smarting and watering so furiously I thought, at first, that they were bleeding.

Still, I enjoyed the warm current of air that breathed through the open window, wafting the scent of blood and flowers from Les Halles. If I concentrated—only a slight pressure of focus inside my head, like clenching a muscle—the smells began to distinguish themselves quite clearly. Anchovies, blood puddings, lilies, apples, calf's brains, butter, mint and lavender, and above all, hundreds and thousands of different kinds of excrement. When Maria came into my room, I was sprawled on my bed, laughing and crying, drunk on pure sensation.

"Get up," she said quite sternly, "and put on your clothes. You were almost in direct sunlight."

"Would it kill me?" I asked in a dreamy way.

"If it touched you long enough, yes, it would."

"So I am not immortal?" Instantly, I felt shame for the note of pure hopeful joy in my voice.

Maria arched her eyebrow at me and blinked, and I could hear her, very faintly, thinking, *I cannot believe he said that. How more useless could he be?* But aloud she said, "I did not say *how* long. Now get up. You have all the time in the world to lie there and gorge yourself on the smell of shit. We have work to do."

"Work?" I said, rolling over into a sitting position.

"Yes, I know it's a strange and foreign concept to you, my most precious lapdog. We must acquire a new home immediately; we are no longer safe here."

"Why?" I whined, forgetting myself again. "It's day-time!"

The eyebrow arched again. I attempted to concentrate on her thoughts the way I had concentrated on the scent of Les Halles, but I was not strong enough or fast enough, and I was mute to all but that my ears could receive. "That, my little one, is why there are curtains.

While it is light, we must pack our things; later, we will go out and acquire a new home. That means I must go to the bank, and that means that, as far as any of them know, you and Georgina are married, and I am your elder sister. We are now Monsieur, Madame, and Mademoiselle Grise. Don't you remember the letters I gave you last week? I imagine you were distracted, contemplating your death as you were." She opened her fan and fluttered it briefly at her neck. "And, Orfeo, stay out of my mind unless I want you there. It's very rude to eavesdrop."

I could hardly pay attention to what she said; all my senses were suddenly, alarmingly keen, and I shuddered with the violence of my perceptions. I felt my fingernails growing, stiffening, cell by cell. Maria still glowed before me, though the lines in her face were more pronounced in daylight, and her eyes looked more like oiled glass than flesh. And her smell! Georgina smelled of almost nothing, even in the exertions of sex, but Maria had an unmistakable, rich, peculiar, half-delicious, half-morbid scent.

"You're . . . bleeding," I said.

She narrowed her eyes at me, her slight smile bitter. "I am always bleeding," she replied, and left me.

I dressed myself, shaking. I despaired of being able to survive for the rest of time when I could hear and smell and see everything with a shocking acuity. It gave me nausea. I closed my eyes and took deep breaths, guessing that shutting off at least one sense would help me gain a sense of control. Presently, Georgina appeared, her hair braided but unpinned, wearing the white lace gown of our first encounter. She frowned at the strip of sunlight coming through my window and drew the curtains, hissing faintly with pain from the sun. As quickly as the burn had occurred, it vanished.

I saw all of this through her eyes.

"Is it true?" I asked her, shuddering. "Is Maria—"

She put her arms around me and kissed the back of my neck. "Yes," she replied softly. "We are held at the state of our transformation for all time. Maria was menstruating, and thus she continues. I was not, and so I never shall again."

"How horrible to bleed always!" I whispered.

"How like a man! It is not horrible. It is a natural state for a woman. It does not trouble her, and it pleases *me* very much."

I was aghast. Georgina laughed. "My Orfeo. You shall learn by doing, and by doing, you shall learn," she said to me. "This is a grand and terrible world that we inhabit. All blood is valuable. Do hurry with your packing, and then come and help roll the tapestries. It won't be hard for you, but you must, of course, be careful. If we are finished before nightfall, you may sleep for a short while; believe me, you will want to. Staying awake all day is hard for anyone, and although I know you think you are twenty-one, you are a newborn. If you were not, it would be better for you to stay awake; we must go away from here, as soon as possible. I shan't sleep."

"Georgie . . . I can't control my mind," I whispered. "I'm overwhelmed."

She smiled sadly. "You can, and you will."

In Georgina's bed, as the late-summer afternoon unwound itself into a fiery dusk, I slept and dreamt. One hundred twenty years later, I still wish I hadn't given in to my sudden, if anticipated, profound fatigue. I had assumed that with the transformation, since all parts of me had been improved and all my physical imperfections smoothed away, my mind would also be cleansed of its own horrible imaginings. But how we are, when we are changed, is how we shall remain for all time.

Just a flicker of it remains: Mamma, in her grave,

opening her eyes and staring at me. "May God save you! May God save you!" Then the violation. So simple, yet so horrifying.

I woke violently, my hands at my throat trying to wrest the air back into my lungs, and fell upon Georgina, who lay next to me, stroking my forehead. She lay still for a moment, even while I pierced her neck with my fangs and drew deeply upon her blood, but then struck me away with her wrist. I went skidding like a rag doll across the floor to the opposite wall.

"Control yourself!" she shouted. My eardrums caved but did not burst; the glass vase on the table next to the couch, full of dead roses and foul water, was not so fortunate. I stared at the cut glass collapsing into shards as surely as if it had been struck with a brick. I could see each individual shard tumbling and pirouetting through the air, each gobbet of water leaping forth, every shriveled petal of every rose. I was too fascinated to be frightened, or even to feel the pain of the blow.

Georgie wiped her neck with the side of her hand, frowning at the droplets blackening on her bodice, and sighed. "We all have nightmares. Every one of us. Everything that lives has nightmares," she said in a quieter tone. "Do not let them control you. They are a part of you, and nothing to fear." I stared at the dirty water, speckled with mildew, crawling across the floor at me. "I know you need blood, but don't take it from me. I need it. Or, at least, don't take it from me without asking." She slid her hand up her thigh, hiking her skirt above her ankle. "I shall, I think, give it when asked politely. You are a very, very, very pretty little bloodsucker."

"Can I do *that* with my voice?" I asked in a whisper.

"Probably not yet," she replied. Maria swept into the room with a look of concern. Georgina gave her a reassuring kiss. "Though, if you keep stealing our blood, it won't be long."

88

Maria stared at me disapprovingly. "Orfeo!"

"I didn't steal . . ." I rose from the floor, licking the inside of my lips and my teeth. I had the fangs now—no longer than my canine teeth had been before, but sharper and more pointed. With the slightest pressure, I punctured my own tongue so cleanly that it barely hurt. Then I bit through the inside of my lip, at the corner of my mouth. The wounds did not seem to bleed.

"He's going to be useless today," Maria said. "Perhaps we can pass him off as an idiot."

"He's in shock," Georgina suggested. "We must make up a story. Um, let's see . . . his beloved elder brother died this morning. Poor M. Grise. He is mad with grief." She smiled at me to blunt the sting of her words.

"Excellent," said Maria. "You *are* so good at this. I just go in and kill everyone, but your methods are so much more subtle." She turned with a chuckle to Georgina and caressed her neck where I had bitten her. It showed no mark. "Come and set my hair. And you, miscreant, go to the kitchen, and get your own blood."

In the kitchen, the last remaining servant, a deaf little maid named Carmina, sat motionless on a stool with her back to the cabinets. The stool was an island in a small sea of blood, leaking from the back of her neck where a chef's knife throbbed gently in time with her heartbeat. I sensed no fear or pain from her; her spinal column had been severed, and her life would not continue much longer than a minute. I stood beside her and pulled out the knife, unable to resist licking the sharp blade clean, then I put my mouth to the neatly cut, gently welling wound.

Her blood tasted of resignation, sadness, and darkness.

I was indeed useless that night. I could only walk if I wasn't thinking about it. I did not trust my voice in the company of the fragile-eared mortals, and so remained mute, only nodding stupidly when anyone asked me for a response.

And oh, the mortals! I had only just departed from their ranks, and yet they already seemed so alien to me. They stank so robustly that I wondered how I ever stood it before, and yet their stench was so rich and warm and full of information that I treasured it like ambergris. M. Trèbute, the carriage driver, took vast quantities of poor-quality snuff, and enjoyed garlic butter and whores with syphilis. Laurel and Laurel, the realtors, who seemed not to mind at all having a business meeting at eight o'clock in the evening, had both engaged in sodomy less than an hour before our appointment, though not with each other. The little girl outside the tobacconists' had a smudge of fresh oil paint on the heel of her shoe, and a chunk of horsehide in her mouth, which she chewed to stave off hunger. It was all I could do to resist seizing her and drawing her into my arms for a fatal kiss; if I am not mistaken, both my companions bolstered my willpower with their own.

By one in the morning, the Grise household had taken up residence in a large apartment on the third floor of a building on the side of a hill, with a splendid view that stretched the gold-flecked tapestry of Paris before us. I stood on the balcony and watched a watery moon draw closer to the toothed horizon, exhausted and exalted by turns. Outside the city, the noise of carriages and shouts receded to a murmur, and the quiet soaked into me like a balm, soothing my overworked auditory sense. My eyes still gathered every detail, relevant or no, and my clothes bothered me so much that I took them off, right there on the balcony.

In the drawing room behind me, Maria and Georgina laughed. "Orphée, the famous bawd!" Maria called. "He shan't remain clothed a moment longer than necessary!

Look upon his legendary rib cage and the hipbones that carved a thousand joints!"

"Why do you mock me?" I asked wearily. I turned to face them, sprawled on the couches with their corsets unlaced and their hair freed of its pins and bonnets. "Can you not help me? You have thrown me to the lions. Please. You have knowledge of this life which I have only guessed at, and I find that what I know is insufficient."

"Is it not always the way?" Maria mused. "What we think we know is inaccurate, and what we do know is paltry."

"Maria," admonished Georgina. "Your longevity has cost you your compassion. Take pity on the poor baby; his suffering is plain to see." To me, she held out her hand. "Come—sit by us, and stop putting on a free show for all the world. They ought to pay you in chests of gold for baring your lovely body to them."

"Forgive me, Orphée," Maria said gently.

I collapsed at their feet and laid my head upon their mingled petticoats, still carrying a scent of lemon oil and snuff from the interior of the carriage. Both set upon stroking my hair, bringing relaxation and calm, separating and clarifying my senses. Maria even bent and kissed my temple with her cold, silken lips. "Focus your mind," she whispered against my ear. "You must exercise it, yes, like a muscle. Your ability is vast; your potential ability, vaster still. But you must learn to walk before you learn to fly."

"Learn to use what you perceive," Georgina continued. "Your perceptions are powerful tools, even more so than the strength you can draw from your body. If you control the flow of your senses, you will find that you can control the senses of others."

"If you don't wish to be seen, you won't be seen."

"If you wish to be seen as other than you are, it will be."

"But listen to your hunger. It speaks the ultimate truth, which can be ignored, but never refuted. You must drink blood. Nothing else will nourish you."

"Must I kill?" I asked.

"No," said Georgie, kissing my hair.

"Not necessarily," said Maria. "But you will. As you already have. This is a form of self-control very difficult to attain. But you must, or you risk undue attention."

"If you must kill, please do it outside the home," Georgie added. "We just moved in here. Montmartre is not so dense as Paris, but its shadows are longer."

"Can we go out now?" I asked, raising my head. "Educate me. Train me. Show me how it's done."

La Vie Nouvelle

From the balcony of an apartment on the side of a hill, I watched Paris. Each evening I watched the horizon swallow the sun, and each morning I turned, shuddering, from the sun's return, quivering with distaste and shame, as from the sight of an old lover coming up the street.

Befriending (or manipulating; I hardly know the difference anymore) Ollier, a young carriage driver whose mother lived a few floors above us, the ladies and I were in possession of a convenient method for returning to the streets of central Paris to enjoy its nightlife, in different cafés and playhouses than the ones we had frequented before. I bid a solemn farewell to my favorite restaurant, passing by it in Ollier's carriage; I could have gone in disguised, but I wanted to be known as myself, as the young Macaroni, and that I could not do. For all the staff knew, the entire household of the house on the Rue du F— had vanished, servants and all. This was not unusual enough to garner suspicion in the constantly transforming Paris.

I missed the soup, but there were other restaurants in other streets where I had never gone. I soon began to enjoy visiting strange places, though my appetite for good food was not as hearty as it had been. Indeed, after my first meal's appearance, essentially unchanged from the state in which I swallowed it, from my rear end, I nearly swore off all food forever.

Instead of gustatory pleasures, the restaurants afforded a fascinating view of Parisians going about their usual business, eating and exchanging money and viewpoints. Georgina preferred establishments full of young radicals, full of anger and hatred of the reestablished Bourbon regime and talk of eternal revolution; Maria chose the dining rooms and chambers of the wealthy and titled, where the bedecked ladies waltzed with cruel-faced, stylish men, and scurrying staff served every whim.

We all enjoyed the dark brasseries and taverns, the air perfumed with the licorice scent of the popular and readily available absinthe. Maria could draw a young woman toward her as inexorably as the tide, and immediately set upon her with flattery and coins. Some of the girls were frightened away and fled to safer corners of the room, but a sizable proportion were all too happy to sit with the generous ladies and the handsome young gentleman. And, as the atmosphere became smoky and dim, they made no protest when, one after another, we would pierce and sip from her wrist or her throat.

The first time we tried this was a mild disaster. I was still very young—a week or so, at most. And I killed the girl by accident. She just tasted so good: garlic, bay leaves, excitement, and grain alcohol. I became drunk and slipped away into a reverie, and I didn't notice that her heart had stopped beating. Georgie and Maria, who were drunk themselves, were occupied in kissing each other, and knew nothing else. I pulled my mouth away from the dancing girl's wrist and stared in some horror at how blue her lips and fingernails were. "Help!" I whispered.

"You're on your own," Maria murmured lazily, and continued her kiss. In my mind I could feel Georgina's half-amused, half-sympathetic laugh.

The dancing girl's blood still surged merrily in mine. Marie-France was her name; she was an artist's model, infamous as a very heavy drinker with a tendency to fall asleep behind the bar at the end of the night. I wrapped her arms around me and stood up with her, making vague amorous noises. She was taller than I; her head flopped backward, her mouth open. I gave her body a quick jerk, and her head slumped forward onto my shoulder. I slid sideways out of the tavern through the side door, carrying her still-negligible deadweight before me, with her back to the room. Outside, I brought her around to the back where garbage was collected. Unfortunately, Marie-France and I were not alone; four young roughs stood urinating against the wall of the next building. One of them turned his head, saw us, and grunted.

"You going to stick it in her?" he said, far too loudly. The other men turned around and snickered nastily.

"Yes," I responded, not knowing what else to say. "Do you want to watch?" I focused as hard as I could to tell them that they didn't.

One of the men doubled over and vomited on the flagstones, and the others staggered with their hands to their foreheads. "Let's go, brothers," their leader said through gritted teeth, trying not to vomit himself. They helped their sick comrade out of the alleyway and down the street. Before they had gone more than ten yards, all four of them dropped to the ground, bleeding from the eyes, ears, nose, and mouth.

Oh, I thought. *That's too much.*

I disordered Marie-France's clothes and laid her against the wall, out of the way of the mess, checked my shirtfront, and returned to the tavern through the front door. Maria and Georgina remained as they had been, embracing, with their tongues in each other's mouth. I took a swallow of my wine and stared, uncomfortably sober, into the fire.

Well done, said Maria, her mouth still engaged. *I would have killed them immediately.*

"That's the difference between us, then, isn't it?" I spoke bitterly. "And would you have killed them had they been women?"

That got her attention. "Women would have never been in such a situation," she responded.

"No, women have more subtle ways of attacking," I said.

"Are you arguing?" asked Georgina, her voice lilting. "Over gender? How revolutionary of you! We ought to be taking our leave, anyway. Tut-tut. Shame on you both. Everyone knows women are far more savage than men."

It was as though she had uttered a challenge, which Maria and I both eagerly accepted. We had no need to be together when we killed; I would always think of her and know she could see my actions. Many times I would be walking down the stairs to the garden or reading a newspaper, and pause, seemingly staring into space, but in my mind watching Maria lure an unwary civil servant or *grisette* to a premature death. I could feel the presence of another mind while I tasted the warm blood flowing from a victim's throat, admonishing me gently, *Remember, not too much!*

While Maria and I engaged in our brutal and amoral competition out on the streets, Georgina had taken to bringing girls home. She thought of it as "fishing," catching the sweet, confused young things fresh from the country, in search of a city job to support an impoverished family in Auxerre or Crécy. Georgie fed each girl and made love to her, then sipped a mouthful of her blood in the guise of an embrace. Then the unwitting creature was released back into the wild, with a full stomach, a headache, and a vague memory of a beautiful lady in the night. Over the course of five years, though she needed to go a-fishing several times a day, Georgina never brought death to anyone. I had much less self-control; I gorged myself on blood to the point of my victims' deaths nearly every night. I moved through the night, a smiling, gentle plague, killing hundreds, without pain or fear, throughout the city.

Maria did not kill by draining blood. She needed much less blood than either Georgina or I; she brought violence, and barely deigned to take a taste. There was no mystery surrounding the deaths of her victims: They were drowned, their heads were bashed in with stones, their necks were broken. Maria displayed all of this to us, her children.

"You are like the government," Georgina accused her. "You use excessive violence to no useful end. You waste life."

"Ha! Your idea of an insult is to compare me with the court of Charles?"

"It was not meant as an insult, merely an observation. Charles is a tyrant, his cabinet are pirates, and his soldiers, homicidal idiots."

"Someday you will attain maturity" was Maria's arch refrain. And Georgina's reply, the next verse in the familiar song, was "I hope that I never shall."

Fortunately for me, I no longer felt physical pain when they quarreled, merely annoyance and a helpless dismay. I knew that their love and companionship were in no danger of breaking apart, and besides, gem-studded Paris waited for me down the hill. Without a word or gesture, I left the apartment and swept down the stairs onto the street, where Ollier leaned against his carriage. He had no other customers; we supported him entirely, and he was at our service at all times. He stood erect as he saw me coming, and climbed onto the driver's seat. "What is Monsieur's pleasure this evening?" he asked smartly.

I let my eyes rove over him, spreading a web of flattery that was better, to him, than a purse of francs. For what is the purpose of money but to acquire things to make ourselves feel better? When I stood before him, Ollier had all the contentment in the world. "Take me to the Quartier Latin," I replied. "Drop me off anywhere. I will find my own way home."

I enjoyed my attempts to get lost; I never succeeded.

I discovered miraculous and terrible things about myself and my new power. I could run faster than the swiftest human athlete, and jump like my old namesake, the hare—and all of it soundlessly! I could balance a sewing needle on the tip of my finger for twenty minutes without a waver, then crush a paving stone with the same hand. I could focus on a single mind, many miles away, at any hour of the night, and bring him, not at all confused about his motives, to where I sat.

And I thought: *Ah, Georgina, I see.*

The young men of Paris were drawn to me. Many did not recognize the impulses that attracted them; many more did not wish to acknowledge them. I did not lure all of them; a large proportion came to me of their own accord, and spoke to me, either boldly or furtively, about what pleasures they imagined in my company. Hoping, in vain, that I would not be spied upon by my female counterparts, I occasionally indulged these mortal men's desires, as long as they were not too elaborate, and usually they were not; their fear of discovery was much more acute than my own. Sometimes I did not even slake my thirst, especially upon the ones I liked, as my control over how much blood I took was not as strong as it should have been. It seemed so much of a waste to hold the corpse of a medical student with an angelic face and a passion for the love poems of Dante Alighieri, having helplessly enjoyed the taste of his thoughts through to his final oblivion.

My wish for privacy in the fulfillment of these obscure lusts was strong enough that I washed my face and hands after these encounters, though the smell of male saliva and genitals could never be completely washed away, as I had no scent to mask it.

Still, I persisted. I needed something of my own, something that could not and would not be shared. I was selfish with myself sometimes. I had enough mornings of coming home to find Georgina and Maria, still "entertaining" their catch of the day on the balcony parlor, Georgina smelling of so many different women that I grew dizzy trying to distinguish them all, and Maria's white gloves flung over the fire grate, stiff and brown with blood.

"Ah, my brother Orphée, draw the curtains, would you?"

"I am not French, I am Italian. It's *Orfeo*. My name is Orfeo. Orfeo Ricari." My carping sounded boneless, even to my own ears, and it fueled my anger.

"What a fine sense of humor M. Grise has. Don't listen to him." Simultaneously, a cold invisible claw wrapped itself around my scrotum. *Speak well in company, little greyhound, or I shall have to be very stern indeed.*

What choice did I have? I drew the curtains.

Chicot

An elegant late supper, after a night at the opera, transformed our flat into a sparkling, supernatural garden of flickering candles and the rich scents of autumn flowers. Maria had had a desire to entertain, and had spent the money necessary to lure the minor viscounts and duchesses out to our Montmartre fantasy.

I dressed for company in the latest fashions, newly arrived from London. I had about eight layers of ruffle frothing at my chest, the starched and pressed cravat forced my chin up for the proper haughty demeanor, and instead of gilt buttons, a double row of tiny pewter frogs performed the same task. Maria stood with a watchful eye as my valet made last-minute adjustments to my trouser stirrups and dabbed my high-topped shoes with a soft cloth. Chambeau was a voiceless old thing, his eyes failing him, but with a fine, sure touch and all his family long dead—perfect for our purposes.

"Where does all your money come from, Maria?" I asked, half daft with boredom. I wanted to be outside, in the vineyards, chasing rats and rabbits. I told myself that my activities assisted the nuns by protecting their vines, but I just did it for pleasure, drinking blood only from the healthiest animals I caught, and feasting on their primitive terror.

"Orfeo. That's a very rude question." Maria snapped her fingers, and Chambeau bowed and hurried from the room. "I have had it for some time," Maria continued, "from the sale of properties that I have owned. I own several now. As you know, I still own the house on the Rue d'F—. We are doing quite well."

I stared at the young dandy in the looking glass. I thought of myself as a man, and a man growing old, with more patience on the surface and much, much less underneath, and a creeping dread about the future that I had never before experienced; and yet what reflected back, and moved when I thought to move, was beardless and wide-eyed, like a first-year student. Each time I looked into a mirror, I felt as though I hurtled backward in time.

Maria's reflected hand plucked a microscopic fragment of white lint from my coffee-colored coat. "You look extremely handsome," she said.

She spoke to the boy in the looking glass, not the man inside me. "I have no money of my own whatsoever," I mused.

"Are you not heir to your family's estate?" she asked.

"Probably not anymore," I admitted. "It has been fifteen years. Undoubtedly, I've been given up for dead. Or at least disowned."

She tutted. "Nonsense. You're the only son. I shall send an inquiry towards its purchase." She dabbed her fingertip against her tongue and set a curl against my temple, just so.

I slapped her hand away from me. "Don't," I said. "Leave it alone."

She backed away with a smile, fluttering her fan.

"Take the dead ones' money," she said. "They're dead; they don't need it anymore. When I think of all the money you left in the gutters—tsk! tsk!"

"What makes you think I left it? I took it," I snapped, then admitted, "I just didn't keep it for very long. There was never very much." But oh, how my bookshelves groaned with their burdens, and how the wine flowed in the taverns, and in the blood of my subsequent victims!

"Oh, alas, poor Orphée, never very much in the pockets of your students and poets! Perhaps you should seek out a higher class of game. It is such a shame when a man of quality like yourself should have to subsist upon the blood of ruffians."

"It suits *you* well, my lady," I pointed out.

"Ah! *Touché*, M. Grise." She chuckled and bowed to me, miming a fencing blade. "I salute. Please join us in the waiting room. It is almost ten o'clock."

If I *had* had a blade, I would have run her through. But no; my father's blade had been stolen by that Aostan slut with the bad skin, a lifetime and a half ago. I rubbed furiously at the perfectly placed spit curl until it frizzed and stuck out straight from the side of my head, then clicked my heels on the floor and walked down the hall to the waiting room.

Georgina saw my rebellious hair and blinked calmly, pursing her lips. Only one who knew her as intimately as I could have known that she was holding back cackles of laughter.

"Ah! My beautiful wife." I sat next to her on the long sofa and kissed the back of her hand. "You are as Venus in the night sky," I said, partially showing off and partially sincere.

Georgina wore her hair wrapped into a voluptuous turban made of heavy ivory-colored velvet, with only a few wispy dark curls around her face. It was a style that had passed somewhat out of fashion, but no one could deny that the effect was striking, with her long thin neck, great dark eyes, and birdlike shoulders. I hope that she has seen the twentieth century, where she would be famous the world over for those dreamy, exotic looks.

Maria, on the other hand, was, as always, the epitome of fashion, rounded generously all over, yet without a hint of excess, her waist corseted into a tight, sinuous line and her puffy gigot sleeves emphasizing the daintiness of her hands. Her saffron-yellow dress was trimmed with gleaming green embroidery and pearls no larger than grains of sand. The shimmering golden curls that framed her face served only to make the silk finish of the dress seem dull in comparison. "And I? And I?" she demanded, with such near-hysteria I knew that she was teasing me.

"And you? My lady." I smirked lightly, and accepted her out-thrust extremity. "My lady, you *are* the sky."

"Oh, mincemeat," Georgie scoffed. "But you *do* look good. Both of you. I am truly the most fortunate woman in the world." Her tender glance traveled between us, binding us with a silken thread of devotion, and my earlier annoyance at Maria dissolved, leaving me grateful and humble. I had gone from the bloody boots and the gutters of Ivry to a sumptuous sitting room in Montmartre, the company of gorgeous women, and tiny pewter frogs on my coat. It was not bad.

The clock struck, and the guests began to arrive.

I had been in Maria's company for long enough not to be dazzled by the infinity of minor titles and curious names, and I quickly tuned out the litany of announced arrivals and concentrated on scanning the minds of the mortals who had obliviously walked into this lionesses' den. None of them had any idea of our true natures, knowing only that Maria was an elegant lady with property, a title, and an immaculate, if unusual, reputation.

In fact, all of our invited guests were completely mesmerized, and had accepted all that Maria had told or suggested to them without a flicker of suspicion. Part of it was her longevity-augmented power, and part of it was simply their own willingness to be blinded. Indeed, it was easier to pass unnoticed as an inhuman among the upper class; all that was necessary was the observance of a set of rules and anticipations, and a gentle unspoken urge to believe.

I was surprised to note that none of our guests had ever slept with Georgie; I had begun to doubt that there was anyone left in Paris who had not tussled with the insatiable radical. Then I realized that, of course, none of them would ever share company with the scruffy, noisy "anarchists" who crowded the cafés of the Latin Quarter, and Georgie would be similarly repulsed by the royalists. As it was, they were fascinated by the lanky, languid Polish girl in her velvet turban and red-ribboned white dress, and her unrestrained laugh, relaxing on the sofa like a courtesan. It was only with effort that I remembered that I was supposed to act as her husband, and not simply as a besotted suitor.

At dinner, seated together, I drank in her gaze and the sight of her powdered face and reddened lips, and ignored my empty plates and glasses. Our highborn guests garnered no more of my attention. I kissed her fingers, long and flutelike in white crocheted gloves, and she stroked my temple, taming my rebellious hair. "Do we get to kill them?" I whispered in her ear. "Please say yes."

Maria, in midconversation, glanced over at me with an arched eyebrow.

Georgie held her head against my lips for a second, smiling. At once she straightened bolt upright in her chair and stared sharply at the doorway. I followed her gaze but saw only the butler, his arms crossed behind him, his face a blank servant's mask. Her skin could not go paler than it already was, but I felt that her stomach had just dropped inside her. "What is it?" I asked.

Georgina said nothing but rose as silently as a fog from her chair. None of the guests seemed to have noted her agitation or her movement; she was veiled to them, but not to me. She vanished from the room in the blink of an eye.

Now I felt it, too. A prickling ran up my spine, then down, then spread throughout my senses, lulling to a mellow but menacing vibration that affected all I saw or heard or felt.

A new presence, inhuman as we three, approached; was perhaps already inside, making itself at home.

The power, the breathtaking power!

Maria still smiled and chatted with the guests, but she was aware as well. I had not felt this alien sensation in years; I had grown used to the frequency and hum of the presence of Georgina—playing always like a low note in my mind—and the stronger, deeper, more ancient one of Maria. But this mode was different—at once airy and heavily minor.

Another one! Another one like us!

Without remembering to disguise myself, I set down my napkin and stood up. The eyes of every dinner guest clapped onto me; I felt naked. Maria blinked at me, pretending to be surprised. "Dear brother, where are you going?" she inquired mildly.

I could think of no way to explain. Georgie's absence was now noted as well. "Excuse me, I must attend my wife," I mumbled, bowing briefly and following Georgie's footsteps past the unruffled, expressionless butler, whose thoughts rang out: *Where the devil is he going?*

I hastened to the balcony parlor, my heart thudding anxiously in my chest. Had I genuinely thought that we

were the only ones? Vampires are made, not born! Even
Maria must have come from somewhere! But I knew,
even before I had entered the room, that Maria had not
sprung from this source. They were not related, as it
were.

What other knowledge had escaped me? Just like a
youth, I had mistakenly figured I knew it all.

Georgie sat, gazing up fondly at a plainly dressed
gentleman of medium height, his unfashionably long
dark hair thinning on top and drawn back in a queue,
and his hat held in a gloved hand behind his back. He
stood before her, but not intimately near. He shone
faintly, less brightly than either of the women, but unmistakably to my keen eyes.

Be wary and on good manners, young man, came the
voice in my head, in no human language but as direct as
a bolt of lightning. *I have more power in my smallest finger
than you have in your entire body.* I did not doubt it.

"Ah, Orfeo," Georgina said, glancing over at me. "I
didn't think you would sit still for long. May I introduce
you to M. Arthur Chicot? Arthur, this is Orfeo Ricari.
He is our newest."

I stared, as silent and rude as a country child. M.
Chicot was not particularly handsome, but I thought I
would never grow weary of looking at him; his very
countenance was soothing and gentle, much as Maria's
was dangerously lovely, and Georgina's wild. His deep-
set dark eyes were mild, melancholy, and quite beautiful, and he wore a slight smile that seemed to be his
usual expression, based on the lines drawn into the skin
by the corners of his mouth. How wonderful it would
have been to have had *him* as my childhood instructor,
and not the shocking, wicked beauty of Lorenzo Mercetti D'Aragón!

"Your perceptions are keen, Master Ricari. I *am* a
teacher," said Chicot to me. "Unfortunately, I know

nothing of English literature, so I would not have been well-suited to your inclinations. You may well have learned more of the world from the tutor you had." His accent was strange to my Paris-trained ear. He was from the southwest countryside that jutted into the Bay of Biscay, and I caught the remembrance of the scent of Bordeaux vineyards in his thoughts.

"Were you invited?" I spoke at last.

Georgie laughed her sprightly laugh. "Oh, Orfeo. You are the rudest, most inappropriate boy I've ever known. Chicot doesn't need an invitation. He is a friend. Not to mention that he may go wherever he pleases, and far be it from me to prevent his passage."

I resisted the urge to sit, but I did grasp his gloved hand in mine. Even through the glove I felt the extraordinary strength in his grip. "I did not mean it that way, Georgie. I meant only—why tonight? Why have I never seen another . . . before? Are there more of you?"

Chicot laughed, becoming alluring in the process. "Oh my, you are young, aren't you? In every way. Don't worry, Ricari, I won't hold it against you. We were all young once. I remember when your girl 'Georgie' was young. It was like yesterday. It might as well have been yesterday. Always the questions, and with answers come more questions. You'll get tired of them soon enough."

He held up his hand to silence the apologies that I had not yet spoken. "You have barely even had time to understand the parameters of the human life, let alone this other existence that we share. Yes, most certainly there are others. Have you never seen them? We may choose to hide ourselves from them—" He angled his head toward the doorway. "But we cannot completely hide ourselves from each other. Come, take a look! You will see their lights."

Chicot led me to the balcony and faced me toward Paris. "Look," he said, "and concentrate. We all shine."

He removed his left glove and laid his ice-cold hand against the back of my neck. At once my perceptions sharpened, focused through his lens.

Among the glimmering lights of fires and torches that sparkled on the warp and weft of the streets of Paris, I made out faint, darting, pale dots that quickly appeared and, as quickly, were swallowed by the shadows, only to emerge again, like fireflies gliding through leaves of grass. "There are dozens of them!" I whispered.

"At my last count, one hundred seven in Paris. You make one hundred eight." He removed his hand, and I turned to face his perennial mild smile. "You see, I keep track. I catalogue. I am a sort of census-taker of the undead."

"Undead?" I echoed. "But we are alive, are we not?"

"Did you survive?" Chicot's eyes narrowed. "I know my mortal body did not survive the transformation. Nothing could. If I did not survive, I must be dead; and yet I have animation. I can think of no better word."

"But it sounds terrible," I said.

"The transformation is terrible," Chicot said. "Do you not remember it?"

Maria entered then, the train of her lemon-ice dress rustling against the floorboards. She and Chicot embraced each other at arm's length and briefly kissed the other on both cheeks. "From one side of Paris to the other," she said. "Thank you for granting us your presence."

"Granting? My lady, you are too kind." Chicot's eyes sparkled with a mixture of malice and admiration, and something like wistfulness. "The introduction of Monsieur Ricari demanded my presence. I almost suspect you create new whelps just to get me to come around."

"That's a horrid thing to say," Maria retorted prettily, only to be met by Chicot's mock-innocent blinking. I looked to Georgie for clarification, but my lover seemed as baffled as myself. This matter went back further than either of us. I finally sat next to Georgina, and she enfolded me in her ribbon-trimmed shawl and rested her head against mine.

Maria and Chicot both stripped off their gloves and grasped each other's hands. They remained still in this way for quite some time, lost in silent communication, a closed book in two volumes. I occupied myself in removing Georgie's turban and combing out her hair with my fingernails, careful not to nick her scalp with my sharp edges.

"One hundred eight," came Maria's low voice. She and Chicot had separated their hands and now busied themselves sheathing them with gloves. "How is that? There should be one hundred ten."

"Dr. Tern has gone to Morocco," Chicot said. "And La Levant . . . La Levant is no more."

Maria looked appalled. "Dead?"

Chicot gave a single, grave nod.

"How?" I cut in. Georgie pinched me lightly. I pinched her back. "Don't try to silence me. I must ask questions, or I will never learn anything. Isn't that correct, monsieur?"

"That is correct." His eyes bored into Georgina, and she bowed her head. "Her head was severed from her body with the blade of an ax, wielded by her human slave. I witnessed this, unbeknownst to those involved—if La Levant knew I was there, I might have tasted doom myself. But her thoughts were focused on a single point." His eyes sought me, and his expression chilled me to the bone.

"Escape."

I was sufficiently horrified not to speak further. Maria tutted. "Ah, she was mad," she surmised. "She has always been mad, living outside society, but just on its fringes, like a rat that survives on garbage. Ah well, this is the best city on earth for such a life."

"Ah, madame, you have not been to Calcutta." Chicot's countenance assumed its previous gentle amusement. "As I recall, you refused my invitation, preferring instead to dine in the company of Antoinette."

"For me, the choice was clear," Maria said. "A vermin-infested marine journey to the foulest place in the world, or champagne and sherbets with the Queen. I make no apologies, monsieur."

"What of our dinner guests?" I asked. "Are they unattended?"

"You have no sense of time, I see, little greyhound. All the guests but one have supped and gone," Maria said. "And with your permission, our final guest may have his refreshment." She bowed to M. Chicot, who returned the gesture, his smile growing. When his lips drew back, I saw rows of sharp, yellow-brown teeth, dampened with the passage of a thick, purplish tongue.

In the dining room, a plump, aging banker dozed, his head nodding and jerking in drunken half-sleep. From the doorway, I could see the waves of alcohol fumes rising from his bald head, and when he hiccuped, I could taste his bile in my mouth. Not deterred in the slightest, Chicot walked to the banker, pulled the man's head back by the thin curls spread across the back of his fat neck, and put those yellow teeth to swift, slashing use. Blood poured into the empty plate and across the tablecloth. The banker's eyes shot open and he struggled against the fatal embrace of Chicot, but his wriggling was blessedly brief. The fat man limply relaxed to the tune of avid suckling.

"Ah," said Maria indulgently. "I do so love to entertain."

Chicot straightened up and wiped his mouth with a

black muslin handkerchief. He looked much younger with his face flushed ruddy. "Thank you, madame," he said to Maria, slurring a little, and weaving gently as the alcohol prodded him. "You still have superb taste in claret. And with your permission, I would like to visit the cemetery grounds in the company of your two beautiful children."

Georgie and I, who had watched this from the doorway, traded a glance. Her smile broke out dazzling. "Splendid," she said. "Maria?"

Maria raised her eyebrows, but her face was pleased and peaceful. "Granted, Arthur," she said. "Have them home by dawn."

We left the building and wandered up the stairs that led toward the church and the graveyard. "Wait," said Georgie as we approached the cemetery gates. "Feo, would you unlace my corset? These things are barbaric; I feel like a string-wrapped roast." Chicot and I laughed, and I unbuttoned and flipped Georgie's dress over her head to allow me access to her corset strings. Chicot said nothing, but I knew that he enjoyed the sight of her lace-pantalooned thighs as much as I did.

We progressed into the cemetery, crowned with trees and smelling pleasantly of autumn dust. Some graves were quite fresh, but we passed by them in favor of the older crypts and wrought-iron cribbed resting places. Chicot took a seat on a concrete slab and stared up at the stars. "Ah, Calvaire, I recall when the first body was laid in your arms," he sighed. "Now you are almost full. They don't rot as fast as they should. Come, sit by me, you two. I have a gift for you."

I looked at the man. He held nothing, having replaced his hat upon his head, and having little room in his coat for hiding. Georgie eagerly took a place next to him, wrestling her dress out of the way of her legs. She seized me and dragged me into her lap, where I fit very well in the space between her narrow thighs, and she kissed the back of my head.

Chicot gave us a searching look. "How are things with Maria?" he asked.

"I love her," I answered immediately.

"As do I," Georgina responded. "But at times she is difficult."

"She is older than both of you combined," Chicot admitted.

"Is she older than you?" I asked, and caught Georgie's hand before she could pinch me again.

Chicot laughed. "No," he admitted slowly. "Almost. We are contemporaries, as it were. We arrived in Paris at nearly the same time, and circled one another like tigers in a cage, wondering if the city was large enough to support us both. But Paris is miraculous; it is as large as one needs it to be. And of course, even then, we weren't the only ones. It became my interest to know exactly how many, and who they were, and how they lived. I am like Maria in that I dislike anarchy and obscurity and I enjoy knowledge. Unlike Maria, I am able to concede control at times. I understand what makes her this way: Spending thirty-six years of one's life living under another's rule gives one a certain attachment to one's own wishes. That does not mean that I believe that she is always right, or always just."

Georgina's wordless, indignant answering scoff was all the agreement necessary.

"But it is thirty-six years out of a score of generations, and she has become ever more inflexible. And I like you young ones. It is becoming clearer to me that the world Maria and I know no longer exists, and shall not again for another score of generations. Therefore, I propose a way to narrow the gap in abilities between you and her, so that you may have more power to do what you yourself believe to be correct, and be less inclined to give her control out of fear or uncertainty in your own ability. I know she does not share her blood evenly between you."

"Share blood?" I asked. "Maria has never shared her blood with me. That is, not since the first time, of course."

"But not 'of course,'" Chicot said. "She no had reason to perform the act in that way. I still do not fully comprehend her reasoning in that, except, again, as an element of control."

"Or love," said Georgina.

"Or love," Chicot agreed. "And she does love you, Orfeo. She loves you very deeply. And yet she also absolutely requires control at all times. Having you directly linked to her ensures that. I have no doubt that you have experienced this control." He smiled at me, and I thought of the ghost hand that threatened to unman me, and added a scoff of my own. "If you haven't yet, you shall."

"I regularly taste the blood of Maria's womb," Georgina volunteered.

"Yes," said Chicot a little wistfully, and I saw that he did not find the method as distasteful to imagine as I did. I resolved myself to think on it again. "And accordingly, you are stronger than your age would suggest. But not enough to lessen the disparity." He unbuttoned his sleeve cuff and rolled the fabric above his elbow. His forearm was sinewy and muscular under skin as pale as sea foam. "Drink from me," he said. "First you, Orfeo. I will stop you well in advance of any danger."

His blood came eagerly to a touch of my fangs.

Wine and salt and a faint, delicious taste of pain—

What a lovely childhood in Gironde by the sea! A dark-haired boy with sisters and brothers and massive shaggy retriever-dogs, running along the strand in sunlight so blazing and total that it burned my eyes just to share his recollection. His knowledge was of trees and plants and medicine, of the alchemy of transforming dry brown twigs and tiny blossoms into tinctures that could cure or kill or erase pain from the limbs while leaving the mind clear. He knew the names of more flowers than I had ever known existed, and the properties of seaweeds and the nodules on the roots of growing things. He married a girl with hair the color of cedar bark, who left him and their infant child for an English sailor. When the child fell ill, Chicot traveled to Bordeaux in search of a cure. Instead, the naturalist found the supernatural, and an infinite ocean of grief and hunger.

Hunger.

Chicot yanked back my head the same way he had that of the banker. "Enough, my son," he insisted, gently but firmly. I watched the echoes of his voice, the sound waves deforming the air, diminish themselves into invisible infinity. He stood up and moved slightly away, putting his punctured wrist up to his mouth. He glowed like a gas flame, as did I. I groaned and pressed my head between my palms, willing the power to recede inside me, and Chicot leaned back against the wall, only the whites of his eyes showing below heavy lids. "Georgina . . . if you would like some, this is the time."

I collapsed to the leaf-strewn earth, writhing and twitching as the blood coursed through my stomach into my veins. I tore up handfuls of grass in an effort to regain control over myself, watering the new wounds in the earth with my bloody saliva. The grass shriveled and blackened instantly where the blood and spit touched it.

Georgina held Chicot against her in a swooning embrace, her mouth pushed against his neck. Chicot's face twisted in an orgasmic grimace, and low carnal moans fell from his lips. "Oh, Georgina, oh, Georgina, enough," he whispered. "Enough."

I struggled to my feet and gently pulled Georgina away from him. She immediately pressed her lips against his and kissed him passionately, and he did not shirk but returned her kiss. I ran my hands up under her dress, grasped her hips, and dragged her away, pushing her down onto the concrete slab still warm from where we had sat. A few flicks of my claws laid her pantaloons aside in tatters, and I drove my knee against her groin fiercely, crushing my lips against hers. "Me now," I said inside her mouth. "While we still have this."

She rubbed herself against my knee, arching her back, her orgasm shuddering through us both like a sudden violent chill. Caught in a diamond chain of cresting climaxes, I did not startle at the touch of Chicot's hands against my back, pressing me farther into her, directing me. "Yes, now," he whispered, bent over, caressing Georgina's ear with his lips. "Let me give you this. This. This is my gift. This is my true task."

For that hour, we three were one, and when dawn came, I was both sorry and relieved to see him go. Georgie and I went straight to our own rooms, to distill our separate thoughts from the sea of the experiences and emotions of others.

Revolution

I spent the entirety of the July revolution (all two and a half days of it) hiding in the Cimetière du Calvaire.

I had found a pleasing stone mausoleum, mostly empty, to make my temporary residence and clubhouse; I brought candles and books and a pair of opera glasses, so as to keep an eye on the dramatic plumes of smoke rising from the city. I did not know if the violence would spread across Paris to the village of Montmartre, but I wanted to have a head start in escaping if it did.

Georgina had gone to join her fellow revolutionaries at their barricades. Maria remained inside the apartment, fretting silently and trying to pretend unconcern. All of the servants had deserted us, and I grew weary of having to fetch and carry for Maria, to try to set her hair in the way she preferred, and set the warming iron on the bed. So I stormed out, secretly hoping she would follow. She did not, too preoccupied in thoughts of her lover, and I joined her, in privacy, in fretting.

I sat in the semidarkness of the warm summer evening and calmed myself by reciting the rosary. As I relaxed, I reached out to Georgie's mind, demanding that she let me know that she survived, and was not lying in distress with dreadful sunburns turning her fine pale skin to red leather.

At once I received an answer: Georgina lay in bed with the sister of a *montagnard*, providing distraction so that the young woman would not worry about her radical brother. *I provide comfort, not perdition*, she assured me. *You should not hide; come into the city and join us.* Softly, through her ears, filtered the sound of ecstatic panting.

I could not resist a smile, or a flutter of arousal, both of which I shared with Georgina. *I am quite content to remain here, thank you.*

Suit yourself; this woman is exquisite. I shall return, mostly intact, my sweet Monsieur Grise!

Like a door being shut in my face, the connection disappeared, and I was left alone with the dusty, moldering corpses. I cannot say I preferred their company to that of my lover, but it was preferable to the thought of leaving the calm and safety of the cemetery, with the scent of ripening grapes from the nearby convent's vineyards.

It was there, in the mausoleum, that I first experienced the shocking fullness of memory that is the eternal curse of the vampire. The smell of the vineyards brought with it the first thoughts of the Fattorio di Ricari I had had in more than ten years: the taste of our wines, the sun-drenched hills, the flavor of milk-and-honey.

The cemetery itself reminded me of my mother's passing, which, due to my foolishness, immaturity, and cowardice, I had not witnessed. Lying against cold stone, my eyes unfocused in the near-total darkness, I thought of my mother's embrace, her calm, sad eyes, the sound of her voice, like bells blown from dark-brown glass. I remembered these things, but I felt hopelessly distant from my mother, not merely by distance or my continued life; I felt as though I hardly knew this woman. "Mamma" had been substituted in my thoughts by Maria. I felt more that I had been birthed through Maria's bloody thighs, and when I tried to recall the specific details of my birth mother, I had clearer images of Maria's lips against my forehead, and my clumsy attempts to set her smooth golden hair.

Consumed with desperate loneliness, I sent out my thoughts, searching even for Lorenzo, but found nothing. Either he was too far away or he was dead; but he was not within my scope of perception. I tried, as well, to find Elena, but it was the same; I heard only the worry of Maria, the satisfied lust of Georgie, and a background roar of all the excited and terrified minds in Paris.

In an attempt to distract myself from crushing self-pity, I leafed through the pages of my copy of *The Bride of Abydos*, a rare early Byron work that Georgina had proudly located for me. There was love of a sister contained within those pages, but my eyes blurred with tears before I could find the passage. Byron was dead and I had hardly cared before that moment. I now wished that I could find his body and revive it, and demand of it the answers which had eluded me thus far.

Why did he love me? Why did he leave me? Did I hurt her? Did I betray her? Is this the nature of my damnation?

I prayed to Holy Mary and Jesus to rescind my life, but they did not deign to grant this childish, selfish request.

When Georgina returned the day after the monarchy had fallen, her hair was cropped short and she wore the trousers, blouse, and jacket of a stone laborer. Although I felt it was Georgina—that same lean, cat-eyed, humorous face winked from under a greasy soldier's cap, her body still radiant—for a moment I did not recognize the tall, thin young man who strode in heavy boots into our apartment. "I have returned," the young man announced in the husky-sweet accented voice of Georgina.

"What have you done with your hair?" Maria and I cried in unison.

"Oh, please. It will grow back, if I want," said Georgina, doffing the cap and running her fingers through cropped dark strands, now shorter than my own. "I took this disguise in order to better meld myself with the republicans. You would be surprised; I am not the only woman wearing trousers who built the barricades."

"That is idiotically reckless," Maria snapped. Her lips were pinched and white.

Georgina rolled her eyes. "It is safer and more sensible than trying to do the same in a gown by Madame Palmyre. I was never in any danger; you underestimate me, my diamond. Have I not the same strength that you have?"

"Your strength will not protect you from a cannon shot that knocks off your head!"

"I was never in any danger. Why won't you listen to me? At least I care about something more genuine than the curls in my hair and the timing of His Majesty's shits—"

Furious, Maria struck Georgie in the face with the back of her hand. Gobbets of blood and teeth flew out of Georgie's mouth and spattered against the parquet floor, and Georgie fell to her knees. Thoughtlessly, I dove for the loosened teeth, only to find them disintegrating into gray jelly among the blackening spots of blood.

"I fought for your freedom." Georgina's voice came muffled through her ruined, dripping mouth. "I stood up for all our freedoms. I saw innocent men ripped in half from the bullets of palace guards. I set paving stones until my hands bled because I believe that we can be free and we can remake the world. You are a fragment of a dynasty that was destroyed hundreds of years ago; your time is over."

"You talk like them," Maria hissed. Her heart contained a maelstrom of conflicting emotions, but pride, as always, triumphed over all. "You are delusional, like them. You cannot remake the world. The world is made and there is no remaking it!"

Georgina rose to her feet again. Her cheek was bruised and her lip still split, but the drying blood had sealed it up, and I could see the skin healing, even from down upon the floor. "I am willing to take the chance that there is," she said. "Because I have had enough of silence and acceptance while the corruption of the government is allowed to flourish. They are consuming and destroying all of Europe. The nobility gulps caviar while the children of the working class starve. They will seize our very lives if given a chance. Nothing can change unless we make it change." The bruises on her face faded to nothingness, and her eyes flashed black fire. "We will remake France. By force if necessary."

I also rose to my feet, and stood between them, my eyes on Maria. "Please, Maria, don't ever beat her again," I said. "Or I shall have to die defending her honor, even against you, my lady."

"I would not kill you to make a point, little greyhound," said Maria, chastened. She trembled, and would not meet my eyes. "I am . . . I have been . . . Oh, my dearest love, you have nearly killed me with worry!"

Georgina embraced us both, pressing me between them, enclosed in her arms. Maria put her arms around me from behind. I relaxed into the sweet suffocation as they kissed, my face pillowed on Georgie's breasts, bound tightly against her ribs with a linen cloth under her blouse. "My love, we cannot die that way," Georgina whispered, a shivery current running between us through the vibration of her voice. "You should know that. We would both be dead a thousand times over by now. But I wouldn't let anything happen to me; I love you too much."

In this tender moment, I did not mention, or allow to be perceived, how overwhelmingly erotic the sight of Georgina in men's clothing had been to me.

I am a mercenary of desire, a naughty, sneaking child to the last.

To her credit, Maria did not gloat when, two weeks later, Louis-Phillipe was inserted as the King of France, destroying the more radical factions' dream of a truly democratic republic. Georgina stood on the balcony, her cruelly short hair obscene in contrast to her flowing red dress with yellow lace cuffs and collar, her face hard and expressionless. Her disappointment tasted like iron in my mouth. "Another bloody king," she muttered, crumpling her newspaper and throwing it over the balcony. It landed in the fountain and sank. "This will never do."

"As long as there are fighters like you, it never will. Have patience. These things don't happen overnight. Democracy requires work; of course there will be pauses along the road. Do not let your idealism blind you to the true goal."

My Georgie turned and threw her arms around me. "Oh, Feo," she teased, "have you become a republican?"

Rather than answer her, either to lie and say I shared her radicalism, or to speak the truth that politics mattered little to me, and that injustice, the vicious heart of existence, never died, I kissed Georgina's red, salted lips until I could no longer taste her tears. "I fight for those like us, you see," she murmured against my mouth, "those of us who are different, who do nothing wrong, but who are hated for what we are."

I shushed her, and kissed her more avidly. Her expected response was gratifyingly swift. Together we returned to the apartment and the couch in the sitting room, and shrugged off the garments that defined us but did not describe us. This was easier than it might seem, since Georgina had not bothered with wearing a corset since returning from the barricades.

She straddled me, as though she were a rider and my loins her saddle, and grinned. "Do you like that I'm a boy now?" she purred.

"You will never be a boy, even if your head was shaven," I replied, squeezing her breast. Against her creamy flesh, my elongated, darkened fingernails appeared as the savage talons of an eagle. To dissolve the unease caused by this distasteful sight, I turned her so that I rose above her, nudging my knees between her thighs. "No boy could ever have skin like yours, or a smile like yours, or a sweet rose like yours."

"Oh, perhaps sweeter . . ."

"Never, my George. Never. There will never be anyone like you."

She smiled wistfully. "George . . . Ha . . . I like that." *I have become a stranger. Where has Jadzia gone? To the same place as the skinny little hare? How we change, we changeless ones!* She kissed those thoughts into my throat. "I do sometimes wish I could be a boy, just for you—there is so much that I want to do to you."

"Yes? Well, treat me as the boys at Les Halles would."

Georgina laughed heartily. "For maximum verisimilitude, you have to be standing against a wall with your trousers unfastened." I laughed too; the idea of putting on clothes so recently shed was plainly absurd. But the sudden sharp desire to create the scene overcame me, and I stood up and donned my trousers.

She stared at me, astonished for a moment. Then her attention was engaged. "Against the wall," she murmured, slouching her shoulders and pouting, tousling her hair with her fingertips till she looked like a youth, albeit one with a very old soul. "Thirty sous for my head, forty for my arse."

"How much for your hand?" I teased, watching her take to her knees before me.

She rolled her eyes indignantly. "My hand? Monsieur, please. Go talk to André over there, he's desperate." With a wink, she bent her mouth over me.

For a while, I was transported with a keen joy that no Les Halles boy-prostitute or Sorbonne angel could produce in me. It should not have been different, and yet it was; no one was or ever can be like Georgina. Every pinpoint of contact bloomed unique and perfect. Is it not always thus—in love, or the next-best thing? And is this not how a man too often defines love?

A burning impatience flared in me, and I could be still no longer. "Stand up," I told her, giving her my hand. She stood, and I slipped my hand between her thighs, where the dense hair rustled like silk when brushed. "Oh, you have this! How much for your pretty cunt?"

"All the world, monsieur," she said, eyelashes aflutter.

"I have that," I replied, and bent her over the couch.

Her roaring, lusty laughter was infectious. Always, we laughed while we screwed, pinched each other, tickled each other, let our happy tears run rampant over the other's skin. For this reason, it was some time before either of us noticed Maria standing in the doorway, curiously observing us. In over a decade, she had never interrupted us *in flagrante delicto*; we were always aware of each other, so there was simply no excuse.

I sat up abruptly, interrupting Georgina's orgasm, and had reflexively hidden my nakedness behind hers before I'd even had a chance to think. "Damn you! What's your problem?" Georgie smacked my bottom impatiently, then looked across the room. "Oh," she added.

"Pray continue," said Maria quietly.

"I don't think he can," Georgie said. She was absolutely correct.

"That's a shame." Maria shrugged. "It's quite an entertaining show to see my lady transformed into a prick-sucking alley cat. She does it surprisingly well."

"Up your arse," Georgina huffed, gathering the lacy folds of her dress around her. She marched up to Maria, threw back her head, and declared, *"You don't own me,"* before quitting the room and slamming the door to her own bedroom.

I thought to myself that I might not ever be able to continue, ever again.

Maria arched her eyebrow at me. "I *do* own *you*," she remarked lightly. "Please, come, and take a letter for me. I wish to invite a gentlewoman of nobility for supper at our home."

I could have smashed the divan into splinters, or told Maria that I shat on her letters to women of nobility and she should learn how to write legibly. But I did not. It was as if I bore Georgina's shame on her behalf, and performed as the quiet, dutiful servant that Maria desired. And yet neither was entirely true. At that time, I think that doing as Maria requested was the simplest course of action and the best way of restoring any level of dignity to myself. I was the house cat that has gotten its tail caught in the door in front of a room full of people, that elegantly walks under the dining room table and grooms every inch of its fur twice, just to make sure.

Avalanche

8 January 1847, Paris
My dearest Jozef,

    Please forgive my horrendous delay in writing to you these last six months. Terrible events have made it impossible even for me to set pen to paper for an unbearably long time, and now that I have sharpened my quill and blackened its tip, I find myself so blinded with tears, even to recall my recent history, that I have had to start on a new page.

    The Kaffir is dead. Yes, dead! Or perhaps he is not—for no body was ever recovered from the snow that destroyed our mountain palace. But if not—how horrible to live crushed under a mountain of ice! I recall with wonder how we would dance under the falling snowflakes, and catch them harmlessly upon our tongues, and yet this very same substance can crush out hopes, dreams, sunlight, even a man's life. Have you ever seen an avalanche? I imagine that you have not; Cracow has no knowledge of such a monstrous and random event, caused by nothing more heinous than the sneeze of a foolish woman. Imagine if you can—a thousand tons of vengeful snow, moving as swiftly and inexorably as a steam engine down a steep and rugged mountain side, reducing houses, carriages, horses, and men to mangled tatters! My dearest Kaffir! Gone! Dead and buried in an icy tomb, never to be recovered in this life!

The Kaffir and I were out on the mountainside near our summer cottage, digging through a recent wet snowfall to where we had recently seen new-sprung berries, and we desired to pick them and eat them frozen—we have many times enjoyed the delicacy in our Alpine paradise. But the snow was too new and too fragile, and I had caught a touch of cold, which made me sneeze. At once, we felt the ground quake beneath us, and before I could do more than let out a gasp, white warhorses of frozen fury snatched us away from each other, flinging me one way and he the other. We slid away from one another, our hands outstretched; I fell through an air pocket between slanted trees, and the branches formed a shelter over which the snow collapsed as heavy as stone. Striking my head against the trunk of one of these trees, I lost my senses, for which I cannot decide if I am grateful or bitter—grateful that I did not see the destruction, yet bitter that I could do nothing to prevent it.

When I regained consciousness, I clawed my way from the strangling white prison with my fingers, though it took me a day and a night, and emerged to a singular white expanse of blank silence. The Kaffir had vanished utterly! I could make out no trace of the cottage, nor the young trees that ringed it, nor the pond where the Kaffir caught fish and I washed our garments. There was truly nothing left of the life that we created together. I managed to stagger up the mountainside to a way station closer to the summit, and was there received by the fine *mountaineers who staff that place, and they warmed me before their fire and gave me food and drink. I had been unconscious for more than two days, and I survived only by a miracle. They themselves had lost six of their number to the avalanche, and another two in attempts to locate and rescue any snowbound people. They had no women's clothing there, so I was moved to attire myself in their own spare trousers and jackets, as my own clothes were in ruins. I nearly lost four toes to frostbite, but after soaking my feet in cold water for two days, the extremities recovered. But oh, my heart never shall!*

I have since that time taken residence at a convent outside Paris, and I do believe I shall remain there while I recover my strength. The sisters of St. Pierre are most kind and gracious, though, as you can well imagine, I cannot very well observe their own vows of silence. Nonetheless, my youthful vigor and volume has been greatly lessened by the loss of my love. Can you imagine—Jadzia the Siren, reduced to quiet prayers and louder sighs of woe!

Ah, such is the curse of getting old.

I beg you to send me your best wishes, and to accept mine for yourself, Anna, Jerzy, Zuzanna, Tomas, and little Fryderyk. I shall write again soon.

> *All my love,*
> *Jadzia*

This letter was returned unopened, wrapped in another letter in a hasty and scrawling hand. Georgie would not let me see this other letter, but stood with her back to me, her coat held tightly around her, her eyes scanning the paper and her mind closed. I looked away, up the darkened street around a crooked corner from the church of St. J—, where she had mesmerized the clergy into receiving correspondence for her. I needed no supernatural power to see that she was upset, and so upset that she wished to conceal the intensity of it.

She had never before made an effort to hide her emotions from me. (Though, sometimes, I wished that she would.) At last she straightened her head, folded the letter, and shoved it into her pocket. "Jozef is dead," she announced flatly, her chin jutting out to keep her lips from trembling. She wore trousers, boots, a shapeless hat, and a rough jacket, but she had never looked more like a little girl, trying to understand that he wasn't coming back, ever, no matter what. "And my niece Zuzanna was prudent enough not to read what I wrote to him. See? It's still sealed. She sent me her best wishes. She is a good child." Her tight smile hardly deserved the name. "I have a locket with a miniature of her. She painted it herself." The smile collapsed. "Now she hasn't got a father."

"Oh, George," I said, holding out my arms, but she shook her head and moved away.

"No, no, no. No matter. Don't feel sorry for me; death does come. He hit his head falling out of a tree." She gave a single hoot of laughter. "That Jozef— climbing trees at his age! Sixty-five years old and a grandfather twice. We are much alike, he and I." She put her two forefingers into her mouth and bit her claws with her fangs, a habit that she had recently acquired. "What must he think of me now?"

I thought of Vito and realized that many decades had passed since I last saw him standing before me, perfect and shining. Lorenzo, like a leech, had bled him from me. "He loves you, wherever he is."

"Heh. He is dead and in the ground. Who knows if he still loves anything." She bit her lip and set her face into a stern and boyish configuration. "Let us away. We have work to do. And remember, do not call me George; you must call me Jerzy. Jerzy Dolski. Remember your role."

"Yes, my dear," I said without thinking. Worshipers leaving evening Mass passed as the words left my lips, and gave us a curious stare; two students, the grubby one the beloved of the dandy, all in the shadow of the church. I gave them a smile and twisted the high collar of my shirt into a defiant point. If only they knew the half of it!

The crowded café was a warm and welcome respite out of the chilly, biting October wind, despite its stink of burnt coffee, sour hashish smoke, and cook fires extinguished with urine. Georgina scanned the room, eyes narrowed, then pointed to the left. "There they are. Let's join them."

At a round table sat three men, two young, one old, all with furrows of concentration marked deep and permanent on their foreheads. Georgie strode up and shook hands with them all as I followed slowly behind her. "This is my colleague, Grise," she was saying, indicating me. "He is a translator, and assists me with shaping my ideas into a higher ideal of the French language. He works with me, but I get to take all the credit. A fine arrangement! Ha, ha. Grise, these are Frederic Lotte, Jean-Pierre Villon, and Théodore Soltan, the publishers of *Les letters solidarité*."

I shook hands as well, and took a seat on the edge of the table, half turned toward the room, drinking in the atmosphere and the blazing heat from the fireplace. I did not desire these men's attention; it was enough that they noted my mere presence, and they paid no mind to me whatsoever. My own attention was absorbed by the dandies in their fawn-colored trousers, the ladies of diminished virtue with red lip-paint purpled by wine, the artists with white and fragile wrists like a hard season's parsnips. In the years before the debut of *La Bohème*, they were not yet aware of their part in history, and as such, were bearable. I could already tell that this fascinating mosaic would soon be extinct; it was too pretty, too bizarre, to be more than tenuous. It was like a dream, the facts easily distorted in recollection.

Georgina proudly drew a roll of paper from her shoulder bag and laid it on the table in front of the men. The pages were rapidly snatched up and perused. "I have written many more," she said. "I brought the best, in M. Grise's opinion. You don't have to publish them all at once, but at your convenience."

"I am glad you have that perspective," said the man introduced as Villon, his mouth full of black bread, "for we could not possibly devote space to all of them in a single issue. This is enough for ten." His eyes nonetheless greedily scanned the writing, forgetting the wineglass already raised toward his lips. Georgie wiggled in her chair and rubbed her hands together, controlling her grins with difficulty. "Yet I wish we did have the space; this is excellent work. Though . . . I must say, you devote rather a lot of text to the plight of Poland."

Soltan plucked the pages away from the other man and peered into them, his heavy black eyebrows knitting themselves into a single one. His thick, full beard stank of pipe smoke. "Not an excessive amount, in my opinion," he grunted. "It is difficult to overstate."

"I agree," Georgina put in.

A plump, pretty waitress in a blue kerchief approached our table. "Jadz-Jerzy," I said, hastily swallowing the instinctive "darling," "will you drink?"

"Water, please," said Georgina brightly. "Like Murger. Oh, and a pipe."

I ordered spirits, amused at Georgina's performance as the youthful social revolutionary, supposedly too poor to drink wine but eager for the prop of the tobacco pipe and the romantically shrouding smoke. The waitress smiled and curtsied, and thought to herself, *That's a woman in a man's getup, or I'll be deuced.*

I did not follow the debate that raged between Georgie and the editors, nor the gossip about the various radical groups that formed, swelled, and were suppressed or fell apart. It amused me, however, that she might have easily bent them to her will but chose instead to leave them with their own opinions, attempting to change their minds through philosophy. As long as her disguise protected her, she was content to accept humanity as it was. While I felt the sting of injustice in the necessity for Georgina's deception, she did not mind, and in fact welcomed the freedom from a female's restrictive clothing and ladylike manners. And her colleagues at the newspaper had no idea that this impulsive young Polish student was a girl (and a deadly angel) underneath her layers of grime and bluster.

The Poland debate raged on for an hour, forming a layer of animated background noise to accompany my human sightseeing. My ears did prick up at the invitation to an evening's pleasure at the home of M. Lotte the fortnight after, coinciding with the release of the next issue of the newspaper. "We shall have food, wine, and discussion," Lotte said, "music, and poetry, and attractive young girls." He wiggled his eyebrows at George, who did not have to pretend excitement. "And you should come, too, Grise. Dance and get into an argument. Put a little color in those white cheeks of yours."

"I am honored," I replied. "I would be delighted to attend, since you assure me there will be poetry *and* music. All in the same place—how extraordinary!"

As we walked into the river-reeking wind after we left, Georgina got cross with me. "Why must you be so inappropriate all the time?" she snapped.

That's interesting, coming from you, I mused silently. "I thought you liked that about me," I said.

"This is different. Having my work published means

a great deal to me. I give my essays a great deal of thought, and when I display them, prominent thinkers are impressed. Did you hear them? They wish they could publish them all."

Prominent thinkers? A trio of fringe-dwelling, failed academics with a stolen printing press? "I never said that it wasn't important, or that your writing isn't clever. I was just being myself," I said. "I did not hinder you in any way. M. Lotte was not offended by me and he suspects nothing—and I propped you up. I don't know if you noticed; your concentration was slipping. Your breasts were practically heaving."

You bastard, Orfeo! Her cheeks burned with rage, and immediately I was stricken with headache. "They were *not*! Clever? Is that what you think? You don't understand anything, do you?" She whirled to face me, her hands balled into fists. "Why can't you be serious? Don't you care about anything?"

I stared at her openmouthed; she impotently beat her thighs with her fists, and turned, again and again, as if looking for an escape route. I seized her by the shoulders and gave her a gentle shake, then pulled her into my arms, embracing her in lieu of slapping her. At once, she dissolved into grief-stricken tears. "You don't have to hide when you're with me," I said, holding her as tightly as I dared. "You don't have to be something you're not with me. I feel what you feel."

"I just want things to change. I want things to be more fair. Because right now, nothing is fair. Nothing is just." She cried on my shoulder during the whole long, shuddery ride home.

The following fortnight gripped her tightly in the black fist of grief and mourning. She did not leave the apartment, and for the first few nights did not even leave her bedchamber, taking no blood. She moved from couch to couch in every room, sitting, sprawling, staring at the walls, weeping and sobbing, and reading from a threadbare book of fairy stories that she had kept since her childhood, fifty years previous. Maria and I took turns staying with her, though neither of us particularly wanted to, as George felt no particular need to keep her emotions to herself anymore. She struck us with headaches, nausea, stabbing pains in the stomach, and a blanketing gloom. Whoever was in the room was fair game. The naive servants were miserable and refused to look after her. Even attending Mass and contemplating the sufferings of Christ was more cheerful.

On the appointed date of Lotte's soiree, I woke from sleep in anticipation of being immediately swamped with sadness, but the ether was clear. I donned my dressing gown and tiptoed to George's room, to find her humming as she wrapped the linen over her breasts. "Ah, Orfeo, just in time—will you hold this while I pin it? Or pin it while I hold it?"

I allowed her to pin. "How are you feeling?" I ventured.

"Oh, all right," she said, frowning a little. "You know. There is a giant hole in my heart that will never heal. But well enough."

"I have . . . nothing to compare it to," I confessed.

"Oh, you do. Your heart is riddled with holes. I only wish I could handle it as gracefully as you do."

"*This* is graceful?" I joked, gesturing toward my mussed hair and thin, drawn morning face. I needed a drink.

She pulled a dirty white singlet on over the pinned linen, and a clean white shirt over that. "But you know, I am still alive. I still have things to do. We have a gathering to attend at the home of M. Lotte."

I smiled. "They shall have poetry *and* music."

"Don't forget the pretty girls." Georgina added a black coat, one of mine that had been retailored by Georgina herself. "I shall wear black, however. And I would be very pleased if you would do so as well."

"Actually . . . I had a mind to wear my green coat." I had been wearing black all week, but I suppose she hadn't noticed. "I just got it, and I haven't had a chance to wear it yet."

"And *your* brother died fifty years ago, so why should you mourn?" she sniffed. "Fine. Wear your green coat. Can you be ready in one hour? I know that is challenging for you."

I had never wanted to slap someone so hard in all my life. Instead, I gave her a nod and a smile and backed out of the room.

Maria came in with the new valet, Gruetter, and my new green coat. Gruetter laid out the coat to display it to me, but I could hardly appreciate the shimmering pine-colored sized wool that had so enchanted me at the tailor's shop the week before. "She's turning into you," I spat at Maria's reflection in the looking glass.

Maria frowned, and touched Gruetter on the left shoulder. Having received his signal, he silently left and closed the door behind him. Maria smoothly took his place and continued buttoning my shirt cuff. I immediately regretted having spoken. "What do you mean?" she asked me mildly.

"She's ordering me around," I said, "telling me what to do, speaking down to me. All those things that you usually do."

"She believes that she is right," she replied, unruffled. "As do I. As do you."

"Yes, but—"

"She realizes that she is sixty years old and her brother is dead. Pray for her, don't judge her."

"I do, and I don't." I sighed. Maria brushed my cuffs with the soft little broom, then set to tying my loose cravat of pale pink silk perfumed with rose water. "I do not know how to mourn on another's behalf, and I resent the implication that I should or else I do not love her."

"You have given in to her too much in the past; she expects you to agree enthusiastically to any idea she has. This was bound to happen sooner or later." She smoothed the front of my coat. "This *is* very handsome. The seams are all but invisible. Is it one of Mister Wembledowns's, in Montparnasse?"

"Quite so. You have an eye for fashion," I said, nodding.

Maria grinned. "I did the same thing as you last week—I went window-shopping. I also have new plumage that I am eager to display. But with both of you out this evening, I shall stay home in my nightgown and bonnet, do absolutely nothing, and thoroughly enjoy myself." She brushed her cheek against mine in lieu of a kiss, then rubbed a minim of rouge on my cheekbones. "There. Now you look splendid. And remember, if you want to leave, you can—she doesn't own you."

I thought on this, swaying back and forth in Ollier's carriage, my eyes fixed on the window and the rushing landscape outside. Georgina said nothing for a very long time; she was silent until we crossed the river. "Feo, what's the matter?" she asked. When my reply was not instantaneous, she grasped my arm and rubbed it lovingly, then slumped back into the seat. "It's all right. I know you're cross. But it's ridiculous! Let us be as we were. Let us be friends."

"Were we friends?" I asked, not looking at her but at her reflection in the window.

She had not had time to dirty her face to make it look somewhat more masculine, and the sadness in her soft reflection tore at my heart. "Weren't we?" she responded in a whisper.

I took her hands in mine. "Yes, yes; I apologize. I'm being terrible. I'm feeling sorry for myself so that I don't have to feel sorry for you, which I am afraid would swamp me. Because I do love you so much. I want so much for your happiness—only your happiness, darling."

We kissed for the first time in fifteen nights, and the sky was clear and pricked with stars, and how beautifully the lights of Paris shone! Ollier pulled the horses up, and we stopped and Ollier opened the door (but, as part of the charade, did not assist Georgina onto the street). As I joined her, she bent to the street, then straightened her back and rubbed her cheeks and forehead with her dirtied hands. Immediately, she became a grubby Bohemian youth, fresh-faced, intelligent, and restless, striding with head held high into the house of an independent newspaper publisher.

M. Lotte had come into some amount of money five years before, and immediately left his job at a prominent bourgeois business newspaper to start his own, republican publication. Unfortunately for M. Lotte, he was an extremely poor writer and had to acquire likeminded and talented men to serve as his staff. This process had taken two and a half years. *Les lettres solidarité* had managed to produce two issues in four months, with the help of the well-connected, zealously radical M. Villon and the prolific and equally zealous Pole, M. Soltan. But Lotte himself skirted the edge of bourgeoisie, with his medium-sized house, his eager smile and well-bred manners, and the kind of money necessary to hold soirees.

That kind of easy, unostentatious wealth must have come as a godsend to the dozens of artists, musicians, actors, pamphlet writers, spiritualists, and assorted ec-

YES! ☐

Sign me up for the Leisure Horror Book Club and send my TWO FREE BOOKS! If I choose to stay in the club, I will pay only $8.50* each month, a savings of $5.48!

YES! ☐

Sign me up for the Leisure Thriller Book Club and send my TWO FREE BOOKS! If I choose to stay in the club, I will pay only $8.50* each month, a savings of $5.48!

NAME: _____

ADDRESS: _____

_____

TELEPHONE: _____

E-MAIL: _____

☐ **I WANT TO PAY BY CREDIT CARD.**

☐ VISA   ☐ MasterCard   ☐ DISCOVER

ACCOUNT #: _____

EXPIRATION DATE: _____

SIGNATURE: _____

Send this card along with $2.00 shipping & handling for each club you wish to join, to:

Horror/Thriller Book Clubs
20 Academy Street
Norwalk, CT 06850-4032

Or fax (must include credit card information!) to: 610.995.9274. You can also sign up online at www.dorchesterpub.com.

*Plus $2.00 for shipping. Offer open to residents of the U.S. and Canada only. Canadian residents please call 1.800.481.9191 for pricing information.

If under 18, a parent or guardian must sign. Terms, prices and conditions subject to change. Subscription subject to acceptance. Dorchester Publishing reserves the right to reject any order or cancel any subscription.

JOIN NOW!

centrics that crowded the foyer and the sitting room. I stared with fascination at a woman dressed in Oriental costume of sari and trousers, with her feet bare and her hands dyed orange; blond hair peeked from under a dazzling shawl of electric blue. Another carried a tiny, yelping dog in a small wicker basket with a lid, from which the dog occasionally popped its head to receive tidbits from the fingers of its mistress. Artists' models leaned against walls next to the stacks of paintings they had inspired, there being more artworks than room on the walls.

There did not seem to be a table at which to sit (food was laid out on a long buffet table in the kitchen), nor a stage at which to stare (a poet expounded about mackerel and freedom from his post on a wooden chair, while no one listened), thus, pleasantly disoriented, I wandered slowly throughout the open wing of the house. George was nowhere to be seen. I stood at the back of the room farthest from the front door and waited for one of the guests to approach me. I had not yet satisfied my hunger, and my temper grew short.

I did not have to wait long; a little model, short enough to look up to me, walked up to me and said, "Excuse me, monsieur, but you look as though you need a glass of wine. I need one too—shall we go together?" She offered me her dainty arm.

Her name was Ondine. I led her outside, into a small copse of trees, and held her for a while. I allowed myself only a taste, but she swooned and flopped like a sturgeon in my arms. She did not get enough to eat, and her blood was thin and melancholy, flavored with hunger, frustrated love, and impossible romantic dreams. I settled her gently onto her backside in the short grass, rubbing her hands with mine and calling her name to ease her back to consciousness.

She recovered at once and blinked at me insensibly. "What am I doing out here? Who are you? I came with M. Nerval."

"I suppose you should find him again, then," I said starchily, and she collected herself and staggered back inside, convinced that she had drunk too much wine. I was pleased at my restraint, and restored through even a small sip of blood. It would not satisfy me all night, but I hoped it might last for long enough to pay my respects to M. Lotte, for Georgina's sake. I had sent Ollier away to pick up other fares for the night, since if either of us needed him again, we could call to him, with our minds, anywhere he was.

I had been outdoors for longer than I had imagined; something in the atmosphere of the party had changed in my absence. I had some difficulty reentering the house through the side door I had so recently exited. Several clumps of guests had clotted into a single mass, all pointing toward the drawing room, two rooms away. I felt that where the attention focused, Georgina was at its center, and I slid and wormed my way swiftly through the mass of people. I feared that she was making a scene, or had been discovered through any of her disguises, but I sensed no anxiety from her, only delighted fascination.

I found George transfixed before the true focus of attention: a girl approximately eighteen years of age, wearing something of a ragtag Gypsy costume, all scarves, skirts, and tiny bells. She had skin of a tawny-brown color, like tea with milk, hair barely a shade darker, and pale-violet eyes. She sang a sprightly folk song with good voice, accompanied by a skillfully played piano, and swishing her skirts around her peeping ankles. It was a pretty sight; in October of that year, any illumination in the darkness was providential.

I applauded the end of one song, but slipped away again as another song began. There was dancing, and I wasn't in the mood even to watch. I needed more blood, and Georgie wasn't going anywhere. I needed to find Lotte (and avoid Ondine), and make my escape into the three miles of anonymous possibility between here and home.

Four more victims of a painless sip came to me easily. I learned a great deal more about Lotte's guests than I could have gleaned by conversation. The newspaper was indeed much more well-known than I had assumed, and actually had some members of the government suspicious. But nothing had thus far happened, which made Lotte, Villon, and Soltan bold. Their plans for the next issue of the newspaper included many outrageous writings—calls for the dismantling and democratizing of the government, collectivism, and universal suffrage. It was madness, as implausible as a fairy story; tales to amuse hungry children to keep their minds off their growling bellies.

At last I managed to find Lotte, sneaking out of the servants' quarters with his trousers fastened the wrong way and his chestnut hair mussed. "Ah? Ah, yes, M. Grise, thank you for attending. You *do* seem to have gained some color in your cheeks!"

I gave him a smile that showed my fangs. "Yes, I have been making the acquaintances of your— acquaintances."

Lotte blinked and frowned for a moment, then his beaming social demeanor returned. "Ah? Ah! Yes, indeed, they are a mixed bag, are they not? I do know a great many talented people. Did you hear Mademoiselle Lefeu sing? She always charms everyone."

"Who?" I asked politely.

"Oh, I simply must introduce you. Charming, charming girl! I think you may have a great deal in common, coming from more southern climes than these. . . ." Lotte ducked away into the other room, and I followed him curiously, wondering what attributes he imagined that I had.

In the room with the piano, someone else now played the third movement of Mozart's Paris Symphony with all the delicacy of a blacksmith hammering steel, and the singing Gypsy girl sat on a couch with Georgina, deeply enmeshed in conversation. The blazing candle-light illuminated their proximal faces, one dark and the other radiant moonlight. Lotte bent over them and spoke under the ringing of the piano and the thunder of wine-heightened voices. "Rosy, I want you to meet M. Grise, a colleague of our friend Dolski. That's him, standing right there."

The dusky girl followed the indicated line of Lotte's walking stick to me, with her strange pale eyes held wide open so that the whites could be seen under the irises. She looked hopelessly innocent, guileless as a kitten, the little bells of her bracelet tinkling as she brushed a lock of hair from her forehead. Georgina's face spoke of a longing that I knew; it was probably the way that I looked at her.

The girls rose from the couch and walked with Lotte back to me. Lotte made a slight bow in my direction. "Grise, I would like you to meet Mme. Rosée Lefeu. Her father is Renaud Lefeu, the esteemed world traveler, who has been kind enough to write an essay for the next issue of the newspaper. Where is he?"

"He is here somewhere," said the girl, looking around the room at the swaying mass of anarchically dancing people. When she was closer, I saw that her brownness was not caused by any sunburn, but was hers alone, her skin as smooth and delicate as the petals of an orchid. "I am called Rosy."

140

"This is M. Orphée Grise. He is a partner of M. Dolski."

I bowed and accepted her dimpled hand, with its attendant music. I wanted to lick her, to crush her delicacy to me and hear the snapping of young bones. She smelled strongly of clove and cinnamon—clove on her breath, cinnamon melting through the pores of her skin, due to a high level of those spices in her diet. She smelled of the Orient. She was like no woman I had ever before encountered; she did not seem entirely human, as I previously envisioned "humanity." She seemed, instead, a figure from myth: Cleopatra, Cassiopeia, Chryseis the Golden.

Yet she was just a girl.

"Your costume is utterly charming," I said. "Did you buy it entire from a Gypsy woman?"

Rosy frowned slightly. "I have collected and assembled it myself," she said, "taking what I liked from every place I visited. I accompanied my father on most of his travels, you see. It would seem, from your tone of voice, that you have a low opinion of the Gypsies. Why the dislike?"

I was caught completely off guard. I saw one side of Georgie's mouth smile. "I have none," I said hastily. "I have never had much interaction with them . . ."

"You ought to reexamine your prejudice," said Rosy Lefeu, "as a foreigner living in Paris."

"I don't think that's entirely fair," Georgie said mildly, and instantly Rosy turned to her with a tender expression. "We are all foreigners here." Rosy blinked, and the entire argument had vanished from her mind, while I still stood, my mouth hanging open, as I struggled to think of something to say. Georgie turned back to me. "We were talking of her travels," she said, "and their fascinating variety. Do you know that Mme. Lefeu has been down the very southernmost tip of Africa? And to Japan, and Persia . . . and America!"

"Marvelous," I said, then awkwardly added, "You sing beautifully." It was an exaggeration, and I am afraid it came out of me sounding extremely insincere. I saw a spark ignited in Rosy's eyes, but then Georgie touched her arm and immediately Rosy gentled.

"Thank you, M. Grise. I am glad you enjoyed it. Singing is what I love most. I take lessons from one of your countrymen, Signor Orinelli."

"I shall look him up," I offered. "My voice would benefit from training. My mother was a coloratura, but I inherited little of her ability."

Georgie stared at me. I felt strange; why had I felt compelled to tell her something personal about myself, exposing the Ricari underneath the gray cloak of obfuscation? I had been bewitched.

"Go away, M. Grise," Georgie said, as light as tissue wrapped around a horseshoe. The smile in her voice did not reach her eyes. "I shall enjoy Mme. Lefeu's company for as long as I am able. If you want to be helpful, go find M. Lefeu and make sure he's good and drunk."

Lotte laughed uncomfortably. Rosy continued to gaze up at Georgie's dirty chin. I rubbed my gloved hands together slowly, repeating to myself, *A gentleman does not strike another gentleman unless he seeks a duel. And I don't think I would win.* "Good evening, mademoiselle," I said, taking as deep a bow as I dared. "Gentlemen." I tapped my heels on the floor, turned ninety degrees, and stalked away, still rubbing my hands. I had suddenly gone very cold.

Revelation

That winter, Maria's heart was heavy with memories. She went out less and less, and on her behalf, I wrote many notes of regret to the piles of invitations to holiday balls and banquets that she received. She stared at her wardrobes full of beautiful gowns, hats, and shoes, sighed, and then closed the doors without even touching the garments.

One of the few activities she continued regularly was attending Saturday-evening Mass with me. On Christmas night, she lit nine candles and knelt for a long time before the image of Holy Mother Mary, bent in silent prayer. I splashed holy water across my hands and touched it to my forehead, praying that her melancholy (and my headache) would be soothed.

"Nine candles?" I asked Maria afterward, walking home through drifts of fresh snow, gray from the coal smoke in the air. "May I ask who they are for?"

"They are for my children. The seven children I bore, and the two children that I made," she replied.

I felt deeply touched. "Do you really see me as your child?"

"Of course I do. I made you with my body. Not my child alone, of course—Georgina helped me."

"I thought it was you who helped Georgie."

"No; I know better than she how it is done. I have watched it done incorrectly to someone else, and I could not bear the idea of letting that happen again. It is a most gruesome end. The body unravels, but knows not how to knit itself together again. But it *tries* a few things." She grinned, with a grimace in it. "No, no, greyhound, that would never do."

I had a flash of knowledge as she revisited the distasteful memory. "M. Chicot did *that*?" I said, aghast, nearly retching.

She laughed at my discomfiture. "He had to learn it from someone else; he had no idea. His initial experiments ended quite disastrously. Poor old Chicot; he is a scientist. But he has managed to get it right several times since. He takes care to ensure that his children do not remain too attached to him, otherwise he would run in a pack like a wild dog." I had to stop and close my eyes; Maria's memories had swamped me again, and I saw her, Chicot, and a half-dozen unnatural others, silent skulkers, decimating whole villages, flocking in trees like a murder of crows. Spoken communication was unnecessary. They fed from each other as much as they fed from humans, continually lost in each other's thoughts, addicted to each other. The complex lattice of sexual relations between them dazzled me. "As pleasant as that experience can be for a short while, it always ends badly. . . ."

I shuddered Maria's memory off. "Have you noticed that George has stopped going to church entirely?" I said, opening my eyes and taking a long stride to catch up.

She moved a little farther in the snow before answering. The lace train of her mulberry-colored skirt had become thickly encrusted with soot and ice. "Yes," she said. "As far as I've been able to determine, she considers it a waste of her time. I think she may be flirting with atheism."

I wrinkled my nose. "She is still going about with Rosy Lefeu," I mentioned. "That is where she spends her time. Anyone would think they were courting."

"Perhaps they are," said Maria.

I laughed and shook my head. "Your wit is surpassingly dry today, my mistress."

But Maria was no longer even smiling. "There is something on the air," she announced, holding her head up and dilating her delicate nostrils. "Do you smell it? It is like . . . dried anchovies."

"They are not courting," I pressed. "One woman cannot court another."

"Oh, Orphée," Maria sighed. "You are both so young."

"But it is impossible. It is nonsensical. Georgie just has a mania, that's all; it will pass. Remember when she was obsessed with beaver-pelt hats? She is a girl of quick passions."

"As you say, Orphée. As you say."

I felt cold again, but told myself that it was because of the snow. But the feeling did not dissipate when I stood before the great fireplace with my hands toward the crackling flames, steam rising from my rolled trouser cuffs. It was a feeling of helplessness, like Georgina's Kaffir, sliding down a mountainside on an unstoppable wave, watching helplessly as I rushed away from her.

That part of her letter was my own invention.

"Feo, I need your imagination. You have to tell me how best to kill my husband," she'd said.

* * *

I hardly saw Georgie for weeks. She did most of her writing in cafés, scowling a clay pipe into the corner of her mouth. She did not even come home to sleep each night, which, before, would have nearly paralyzed me with worry; but by the end of the year, I was grateful when I came home and she was not there.

Yet I missed her so terribly when she was absent. In fact, I missed her when she was there. To be specific, I missed *Georgina*; I was quite sick of Jerzy.

The next issue of *Les L.S.* (as they all liked to call it) featured three of her recent opinion pieces and my illustration of a penniless, skeletal flower-girl, which I had not intended as a political metaphor but, with Villon's addition of the caption "Child of the Monarchy," served that purpose. The newspaper still lost money, but that was not really the point, and all the staff celebrated their success.

At the New Year's Eve salon, given at Lotte's home, I met M. Renaud Lefeu at last. He had the stocky build and brown-burned face of a wheat farmer and a short crop of salt-and-pepper wool atop his head. He wore a red fez, and an orange Chinese silk scarf wrapped around his neck. His narrow eyes seemed always fixed on a point in the distance over my shoulder. I thought I would very much like to taste his blood. "Your daughter is a most engaging young creature," I said to him.

"Rosy? Yes, she is an extraordinary young person. She really got into the spirit of traveling—even more so, I think, than I did. When her mother died, she could have chosen to stay in Oran with her nurse, rather than come with me to Japan, but she needed hardly a second to decide to join me. She has learned five languages, and is celebrated for her beauty wherever we go."

"I can well imagine. She has extraordinary coloring; I

have never seen anything like it. I assume her mother was an Algerian native?"

"No; my wife was a Persian, of unusual beauty even for that exquisite race. Nasreen was the greatest woman I've ever known—ancient royalty, quick, brave, and strong. She defied her family to come away with me." Lefeu hurriedly gulped at his glass of ale and twitched his head as if shaking off a fly. "She has been dead for more than ten years, but it seems as if it were yesterday when I last saw her. I have Rosy as a reminder of her, at least. She is much like her mother in appearance and in personality. Nasreen would not stand still when she saw injustice being done. . . ."

Lefeu's voice trailed off. Rosy herself, accompanied by Georgie, approached us then. Her sheer vitality stilled my breath, and every head turned as she passed. Her eyes sparkled with joy, becoming even more beautiful as she turned to Georgie as a flower turns toward the sun. "She must be in love," came a whisper muted by a discreet feather fan.

I could perceive from where I stood that Rosy had fallen prey to that enchantment, that masquerade of love, the mirage of devotion, that clockwork adoration, just as I had twenty years before.

Suddenly, all was illuminated, and my blood boiled with rage.

I was a fool—now a damned, immortal fool!

The process had only slight variation. Despite my own appreciation for Rosy, she was not devoted to me; she would do as I commanded her, but she did not feel that she did it out of love. (Indeed, she barely felt it at all.) But Rosy had never tasted me. Whereas Georgie had poisoned me with the nectars of her sex, Rosy had lost her wits through the fluid medium of the passionate kisses they stole in the privacy and intimacy of Ollier's carriage. Rosy's mind was full of the memory of Georgie's smoke-flavored tongue in her mouth and the sensation of long-fingered hands squeezing her breasts. She had never before experienced such sensations, such blissful tumult, and she did not know how she had ever lived without them.

I knew; I saw all. I remembered. Rosy was a child, as easily plucked as a flower. And yet I had experienced lovemaking; I had experienced lust and sensuality; and yet, I had fallen just as surely, just as completely, just as involuntarily.

But I did not let this realization prevent me from reaching my goal. I stared into Rosy's eyes, pinning her still, while I searched her mind for further details. My stomach churned at how easily she bent to my will. I wanted so much to feel her resist me, even slightly, but it was not within her power, nor within any human's power. She was as easily seduced, as easily misled, as I had been.

I did not want to know the whole of the truth, but I needed it, the way that she needed that very first, most perfect reciprocal lust.

You have kissed this person with your open mouth?

Yes, oh, yes, I live for it.

You have had intercourse with this person?

She hesitated, a little taken aback. *No. Not yet. I will gladly give myself to him. Some nights I despair that it will ever happen, but he is a gentleman.*

I almost laughed. *Do you know that Jerzy is not a man? Is not "Jerzy" at all?*

I don't understand. Then, emerging faintly from her subconscious: *Yes. And I don't care.*

Do you know that this is not a human whom you adore?

I saw it as through veils. She did not know that she knew.

Yes.

Don't you understand, you stupid girl? Are you not afraid? You consort with demons!

"Orphée!" Georgie bellowed, giving me a sharp clap on the shoulder that would have knocked a lesser man over. My concentration collapsed like a house of cards. Before me, Rosy swayed, blinked, shook her head. All she knew was that she had been staring into space, daydreaming about defending her love. "Come with me to the buffet table; Madame Lotte has just made a fresh loaf!" Her pincer grip closed around my arm and all but picked me up and shuffled me into the kitchen. Rosy met her father and gave him a kiss on the cheek, both of them unaware that a savage, shameless violation of her mind had just taken place.

Georgina shoved me into the kitchen pantry and closed the door behind us. In the near-total darkness, I could see little besides her incandescent, smudged face; her eyes were like live coals in snow. "What are you doing?" Georgie demanded.

"What are *you* doing?" I shot back, furious myself. "Why haven't you killed this one? Or set her free?"

"There is no way to do either, nor would I if I could. If she were to die, Lefeu would be devastated. And I cannot set her free, it would—" She cut off, and grimaced at me. "I do not *wish* to set her free. Do you understand, Orfeo?"

I took a deep breath and said, "No, I don't."

"I see" was her response.

"You are playing a very dangerous game. What has brought on your recklessness? You hardly come home during the days; you risk death from sunburn. What if you are discovered while you sleep? And why do you no longer attend Mass?"

Georgie threw back her head and laughed humor-lessly, like a dry snapping twig. "I can't believe you," she said. "Asking me about Mass after you've just put *me* in danger. Opening her mind like that in public—*that* is dangerous, my friend!"

"Oh, shit on that, George, you know very well where the blame lies. Don't you understand? You've got ten years' advantage of this life on me, and even I can see that you are making a terrible mistake."

"Allow me to make it," she said. "Allow me to live my own life and accept my own consequences. This is how I live, how I have always lived. And if you feel so strongly that Rosy is a threat to you, take a moment of thought—" She gave a short bark of incredulous laughter. "A moment of *prayer* to think about why that would be."

"I have no idea!" I said. "I have thought about it, and I cannot find an adequate reason. Everything I do or say seems to anger you. What did I do wrong, George? Why are you punishing me?"

"I am not punishing you," she said. Her voice was strained. "I am just living. I am being myself. I thought you liked that about me."

"I did," I said with a sigh. "Georgina, please, I feel it's only right that you tell me—are you going to transform her?"

"It's midnight," she muttered. She roughly shouldered past me out of the pantry and returned to the party, shouting a hello to some newly arrived guest. I closed the door and sat in the dark among the braided strands of garlic and jars of honey, listening to the sounds of human laughter, human excitement, human hope.

I had never felt so remote from it in all my years.

Conflagration

Revolution. Transformation. Evolution.

How abrupt a Change seems when it comes. The catalyst is perceived, but ignored; there is always some small matter that is more pressing. The coat needs a button replaced, more coal is needed for the stove, an old lady dies in her sleep on a cold February morning, another three illustrations needed immediately for the issue of the newspaper to be handed out in front of the latest campaign banquet. I had spent most of February in my room sketching the tangled shadows cast by a single candle blazing. I was hiding. I kept my mind as closed as I could; I had no desire to know what went on outside the circle of light around my desk.

Ollier's old mother died. Maria sensed it, went up to check on the old woman, verified that she had breathed her last, and braved the overcast day to inform Ollier of his mother's passing. He broke into such vivid and heartfelt tears that Maria even embraced him and let him cry onto her shoulder, tucking her veil firmly into the bodice of her dress. I was already in bed and falling asleep by then, too tired to build a barrier in my mind against the grief that Maria absorbed from Ollier and then radiated out into the atmosphere. I felt my consciousness slip away, wetting my pillow with impersonal tears.

When I awoke at sundown and staggered into the balcony-parlor to check the weather, as I always did, I found Maria and Georgina kneeling on the floor, before Ollier, lying on the couch with one arm limply flung out into space. I blinked stupidly at them, more astonished at seeing them both in the room at the same time, a rare occurrence. Before I could speak, Georgie turned her head to look at me. "Drink of him," she said. "You need it."

I took a mere mouthful from the bend of his elbow and moved across the room, away from them, until I knew if I could trust myself. "I don't want to kill him," I said, his fresh warm blood rushing into mine, stirring and heating it like pouring hot milk into cold soup. Ollier ate a great deal of black pepper, garlic, goose livers, and mint, and he did not smoke, so his blood was always delicious. Today's taste, however, was peculiarly bitter. I sank down onto another couch, opposite them.

"It's too late," Maria said. "He won't last the night."

The strange taste, dispersed among the cream and spice, at last occurred to me. "Opium," I said, already feeling chemical gravity weighting my freshly awakened limbs into the upholstery of the couch. "Raw opium, massive amounts . . . why would he do that?"

"He loved his mother," Maria said with a faint shrug. Her cheeks were ruddy with the recent ingestion of his blood, and her hair fell in a great sloppy mass of gold across her shoulders, pooling in her lap. "He has no other family. Unless you count us."

I crawled back to where they were and grasped Ollier's wrist again. His head turned toward me; his eyes were open, even if only as narrow slits. I noticed for the first time that his eyelashes contained gray hairs. "M. Ricari," he whispered, smiling a little. "I had hoped to see you before I went."

"Why did you do this?" I asked, chafing his arm to circulate his blood. Of course, this could no longer be beneficial, but I felt I had to do something to keep him warm, comfort him, provide him with genial company. "Who's going to drive us?" I added with a laugh, and kissed his hand.

"You never needed me to begin with," he said. "I've seen you fly, monsieur; I've seen the Lady Georgina—or is it Jerzy now? Forgive me if I slip, my lady."

Georgie smiled reassuringly and touched his forehead. "You may call me whatever you wish."

Ollier opened his eyes wider then, but he could no longer see us. He only said once more: "I have seen you fly," and then he closed his eyes and sighed away his soul.

"Quickly," said Maria, "don't let him get cold."

Afterward, I felt compelled to go outside onto the balcony, though I was barely half-dressed and the wind was bitter. The opium made me nauseous yet apathetic. Those are two sensations that I dislike intensely. I put my face to the wind and stared down at the unraveling tapestry of Paris. The sun did not set; the gray gloom merely darkened to an inky lead, rendering the world in charcoal monotone. I had not seen the moon or stars for weeks. Determined to create my own light, I grasped the crucifix that rested against my heart, and thought of Ollier's soul and his *foie gras*, and laughed— one of the purest prayers I have ever performed.

I returned to the apartment once I had taken command of my nausea. Ollier lay dead on the fuchsia couch, his arms folded peacefully across his chest. His jawline sagged, his ears were large and growing wiry hairs, his rein-toughened hands were covered in scars, and his knuckles bulged gnarled and twisted where they had been broken and rebroken in tavern brawls. I had simply not noticed that he grew old; he was forty-eight, but the young man only saw the young man.

We were the same age.

Maria had stoked the huge fireplace in the kitchen, bringing blazing warmth. I joined the two women there, reclining on the fur rug before the fire. Now that the nausea had passed, the opium left only a delectable heaviness, dreaminess, and relaxation, best experienced in a warm, dark room on a soft surface. "So did he just come in and say 'I am ending my life, please consume me'? Or did you take your own initiative?" I asked, glancing over my shoulder at Maria.

"Don't look at me," Maria replied archly. "Do you just assume that any unconscionable act in Montmartre bears my signature? Even the ones that exist only in your own mind?"

I laughed. "Pardon me, it was just a reflex."

"You can blame your wife," said Maria, yawning.

Georgina gave a brief sneer. She had obviously gotten the lion's share of Ollier and opium; nausea still wrung her insides. "You might as well blame God for taking away people's mothers. Or for making a carriage driver depressed enough to eat a thousand grains of opium on the doorstep of his employer. He plainly wanted to be found by one of us; again, why would he have waited till sundown? Madame Ollier was dead this dawn, and he knew she was dead by ten o'clock. Right, Maria?" Georgie looked to her, and Maria gave a single, sedate nod. "So he goes about driving, takes a stop at the apothecary's, buys enough opium to kill a horse, and then returns here."

"Maybe he wanted to become one of us," I mused.

They both stared at me, as though I'd suggested

something outlandish. "He did not," Georgina stated with authority.

"Did you make sure?" I said.

"As sure as I could" was her cutting response. She turned her head away from me, closing her eyes. "Leave me alone, Orfeo. Do not lash out from grief."

I stood up, thinking to scream a much more vicious accusation back at her, but I felt so dizzy as soon as I took to my feet that retaliation fled from my mind. I stood by the fireplace, my hand resting against the mantel, staring into the blasting flames until I thought my eyes would melt. "I'm going back to the balcony," I said, more to myself than to the women. "I have gotten too hot."

I wondered if I would be caught in this pattern of indoors-outdoors all night, as I chipped away at a paper-thin coating of ice on the railings with my overgrown claws. It was time to make the final decision to cut them, or not to cut and let them grow as long as they liked. They grew very slowly. Would they regulate themselves, or grow out longer and longer? Still so many things I did not know. I did not know what to say to Georgie that would explain to her why I had to keep rushing from the room whenever she was there, to keep from striking her. Instead, I ran off to be alone; in privacy I fantasized about being able to scream a terrible scream at her, the cry I'd held inside me for twenty years, ashamed of it and afraid to release it. I feared its power, now banked and building; when I let it out, it would destroy everything in my path, including her hypocrisy and her wrongheadedness. If it destroyed her in the process, so be it.

I imagined her being ripped to pieces, exploding the way the glass vase had exploded, but the image gave me no pleasure. The image bore too close a resemblance to

the vision of her being torn apart by gunfire or dynamite that had haunted me since she first ran away to
build barricades.

The wind paused entirely for a moment, and on its
next breath I caught the scent of human fear rising
from the sloping street below us. I peered through the
railings, willing my lazy eyes to focus. Taking the steps
two at a time, holding her full skirts in her hands, a lone
woman ran up toward the building, her breath leaving
hot puffs of steam with every fourth step. Instantly, I
recognized the strong, cinnamon scent of Rosy Lefeu.
Startled, I shouted down, "Rosy! What are you doing
here? Why are you alone?"

"Let me in, Ricari," she shouted back. "I must see
Jerzy!" Her voice was tight and high, and she hammered
on the door with her hand. Before I could reply, the
housemaid had opened the door and Rosy disappeared
inside.

I turned and rushed back into the tropical apartment
in time to meet Rosy, who had seemingly run up the
mezzanine stairs as well. I led her into the kitchen, and
she collapsed, breathing with difficulty, onto a chair.
Georgie immediately loosened Rosy's corset strings and
fanned her with a wooden spoon. Maria turned her
head and watched them with no expression on her face,
but her mind in such a tumult that I could distinguish
nothing. I stood in the doorway, bemusedly watching all
at once.

"What are you doing here?" Georgie whispered. "I
told you never to come here!"

Rosy half sat up, gazing at Georgina, her eyes wide
with desperation. "Oh, Jerzy! Don't be angry! I had
to . . ." she began, then let her eyes travel down
Georgie's body, across the white flannel gown, the
slight, but definite, swelling of breasts and hips beneath,
and back at her luminescent pale face and close-cropped

hair. Georgina's face appeared unmistakably feminine when it was clean, but with the voluptuous, delicate Rosy next to her, Georgie still looked like a boy in a dress.

And her spindle-fingered, clawed hands, still resting on either side of Rosy's body, did not appear at all human.

Rosy swallowed hard and closed her eyes, fighting off her confusion in deference to her true message. "My father—they've arrested my father!"

"What?" Georgina blinked, trying to shake off the opium haze. She could not, any more than Ollier could; she would be intoxicated for at least another several hours. "They can't have . . . they have no right . . . what are the charges?"

"Sedition, of course," Rosy said slowly. "He has been wanted as a deserter since . . . I . . . What is the matter with you? Are you ill?"

"Opium," I said, coming into the room. I sat next to Maria on the rug. "Rather a lot of it. Rather more than we bargained for. It is a most unpredictable drug. Maria, may I present Mademoiselle Rosy Lefeu. Rosy, this is Mademoiselle Grise. My sister." I could not suppress a sarcastic laugh, though I immediately regretted it.

Rosy, recovered from her exertions, sat up completely, moving Georgie's familiar hand out of her lap. "Oh," she said hesitantly, "how do you do. I was unaware that you had a sister, M. Grise."

"I've got a sister and a wife and everything," I muttered.

"Shut up, Orfeo." Georgie blinked her left eye at me. She was trying to blink both eyes, but only the left one responded to her command. "This is very serious!"

"It is even more serious than you think," Rosy replied. "I heard, while I was on my way here, that M. Soltan has been taken as well. I believe they will arrest

M. Lotte in the morning, and M. Villon if they can lay hands on him. And they will come for you. I do not know if the others have been warned; there were very few witnesses, and . . ." Rosy's eyes filled with tears. "They just came in while we ate supper, and took him away. They're going to kill him!"

"No, they're not," said George firmly. "We won't let them."

"What are *you* going to do about it?" Maria cut in, her voice sharper than I thought possible at this stage. Her age gave her strength even against a near-toxic dose of opium. Or perhaps she had not drunk as deeply of Ollier's blood? "Storm the conciergerie with a party of rescue pirates in Turkish costume? Say good-bye; the man is as good as dead. And good riddance to the lot of them."

"I have never met you before," said Rosy Lefeu, her chin trembling and a single tear streaking her blushing cheek, "but I can already tell that you are cruel, cold, and bitter."

Maria widened her eyes and smiled brightly, but Rosy did not correctly interpret that signal of aggression. A tiger always grins before she attacks. "Is that what you think, young lady? For voicing a doubt that there is anything that two young *girls* can do to save your father from imprisonment and the guillotine?" I wish that she had not said that with such relish, for I could not help laughing. Certainly, it was the nihilistic laughter that I am prone to at the worst moments, but it did not help to restore calm or rationality.

Rosy continued, "You are cruel to jeer at me on this, the most tragic of days! Think of your own father being snatched from his home in the middle of a meal! I am willing to bet one million francs that you cannot do it— compassion requires a heart! Compassion requires belief! You stopped believing in anything long ago. You stopped loving anything long ago."

I begged, "Shut up, now, Rosy, you don't know what you're playing with."

Maria's chilling laugh brought back my nausea. "You are blind, my child," she said, "if you think I have stopped loving." She twisted her hair up into a bun. "Now, Georgina, please advise the young lady to leave. I would like a word with you."

"I will not," said Georgie.

"Would someone please explain what is going on here?" Rosy said.

"I told you to shut up," I said more forcefully, and her mouth closed tight; but her face grew redder and redder as she struggled to speak. "It's for your own good."

It was too late.

Lifting Rosy from the couch, Georgina stood up and, keeping her eyes on Maria, they left the room. Maria fell over laughing, clapping her hands with delight. "What does she think that's going to do?" she cried. "The walls are paper thin—we could hear you without listening!" She rolled along the rug, tangling herself in her nightdress, then paused and looked at me with one wild tail of loose blond hair straggling over her face. She looked as mad and gleeful as a little girl. I stood again, warming my hands in the glow of the fire. We both listened.

In Georgina's bedchamber, Rosy was asking, "Does my father know that you are a woman?"

"No," said Georgie. "He must never know."

A thick-throated sigh. "Oh, worry not on that account. He most likely never will; he will be dead in six weeks. The newspaper cannot continue. The organization cannot continue," Rosy insisted. "If M. Lotte wants to avoid the guillotine, he will have to flee. We shall all have to flee. What are we going to do? What am *I* going to do? I have no guardian, and . . . and I had assumed, I had planned, to become your wife. And now—" Her voice broke off in a sob. Maria and I glanced at each other, but I could not hold her terrifying gaze.

"I am sorry. But I do love you. I do love you, and I would gladly take you as my wife if . . . if such things were possible."

Maria's claws ripped a long tear along the rug. "No," she hissed. "No. She will not do this to me."

"I do not want to be a woman's wife. I want to be *your* wife."

"My love, I will not ever let anything happen to you. I will take you away from here with me. But we must act quickly."

Maria put her fingertips to her temples and drew them slowly down her face. Her claws sliced deep into the skin, and blood poured down her jaw and into the neckline of her gown. The blood darkened and dried instantly, and the cuts on her face sealed themselves over, but I could smell her pain. "She will not do this. You were one thing. This—" She stood up slowly, steadying herself. "This will not do."

"Maria!" I croaked, but my limbs were filled with wet sand, and almost immediately I was mesmerized again by the constant transformations of the fire. I was powerless against the feverish fascination of the rhythmic hallucinations. I saw the Alpine crags grow, warp, and melt in the shapes of the flames; I saw the rabbit trapped in ice; I saw the twinkling skyline of Paris repeating itself into infinity. All the while, I repeated to myself: *Do something. Use your power. Move your mind, if not your whole body.*

When at last I succeeded in my struggle to turn my

perception outward, I saw Maria's bare white feet, toes crowned with iron claws, flashing along the hall carpet.

Escape, Rosy, I thought. *Get out now.* Rosy looked toward the doorway and took a step, then turned back to Georgina for one last look.

At last, she had grown the power to resist me.

Georgie held the sobbing Rosy close to her and gently kissed the young girl's hair, lost in its infinite, magical scent, and thus she did not notice Maria's lightning entrance until Maria was upon her. I felt Georgina's vertigo as she was spun around and hurled to the floor by Maria's blow, and I heard Rosy's scream through the walls and through three pairs of eardrums.

I fell to my knees on the rug, seized with nausea, and retched a mouthful of blood onto the flagstones. Half of the blood shot from my nostrils. "Stop it," I shouted; it reached my ears as a burbling moan. Blood clotted instantly inside my nose, and in another instant had been reabsorbed into my body. When I tried to smooth my hair away from my face, I was shaking so hard that I cut my temples with my fingernails.

Rosy Lefeu stared at her own heart, still twitching and oozing, held in the palm of Maria's dripping scarlet hand. She had not really felt any pain—it happened too quickly—and she did not recognize her heart outside of herself. But she felt suddenly faint, confused, sleepy.

"Never imagine that I do not love," Maria said softly, crushing the organ into jelly. Rosy blinked at it, but before she could blink again, toppled over dead, next to Georgina. Georgina sprawled along the floor, frozen in shock, gritting her teeth against the pain of skin healing around the sharp edge of a broken bone jutting from her wrist.

"Never imagine that I do not love," Maria whispered. Georgina stared at her. Maria knelt beside the injured

Georgie, kissed her forehead, and grasped the broken arm. With a faint grunt, she smacked the two halves back into place with her palms. Georgina's scream drove agony into my belly like the blade of a broadsword.

"There," said Maria. "All better."

I lay on the blood-spattered rug, pushing my face into the heavy gray sheepskin and fluttering my hands underneath me, searching for my rosary. I could not find it with my numb fingers.

Georgina looked at Rosy.

"She might still be good," Maria said. "Don't let her go to waste."

"You," said Georgina, and slid away, across the floor, toward her bed.

"Did she mean so terribly much?" Maria mused lightly. "You only knew her for five months. How could you—your *wife*, Georgina, my love? You led her to believe that you would marry her? Are you out of your mind?"

"You," said Georgina again, this time punctuated with the same joyless whinny of a laugh that I had previewed. I heard her scuttling in her wardrobe.

"Oh, are you going somewhere? Are you actually going to attire yourself in the garments of the weaker sex?" Maria laughed. "Ah, no, I hadn't thought so. I have never known a woman who despised corsets as much as you. You never did move past the fashions of the Empire, did you?"

A pause. Maria's voice came more faintly; I was losing my perceptions as I slid deeper into the effects of the drug. The chaotic pattern of the sheep's hair rug had arranged itself into a lattice of infernal logic and complexity, and I could see, magnify, and move about the pattern when I closed my eyes. "Oh, Georgina, my love, I have been so indulgent all these years. But you really have gone too far this time. I had to put a stop to all of this nonsense. I have allowed your radicalism and your agitation and your wildness, but to deceive that girl was simply cruel. And I would like to know if you have taken a turn for the cruel; it's only polite that I, as your companion, should know."

I closed my eyes and traveled into the lattice, which unraveled itself, knit itself into a rope, and wound itself around my neck. When I tried to open my eyes, the rope pulled strangling-tight. I tried to call out, if not with my voice, at least with my mind; but I heard no response, and I do not think that either heard me.

I felt rather than heard the slow, heavy tread of Georgina's boots on the hall rug, and then approaching me through the kitchen and pausing right beside my head. I lay helpless.

"Good-bye, Orfeo," Georgie said. "You should not have lain down."

When I woke again, I could hear war.

I still lay before the roaring fireplace, but the logs were bright and new, giving off enormous heat. The trail of blood that I had expelled was reduced to sticky black ash. I smelled putrefaction.

Maria sat in the chair behind me, dressed in white taffeta, her hair undone. She stared into the fire without seeing it.

"Is Ollier still there?" I asked.

Maria nodded.

"Rosy?"

She looked at me and smiled briefly.

I stood up, the opium hardly more than a memory in my bloodstream. I felt a profound lack, an absence of ambient sound. The loss of a presence. "Where's George?"

"Look and see," Maria replied.

I sent out my thoughts and found nothing. She was not in the apartment; she was not in Montmartre; she was not in Paris. "Is she dead?" I asked in a panic.

"No, she's not dead. I wish she were." Maria stood up and poked at the fire logs until they roared. "I wish I had killed her when I first thought to do it."

"Maria, no—"

"No, little greyhound. You should go too. Gather your books; gather your handsome coats and your walking stick. Go down and watch the destruction. Destruction is always entertaining. And we are lucky enough to rise above it. It's not our world that is being destroyed. Or . . . perhaps it is." She frowned. "Perhaps our world ended a long time ago. Or perhaps just mine."

"Maria!" I cried.

"Go!" she commanded; she racked me with headache until I had gotten dressed and packed a trio of cases of papers, books, and linens from her room and mine. I slipped the watercolor portrait of Maria between two folded bedsheets. I thought to take a last morbid look at Rosy and the hole in her breast, but another stab of pain advised me against it. I did glance down the hall to the balcony-parlor, and saw bodies of all our servants piled atop one another, with the housemaid balanced on top, like a garnish.

Maria brought me back to the kitchen, my bags in a pile outside the doorway. "Come, embrace me, my child," she said, holding out her arms. I crossed to her and held her cool, yielding form for a long moment, then she pushed me away slightly and brought her hand up to her chin.

The razor was so keen it did not even make a sound. The flesh simply parted, the skin peeled back, and her jugular vein opened and soaked us both.

Drink, boy.

I wrapped my mouth around the wound she had

made and sucked gently, not wishing to turn the wound inside-out with too much force. My caution was unnecessary; I felt her skin closing again under my tongue. Oh, but in the meantime, I gulped down mouthfuls of dense, freshly fed, ancient blood, so powerful that I felt it nourishing all of the tiniest cells and capillaries of my body, flushing my face and erecting my sex. She held me tightly against her, not minding my reflexive arousal, loving it even, in the same half-disgusted way that a mother loves her smelly infant. She had consumed all the blood of all the servants; each consciousness had lost the greater part of its individuality, subsumed under her own.

When her injury had closed completely, I kissed her hair. "I love you," I said.

"And I you, Orfeo," she replied. "Now go. And don't come back." She was greatly weakened from the loss of blood, and the lines of her face deepened and took on greater shadows. I broke away from her, and she staggered; I would gladly have taken her back into my arms, but she shoved me away with her remaining strength. I walked away. There was no longer anything I could do.

I bent to pick up my cases but glanced inside the kitchen. Maria stood silhouetted against the blaze, backing slowly across the hearth, across the flagstones. When she put her foot into the coals, she hissed and flinched.

"No!" I cried. But she did not hear me.

The white taffeta sucked up the flames as a sponge absorbs water, passing it, almost instantaneously, throughout its entire form, swelling it, dilating it. Her golden curtain of hair flew out, flowed up, floated and vaporized at once. The air rushed out of her lungs in a long, piercing scream, her breath pushing fire out into the room, sparking the fur rug, igniting the heavily varnished kitchen chair.

I fled down the hall and down the stairs.

"Fire!" I shouted as I rushed through the front door. "Fire!" I cried to the stars above, for I saw no one; the streets near our house lay eerily deserted. I seemed to be the only being left alive in the world.

In my panic I leapt, cases and all, thirty feet down the hill and hit the ground still running. I did not stop to speak or think or take a breath until I reached the westernmost edge of the city. I wanted to escape it entirely, but the sight of the last brasserie in Les Batignolles, on the edge of the cemetery, kept me from taking another step. Where would I go to escape the memory of Maria's beautiful face being charred to the skull? Where could I find Georgie, out in the vastness of the world outside the city? Where could I mourn in peace? There was nowhere to go; all I had was Paris.

And Paris burned.

La vie Parisienne

I walked in widening circles until sunrise, without destination or idea, adrift in the shallows of chaos.

I had grown so used to the women. I had kept a similar daily routine for two decades, in the same neighborhood, employing the same comfortable, reflexive deceptions that now crumbled uselessly away. That was the hardest loss, even harder than the loss of love. They were the parameters of my world, the sky and the earth, alpha and omega. At times I had despised them, and despaired of the time when I could escape; and why had I not escaped? I could have just walked away at any time. And yet I never went any further than the cemetery or the Quartier Latin.

Georgina had just walked away.

I had no sense from her but a heavy sorrow that I could hardly distinguish from my own. Somewhere, she was still alive. Maria was not. Maria's individual soul, her unique consciousness humming like a wavelength in the ether, no longer existed. In despair I kept listening for her sound, kept calling out to her, begging her to answer from beyond. I refused to believe that an immortal could be gone, without even a disembodied soul to keep me company.

I had grown used to being suspended in their thoughts, like a babe in the fluids of the womb, struggling to shut them out and form my own thoughts in privacy. Now there was no resistance; now I was free, adrift, in silence, with only my own mind at work, the way it had been. I did not remember having a solitary mind, without the backdrop of the dazzling thought-filaments of Georgina, and Maria's long, elliptical, savage images and motivations. I had been born anew into a still, cold, stabbingly bright world. It was strange, yet oddly natural, as if an additional organ, a gland of pain, had grown in my chest, swollen and pressing into my heart.

On the edge of the city, where the trees still grew wide and massive, I found an empty, deserted coach house, a kilometer or so away from the house it served, on a road so rarely traveled that my feet left pristine prints on the surface of the smooth mud. The chain on the bolted door broke easily in my fingers. Inside was dry and dark, and smelled of old hay, old horses, and older leather, removed over a decade ago. I sat in a wooden groom's chair, left behind, the seat worn to the fibers, and stared out the window at the insipid, colorless morning, freezing rain clotting on last season's ripped and dripping cobwebs. Even the spiders had long since deserted this place.

I slumped paralyzed before the cracked pane all through the day, not seeing what came before me. I had no appetite, and no desire to move or to sleep. I could not even weep; the world wept for me, sending great fat icy blobs that once, in a faraway cloud, had been snowflakes.

* * *

Dusk brought me abruptly to my senses. The rain had stopped, holding itself back in preparation for snow, and the Batignolles stood utterly silent but for the wind murmuring through the naked trees. But my mind was no longer alone.

Chicot was coming.

I sat bolt upright and turned my head until I heard his footsteps, the heavy boots on wet, dead leaves, and the swish of his cloak against the backs of trouser legs. He was a good kilometer away. I thought to myself that if I ran now, he might not be able to catch me and I could remain alone; but the absurdity of that idea occurred to me instantly, and I slapped my own face. I could not outrun Chicot. If he wished to kill me, I would have no choice but to die. And the idea of death appealed to me. He would not be cruel.

Simultaneously, Chicot's consciousness permeated mine like a soft, sweet fog, settling gently inside my own. He walked along the road bounding the grave-yard, eyes closed against the rain, using only his higher senses to guide him toward me. "Ricari, I am here," he spoke aloud. A cold wet wind whipped his hair against his cheek. "There is no need to run."

Resisting the urge to relax, I gathered my body into a knot, toes against the floor, arms locked around knees, ready to spring up and fight. "I ought to be alone," I replied, my voice thick and rusty. "There is nothing more to say. There is nothing more to do."

Chicot appeared before me presently. He had taken a few great leaps along the trees, as silently as a cat, and slipped into the coach house, bringing a brief gust of chillsome air with him through the door. "You are right," he said, tipping rainwater from his hat. "If you must be alone, you must. But you must master your grief; you are all but screaming into the void. Every vampire in Paris can hear you. I was going to leave you alone, but one of *my* elders suggested that I offer my consolation directly." He gave me a slow smile. "I didn't get a wink of sleep today; you should be grateful for my generosity. And our bond—do not forget that. It has saved your life today."

I could not be grateful for surviving. "Where is Georgina?" I asked. "Please tell me that you know. You are so much more powerful than I—surely you can find her and tell her . . ."

Chicot slowly shook his head. "I do not know," he said. "If she does not want to be found, she will not be, by either of us. I am not so much more powerful than you; not anymore."

My mouth remembered the raw contours of Maria's slit throat, and my eyes remembered tears. Chicot removed his wet cloak and stood by, impassive, while I took hold of my grief with both hands and cried until my eyes felt raw and the painful swelling inside me had been slightly relieved. Chicot handed me a miraculously dry handkerchief.

"Rest, and mourn," he said to me. "I shall return tomorrow night, and we should go a-hunting. The Seine," he added, staring into the distance with his mellow smile, "runs red."

"I should leave Paris," I mused. "Before they destroy the place."

"No," said Chicot, as if I'd suggested something wicked. "Not yet."

He reapplied his cloak and hat, gave me a slight bow, and said, "Good night, M. Ricari. Do not despair completely; you now have immense power, and you still have friends. Take comfort in that; friends among the undead are more valuable than diamonds. You will see. *Adieu.*"

Over the course of the next several months, I placed myself into Chicot's excellent care. Fortified by Maria, I found that I needed much less blood than I had before, and blood that I did take gave me enormous energy and power, and vastly improved my mood. Perhaps because of that, I did not take any blood for the first few weeks. I did not want to feel better. It seemed sacrilegious to smile or lift my head. Chicot forced me into it, though, exploiting my rising gut-hunger, and the pliability of the youngest, consumption-stricken daughter of the nearby manor. He initiated the midnight seduction, and the sight of Chicot's jaws dripping with life-sustaining scarlet literally made my mouth water and my stomach growl. "Do her a favor, Ricari," Chicot said to me. "Save her from another year of decline; rescue her while she is still a tender young maiden with corn-silk hair."

She even opened her eyes and said, "Thank you; I couldn't bear it any longer." At her bedside was a well-thumbed copy of Polidori's *The Vampyre*.

"An admirer," mused Chicot, folding the girl's limp arm across her chest.

Throughout the subsequent months, we made short work of the rest of the family and most of their servants.

Chicot also went through all the papers that Maria had made me pack. While I slumped despondently in a corner of my coach house, twisting straws into tinder sticks, Chicot leafed and stacked and hummed, puffing cheerfully on a long clay pipe. At one page, he sat back onto his heels, blinked, crossed himself, and let out a low whistle. "Heh," he said at last. "It is as I suspected. She's left you everything."

"What?" I raised my head.

"All of it—the houses, the property, the estate in Metz, the accounts. I wonder if Georgina knew about this. You are now a most wealthy hermit." He arched his eyebrow at my scruffy, halfhearted beard and torn, muddy clothes. "If I were you, I would go into the city to see how much of this is left, and have it given to you in gold. The currency of the old regime is not worth much anymore, but gold will retain its value. Of course, then we have to find somewhere to keep it."

"Land is more valuable than gold," I said, feeling as though my father were speaking through me. My voice was colorless and flat, and my lips moved of their own volition. "I will retain the properties and acquire more. Bring me materials to write with." When he had done so, I scribbled awhile and told him, "Now you may act as my agent, and take the accounts, and buy what you will with them. Every man should own land."

Chicot laughed. "The last thing in the world I want is property," he said. "I live nowhere; I belong nowhere."

"Take it off my hands, I beg you," I insisted. "I will retain the property I have, but you deserve something for your assistance." I held up my hand to still further argument. "I won't hear it, Chicot; do this for me. Take the bank accounts! Buy yourself a new cloak, a horse . . . Give the money away, for all I care. Buy yourself a woman. Buy all the human slaves you want. You need never hunt again."

"Whyever would I want that? That's the best part of life," Chicot replied; but he accepted the note I handed him and slipped it into his coat. "You will have to come out sometime, unless you mean to entomb yourself here. And believe me, it wouldn't work."

Chicot did convince me to sell the house on the Rue d'F—. I fetched a handsome price from the city planners desperate to demolish the old, cramped, easily barricaded Paris in favor of precision, light, and hygiene. In celebration, Chicot insisted that I join him at Dumarchand's restaurant, near the Varieties, the theater that still showed *La vie Parisienne* to adoring crowds each night. I arrived early, slipped unseen (and unpaid) into the Varieties, and watched the play from the back of the room, amazed to find that my heart still stirred inside me at the plight of fictional characters. I knew in my heart that the fiction was a mere veneer painted over actual lives; I recognized each character from the streets and cafés where I had lived. Like them, I was unchanged, artificially held forever in a single moment in time.

The restaurant Dumarchand's mouth was full, and excess patronage spilled and trickled from the corners. Even I had some difficulty navigating the sea of giant hoop-skirts and snapping, mothlike ladies' fans. I smiled when I thought of what Georgina must think of the imprisonment of hoop skirts. The play had put me into a good humor.

Chicot stood encircled by actors and theatrical producers, purchasing magnums of champagne in a loud, jokingly imperious voice. He wore a coat of green Chinese embroidered silk and pale-pink trousers; his cheeks were enlivened with rouge, his eyes lined in black wax pencil, almost as though he were another actor who had just quit the stage. I hardly recognized him, and it startled me when he embraced me and kissed both my cheeks. "Ah, there you are, Ricari. I had begun to worry that you wouldn't make it in. Won't you have a glass of champagne?"

I blinked at him. "I hardly need it; the atmosphere is intoxicating enough." Indeed, the air reeked of spilled champagne and tobacco smoke, almost completely swamping the delectable scent of garlic and butter, rising yeast, roasted goose, and thyme. "I think, instead, that I should like to dine. Is there a table, or do I have to pick bits out of the kitchen?"

Chicot, his arm still around me, turned me away from the reveling humans and pressed his head gently against mine. *I have taken your suggestion*, his voice in my head came, softer and higher than the sounds produced by his throat. *I have bought a woman.*

"You what?" I jerked away from him.

"Just the one," he said, smiling, a little embarrassed. "Oh, don't worry, I have no intention of mistreating her. Raissa!" He gestured at the gaggle of actors, and a woman broke away from it and approached us with a smile. She was not young, one of the bit-part actresses whose single line I could not recall, with a round, pleasant face, still coated with white and scarlet makeup. She and Chicot looked oddly suited for one another. "Raissa, this is my friend, M. Grise. You have him to thank for this evening's enjoyments."

She curtsied to me, lowering her eyes. "I very much look forward to making your acquaintance," she said, and when she looked up again to meet my eyes, I saw exactly the kind of acquaintance she had in mind.

I looked at Chicot. "Was she very expensive?"

Chicot only chuckled, but his eye twitched warningly as he led Raissa away.

Incensed, I enfolded a pliant young costume girl in my arms and had a deep draft from the side of her neck. I wanted champagne after all.

Later, I followed Chicot back to the house on the Rue d'F—. The sight of it nearly struck me blind with memories. Yet it had changed in the twenty-odd years since we had left it, and I had become M. Grise. The previous inhabitants had only recently quitted the residence, and it retained their scents: the sweat, powder, perfume, and waste of half a dozen families, some with dogs, and the familiar barnyard smell of rabbits and chickens in the courtyard. I stared at the stonework of the doorway; my blood had been scrubbed away, but traces of it remained in the crevices around the hinges. My humanity, reduced to a faded stain!

Chicot was too drunk on champagne-saturated blood

to notice my distress. He danced with his arms about an invisible partner. "Ah, my Raissa, how difficult to part from you and say 'till next time'! I hope I do not accidentally kill her; she is a fine woman indeed, and more than worth eighteen francs a month!"

"Eighteen francs!" I said. "You have made her a rich woman."

"She can make better use of the money than I," Chicot said. He put his coat on the first chair that he saw in the front room, and sat with a heavy sigh. "Ah, Ricari. Take comfort in the fact that this house will no longer be standing by the end of the week. Feel despair as well. You won't be able to forget about it; you will know these details all your life, and nothing you do to forget what's happened will do any good. But if you wish to look upon it to refresh your memory—well, there will be a street here instead. There will be no trace of how you came to being." He yawned. "It is a valuable lesson in your eternality. All passes away in time. . . ."

I went out to the courtyard again and gazed up at the impassive sky, starless and dark, as if the Almighty hid backstage, behind a dusty black velvet curtain, preparing for the next act.

When I returned to the house, Chicot lay limply sprawled on his coat on the chair, head thrown back and mouth open. He was falling asleep, his glow muting away into nothing. As I stood watching nearby, his breathing ceased, all color drained from his skin, and then even the whiteness faded into a dull pale gray. His gums shrank back from his brown-grooved yellow teeth. My own heart nearly stilled in my chest. His flesh lost its muscularity, collapsing and shrinking over his bones, wilting like accelerated autumn leaves, until he resembled a man who had died of starvation. And yet I knew he was not dead; the link between our minds, forged in blood and proximity, remained. He was not yet dreaming, but held in a soft, black, restorative limbo.

"I see," I said to the still house. "This is what you did not let me see! And I . . . I too . . . every night . . . how awful." The gland of pain inside me clenched itself and doubled its output. "I'm sorry, George . . . if you can hear me, I'm sorry . . . I thought you simply didn't love me enough. . . ."

I slid down next to the emaciated Chicot, kissed his marble-cold hand, and rested my head on his thigh. I would be there when he awoke, as he had been for me; and in the meantime, we would see each other in our dreams.

A Generation Come
and Gone

I had no intention of leaving Paris for good when I set out.

I had never really completely reintegrated into society. The sight of all the lively human faces, rich and poor and middle-class, only reinforced my alienation from the minds underneath. Instead of eagerly eavesdropping on their thoughts as I had before, I now sought refuge from the unceasing noise of mundane worry and obsession. It never really varied. Still, I did not feel superior; I knew my own thoughts were as tiresome, and I endeavored to keep them to myself.

Instead of visiting the new restaurants and buildings, I spent my nights in the coach house, writing dull but mathematically precise Latin poems, and painting a pastoral scene with nymphs, horses, and sheep onto a long scroll of uncut paper. Weeks and months would pass without my leaving the coach house, losing myself in tracing intricate details of running water and vines, weakly illuminated by the dull light that fell through the cracked windowpane. The only humans who saw me with any degree of regularity were my bankers, though once in a while I would make my way to the artists' cafés to listen to the heated and outrageous conversations held there. They were the only fresh ideas I had heard in decades. I had no desire to show my work to anyone. I did not fear criticism, only the poison of mediocrity, politics, and commerce. I had all I needed; praise, gold, women, and fame were mine for the taking, but I chose to leave them.

The loss of Georgina had killed my desire for physical intimacy with anyone, male or female, human or undead. I desired only her. My most painful moments occurred when I saw a thin young man, shabbily dressed but with an elegant stride and a loud laugh, or a brash young woman with her dark hair loose, gesturing with a vulgar cigarette; and I would gaze upon them with a sick despair. No man could ever be my George; no woman could ever be my Jadzia.

Chicot was an admirable companion, though our socialization was limited to the parameters of the hunt, and the idle conversations that took place while we stalked unwary, gullible prey through half-demolished streets, and the newly gas-lamp-lit avenues that had once been crooked stone houses. Though he always had a favorite—sometimes bought with francs, sometimes with posies and promises—Chicot could not limit himself to one flavor of blood. Variety was his spice of choice, and variety we had; musky Dutch sailors, syphilitic old whores, clear springlike virgin youths, and dozens of flavors of hashish, laudanum, tobacco, chocolate, and savories. Chicot liked the Les Halles escargot families, with their blood like a buttery, garlicky sea. "You would never know it by my figure, but I am a gourmand," he bragged. "I have tasted an infinity, and I wish to taste an infinity more!"

But eventually, I grew restless in my hermitage, with

twenty feet of golden rolling hills and cerulean river spread out on the floor, daring me to step into it. Though I had a small amount of Batignolles countryside surrounding me outside the coach house, the flora that I illustrated was of a ruder, more exotic species, and the cleft summit of Vesuvius floated on the horizon in my dreams.

"I am homesick for Campania," I told Chicot one evening as we sat, poring over my painting. "I have been painting from memory. I want to see it again. I want to be there again."

"You should," Chicot answered, to my surprise. He had taken to wearing a beard, which only made him look smaller, thinner, and more kindly, his dark eyes sparkling above the heavy thicket of his whiskers. "Truly, you need a holiday; you have been in this ruin for more than twenty years, staring at the walls. And this is a wonderful time of year to travel; the springtime weather has been very kind recently, and the passage is clear. And your Italy is now unified as a single kingdom; think of that!"

I smiled at him, and shooed him aside to roll the painting. I tapped the scroll on the floor to even it; it had never been furled before, and I hoped that the colors would remain fixed and vibrant. "I have seen much," I said. "I know that all earthly unities are temporary. That fact saddens me; I still long for the eternal, the unchanging, the ultimate stability."

"Ah, you are not so very wizened," Chicot said knowingly. "You still have the mind of a young man. What are you—seventy?" He laughed at himself. "Still so young. I wish you safe travels, young man, and I will see you when you return."

The journey was more difficult than I had anticipated, for wholly unanticipated reasons.

I had not yet, in my life, traveled a long way by carriage, and though I had endured the jolting and noise of farm carts for months when I was young and mortal, my heightened senses struggled to cope with the squeaking, creaking boredom. More than anything in the world, I longed to unfurl my painting and continue working on it, though it was as complete as it could be without negating what I had already done. Therefore, somewhat like reading a long novel, I amused myself by silently examining the mind of my driver, a M. Louis-Jacques Regule, and his memories of his mundanely fascinating youth spent in the stables of the Emperor Bonaparte III, looking after the coach horses of the minor nobility. To access these cognitive jewels, I found myself hacking through a jungle of overwhelming worry about the planned war with Germany. He bitterly cursed the Emperor and the Prussians. He knew that when he returned, he would be pressed into service as an infantryman, fighting against men who held no threat to him.

When we arrived in Toulon, I did the only compassionate thing: I shot him dead with two bullets in his forehead, and supped upon his flowing, shock-tinted blood. I, too, had become a connoisseur.

Had I not given any serious thought to the truth that I would never again be able to see the golden hills of Campania wavering under an ocean of sunshine?

It did not seem so. I slept through the increasingly ovenlike days, with stringent direction not to be disturbed, and sprang again into impatient action as soon as the sun was setting. I could barely keep my stinging eyes open against even the declining light. Each time I woke, I cursed the brilliant scarlet sunsets, flaming and fading over the taffeta sea, and redoubled my savagery at night upon the unfortunate and unwary of the city of Naples.

My appetite had returned with ferocity. More than twenty years denied, I slaked my thirst greedily, emboldened by rumors of cholera, scarlet fever, summer agues, and the like. After subsisting on the thick blood of sailors for days on board the ship between Toulon and Naples, the novelty of the Neapolitans refreshed me. Naples was rife with disease, and I grew as addicted to the taste of a new sickness each night as I had to a roster of different entrées at Dumarchand's. Each malady would affect me gently for a few hours—chills, nausea, a fluttering headache, weakness in my limbs—then seep away, leaving me feeling stronger and fitter by minutes. I grew to enjoy the symptoms as though it were a new form of drunkenness, tossing and turning on my bed in a whirlwind of discomfort, my mind painting feverish pictures, knowing that I would be as well as I had been before by the end of the night.

Neapolitans were also prone to killing each other in fits of pique. I regularly saw knife fights and brawls, just passing between the dockside and my cheap hotel in the central district. Finding dead comrades on the street in the mornings (or better yet, whole families, killed stone-dead by cholera before any of them could even leave their homes) was even more common here than in Paris. Their hot tempers bemused me like the aggressive antics of children; though no less fatal, my own methods had become so secretive, so subtle, so distinct.

Nonetheless, I quickly tired of the human intensity of the city. I remained in the crooked brick-oven of Naples for only two nights, and set out toward Piedimonte on foot on the third. I carried only my pocketbook, my pistols, and my painting, and I seemed to skim over the roads and fields with no more effort than a leaf borne on the wind. What relief to leave Naples behind and strike out on my own through the country of my birth! How fine the summer night was! How brilliant the half-full moon, set in a polished obsidian sky! I would see my farm again, honor the grave of my mamma, and settle at least part of the disturbance in my soul.

The hills glowed the same white-gold in the moonlight as they always had, and the single, eldest olive tree, planted at the entrance of the road that led to the farm, had grown thicker and wilder, its branches heavy with immature fruit. I climbed up into the tree and stood out on the highest solid branch, gazing out at the rise where the sheepfold, the house, the vineyards, and the orchards could all be seen at a glance.

Even in the dark I knew that something was wrong. I did not make out the details of the grounds themselves before the awesome quiet began to alarm me. Where were the thoughts of the mortals who lived here? Even sheep had consciousness; where were they? There should have been hundreds of humming sheep-dreams. The vineyards did not look right and the grass in the folds grew tall.

Not a soul, human or animal, flickered in my mind as I walked up the road toward the house, passing the carriage house and stables. The path was strewn in sharp stones; we had always kept it clear. Morningglory vines tangled themselves right across the path, the alabaster trumpet flowers soaking the night with their syrupy scent. I thought of dear old fat Prego, and how he would have stumbled over these vines, and cut his knees upon the stones, and my remorseful heart ached as though I had killed the horse with my own hands.

On the front door of the house, a rain-stained sheet of paper curled away from the carved wood, toward the flowers, toward the moon.

FIEND

Property of the King Victor Emmanuel,
Annexed upon this date, 1 May 1868
No trespassing

Empty. Abandoned and forgotten.

I was struck blind with rage and distress. When I returned to my senses, I found myself, wet-faced, at the door of the little rectory of the church in Piedimonte without remembering how I had gotten there. A bearded old priest opened the door, sleepily rubbing his eyes. I did not recognize him, but I sensed that he had been there for decades. An entire generation had come and gone.

"You are still asleep," I commanded.

He replied slowly, "I am still asleep."

"You will remain asleep, and recall this exchange as a dream. Tell me truthfully what has happened to the Fattorio di Ricari, and you will avoid a nightmare," I demanded.

The priest's eyes drooped closed. "It belongs to Our Majesty King Victor Emmanuel," he murmured. "It was claimed as property of the court of Italy."

"Yes, years ago—but what about before that?"

"It was owned by the family of Zelotti."

"And before that?"

The priest blinked a few times, and his eyeballs shot back and forth under the closed lids. "I was told when I arrived here that it was owned by Captain Vittorio Ricari. That was before my time; I was still in Salerno then. I did not know the Captain. He had a great reputation in this town; he was spoken of frequently for a while. Years ago. He is all but forgotten now but for Brother Luigi, who manages the holy oils. He is always reminiscing about Captain Ricari's oils; they were the finest."

I felt panicky and sick, and I cut into the old man's recollection, which could go on forever. "Who was Zelotti?"

"The elder?" the priest asked, but then he grasped my meaning. "Sr. Zelotti married the daughter of Captain Ricari."

"Which daughter?" I whispered through dry lips.

"The eldest," mumbled the priest, smiling. "Signora Maria Elena. She was a most beautiful, capable woman and a fine mother."

So many questions filled my mind, and demanded answers from his, that the poor man struggled and twitched, strung between the non-sense of sleep and the fractured logic of my questioning. *Did they have many children? Was this Zelotti handsome? More handsome than I? Did the farm prosper or fail? Was I ever mentioned, or did I simply disappear?* The only words that finally passed my lips sounded like the guilty plea of a condemned man.

"Did she love him?"

The priest relaxed a little, and sighed heavily in his sleep. "She bore him three fine sons," he answered. "He was not cruel to her. Their marriage was advantageous, and prosperous, for a time. One child in the grips of the devil's temptations, and all their prosperity was in vain . . ."

I could not bear any more. "That's enough. Go back to bed." The priest shrugged a little and raised his arm to close the door. "You will dream of the ghosts of sheep," I said to him. "Good night."

I turned around and wandered back toward the farm with my face in my hands. Abruptly, I changed my course and walked back to the church, and the grave-yard surrounding it. I thought, *I must drink it all at once and get it over with. I must do this. If I feel as though I am dying, it is because I am.*

The Ricari mausoleum stood almost precisely as I remembered it: golden-yellow marble, as tall as I was, deftly carved, guarding over the plot of graves. However, now both of my parents' names had joined the ranks of grandfathers and great-uncles, and of my brother Vittorio. There was a place for me next to him, too—a blank spot on the marble, to the left and below my father's, awaiting the inscription of my name.

Elena was not here; of course, she would not be— she was a Zelotti now, and a mother of Zelottis. I felt that I hated all Zelottis in Creation, both the pious and the profane, with a viciousness like the crackling madness of rabies. I placed my hands against the chilly carved granite, crossed swords and grapevines and books cut into the rough surface, and prayed to the God of Job to take retribution against them. And yet—I slumped down the mausoleum wall and fell into a heap on the grass—God had already granted my wish; they had been ruined, and ended their lives unhappily.

Could I ask for a better, more efficient method if I begged it from Satan himself?

And had I not?

The next day, the village stonecutter rode out in the scorching heat of the day with his tools and added my name to its place on the surface of the mausoleum. When his wife asked him where he had been upon his return, he had no memory of having ever risen from bed that morning.

By then, I was halfway up the Voltorno, headed away from golden Campania hills and the drifting ashes of my painted dreams of the past.

My second trip to Switzerland was much more comfortable than my first, though no less painful. Money acted as a superb lubricant and cushion, guaranteeing a fine carriage and soft beds that I did not utilize, preferring to rest my penitent bones upon a hard floor, with the bedding wrapped around me like a shroud.

My hunger grew demanding again, and I was too befogged in despair to attempt to control it. The mortals would die anyway, sooner or later, probably sooner; and I was rarely cruel. If I had to decimate an entire family for an undisturbed and sheltered day of sleep, I was more than capable, but I did not seek the opportunity.

At length, after a meandering journey of a score of months, I felt that my spirit had lightened to a less impenetrable darkness. I thought I had been looking directly at my soul, but I had been glancing past it to the gloom of the grave, which did not describe my entirety. I had barely been conscious of my destination; I allowed myself to be drawn to it, as naturally as a bird flies south in September.

And, as if stepping out into the Holy Land, I came again to Geneva. It stood as calm and gay and secure as ever, insulated by the toilsome Alps. War seemed alien here. The peace soothed me; I was safe in its sanctity at the apex of the mad continent while the conflicts swirled about, around and below us, but as far away as legend.

I settled my deeds and money in the banking system there, and froze it tight, removing even my own access to my accounts. I would have to become someone else, and come back for it, if I wanted it; I locked it into a trust to mature for twenty years, to be accessed only by Orfeo V. Ricari. Signed, M. Grise. By then, my French was so seamless that the bankers had no idea that I was not a Parisian gentleman, entrusted with valuable property and exceptional wealth, and with a quirky eccentricity about meeting times. My requests were not unusual at this time; many noblemen had retreated over the Alps, intending to keep their wealth intact. And the soundness of my money was quite beyond suspicion.

Once this unpleasant responsibility had been resolved, I retraced the steps through Geneva I had taken
with Lorenzo. A lifetime ago—two lifetimes!—I had
come with him in pursuit of our hero, the poet Lord
Byron. I had sought to touch the hem of his robe and
receive absolution for my sin of mediocrity. I had bet
my soul and lost; but here was another chance to at least
take in the glory of history with my eyes. I sought the
magic castle, the now-famed Villa Diodati, which together we had never perceived; I would not be denied
the culmination of the pilgrimage a second time.

Byron had died a lifetime ago, but the Villa Diodati
still stood, golden and gorgeous on its carefully maintained grounds, the waters of the lake reflecting on its
face like a pretty girl angling her looking glass. The
night when I arrived was clear but windy, whipping
froth across the lake surface and bending the young
leaves on the trees. A storm approached from the
northwest, massing the fleecy pearled clouds in a layer
over the moon. Spring had grown impatient with the
soft, mild weather of the last several days, and the air
trembled with dips and swells of atmospheric pressure.
I guided my little stolen rowboat with swelling joy, my
eyes drinking in the sight of the columns of the man-
sion against its cape of black swansdown, restraining my
delighted, horrified laughter in the face of its magnifi-
cence. At last I had made it, though the journey had
taken sixty years and cost me my life.

The air was just air; the house was just a house.

I flung myself onto the cropped grass, several yards
away from the house itself, and gave vent to my emotions. My claws rent great furrows in the manicured
lawn, tearing the earth itself; I grasped handfuls of sod
and flung them behind me, back into the water,
scrubbed the dirt into my face and into my hands and
my expensive, if travel-worn, elegant clothes. I rent the

hair from my scalp in great handfuls. I threw my shoes into the waters of the lake and ran about on the grass in my bare animal feet, spinning myself in dizzy circles until the ground rose up to meet me, hold me down, clasp me and calm me by force. *You still exist, Orfeo Ricari*, it said, thrumming through the aching of my bruised bones. *You cannot escape my gravity; you are an organism, a natural creature. You belong here. The earth is your home. Be glad of my protection, for there is no place for you in Heaven.*

Reintegration

The best and worst thing about the countryside bounding Geneva is its illusion of changelessness, hidden behind the explicit variation of the seasons. Before I had much noticed, the new century began, and Europe went to war with itself. I think I slept through most of it. Sometimes I lay down to sleep in my cellar when the cherry blossoms were fresh, bountiful and fragrant, and when I woke up, the fruits had emerged, like tiny green pebbles, each containing a moment that had passed me by.

I took no more notice of the conversations of mortals than an animal would; what could human concerns interest a creature who had seen a hundred years and more? No war could touch me; no ideology could seduce me. Cologny was gorgeous and immutable, its mountain skies clear. I lived as a ghost, silent and veiled, catching mice in closets, warming myself beside the fire so that I would cast no solid shadow, comfortable in my feral and insular nature. Almost every day, I read a different book from the villa's superb library, sensually thrilled at the idea that perhaps Percy, or Mary or the Doctor, or even Lord Byron himself, had once touched those same pages. I even translated some of the Italian history and political science texts, and had them published from London under my real name, sending the small payments directly to my Geneva account, conducting all business, a few pages at a time, through the mail. I had no need of money or recognition, only mental occupation. After a while, even the need to write or translate dissipated, and I spent my days reading, tucked into a crook of an old tree, watching the infinite change and stability of Nature.

I had died and gone to Heaven.

And yet a physical Heaven meant nothing to a soul still in turmoil and a mind still imbued with the ability to learn. And somehow I'd managed to read every one of the thousands of books in the library.

I grew bored in Paradise.

Thus, I said farewell to the Villa and the grounds and the lake, and took my ragged, naked self into Cologny to be reborn. I stood in the village square as dusk fell, wearing only my long hair and a thorough coating of dirt, and stared around me; villagers passed by me, talking quietly among themselves on their way toward the tavern or home from it. I must have been as transparent as the air, for none of them even glanced uneasily in my direction. I could not resist an audible laugh, which made a few persons turn around and look, but they saw nothing.

In hardly any time at all, I had acquired clothing and shoes from a shop that sold them ready-made, imported from Paris. I had to try on dozens of pairs of shoes before I found ones that fit. The shoes and clothes were ugly and cheap, and I had not worn anything since my coat and trousers had been worn to rags and reduced to moldy shreds, and I felt an agony of discomfort as I walked out, dressed and shod, into the street. I breathed carefully and tried to relax, imagining that I lay upon a bed of nails and my resistance would only cause me further pain. I had worn clothing every day for eighty years, and I committed myself to learning to do so once more.

A barbershop stood, its doors closed and shutters drawn, a few doors down from the clothes shop. I stood staring at the facade, attempting to discover a way inside as smoothly as I had gained entry to the clothier's. Before I could, the barber had returned from the tavern, staggering and chuckling to himself. He blinked at my appearance. "You will cut my hair, please," I said, frisking him until I found his keys and leading him inside.

"Who are you?" he asked blearily, his breath blasting schnapps vapors toward me. "Wait, *where* are you? Who has spoken? Oh, there you are . . ." He fumbled against a wall until he found a lamp, and switched it on, flooding the glass bulb inside with electric light.

I stared at the lightbulb, momentarily dazzled. The barber stared at my sharp-drawn shadow against the wall and rubbed his eyes, seemingly unable to connect the shadow to the form that cast it. When he attempted to light another lamp, he stumbled over one of his chairs and barked his shin. I shook off my fascination and gave him a searching look. He slumped down in the chair and put his hand over his mouth, seized with violent hiccups. I said, "It doesn't matter who I am. You have never seen me before, and you will never see me again. And never mind; do not cut my hair. You're in no state. I will do it myself. That way, I won't have to pay you."

I glanced into one of his mirrors, and saw a face so pale and ragged that I hardly recognized it as my own. The beard did not help matters. To the barber, though, I wavered in and out of perceptibility.

My matted hair was very difficult to cut; I first

braided it, then chopped through it at the nape with his stoutest scissors. The barber sat there and gaped at me, rubbing his eyes again and again. I tossed the braid into his barber's chair. It resembled a dead ferret, and the barber shrank back from it, as though it threatened to bite him. I pitied him, but I laughed at him anyway, as I lathered and shaved my own face before the glass. "Once upon a time, a highly paid manservant did this for me," I mused. "That was before you were born." And underneath the dirty eiderdown lay the face of Orfeo Giuseppi Vittorio Ricari, entirely unchanged: a nose still keen, the slight overbite, a wild hare's ears, enormous eyes that caught and held the light in a crystal lattice. How ironic that I should have to die and be reborn to witness the beauty of my face!

"There you are again," I said, adding a smile to the face. My fangs had grown long and pointed; I would have to adjust my lips so that they did not show so much.

In the chair, my severed hair had crumbled into a snake of colorless dust.

I thanked the trembling barber and suggested that he forget our encounter, then took off my shoes and ventured to Geneva on foot.

I had not been back in many years—not since before the War—but I unfailingly retraced my steps to city and the bank where I had assigned my money. Of course, the bank was closed, but nearby, I saw the cheerful lights of a café, just now bringing the tables in for the night.

I gently seized the arm of the young girl who gathered chairs. She stared at me with an uneasy expression; I supposed I had walked up with greater haste than I had noticed. I made sure to relax my grip to the lightest of contacts. I could snap her arm like a matchstick. "Do you know the manager of that bank?" I asked her mildly.

Instantly, she relaxed and even smiled at me. "Of

course. Monsieur Otto; he comes here every day for lunch and dinner. He has no wife to cook for him, you see. . . ."

"Where does he live?"

She told me the precise address, for she had visited him there many times, bringing him food and trying to look like a pleasing future wife. I gave her neck a little kiss—just a tiny prick and a taste of her longing—and released her. She sat in one of the chairs and stared into the indigo distance, savoring her moment of pleasure, thinking of the bank manager.

I roused the man (who was, shamefully, not at all interested in the waitress) from bed and brought him to the bank. "I am Orfeo Ricari," I told him. "I have come to make a withdrawal on my funds." The bank manager, still mostly asleep, nodded at me and drew up the appropriate papers.

I kept him up until dawn. I withdrew the majority of the money at that bank, both pleased and horrified at how much interest had built up while I had been reading Hesiod and throwing cherries out of the tree at the villa's tourists. I now held a million in certificates and a thousand francs in cash. I withdrew three-quarters of the funds. The bank manager kindly gave them all to me in a stout leather briefcase. "Thank you for your continued patronage," he said with a yawn. "The funny thing is, the bank expected you twenty years ago."

"I had hardly been born twenty years ago," I said.

I spent the entire day in the basement of the university library, reading every newspaper and magazine that I could comprehend. Even after I had read them, I could barely absorb how much had happened, how much I had missed. There was not enough time to take it all in. I would have to step lightly, remembering the bed of nails, and keep my eyes open.

My head reeling with information, I sat alone on the shores of the Lake of Geneva for a few hours, watching the water's color change as night fell. I was hungry from all the mental work I'd done and from staying awake all day. I had to struggle to recall the last time I'd done that; I was rather more prone to oversleep at the Villa. Modern human existence excited me too much to sleep. I did not know if I would ever feel safe enough to sleep again, and I wasn't sure if I wanted to. I wanted this danger. I wanted awareness, even of the negative things. This was the coming home I had sought; the Fattorio di Ricari had been only a diminished shell. Returning to my origins meant mixing with humanity.

After darkness fell, I found a little smoke-filled social club with a bar, a stage, and four tables, located in the basement of a block of shops. The place was full of students, in the midst of a quiet stage of being very drunk, between outbursts. It seemed a promising location; one of these youths shouldn't miss a mouthful or two of his bloodstream.

On the stage, a man and a girl shared a cigarette and a bottle and shouted a dialogue from typewritten sheets of paper. The girl's pale-brown hair was cut almost as short as George's had been, but she wore a long muslin dress with a printed sash, and scarlet paint on her thin lips. The young man's lips were red, too, from sharing the stained bottle; he wore a dirty white undershirt, suspenders, and the same pants I wore. Their hair and clothes were so disheveled, they looked as though they had been interrupted in the middle of lovemaking and forced at knifepoint to get dressed and read poetry.

I stared at them with horrified delight. They were hideous yet vibrant, trembling with nervous energy, the scent of adrenaline pouring from them. Their dialogue made no sense whatsoever; it consisted of nothing but repetition of the most trite phrases, screamed at top volume. But its pure vitality and noise interested me despite its lack of grace. When they had finished their piece, with no reaction from the anesthetized audience, they stepped off the stage and back up to the bar, next to me. Both of them looked at me expectantly, unconscious of having been summoned.

"Sit with me," I said. "Tell me about your art. I will buy you a bottle—what will you have?"

They slumped into chairs beside me, as if they had been deflated, and asked for vodka. "That is all I ever drink," said the girl, a curious accent in her French. She looked me squarely in the eye, startling me. "Yes, I am German," she spat out, as though expecting a fight.

"How marvelous," I replied mildly. "Tell me all about it."

I poured, and they talked. She was Liesl, and she had come from Berlin to take a late-summer holiday. He was Freddy, and he lived in Geneva. They were both actors, and they were in love, though they barely looked at each other. Neither of them had any money, so they remained here at the club, which was owned by Freddy's uncle, and drank all day. "There is nothing else to do," Liesl complained. "There is no proper theater to speak of in this city; this is the worst, most boring holiday I've ever taken. I cannot wait for this month to be over so I can go back to Berlin!" At that, Freddy looked sad, and I understood why they didn't look at each other.

"Is Berlin so wondrous?" I asked. "I've never been there."

The animation returned to Liesl's face; she was almost pretty when she smiled in that manic way, with her pale, greenish eyes sparkling like fireworks, and her mouth a broad rectangular frame around her red-stained teeth. "It is the worst place in the world," she said dreamily, "it's gray and miserable and terribly unfair. Life is cheap. Gangsters have the control over the entire city. You have to grab what you want and go, go, go!" Grinning with delight, she lit a fresh cigarette and gave it to Freddy. "You really learn what you're fit for in that place. When I was there this spring, I was in two plays at once, and even getting paid for one of them! It was splendid." She spoke the last of it in German—*Es war prächtig*—and I understood it at once and was absolutely enchanted. She grimaced a little, embarrassed, at my beaming smile. "I miss the disgusting old place; I keep speaking in German. It drives poor Freddy crazy. He has never been paid for acting; he does it for the love of it, don't you, Freddy?" Liesl gave her gentleman a kick under the table, and he punched her arm, all quite lovingly. "I want him to come to Berlin with me when I return. He would find work, I know it."

I looked at Freddy, slouching underneath his cap, mouthing the cigarette, and saw nothing to lead me to believe that he had any talent whatsoever. "I think you should go with her," I said to him.

"I haven't the money to go," he said. "And I don't want to go."

"Even for Liesl?"

Freddy grimaced again, as though he'd had a sudden cramp.

"He's afraid of Germany," said Liesl. "I don't blame him; I am afraid of Germany, too. But it is fear that helps us live."

"I am Swiss," he said stolidly. "We have no fear."

Liesl shrugged at me, as if to say, *I rest my case.*

And yet I could taste fear in both of them; delicious; my favorite drug. It was not I they feared. Neither of them knew or remembered what had happened in the piss-stinking stairwell. Their fear was far more universal and more ingrained. I would learn to recognize this special signature in the blood of all of the twentieth century's children, this taste of permanent uncertainty.

* * *

Two weeks later, I rode a train for the first time, with the newly outfitted Liesl by my side, bound for Berlin.

Freddy had been most understanding. Germany was simply too frightening a prospect for him, after all; and Liesl was "going places," and he oughtn't to stand in her way, particularly not when a rich, adventurous gentleman, who seemed to have no possessive desire toward her, had offered to pay all her expenses simply for the pleasure of her company.

I truly did need Liesl, for the prospect of riding in the belly of the great, belching, violent beast had unsettled me terribly. I had seen them from a great distance in Paris and read about the modern railways, but the elephantine mass of the immediate reality was quite another matter. The sharp steel wheels and the tracks reminded me uncomfortably of the guillotine, and I could not keep from my mind the image of a woman in its path, tied to the crossbeams, being sliced into pieces. I mentally calculated how many pieces, and what state they would be in when the entire hundred-foot length of all the cars had passed.

Liesl was unconcerned; she had ridden trains "hundreds of times," she claimed, and found it all quite invigorating. She dragged me happily into my private chamber, with bunks built into the walls for us to sleep upon. "Look at all of this! I have never seen a first-class berth; how impossibly fine, how gorgeous!" It seemed to me a well-outfitted, excruciatingly clean prison.

I had my hair cut more precisely, and purchased much finer clothes, and patiently lent my money toward Liesl's appetite for lingerie, dresses, and hats. In the berth, I watched her spread out her new plunder on the bunks, cooing and petting the fabrics as though they were living pets. "Pack up your things again," I said, "this is my room."

She raised her eyebrows at me. "I thought this was for the both of us?"

"No—! I must sleep alone. You have your own room next door." I showed her the fine print on her ticket.

She made an impatient ticking sound with her teeth and cheeks, and folded her things as slowly as possible. "I thought you Italians were hot-blooded," she grumbled.

That night, neither of us slept. After I had gained the peculiar version of sea legs necessary to walk inside the moving train, and Liesl had changed into a new gown, we spent the rest of the time in the saloon car, drinking and playing cards. I wore a carefully cultivated slight smile all throughout the night, trying not to be too alarmed at how short some of the women's dresses were; the room seemed full of ankles and knees, enclosed in translucent, dun-colored stockings. Also appalling and strange and wonderful were the uniformed American soldiers traveling with us, most of them with pretty young American and French and German wives. The soldiers spoke a crude, half-swallowed English in loud, harsh voices, had dreadful table manners, and got very drunk very quickly. Some of them tried to dance in the narrow space between dining tables, jostling the cham-pagne from our glasses. They were wild with survival.

The Americans taught the rest of us poker, and I learned quickly and played well, even without cheating. Liesl played terribly, and quickly lost all the money I had given her, which I won back in twenty rapid hands of a game called Texas Hold 'Em. The ranking officer in the saloon car eyed me suspiciously. "You ain't no cardsharp, are ya?" he asked me in English.

I had to access his mind to understand him, and then I blinked and smiled innocently. "No, I ain't no shark," I replied, mimicking his accent exactly. This comment garnered a huge laugh from the Americans.

"You wouldn't be makin' fun of me, now, would you?"

"No, no," I said, patting his hand with my gloved one. "I just learn rapidly." His thin, freckled face immediately broke into a smile.

"Hey, you're not too shabby at poker! Is that how you made all your money?"

"No, I made it the old-fashioned way; someone left it to me."

After that all the men were my friends, no matter how much of their money I won from them. Liesl was not the only woman who gazed at me with hunger and admiration in her eyes.

I considered my reintegration into society to be a complete success.

Shorthand for Hamlet

We arrived in Berlin at last, in the cloudy afternoon, and I draped my hat in a veil of gauze, like a tropical explorer, and donned dark eyeglasses. These physical preparations did not suffice to shield me from the chaos of the capital of Prussia. I had not ever been in a city so large and dense, and I was wholly unprepared for the cacophony of a million minds, all working at a frenzied pace.

Upon Liesl's advice, I took a room at the Hotel Adlon, supposedly the best hotel in all of Germany. I did not doubt it; I stood dazzled by the ornate facade and the brilliance of the electric lights, while a small army of scurrying men snatched our bags away and carried them up to my room. "It's in the middle of everything," she said. "They call it the little Switzerland; you should be right at home there." She did not allow me to linger in my luxurious suite, staring at the strange twisted lions and dragons that served as table legs and wondering at the bathing-room floor, which was so clean I could see my reflection in it. "Drop your bag and come out with me! Come see my theater! Come see my city!"

Berlin "bustled." Naples did not bustle; it seethed like a nest of maggots. Paris was more muscular and deliberate than either. The pace of Berlin was fast, electric, modern, and callous; it did not slow as we passed through the elegance of the Unter der Linden on our way to the Potsdamer-Platz, but it did get noticeably dirtier and poorer. Automobiles careened through the streets, blowing their horns incessantly, jockeying for space with streetcars and pedestrians. There were no more horse-drawn carriages, at least, not that I saw, and the usual street stink of horsedung had been replaced with the choking exhaust from the motorcars.

I had a moment of doubt about whether I could endure this chaos, but it did not last, while Liesl caught my arm and pulled me through the ranks of cars, as nimbly as a squirrel. "Don't just stand there staring, or you'll get run over," she shouted. "I've seen it happen, right here."

I got one last glimpse of the Brandenburger Tor, standing like the disembodied head of a Roman legislative building, before Liesl shoved me into the back of a motorcar.

I surmised that this was a taxicab when she shouted for the driver to take us to "Julian's, *auf* Wedding," then collapsed into the seat next to me with her wide rectangular grin. "Julian's is where I worked as an actress this spring, before I had to go to Geneva. I should never have gone, but I had to get away from here for a while. I guess it's all for the best; if I hadn't gone to Geneva, I never would have met you, darling."

I smiled at her in reply, and thought about her under the wheels of the train. "Please speak in German from now on," I asked her in German. "I learn faster when I am forced to speak it." Of course, by now, with all the minds buffeting mine, I was fairly fluent.

"With pleasure!" she replied, and gave my arm a vigorous squeeze. She must have left bruises on poor Freddy.

Julian's was a medium-sized dinner theater with threadbare violet velvet curtains closed on its stage, and a queer little old man playing piano with great energy in the small orchestra pit. Every table was full, and at least thirty other people strolled about, moving sideways between tables and chatting. The man at the door embraced Liesl warmly, then turned to me and growled, "Ten marks admission."

"Oh, Hans, don't be cruel; he's with me. He'll pay you next time. He's as wealthy as a sheikh. And as seductive."

I smiled at Hans, too. "She is correct," I said.

Hans's expression did not soften. "Your German is shitty, foreigner," he said, but waved us in, applying a firm slap to Liesl's bottom.

"Don't listen to Hans; he hates anyone who is not German. There are so many people living here who are not German; it is so terrible for the economy."

I took advantage of Liesl's homecoming embraces to slip away from her and out of the club. I wanted to see the sky and reorient myself on solid ground. I still felt as though I sped along at high velocity, imprisoned inside millions of luxurious minds. I challenged myself to find my way back to the Adlon. This was accomplished so easily that it barely gave me any satisfaction; I still could not get lost.

I stood with my legs balanced against a motionless motorcar across the street from the hotel and stared at the people going in and out. How drastically fashions had changed from country to city! The women looked like columns draped in gauze and bedecked with diamonds, the movements of their heads strangely insectile. Fortunately, the men's suit had not undergone the same drastic metamorphosis; men had not started wearing frocks, at least. I swiftly determined that the women who wore fur coats, though it was a balmy night in late August, were successful prostitutes; the men accompanying them were the same politicians, business owners, opera conductors that I had earlier seen with their more tastefully shawled wives. An orchestra in the lobby performed a punchy song of welcome, never ending, just reaching the end of the composition and starting at the beginning without pause.

Finally, I went up to my room and paced around its perimeter. Only a week previous, I had been sleeping in the turnip cellar of the Villa Diodati, wrapping my long hair over my shoulders for warmth, subsisting mainly on the blood from rats, voles, and pigeons; now my blanket was made of Chinese silk and eiderdown, and a bottle of complimentary champagne had melted the ice in its ornate silver bucket by the window. At least the windows were curtained in thick, heavy red velvet.

Most shocking to me, I had a bathroom with a bathtub in it, and when I turned on a tap, clear water rushed out as though the most infinite, pure well had been tapped in the basement.

I filled the tub halfway, stripped off, and sank into the cold water until it covered me entirely. It was only with great reluctance that I resurfaced to take a breath. How pleasant the modern world was; how much of its growth and change I had missed!

I heard a persistent knocking on the door to my suite when I sat up. Too annoyed to dry myself off or find clothing, I stormed to the door and opened it, naked and dripping and covered in goose pimples. Liesl stood there, slouching, with a lit cigarette smoldering between her fingertips; she stared at me and clapped her hands over her mouth. I pulled her into my room and shut the door.

"Liesl—"

"I know, this is your room; and you didn't get one for me, I notice. Where am I supposed to go? I don't have anywhere to stay in Berlin yet. I only need a couple of nights; it won't cost you any extra." She let her eyes travel over me. "Oh, my. Are you going to get dressed?"

"I don't see why I need to in the privacy of my own, private room."

"Oh, if you think this is private, you are stupid. With all the politicians in here, every room is bugged. Oh, Herr Ricari, do let me stay; just for a few nights, please? I promise I'll make it worth your while." She hiked the skirt of her frock to display the tops of her stockings.

"What makes you think I want you, child?" I said starkly. "I am in no mood to be indulgent right now, Liesl; I suggest you find somewhere else to stay tonight. Now get out at once."

Of course, Liesl had no choice but to obey me. I sat on the edge of my bed and sighed, then returned to my bath for a while. Instead of being refreshing, now it was displeasingly cold. I scrubbed myself thoroughly with the perfumed soap provided by the hotel, dried myself with their velvety-soft towels, and went to sleep several hours early in the cool, sweetly perfumed total darkness. It might have been the best sleep I've ever gotten.

When I came down at dusk, willing to give Berlin another try now that I had rested, I found Liesl outside the hotel, staring up at the window of my third-floor room. She jumped when I spoke to her, then threw her arms around me. "Finally, you're up!" she exclaimed breathlessly. I could tell by the way her eyes looked that she had not gone anywhere to sleep the night before; that she'd just stood outside on the pavement, waiting for me. "Come on, baby, let's go! I have so much to show you!"

I felt a little sick, a little sorry for her, and very hungry. I could take her, but I didn't want to; not her. "All right," I said, "let's go."

Liesl didn't seem to have noticed the fact that she had been rejected, then waited outside for me all night. She was as full of pep and chatter as always. "Look, Hans gave me some wonderful cocaine last night. It's the real thing, none of that baby-powder stuff, and incredibly pure. Here, try some." I shook my head with a grimace. "Oh, you don't like it? I didn't like it either, at first. Later I found out that it was just bad cocaine. Hans gets his from Aztec Jan; he brought back about twenty pounds of it from Mexico, absolutely pure, the very best. It helps to keep me going."

"Are we going to another theater?"

"Yes, I thought so. . . . Julian's is so . . . you know. It's just a place where I know everyone. I will be able to start work there again on Monday."

"As an actress?"

"Well, no, as a coat-check girl. But I've acted before; I've been a chorus girl. If they need someone to step in, they know where to look. No, tonight, we're going to the Streitpunkt. Tonight there will be a Dada performance."

"A what?"

She blinked at me, as if I were slow. "You will know when you see it."

I did not know when I saw it. None of it made any sense, from the curious, obscene, ridiculous costumes made out of papîer-maché and cardboard, to the random blasts of saxophone music played by a naked man who periodically ran across the stage, to the language, which was nothing I'd ever heard. I was glad we had sat at the very back, behind a pillar, so I could shield my eyes. "This is horrible," I whispered to Liesl, who watched everything with her usual delighted expression.

"Yes!" she agreed cheerfully.

At the culmination, a tall, thin young man with a long, shaggy mane of black hair took the stage, and the rest of the performers drifted away. He wore the black tights and doublet, iconic shorthand for Hamlet, the Prince of Denmark, but the costume had obviously been made for a much larger man, quite a long time ago; the doublet hung open limply, and the baggy tights were laddered and threadbare. He held a leaf of paper in one hand but never looked at it; he continued to speak the nonsense to which we'd just been treated, but coming from his throat it was different. He had a beautiful, utterly masculine tenor speaking voice that easily filled the theater without any visible effort on his part, and his stage presence, with his long, thin limbs like rain-soaked twigs, his large head and broad shoulders, was the strongest I had ever experienced.

I actually rubbed my temples, momentarily doubting my sanity. It could not be—but how he resembled . . . !

With the white paint on his face, the sly dark eyes reduced to shadows, his wide mouth a dark double bow, the proud, sensual slump to his shoulders, and the muscles outlined along his slender, agile frame, I saw Lorenzo, transformed into an undead creature such as I!

But it could not be. The glow that emanated from him appeared supernatural, though I could see that it was only the dim inadequate stage light reflecting from his iridescent makeup, the handsomeness of his features, and the resonant power of his voice. It was his voice, more than anything, that redrew this actor in my mind and erased the shadow of Lorenzo once and all. This Berliner's voice was a semitone higher, biting off the edges of the words, and it lacked the fine edge of sarcasm that shaped every word Lorenzo said.

When I attempted to gain access to the actor's mind, I saw only light.

That was that. And Almighty Father, forgive me.

At last, he gave a smirk and a shrug, and a wave of disregard of the paper he held. "I reject this shit called language," he said in English, and lit a match under the sheet. In a flash, it vanished, to thunderous applause and cheering from the audience. The actor bowed very deeply, then spit on the front row of the theater and stalked back into the wings, grinning and wiggling his rear like a saucy showgirl.

"Isn't he wonderfully talented?" said Liesl, turning and crushing my shoulder in her hands. "I'm so glad he's still here. He was talking about leaving Berlin; things are so difficult here. But there's no other place for him in the world; no other city could contain him! No other city would tolerate him, if truth be told."

"Who is he?" I asked, a little breathless myself.

She seemed surprised that I didn't know, though she knew that I had never been to Germany before. "Oh, but that's Danny Blum. He's going to become famous someday if it kills him; he's not such a bad singer. He's a better singer than he is an artist, though he'd tell you exactly the opposite."

"Would you introduce us?"

To my surprise, Liesl laughed so hard that seltzer ran up into her nose, and I had to tap her back several times before she could stop coughing. "No, I'm afraid I can't," she said, wiping her streaming eyes. "We are enemies. We were in love once, and we both betrayed one another on the same night. He went with Eva, and I with Charlie. We fought and fought that night; I broke his nose! I said I would change his face for him, and I did! Isn't it hilarious?"

Jemiah Jefferson

I was too bemused to dispute her; all around us, in a soft buzz, like layers of sheer silken veils, came the name again and again, on dozens of pairs of lips: *Danny. Daniel. Daniel Blum.*

Through Black Smoke

In almost no time at all, I found myself as a patron of smaller Berlin theater.

I provided money for the printing of advertising posters for the show containing Liesl's new role at Julian's, and when the costumes for the play were stolen one night, I paid for replacements, rented from the costume department at the Ufa Film Studios. The manager at Julian's, a congested man named Werner Luft, was delighted at the larger audiences, brought in by leafleting all over the city, and begged me to continue my philanthropy. The two costume girls were also grateful, and offered their bodies to me in recompense. I only smiled, and convinced them that it was not me that they wanted, but each other.

Berlin brought out my playful tendencies. Besides, one of them was tall and thin and the other short, round, and blond; it only seemed right that they should fall in love for a while.

It was all merely an ineffectual distraction. Try as I might, making enjoyable mischief, seeing all of the motion-picture shows in the brown-plush darkness at the Zoo-Palast, and compulsively buying "driving gloves" until I had two pairs for each day of the week, I was unable to get Daniel Blum out of my mind. I looked for him everywhere; how large could Berlin be? Yet he was as elusive, and as spectacular, as a white stag in a dense forest. No other man resembled him even slightly. I theorized that it was not the person of this singular gentleman that obsessed me, that it was instead the dazzle of stage lights reflecting from white makeup. So I combed the theaters, and saw scores of plays and performances, hoping against hope that the threadbare nonsense Hamlet would emerge from the shadows and take the boards.

He never did.

I heard of him, though, constantly, from all of Liesl's theatrical comrades. His reputation was as immense and varied as Europe itself. Not a single person held a uni-lateral position on the matter of Danny Blum; everyone seemed to both love and despise him, respect him and denigrate him by turns. Liesl was far from being the only girl whose trust he betrayed, and by the expres-sions of some of her male comrades when this subject was discussed, he did not discriminate on the basis of sex. I wished I hadn't known that.

He was a good singer; he had a voice like a toad. He dressed with verve and artistry; he looked like a circus clown, an old whore, a madman. He was a Jew, a Com-munist, a gangster; no, he wasn't. The only thing that could be agreed upon was that he was not present.

"He was just here an hour ago," they'd say, ordering another round of drinks on my tab.

I wandered the deserted nighttime streets around the official buildings of the centermost district of Mitte, adjusting myself to the future-present in relative calm and quiet. So many things impressed and frightened and intrigued me, and in the company of humans, I could not express my astonishment. I spent a great deal of time devising ingenious ways to get the humans to perform certain tasks for me so I could see how they were done. Also, once again, I was a foreigner, and my ignorance about the basics of German culture found an excuse. But at night, out on my own, I could listen, observe, and laugh.

But I had not come to Berlin to be alone; I came to see the sights of a fresh, dangerous new world. I moved out of my costly suite at the Adlon and into a less sumptuous, but still elegant, two-room flat on the second floor of a quality boardinghouse near the Tiergarten, so I could look at something green in the midst of the slate avenues of the city. With greater quiet at home, going out at night seemed more attractive. I found myself particularly drawn to the newly opened, huge entertainment complex, Haus Vaterland, four stories of sparkling restaurants, dance halls, cabarets, and sideshows, located at the frantic heart of the Potsdamer-Platz. Open until three in the morning, it became the place where I would begin each night. It was so vulgar and overdone that the air itself seemed thick and sleazy, though it supposedly catered to families. I would wait for the inevitable Liesl to find me; I sat in a different restaurant each night, challenging her. It did not matter. She was as keen as a bloodhound, and naturally so; aside from that first drink of blood from her neck, I had hardly even touched her, and she should not have been as attached as she was. I had never even kissed her.

If I was in the mood to see Liesl, we would stay at Vaterland until closing, and then I would see her home in a taxi and compel her to get a good morning's sleep. If I wasn't, I took her to one or another of the numerous clubs, and then I would disappear while she was distracted. We started out in the nicer cabarets and taverns, but as autumn became winter, I sought the strange and uneasy thrills that could be found in the gangster bars and transvestite clubs.

Our first visit was Liesl's idea. She met me in the Tuscan plaza café at Vaterland, wearing a blue serge men's business suit, her curly light-brown hair slicked onto her skull with Vaseline. The look did not flatter her, but it inevitably excited me nonetheless, and I wondered if I might find her attractive after all. "Yes. It is I, Herr Wankelmut. I am dressed appropriately for the Mikado," she said to me, her voice clumsily gruff. It was all I could do to suppress a laugh. My attraction evaporated. She bent to me and gave me a wink. "Fooled you! It's me, Liesl! Come and join me for a drink. This place is a scream."

In the taxi, she anxiously awaited my response. When I offered none, enjoying too much her squirming and fidgeting with the crotch of her trousers, she punched me in the arm. "Well, aren't you shocked?" she demanded.

"Oh, no, not at all. I've seen women dressed as men before."

"Oh, you have?" she replied, crestfallen. "Where? When? Obviously not in Geneva! In Paris?"

"None of your business. But you look smashing, don't worry."

We alit from the taxi and walked into a peculiar and beautiful world that literally took my breath away at first glance.

I excused myself from Liesl once she had found a table, and stood in the back of the room, concealing myself from human eyes so that no one would notice me goggling at the spectacle. Along with the usual upscale cocktail crowd, there were girls dressed as men, men dressed as women, and some I could not distinguish at a glance, laughing and shouting and staring at one another and ignoring one another, against a backdrop of red lacquer screens and scrolls of Japanese watercolor painting. Some of the men wore evening gowns scintillating with rhinestones, while others had merely put on a workaday blouse and skirt and a tatty wig. The women in men's suits were dazzlingly handsome, each and every one, willowy girls with rouge and watch fobs. In comparison to them, Liesl was dumpy and amateurish in her obviously borrowed *burgher's* suit. This was not theater, not boys playing as girls in Shakespeare; this was life; this was reality. And yet it was as far from the reality that existed outside as possible.

My mind reeled. The cafés of Berlin were one massive stage, dizzying with special effects, curious makeup, and gorgeous, outlandish costumes, with the hostile, cold winter world a few feet over the threshold. Even I had a part to play on it, but I did not know my lines, or my marks, or who the director was.

"Dance with me," said a young man in curly platinum-blond wig, cheap baubles, flaking red lipstick, and a skirt full enough to hide any untoward protuberances. His eyes were glassy and heavy-lidded, but he had seen me, and the black stubble on his forearms overwhelmed me with amusement and pity. So I accepted. He tried to pick my pocket, but I caught his hand and pressed it to my buttock tightly instead, smiling at him.

"Ah, ah, ah—it is I who shall steal from you," I said.

From a distance, it appeared that we were deeply enmeshed in each other, locked and swaying together on the dance floor to the waxy sounds of the trombone and out-of-tune piano. Instead, I drew droplets of blood, cloudy with the poison of fatigue, from the four tiny puncture wounds I'd nipped into his neck. He had been dancing all night in high heels, trying to win patronage from the club itself; when he'd arrived that night, he looked as perfect as a film star. Underneath the flared skirt, his penis poked against me, as hard as a wooden ruler, and he mumbled into my ear, "Yes . . . my sweet . . . kiss me again. . . ."

When his erection had gone, I knew that I was done with him; so I walked with him back over to the bar seating area and handed him five marks. "Buy yourself some better lipstick," I told him, and his comrades, listening, howled with laughter.

I returned to the table where Liesl sat, her brow as black as thunder. "See what you've done?" she complained. "Leaving me all alone like that while you danced with that repulsive line-boy Simon!"

"What have I done?" I asked mildly, a little flushed and smug. Simon had tasted good in those tiny amounts, like individual grains of caviar.

"You left me alone here, and Danny Blum came right up and spoke to me!"

At once I was alert again, my head threatening to twist itself off my neck, I turned it so suddenly. "He was here? Where is he?"

She drew upon her cigarette languidly. "He's gone, of course! I told him he could stick his head up his asshole if he's so awfully special."

My vision blurred with the effort required to contain my annoyance and not tear Liesl's throat out. "Oh, Liesl, you are not to do that again, do you understand? I should like to meet this young man Blum." She made as if to protest, but I placed my fingertip flat against her forehead and stared into her eyes. "I think you can make it happen." Her face assumed an expression of pain and alarm, and I adjusted the force of my directed thought until her face went blank. I didn't want to hurt her if I didn't have to, and I could blast her mind to flinders just by wishing it so. "Do you know where he is now?"

"No," she said mechanically.

"Dammit, Liesl." I relaxed and looked away, cracking my knuckles under my paper-thin kidskin gloves. Liesl shook her head and began to cry softly. She no doubt had a terrible headache, but I was in no mood for indulgence. "Stop being such a baby. You're lucky I didn't hurt you. You're going to find Daniel Blum for me. It won't be difficult."

"You want him, and you don't want me," she wept. So it wasn't about the headache. "You don't like women at all, do you?"

I felt embarrassed for her. "I do like women," I said, "exceptional women, women who are not like other women."

"But you like boys more."

I truthfully admitted that I did, partially to hurt her feelings and cure her lovesickness for me, and partially because it felt right to say it aloud, in that environment, among the Oriental lanterns and slick-haired women in morning jackets, dancing with one another without fear or furtiveness. "I am more susceptible to the charms of boys," I said, "whereas I despair of ever finding a woman comparable to . . ." I shrugged rather than speak their names, or decide on one to mention. I could almost see them as a single being: *Maria Elena Georgina*. If you combined them, they produced me. "That's all in the past. You should not trouble yourself over me. You could have a dozen boyfriends if you wanted. The only thing you need to do for me is to find Danny Blum, so that I can meet him."

"But I hate him," she insisted. "He broke my heart when he left me for that bitch Eva. Besides, he's a dirty cross-dresser and a pervert."

I smiled at her reflexive hypocrisy. But I knew that she would obey me. She had no choice.

* * *

I kept missing him by moments, and I almost wondered if Daniel Blum was conscious of my desire, and his own desire was to avoid contact.

I found that he vacillated from being an employee of the Grinzing in Haus Vaterland to being banned from the premises. From that point on, I always went to the Grinzing first, but the moment happened to coincide with his fresh unemployment.

At Mass, I prayed that I could set eyes on him again.

My efforts to precisely recall his features infiltrated my dreams. I had begun to dream of Lorenzo again, remembering our time together, the memorization of lessons and the exquisite agony of our unions, ingrained into me as deeply as the Glory Be. But now Lorenzo wore a mask of Daniel Blum's face, made of fine carved ivory that dissolved into steam when it was removed. When that happened, I awoke, groggy and unsatisfied, my limbs as heavy as mud, and if and when I returned to sleep, my dreams were of something else entirely.

When I found that Daniel Blum himself had been slotted to perform on the night before Christmas, at a place called the Dummschwallen, I found that I could not sleep at all.

Oddly, I couldn't bear the thought of going alone, and I felt like enacting a bit of mischief upon my only Berlin acquaintance. I bought Liesl a superb dinner to convince her to accompany me to a performance by her "enemy." Even so, she insisted on bringing along her new boyfriend, a glum youth named Klaus, with a little, crooked, bark-colored mustache that I did not like at all. I hardly cared about the extra expenditure of feeding a stranger, even though Klaus ate enough food to cram a hippopotamus full from stem to stern, but I could not resist punning on his name. "It is short for Nikolaus? Saint Nikolaus? Have you got toys for children in your

knapsack, dear old St. Nick?" I winked and blew cigarette smoke in his direction.

"No, just Klaus," he mumbled, unfazed, his mouth
full of sausage.

"Leave him alone, Ricari," Liesl pled. "He is much
better to me than you are." Klaus and I shared an odd
glance over the laden plates and empty *liebefraumilch*
bottles. "You are a dandy and a coward; you can't even
go to your own seduction by yourself! I thought I'd be
done with him once I told you about the show, but you
insist on dragging me along. I am just about done with
you, too, Herr Ricari. I have no use for men like you
when I have Klaus." She stamped a rosette of lipstick on
his cheek.

"I'll tell Freddy Geneva you said that," I replied.
Klaus frowned at her, and she let out a brittle laugh and
a smile that folded into a pained grimace. I folded the
napkin next to my empty plate. "Come, let's go. I want
to get on with meeting your worst enemy."

I may have held my head up and traded verbal ar-
tillery with Liesl, but inside I quaked, and each step
ached with a private embarrassment. I was nervous
about being in the presence of a mortal! That should
never be—I can control their movements and thoughts
as easily and instinctively as I shave my face. But I had
no control over my fascination, my obsession, with this
man. There was too much of Lorenzo in his appearance, and despite all the blood I'd drawn and the lives
I'd ended, despite all the miles and years that separated
us, Lorenzo still retained a fragment of power over me.
Over a hundred years after the fact, I still wanted to
please him. That realization disgusted me but made it
no less true.

Maybe this time will be different, I thought.

Dummschwallen was located in the district of Prenzlauerberg, which I had not ever visited, at the end of a long, dark, narrow street. The northeastern outskirts of Prenzlauerberg had none of the expensive sheen of Unter der Linden or the economic bustle of the Ku'-damm; this was a neighborhood well on its way to becoming a slum. Only one of the streetlamps seemed to be operational, and the flickering electric light caught the scaly tail of a dog-sized rat, skittering away from the path of our taxi. The street was far from deserted; packs of young men in odd handmade uniforms stood in small knots, talking and laughing among themselves, and female prostitutes of various shapes and ages shared cigarettes and chatted with the boys. "That's the Sträubenhund Ringverein," Klaus said quietly. "Don't worry. I'm friends with them; there won't be any problems."

Liesl looked at him curiously. "Are you working with those gangsters?"

"The Sträubenhund are not gangsters," Klaus maintained in his monotone. "They are an athletic club. They are all gymnasts and sprinters; they represent good health and proper living."

"And bookmaking and the skin trade, no doubt." Liesl sighed, and looked uneasily into the darkness. I heard the sound of a piano playing, incoherent and badly out of tune. There was no sign, and no indication that a theater existed here besides the noise of the piano. A Sträubenhund stood in front of the entrance, toying with a coin strung on a cord, but he nodded at Klaus and moved aside. Liesl tightened her scarf. "In we go. And don't say I've never done anything for you, Ricari."

We stood outside of a covered garage that, through the chemical stench of petrol and paint, retained the smell of the cab horses that had been stabled there ten years before. One of the great stable doors stood ajar, and within, I could make out the flickering of candle flames. Inside, walls, floor, and ceiling had all been painted heavily with dull black paint. A handful of cheap, flimsy wooden chairs had been arranged, seemingly at random, in the space between the door and a stack of black-painted vegetable crates shoved against the far wall. Tallow candles, stuck into two-meter-high wrought-iron candlesticks, clouded the air with their heavy, meaty smoke, and the few people nervously milling around the chairs coughed into their handkerchiefs.

The smoke did not much bother me, so I gave my handkerchief to Klaus to contain his mustached sneezes. I insisted that he keep it. "Happy Christmas," I added.

At last, wavering through drifting smoke, I saw my goal.

At the far rear end of the stage, Daniel Blum did not so much play as attack the piano, hunched over the keys on a chair too tall for the task, his head jerking back and forth with intense concentration. Once I had gotten used to the sound of the awful tone, I could tell that he played quite skillfully, a semi-improvisational American style known as "honky-tonk," without a sheet of music to guide him. He had a crude, spiky crown, fashioned out of sheet tin, cocked at a jaunty angle on top of his rat's nest of inky black hair, a black tuxedo worn over a bright red cummerbund on an otherwise bare torso, and a necklace made of wire strung with shark's teeth.

The light entertainment in Hades consisted of piano torture and a handsome incubus clad in hand-me-downs. I found myself coughing uncontrollably, and I turned back toward the door in search of a moment of fresh air.

But he turned and saw me then, and his pale, smoke-smudged face illumined with pleasure and awe. He knocked over his chair in his haste to reach me, and quite frankly elbowed Liesl aside as he thrust out his hand toward me.

"Please," he begged, "do stay! Shall I put out the candles? I prefer darkness myself, but *ordinary* people need light to be able to see."

His eyes swallowed me. Reluctantly, I accepted his hand, hot to the touch, the long pale fingers encrusted with a filth of coal and paint. I imagined the fingers in my mouth, and I knew he could see it, too.

"I don't need light to see that you're still a sack of shit," Liesl yelled.

Daniel smoothly turned toward Klaus, but keeping his eyes on me, and said, "Sir, I'm sorry, but dogs are not allowed in the theater. I admit that she is a fine-looking pedigreed bitch, but I will have to ask you to remove her."

I expected Klaus to make a violent move, but instead he took Liesl's arm and turned to the door. Liesl's face had gone purple with rage, and she struggled in Klaus's arms, spitting on the floor at the threshold. I watched this with my peripheral vision; my eyes remained locked in Daniel's eyes. He was a mirror reflecting my own fascination back at me, but shifting it slightly, clouding it, perhaps, or warping it into a different shape. I should have actively changed Klaus's mind about attacking Daniel, but I know I did not, for my attention was wholly focused elsewhere. I still don't know why Klaus didn't punch Daniel in the eye, breaking our contact, maybe sparing me, but things happened as they did.

Daniel squeezed my hand between his palms. "I've wanted *so* much to meet you, Herr Ricari."

He was much taller than I, and I could not shake off the thought that my head would fit very nicely under his throat, and my arms around his waist.

"My name is Danny Blum," he added unnecessarily.

"I know," I said, adding, also unnecessarily, "I am Orfeo Ricari."

His eyes shone with open admiration, a kind of astonishment. The sound of my name made him tremble, as though he received a divine sensation. When he repeated it, I felt the same, my changeless self formed by the coalescence of the smoked tones of his voice. "Orfeo . . . ! Orfeo. Of course. It is a pleasure to make your acquaintance. And now that I have made it, I shall never let it go."

Too true, my Lord. Too true.

Conjoining

My head did fit neatly under Daniel's chin, my arms comfortably around his waist.

Our big mouths fit perfectly together.

We fit perfectly inside each other.

He "lived" on the other side of that horrid garage, in a tiny, vertical room that was once a coal shed. He slept standing up, leaning against the wall, wrapped in a filthy, greasy wool blanket stained all over with mud, red lipstick, and black boot polish. "But I don't usually have to sleep here," he said, his lips wrapping themselves around my ear like silk snakes. "Like tonight. Tonight I'm coming home with you. You'd like that, wouldn't you?"

He was thoroughly unemployed, having lost his busboy job at the Grinzing for the last time, and had lived for the last week on scavenging, cocaine dealing, and outright and blatant theft. "I just walk into a place and take what I want and then leave. I never get caught. People are afraid of me. I used to steal from the Grinzing all the time; but I didn't get caught, even there. I got the ax this time for taking off all my clothes in the middle of the dining hall. What could I do? I felt a spider bite me, right here." He clasped my bare hand to his bare hip, where the belly muscles curved toward his groin like the wings of a hawk, and the bone slid under the skin under the press of my hand. "I didn't know where it would strike next. What would you have done?" It was not a rhetorical question; his long, tilted, poison-green eyes demanded an answer, which, my breath stuck in my chest, I could not give.

"You are an offshoot, like me," Daniel said. He held up my hand and swept his tongue along my fingers, from the valley of my thumb to the undersides of my claws. "You are not one of the usual specimens of humanity. You are downright peculiar, if you want to know the truth. You are much too alabaster. You glow in the dark like a will-o'-the-wisp! A will-o'-the-wisp." He said this in English, in love with the sound, pronouncing the consonants in the German fashion, *villozevisp*. It was so beautiful, I was in love with it too. "You are so small and delicate, you look like you could be crushed in my fist. But underneath you are as tough as a willow switch, you're just as cutting; you have laid me open, you gut me and skin me. You are too beautiful for anyone but me."

I bent under him as a willow does under a torrential rain.

"Orpheus, son of Apollo and Calliope." His tongue swept over my throat, and his blunt teeth nipped and pulled at the tight skin. "Was your father a god, and your mother a muse? Yes, I see it in your eyes that it's true. Your voice would charm the stars into falling from the sky to get closer to you. Your Eurydice is underground, and she's not coming back, ever, ever! And that suits me; you can be mine instead."

"Don't you want to be my Eurydice?" I asked in surprise.

He arched his eyebrow. "I would never be so stupid as to look back at you," he retorted. "I'd want to get back to the world with you and I would never let anything jeopardize that, not even a glance at your demigod's ass. No; I don't want to play a dead-end role from myth. I've already got a Hebrew name that doesn't say anything about me. I've never even *seen* a lion. Never mind; forget about it. I was just showing off the fact that I've read something. It's my greatest fault and my greatest gift, that tendency to show off. Where would I be without it; who would I be? I would not exist much at all. How awful it must be to be ordinary and shamble through your life, going to work in a factory, coming home every night and screwing the same old woman, eating your *wurst* and beating your kids and paying taxes, and never seeing the absurdity of it. At least I am aware that what I do is absurd and meaningless." He rubbed my throat with his fingertips and bit it again. "Except for you, of course. I do *you*, and you are sublime. Dammit, why don't you bruise?"

"Try harder," I told him. "Like this."

I bit into him. My fangs smoothly penetrated the hot, pulsing skin over his neck, and simultaneously, his penis penetrated me again; and we rocked, ever so slightly, like a boat on a calm afternoon lake, toes curled, holding our breath. There was almost too much of him; too much, so early. I wanted to tell him that he had no need to be careful with me, but I savored any fragment of the tense pleasure of him inside me. There would be time for much more, and I could wait.

When his hardness waned, I knew I had gone far enough, and I sat up on top of him, my thighs spread across his pointed hipbones and my mouth lusciously wet with him. Daniel had fallen unconscious, his mouth still open in midmoan, his lips pink and glistening from my kisses. His face was uniformly pockmarked like ancient marble, hints of smile lines marking his cheeks, a grainy texture of stubble on the small, variable cleft in his chin. Fine black hairs ringed each of his nipples and trailed down the valley in his torso to the furred oasis of his navel. His skin was a motley patchwork of different scars, from the faded to the newly minted. He was not pretty, and less so without the animation of his active face and the black pearls of his voice; and yet I had never seen anything that I hungered to look upon more.

His blood blended with mine, and I felt the fascination and lust, admiration and curiosity held within his mind and the youth and strength of his body. He had resilience, too—a violent health fed on stolen milk and eggs, thick, frothy beer, and constant hard exercise. His heartbeat had flooded my mouth, growing stronger the more blood I drew.

Smiling to myself, I slid from his body, turned him and raised his right leg, and fitted my dew-moistened prick into his anus, taking his advantage while he lay with his mind in limbo, his limbs helplessly splayed out. I wanted to be inside him as he had been inside me, and I would not wait to ask his permission. I had never been able to perform this act before in all my life, natural or unnatural, and I had always wondered how it would feel; would it be difficult, as it sometimes had been with me at first? But no, there existed no difficulty whatsoever, and I made no effort to be gentle. Indeed, it was perfect, excruciating and grand, almost as if he had been made for me, and my former existence, lived without this incredible sensation, seemed a gray and joyless thing.

No wonder Lorenzo had stolen this innocence from me; no wonder he kept coming back for it, even long after my innocence was lost.

I pushed faint gasps from his throat long before Daniel opened his eyes; he began to frown and grimace, and the moans gained in strength as he regained consciousness. "Oh, my God . . . you little sneak . . . Orfeo . . . please, harder," he whispered. "Oh, my God . . . ! Fuck me like I need to be fucked! I've been waiting for you all my life! Ah—*ow*!" He opened his eyes in shock as my claws accidentally grazed his belly, slicing swiftly into the skin like razor blades. "God of shit, those bastards are sharp!"

I withdrew and bent over him, licking the fresh cuts and tutting sympathetically, with every intention of finishing what I'd started once I'd soothed his pain. But Daniel pinned me to the bedsheets, attacking my penis with his palms and his mouth and probing my anus with his fingers. I mouthed some empty words of protest or struggle, but I was too late, already caught in the sucking vortex of his fingertips, tongue, palate, my spirit sparking and fading like a shooting star falling to earth.

Between convulsions, I saw him watching me with a serious expression.

I kissed his sparkling, sour, wet mouth, but he did not return the pressure, and when I stopped and looked at him, his eyes were open and his face still looked blank. He disentangled himself from me and stood up, staring down at his stomach, where the bleeding scratches had healed to faint, fading, pink hairline seams crossing the semen-veiled trail of hair. Without speaking, he walked into my bathroom and began running the hot-water tap to fill the bathtub.

I lay still, allowing myself to savor the sweetly dying ecstasy of my orgasm, until I heard the water shut off and the low splash of my lover sinking into the tub. I slid down the bed and crawled across the carpet to the bathroom on my hands and knees, passing under a cloud layer of steam from the boiler.

Daniel startled as I appeared suddenly, as if coalescing from the steam, and ducked under the water, his hand clasping his belly where the scratch lines had disappeared entirely. I sat back on my heels like a patient dog, waiting him out, until he surfaced with a gasp a minute later, water streaming through his hair. "My God!" he burst out. "Y-you really *aren't* an ordinary man, are you?"

"I never pretended to be," I replied softly.

"Bullshit!" He spat in his vehemence. "You wear a suit and tie and walk about and go to the theater and hang out with a tramp like Liesl; you pretend to be a man when your ass doesn't even *taste* like anything! You're not a man."

"I don't know what you mean," I said. "I am a man. My ass doesn't taste of anything because I don't eat anything."

"That's disgusting," he muttered.

"I disagree," I said mildly. I gathered burning hot water into my cupped hand and poured it over his shoulders, but when I reached for his hair, he shrank back and slapped my wrist. The wet sting of it only excited me.

He sank back into the water, sighing. "Why did you drink my blood?"

It wasn't an easy question to answer. "Because I wanted to," I said. "I wanted to feel that. I wanted you inside me."

Liar. I heard it inside my head as clearly as if he had screamed it. But I felt no fear from him, just a confusion of anger and lust and a sense of having betrayed himself somehow. "And having my cock inside you isn't enough."

"It isn't, and you know it isn't," I replied as sharply. "And I do *not* lie." *Your cock doesn't tell me what you're thinking. Well, not everything, anyway.* My own thoughts made me smile, belying my harsh tone; I knew he could see the joke.

He had no other choice now. We had fucked, and we had kissed, and he tasted my sexual fluids, and I had his. His heart was mine for as long as I wanted it; he saw the thoughts I wished to share with him, and he felt the way I wanted him to feel.

He started to speak, but instead shook his head and sank back until only his head and red-boiled knees emerged from the water. He did not resist when I reached again toward his head, combing through his matted hair with my fingers, following it with the teeth of a tortoiseshell comb I had taken from the Hotel Adlon. His hair was thick, coarse, and naturally coal-black; once the dirt had been rinsed from it, it became pliable and smooth, lying in a heavy curtain down his neck almost to the shoulders. He closed his eyes while I groomed him, arching his head into my hand.

"You *can* have me, you know," he murmured. "I'll never be able to resist you."

"I *am* a man," I said. "I . . . was a man. I am . . . not what you think of as human anymore. I haven't been for a long time. I am much, much more."

He gave another deep sigh, and an acknowledging nod. He took my free hand and pressed it to his lips.

"I won't let you kill me," he said.

I couldn't resist a laugh. "If I wanted to kill you, there is nothing you could do about it."

"Oh, I think there is," he said, opening his eyes and staring at me. I saw images from films flicker in his mind, and I smiled smugly.

"Oh, I don't think so."

He blinked a few times, then settled back and smiled. He was never afraid. "You fuck well," he said.

"Thank you." I chuckled. "So do you."

"I ought to by now . . . there are more notches in my belt than there is leather—What *are* you doing with

Liesl?" he interrupted himself. "You can do so much better than that!"

"I know I can. We've never been lovers. I met her in Geneva. She seemed to know Berlin well; I wanted a guide."

"I'm a better one," Daniel claimed. He sat up and gathered his hair into a twist behind his head. "Liesl is a pretender; I am the real thing. I can get you anywhere; I can get you anything. You've got money; I've got connections." He relaxed and smiled up at the ceiling. "The world is ours."

I did not wish to follow the path of his thoughts, but I let him go on it, because I loved the sight of his naughty-child smile. "Anyway, she's with Jolly Old Saint Nick now, and good riddance. She is like champagne-vinegar. Did she really break your nose?"

That evoked a laugh. "Yes, she certainly did, and I bruised her tits for her real good—pow! pow! See, my nose was crooked before; she knocked it straight. She's never gotten over that." He laughed loudly. "Bitch. Actually, I couldn't have cared less if she spread her legs for another man; but she's a hypocrite. She can dish it out, but she can't swallow it. I don't care that she's a woman; I beat her! She deserved it!"

He grinned and splashed the water, but his eyes clouded over as he thought of Eva, recalling flashes of kissing her, deflowering her, the feel of her silk stockings and her hair like white-gold feathers. He almost remembered how cruel he had been to her, but stopped himself and recalled something nicer instead, her smile, her laugh.

"I can feel you in my mind," Daniel said, his voice distant. "That's Eva. Do you see her? Wasn't she a looker? Of course I left Liesl for her—who wouldn't? It's not my fault what happened to her."

I pressed my lips against his steamy temple, tasting his hair, his ear, the sandpaper stubble on his jaw, the thoughts that seeped from him. "I was used and thrown away once too."

Lorenzo, insisting, "Recite, Phaedrus," while I held in my scream, begging myself, praying to God, not to come; the journey; the awakening, alone. I felt a shudder pass through Daniel's body as he got all the memories in an instant, stitched together into a single, many-layered image.

"I wouldn't do that to you," he whispered. He took my hand and drew it underneath the water to touch the head of his hardening penis, smooth like a peeled boiled egg on a bed of wet wool. "This is completely different. I won't ever let you go. You want me for your slave? No; you will be mine. I swear it." He looked up at me and grasped my arm as I stepped, hissing, into the scalding bathwater. "I won't let anyone hurt you again; I'll be the one to hurt you. Only I know how to hurt you in the right way, in a way that will make you better, happier, freer. . . . Ah yes, you are mine."

The hot water and his pungent, insistent kisses made me dizzy. "I can destroy you," I panted, "never forget that."

"Shut up," he said, shoving his tongue into my mouth, pausing to touch the points of my fangs with his tongue tip, and filling my mouth with the seawater taste of fragments of blood.

When night fell again, I sent him away with sixty marks to pay the rent he owed on his theater-cum-hovel so that I could attempt to think about what I'd done. I wanted him to take the money and run away, so that I would not have to face him again and make the uncomfortable decision of whether or not I would let him witness me as I slept. It wasn't merely the danger that put me off; it was vanity. I didn't want to look like a dead body in the presence of the vibrant, living Daniel; what would he think of me? What would he do with me?

But I could not resist sleep any longer. I had barely closed my eyes in days, and I had spent the larger part of Christmas Day, when I should have been in Mass, engaging in the most exhausting and delicious sodomy. I picked up my rosary beads from the pile of shed clothes and clutched the ivory to my heart, whispering a plea for forgiveness, but I had fallen asleep before I could say the Apostles' Creed and begin the genuine prayer.

When I awoke, Daniel Blum sat in the chair across the room from the bed, reading a glossy cinema magazine and eating a piece of *stollen*, his lips white with powdered sugar. Judging by the smell of the greasy waxed paper pile next to him, he had made away with an entire Christmas dinner and had saved the *stollen* for last. The smells made my head ache with hunger. He looked over the top of the magazine at me, his jaws slowly and contentedly moving. "I guessed correctly," he said, swallowing. "I knew you weren't dead, because I could still feel you in my mind."

"What if it was only my disembodied soul?" I asked with a yawn. I still held the rosary beads in my hand.

"Soul?" he said. "I don't believe in souls!" He flung down the magazine, stood up, and wiped his mouth. "Has your ass finally recovered from the banging I gave it last week?"

"Last week?" I echoed.

His smile was slow and wicked. "Is this atypical for you? You looked so peaceful. It is Three Kings' Day," he said, "the sixth of January."

I jerked up and put my hands up to my face while my stomach sank. No wonder I was so hungry. "You haven't been sitting there this whole time, have you?"

"No; I have your keys. I have been sitting here all day,

though. I knew you would be awake soon. I could feel it." He approached the bed, slowly, almost shy. He looked wonderful, all in black but for a dirty white satin muffler draped across his shoulders, his hair still clean, hanging in loose waves around his angular face. "Did you miss me?"

"I must go to church," I said, trying not to be caught in his eyes. I knew that if I did, I would be lost.

Daniel spit out a hard little laugh. "Church? I am your church. Get in me and worship." He sprang onto the bed, gently disentangled the rosary beads from my fingers and dropped them onto my bedside table, and devoured my nude body with his hands. I had not even the need to look into his toxic eyes; the merest touch of his hands against my skin was enough.

He stretched out his neck and drew his fingertips over the side, where I could see the artery flutter. "Go on," he purred, "you know you want to."

No self-control.

Heavenly Father, forgive me. He had possessed me.

The Berlin *Schnauze*

I had almost begun to despair of ever leaving my bedroom again, but when we did venture out together, I
wished that we had stayed there, in the safe, warm semidarkness, just the two of us together, speaking more
with our bodies than with our mouths.

But I did want blood, and I did not wish to harm
Daniel by using him as my only source. Already his natural pallor had been heightened from regular bloodlettings, and his formerly tight-fitting trousers now hung
from the ends of his hipbones, constantly threatening
to slide off him entirely. "Just come around me with me
tonight," he said, "see the places I go to."

Daniel took me to his favorite coffee shop, a shabby-
chic, haphazard affair on the Brunnenstrasse, a handful
of healthier blocks away from the Dummschwaller. "It's
watered down into piss," he told me authoritatively,
"but at least it's real coffee and not malt-coffee or fermented weeds. Would you like a cup?"

"No, thank you," I said, cautiously picking my way
through the densely crowded tables to one at the far

end of the room. Daniel smiled and squinted at me lovingly, and fetched his coffee, greeting several acquaintances in a polyglot of Berliner German, French, and English, before joining me.

"Why are you all the way over here? There's an empty table right there." He pointed at the dead center of the room, underneath a precariously dangling but brilliantly illuminated brass chandelier.

"I like to see the room," I said.

"Ah! He likes to watch. I see. I'll remember that, and give you a little striptease next time. By the way, do you have five marks? I owe them for a few weeks; they give me credit." He waited patiently while I withdrew the money. When I had finished handing it to him, I noticed that every eye in the room was now upon us, and upon my wallet with its sheaf of bills peeking out like the dull plumage of a bird long thought extinct.

As soon as he had the money in hand, Daniel went back to the counter and engaged the young girl there in a low conversation, standing with his elbows on the counter. He stuck his rear end out, toward the room, displaying the worn-shiny seat of his trousers clinging to his firm, round buttocks. He waved it back and forth hypnotically, like a snake charmer. Attention shifted from me to it. I had to admit that his rump was fascinating, but after several minutes, I began to feel somewhat deserted. Daniel laughed over and over again, and accepted the countergirl's fingernail, full of white powder, up his nose. Then they kissed. My vision grew blurry again. It would be so easy to kill him, but shaming him would hurt him more.

I snapped my fingers and summoned him without speaking.

He looked over his shoulder with a scowl, but he returned to my table and sat down opposite me. He had some powder on his upper lip. "What do you want? Can't you see that I'm busy?" he asked loudly.

"Busy? Busy flirting with her? I want your attention on me." I focused my eyes on the white smudge on his face.

A slow smile spread across his face, and he wiped his lip with his finger and rubbed the powder onto his gums. "Flirting, was it? Oh, I see. Agatha is a friend of mine; we don't flirt, we visit. Besides, I've already had her." His voice carried effortlessly throughout the café; at the counter, Agatha laughed and shrugged—*What will I ever do with that scoundrel?*—and returned to wiping out coffee cups with a brown-stained rag.

"Who haven't you had?" I asked, a little wearily.

It was plainly a rhetorical question, but Daniel would not be cowed. "Well, let's see. That fellow here; I haven't had him. In fact, I've never seen him before. He must be a tourist. Sir! May I ask where you've come from?"

"Bremen," answered the man with a grin.

"Oh! I *thought* I'd smelled something stupid!"

"Daniel," I protested, rubbing my gloved hands together.

He grinned. "Oh, and let's see, I haven't had her, or her, or her. But they're whores, and there's been syphilis about; you wouldn't want me spreading that to you, would you? Oh yes, and him. I wouldn't have him. I can't abide a man with a thick neck. It makes me think of swine and bulldogs, and who wants to fuck a bull-dog? Wait, don't tell me—I think *she* does. Isn't that your schtick, honey?"

Everyone in the café, including the fellow with the thick neck, laughed. I wanted the earth to swallow me up. I wanted to vanish, but I couldn't, not here, in a crowded public place. Instead I stood up, gave Daniel a stiff bow, and walked out. Laughter followed me. They knew him; they did not know me.

I felt a physical homesickness for Paris.

Daniel followed me immediately, with a sunny smile on his face. "Where are you going? You can take the *Schnauze*, can't you? It's just a lot of bullshit! It's just how we talk around here. It's expected. Oh, my sweetness, don't be jealous, I'm just being foolish, trying to get some color into your cheeks. But that's impossible, isn't it?"

"No, actually, it isn't," I said.

I seized him by the lapels of his tuxedo jacket and dragged him into an alleyway, slamming him against the ice-rimed brickwork. I noted his expression of alarm with great pleasure, lifted his arm, and bit deeply into his wrist, inhaling a great rush of blood from his vein. His eyelids fluttered as he felt the blood leave him, but he only moaned quietly and put the other arm around my shoulders. When I raised my head, he bent down and kissed me, smearing his mouth with his own fresh blood.

"See," I said, "there is color in my cheeks now, isn't there."

"Who do you think you are? I'll fuck you in the ass right here," he threatened, though his voice came out a thin whisper.

"No, you won't," I replied giddily. The drug in his system came into my brain all at once, in a twinkling rush, the pollution flavor of his mouth transferred to mine, numbing my lips and tongue. "You're still sore. You won't be fucking anything for a few days." I let him go and took a step back. He cocked his hip and lazily tossed his hair over his shoulder. He looked so sexy I thought my heart would stop. "Except . . . maybe you should try sooner than that."

"If it was possible to have your dick fall off from too much shagging, it would have happened to me before now." He gazed at me with heavy-lidded eyes. "Oh, Orfeo! I can't believe how good it feels when you bite me. It hurts a teeny-tiny bit, but it's marvelous, like being fucked when you're not quite ready. And I can feel what you feel, just for that one precious moment. . . . Mm-mmm . . . do I taste good?"

"You taste bitter," I said.

He kissed me again. "Like my soul."

Together, eventually, we returned to the coffee shop. The other patrons discreetly did not stare at us as we returned to our table in the back. Daniel picked up his cup of weak coffee and took a sip. "It's gone cold," he said. "You'll have to buy me another cup."

"Wouldn't you rather have a real drink?" I asked, eager to put this place behind me.

"Are you trying to get me drunk? First you suck me dry, then you try to get me drunk. I guess you really *don't* want me to screw you." He softened this with a smile. "All right, let's go where you want to go. I'm no snob."

Off we went to the Peacock, a lesbian bar where Liesl had once taken me, in the sane months before Daniel. Daniel seemed bemused, but even here he was recognized by the uniformed doorman, and by the maîtresse d', an elegant butch in her stern high collar and bare breasts, rouged nipples chilled into tiny hard nubs. As she showed us to a table, she grimly reprimanded Daniel for letting in a draft, then glared at him as he gave her backside a pinch. "Why don't you keep him in line?" she snapped at me, and I answered with a mute shrug.

Many of the tables there were dark and enclosed, across the room from the crowds of Japanese businessmen and politely shocked English tourists, who could nonetheless easily spy upon us. Of course, Daniel was part of the entertainment for which the tourists had come—and paid their five-mark cover charge—in the first place. We were the entertainment as much as the all-girl band, or the dissipated jazz singer muttering her way through "Squeeze Me." Previously, I would have wanted to be near the group of Japanese, as I had never seen more than one at a time, and I wanted to learn their language; but there was Daniel, and Daniel's eyes and Daniel's voice, and not much else truly interested me.

"I think I've begun to figure you out," Daniel said, resting his face on his hand. "I think you're a lesbian."

I laughed. "Do you think so?" I replied. "What makes you think that?" Around us, the women talked and laughed and fought and paired off and kissed each other in the middle of the dance floor, while the Japanese looked on, whispering to each other. "Perhaps I just love beautiful women who like to dress up."

"Go to the theater. I don't know what you get out of this. You're not supposed to want to look at girls at all. You're *schwul*."

I didn't like that word *schwul*—it implied a fitful, overheated sexuality that I did not feel described me at all—but he said it so gently and comfortably, and we were surrounded by overtly deviant behavior, that I could only laugh. It didn't seem so bad. Maybe I was *schwul*. "As are you, my friend, as you well know."

"I am not *schwul*. I am Daniel. I fuck whoever I want to fuck."

I rolled my eyes at him. "And I look at whatever I want to look at. I love women. I adore making love to them. And I love women in love with other women, because I can understand it. I also do as I like. You don't corner the market on that."

He gazed out across the room at a trio of nearly identical young girls, no older than fourteen, their sleek legs encased in shiny nylon stockings and their bodies in short tweed coats with lacy slips peeking from the skirt hems. They sat close together but did not speak to or look at each other. They had been purchased for the night by the Japanese businessmen. "Have you ever thought that you were one or the other and decided to stick to it?" he asked me.

"I have never thought about it," I said. "I don't fall in love very often."

"But who do you like to fuck?" he insisted.

"I like to fuck who I'm in love with," I said. He gave a little scoff. "Yes, love. Try it sometime. It really enhances sex."

"Never touch the stuff," he said dryly.

Liar, I thought. *You are touching it right now, gulping down great heaps of it, and you know it,* and he smiled and wouldn't meet my eyes. "Why don't *you* decide to stick with one or another?" I countered.

He shrugged. "I let my impulses guide me. I live in the present. The past is not my responsibility, and the future is a complete unknown. If I want something, I take it. It is just that simple. No philosophical quandaries, no guilt, no fear."

"That must be nice for you."

"Oh, come now, what have you to fear? You are . . ." He trailed off and wiggled his fingers, digging for the word.

"I am a vampire," I said simply.

His eyes grew wide, and he blinked and stared at me in astonishment. "You are an angel without the fetters of religion. You are myth made flesh. You are the ultimate in human potential. I know what you *are*. I also know what you can do; I just don't understand why you don't do it."

"Like what, pray tell?"

"Like kill," he said.

We engaged in a staring contest. "I do kill," I replied. "When?"

I lost the staring contest, momentarily overwhelmed. Who was this Danny Blum? "Well, when I need to," I said.

"What about when you just want to?"

I laughed, and accepted a cigarette from a passing girl in high-heeled boots and a monocle. "I'd hardly ever stop killing," I said glibly.

"Well, then, you *don't* do as you like." Daniel picked out a handful of cigarettes, two cigars, and a tiny glass vial of cocaine, all of which he shoved into his jacket pockets.

"I don't indulge every impulse I have, no," I said.

"Then you are a phony. You say one thing and do another. It's really too bad. I expected more from you." Daniel tapped a bit of the powder out of the vial onto his fingertip, and up it went.

"I really don't like the way that stuff tastes," I said.

"Then don't do it," said Daniel, treating his other nostril.

"*You* don't do it," I countered, and wrinkled my nose; and he put the top back onto the vial and set it down on the table. He stared at his fingers for a long while, making a series of pained and ecstatic faces as the cocaine took effect, but he did not reach for it again.

"Let's get out of here," he said. "All these *bubis* are making me hostile. Let's go back to the Dummschwaller and do something kinky."

I stood in the bone-chilling cold of Daniel's private room while he gave the cocaine and cigars to one of the Sträubenhund gangsters, in exchange, he said, "for a little privacy for me and my friend." For once, I did not mind being left alone by him. Even this tiny space had been remade in the image of Daniel's mind. The walls had been papered with clippings from newspapers, theater playbills, and film-star magazines; the hollow-eyed, morphine gaze of actors vied for space with scientists, politicians, fashion plates, lurid *Lustmord* photographs, all of it connected with nonsense messages collaged from newspaper headline text. GERMANDERALAD abutted Theda Bara, WÜHOLSMANNERZ captioned Rudolph Valentino; my favorite was a portrait of Hindenberg in a frame of SCHEISSE SCHEISSE SCHEISSE. He did have a talented artistic eye; an aesthetic logic emerged from what, at first, seemed mere childish chaos, a scrapbook blown up with dynamite. "Yes, I see," I said aloud, turning around, staring up at the layered, yellowed collage that reached the ceiling. I stood with the wool blanket puddled around my ankles, the cocaine dissipating from my bloodstream, waiting for him to call for me.

"Come into the theater," he said at last.

I was backstage, as it were; another door led from this room into the theater and directly onto the crates. I passed through the portal into near-total darkness.

Seated on the opposite end of the stage, Daniel flickered into view as he struck a wooden match. His body was surrounded by something pale and wispy and flowing like a glimmering cloud, his lips a vermilion slash. The match sputtered out, leaving me with only the ghostly, negative afterimage. The next match elaborated on the first glance. He wore a sleeveless evening gown of translucent pale-green, bare ivory shoulders, the plunging neckline a glimmering V that showed the wisp of hair right over his heart. The vermilion lips curved as the second match went out. I felt my teeth click against each other in a savage grin.

"Isn't my dress pretty?" said the afterimage.

"It is a filthy rag on your lovely body," I replied.

"Tear it off, then."

I did.

In the midst of Daniel avidly fellating me, the darkness folded itself away as streetlight suddenly flooded into the Dummschwaller. Daniel did not stop, even to open his eyes, but I saw the Sträubenhund staggering with his hand on the door frame and powder on his mustache, bellowing, "This stuff is cut with powdered sugar, Danny!"

I felt my rage distantly, as though it were happening to someone else and the real Orfeo had been reduced to a mere observer.

I stepped away from Daniel's mouth and to the open door in one smooth movement, seizing the Sträubenhund and dragging him inside. "Mistake," I said to his livid, panicked face, just before I clamped my teeth into his neck, my bottom fangs puncturing his trachea and spraying blood and breath into my mouth.

I inhaled him. I became pure instinct, without personality, without thought of morality, let alone the restraint of conscience. My nature propelled me, guided my hands, my mouth, everything. The bitterness of the cocaine could not compete with the smooth, infinite richness of his fear. I longed for that taste, and I had not had it in a long time—certainly Daniel's lusty blood never tasted of terror!

Daniel silently slipped past us and closed the door again, shutting out the tide of streetlight.

In seconds the gangster's struggling and twitching ceased entirely. I opened my fingers and allowed him to slide down the wall into a lifeless heap at my feet. The contents of the vial now swept over me like a vicious, cutting wind. It was more than I had ever had inside me. I knew then that I still had a heart, for the rattling in my chest nearly throttled me. I was grateful for the darkness, for it made the vertigo seem less total; all the same, I stumbled and fell next to the dead man when I tried to take a step. I imagined myself plummeting to Hell, my body flattening as gravity thickened, my heart desperately struggling against it.

Daniel lit another match and stared down at me with

more curiosity than concern. "Oh, Orfeo. I could have told you that would happen," he said. "You should be more careful who you bite." He nudged the Sträubenhund with his silver-slippered toe. The ripped fragments of the dress fluttered in the cold draft; he wore nothing else but the shoes and the lipstick, and his prick hung, still hard, heavy and flushed between his legs. I could see the blood circulating under his skin, the electric heat radiating from his body.

He let the match go out, and I felt his hot breath against my bared lower belly and the touch of his tongue on my engorged and hypersensitive penis.

"I wasn't finished," he whispered, and proceeded to suck me off while I lay delirious, the Sträubenhund's spattered blood soaking into my skin.

When his task was swiftly completed, he dragged the dead man outside, by himself, naked but for the shredded remains of an evening gown and four-inch-high heels. I began to laugh and found it extremely difficult to stop. What a miraculous spectacle! What grace, what beauty, what style—festooned nudity, the original fashion, and unconscionable savagery, the original entertainment!

At last, I returned to my senses. I stood up, buttoned my trousers, and dusted off my legs and elbows. The body had been moved before his fluids could leak, and there was hardly a trace of him having been inside. I scuffed my foot on the floor to obscure any drag marks, all the same. Daniel stalked back inside, lit another match, this time to light a cigarette, and smiled at me with his wicked, womanish lips.

"Where to next, my love?" he asked.

"Can It Be Done?"

We were a fine team of monsters, Danny Blum and I.

I gave myself up for damned and decided to make the best of it.

I stopped going to Saturday-night Mass. Instead, I accompanied Daniel to a different kind of worship at the cinema. Daniel was an aficionado, an avid consumer, and had even worked on a few films himself, and so knew a great deal of the mechanics of creating the sublime illusion. Each weekend, we came to see the moving pictures unfold their silver-and-black alternate reality over a silent and devoted audience, to the strains of a small orchestra or a lone, gamely tinkling piano. It made no difference to Daniel and me whether the picture was good. If the story was well-told and beautiful, we absorbed it, murmuring our admiration in hushed, respectful tones and applauding the end title; if the film was cheap-looking, insipid, or "ordinary," we spent the dim hours with our tongues in each other's mouth and our hands down each other's trousers. By unspoken mutual agreement, everyone was invisible in the flickering half-dark; we were not alone in lovemaking in our seats during the duller pictures. From time to time, I would lean forward to the next row, and though to any curious eye it seemed that I murmured into the ear of another cinema patron, I stole brief, painless mouthfuls of blood to fortify me for the long, mad night yet to come.

Of course, I told Daniel stories of my youth in Italy and my passage to France, and tales of roaming the Parisian street, the artistic and political upheavals, the awkwardness of growing into my new-forged power while remaining a pet to Maria and Georgina. He had little interest in the women, or in M. Chicot, except for the details of their vampire natures; most of all, he wanted to know how it felt to leap over the Seine in one bound, the mechanisms of seduction and deception, the varieties of blood and all that it carried. I prattled on happily, grateful to have an audience, as though I were telling bedtime stories to an enthusiastic child.

Daniel flourished under my care. I kept him well-fed, well-sexed, well-clothed, and intoxicated. Since he had decided that he no longer liked cocaine, he returned to the bottle with a vengeance and smoked forty cigarettes a day. He also enjoyed a pipe of hashish first thing "in the morning" when we woke up, generally around three o'clock in the afternoon. Then he would go to the restaurant on the end of the block where I lived and attack a massive breakfast of rolls, cold beef, honey, plum jam, soft cheese, and coffee. One would imagine that this lifestyle would leave him pale, sick, and obese, but Daniel fairly glowed with health and vitality, growing more beautiful each day.

I remained the same, of course.

He eschewed current men's fashions, preferring a motley hodgepodge of "found" garments, largely stolen, that he altered and combined with a perverse originality. He sewed quite well. "My father was a shoemaker," he explained, "and my uncles were tailors; they taught me sewing when I was just a kid. I was very good at it, of course. I earned lots of money drawing patterns for them and finishing projects. Everyone was horrified when I decided to study art in Zurich instead." He did allow me to purchase him a black frock coat, second-hand, from a costume-shop rummage sale, and then he spent a whole night at home, replacing the plain buttons with big, gaudy rhinestone-encrusted ones. "I stole these from a ladies' dress shop in Zurich seven years ago, and I've been waiting for the perfect use for them. You have an eye for style yourself, Orfeo!"

I found less comprehensible his love of wearing women's evening dresses, and always of the height of fashion, adorned with high-heeled shoes or boots, stockings, jewelry, and heavy makeup. He shaved his legs and forearms. He even painted lacquer on his fingernails. I had to admit that he looked marvelous dressed in this costume. The dissonance aroused me beyond all sense. Other observers had similar reactions of mingled awe, disgust, and desire. He most definitely turned heads wherever we went, and hardly anyone noticed me at all. I took a nervous pleasure in escorting this curious apparition to clubs and taverns, and the cabarets in which he sang popular songs, his stockinged legs cocked open randily on the piano bench.

He had no female alternate identity; he remained Danny-Boy all the time, despite his insistence on plucking his thick eyebrows and wearing red lipstick almost every day, whether his garb was masculine or feminine. Even dressed as a man, he barely resembled the other men enough to deserve the term. He was an odd, unique third sex, as decorative as a woman and as menacing as a madman. Only the boldest dared accuse him of being homosexual, or looking like a circus clown, a condemnation in which I could see a certain truth. But these unwary aesthetes had no idea what they had unleashed. Daniel's rejoinders caused heavy psychological damage. Only once or twice had I cause to intervene in a confrontation; most, like Klaus, simply slunk away with tails between legs, wondering how a stranger could prey so effortlessly upon hidden insecurities and shames.

I could have controlled him more, but I didn't. It was not even particularly hard to do; his very complexity made his mind extremely vulnerable. He thought so many things, so quickly, and his attention had all the permanence of a butterfly in a field of poppies. He was a brilliant, willful, easily distracted child.

I was entertained. I had got what I had left Geneva for, indeed, what I had left Italy for, what I had wanted all along: glamor, excitement, intellectual stimulation, physical love. And miraculously, he was true to me; I would have known if he had slept with someone else. But he genuinely had no desire for others. He appreciated them aesthetically and was lavish with his flirtation, his blatant grabs, and his eyes, but he was always there beside me, kissing and stroking me, when I succumbed to sleep.

Each evening that I awoke, I would remember, *Daniel Blum loves me*, and feel both horrified and blessed: I was blessed in the intensity and sweetness of our love, the tender embraces of comfort he eagerly gave, his nonsensical protectiveness of me, his lightning ability and infinite willingness to learn; and horrified at the guarantee that, before I slept again, he would do something to embarrass, disgust, or offend me.

But oh, what a fine "cowboy" he was!

He guided victims to me with ease and grace, indicating to me with a wink and a surreptitious gesture at his throat which "cattle" he had selected for me. I turned most of them away, but his skills were undeniable. Hapless tourists, suicidal businessmen, young prostitutes addicted to morphine—all were drawn to this strange creature Danny, and with a few kind words and a well-spent mark, they were sent across the room to me. I was appalled, at first, that several of the victims knew exactly the nature of the interaction, and of me, and they were eager for the experience. I did not even have to veil my appearance or my intentions. This was Berlin, and the thrill-seekers had exhausted every experience save that of sensual bloodletting at the hands of an undead gentleman; they were grateful for the opportunity.

I didn't have to make the slightest effort anymore, but when I protested, he silenced me. "Shush, Orfeo. You support me, I support you. Let me do this for you. I'm so good at it and I enjoy it. It's a sport, it's a game. Now that I know the rules, I must play."

And later, in back rooms at parties, in the back of taxicabs, on the filthy floor of the Dummschwallen, physical pleasures still unknown to me were explored to their fullest extent.

I should have known he was in training.

On a cool, rainy afternoon in September, I awoke and opened my eyes to Daniel standing across the room, staring out the window at the Tiergarten trees bending in the wind.

"Danny?" I called. "Come here, love, I'm hungry."

He did not turn around. "We should do it today," he said decisively.

"Do what?" I said, and then, my stomach sinking: "Oh, Danny, no."

"What do you mean, no?" He turned back and sat next to me on the bed, stroking my hair. I frowned at him. "Yes," he insisted softly, his fingertip tracing my ear, "you know it's right. It's what I want. It's what you want."

I opened my mouth to protest, but nothing emerged. He was right; it was what I wanted, something I had imagined myself many times, thinking of how alone I would feel when he had gone, when he had grown old, the way Ollier had done while I hadn't been looking. "But you don't know what you ask," I said at last. "I don't wish this on anyone. It's a terrible thing."

"But you do have the power within you to do this."

I sighed. "Yes," I said. "But it is more horrible than you can possibly imagine."

"Indeed; that's why I must witness it with my own eyes."

"This is not a cloak you throw on over your clothes. This is not a holiday; you don't get to come back. This changes who and what you are to the very . . . to the very marrows of your bones. And then some." I kissed the center of his palm, my mind filling with the agonizing memories of my own transformation, the blood, the terror on the faces of Maria and Georgie, and sent it to him.

When I opened my eyes, his face had gone a shade paler, but he gazed at me steadily, chewing on his bare lower lip.

"The more drastic the transformation, the more painful. I know this. *Can* you do it?" he asked me.

I rolled off the bed, walked to my closet, and began dressing myself. Daniel sat on the bed, watching me, silent. How could he ask me for the one thing I did not wish to give? He had my money, my body, my heart, a key to my apartment. Why must he have it all? Why must he implore me to create catastrophe made flesh? Not to mention making a mess more appropriate to a cat-meat factory than a dwelling.

I looked into my bathroom and stared at the massive bathtub, the smooth round angles of the plumbing pipes, and the immaculate linoleum floor with a drain in the center, nearly directly under the tub itself.

The world had changed since I had been reborn into it.

And if Daniel wanted this life, this wretched eternality, how could I deny him? Let him taste of the pain, and the loss, and the suffering; it would serve him right.

That bastard.

I looked back at Daniel as I slipped on my shoes. "I'll need blood," I said.

He smiled only a little. "I know just the one," he replied.

Liesl lived in an apartment in Prenzlauerberg with a gaggle of other theatrical ladies, either four or six, depending on the season. On the telephone she enthusiastically agreed to my request to come around and see her for a late supper, telling her I would bring champagne. "Your timing is impeccable," she told me. "All my roommates are out at work tonight, and this is my only night off all week. You can stay for only an hour; Klaus will be meeting me at ten o'clock."

I arrived half an hour late, at half past nine. Liesl did not seem put out by my tardiness. Indeed, she looked radiant. Her hair had grown out to a more flattering length, her curls softened into rye-colored waves around her jawline, and she wore hardly any makeup, allowing her summer-browned skin to shine for itself. "You look wonderful. How was your summer?" I asked her, producing the waxed-paper-wrapped champagne bottle from my briefcase and kissing the air next to her cheek.

"It was very good. Klaus and I went on holiday to a health camp in the country, and played tennis and ate fruit all day. It only cost us a hundred marks each for the whole summer. It was nice to get out of this hideous city for a while."

"But not so much as to convince you to return to Geneva."

"Oh, horrors, no, I won't go back there again anytime soon. I was bored out of my mind!"

I uncorked the champagne and poured a measure for her into a tall, thin wine-flute. "It's our only one," she explained. "All the others got broken last New Year's Eve. It was quite a wild party; you really missed out." She sipped and sighed. "Aren't you going to have some? There's an ordinary glass in the cupboard."

"Oh, no, thank you," I said.

"You must drink it all the time," she surmised. "You're probably sick of it. I wish I could be sick of it. Have you ever been poor, Herr Ricari?"

"Yes," I said, "very poor indeed. I hadn't a pot to piss in, nor a window to throw it out." I relaxed upon the sofa, its cushions frayed but cozy, and fingered the multicolored knitted doilies draped over the back. Liesl had knitted them herself, bored at the coat-check station at Julian's. My eyes flitted over the small, net-curtained windows; they opened inward, but the apartment was at streetlevel. No problem. "How are you and Klaus?"

"We're going to be married at Christmas," she said with happy calm, draining her glass and topping it up again.

"Really? How splendid. Many happy returns."

"Thank you. I know that you're still going about with Danny Blum," she countered. "Why?"

"We love each other," I said.

"I don't understand," she said. Her happiness dissolved, and rancor began to wear away her reserve of calm. "He's so awful, so gauche! He'll never really love you, not enough to stay. You've *got* to see that. I don't know how you could give the time of day to that faggot monster."

"Perhaps it is because I am one, too," I said without changing the expression on my face or my mild tone of voice. Let God judge her; I was past that. For now, I could feed upon her anger, let it lend steel to my spine and cold to my blood. "We have more in common than you could possibly know."

Liesl finished her glass of champagne and, keeping her eyes on me, defiantly poured a third. I watched her.

"Drink up," I said, "who knows when you'll have it again?"

Her eyes darted around nervously, but she obeyed, knocking back the effervescent fluid so quickly that she choked. I sprang from my seat on the couch and began to pound her back, first gently, then with increasing force, holding my hand over her mouth. She wanted to scream, but there was too much champagne and saliva blocking her throat; she could only cough. I struck her sharply, precisely, against her kidneys. My hand, over her mouth, caught a spurt of bright scarlet blood.

The clock sweetly chimed three-quarters. Right on time.

I put my mouth to hers, covering it entirely, inhaling her life, the blood and air from her damaged lungs. I slammed my fist against her back to make the blood come faster. I must have all of it, and promptly.

She never even struggled. It hadn't hurt for more than a moment. She had got her heart's desire: a kiss, an openmouthed, rough, passionate champagne kiss, from the sublime Herr Ricari, in her own candlelit drawing room, the jaunty, scratchy sounds of a jazz-music phonograph record, the measured thump of dancing feet on the floor above us. I held her gently in her last moments, whispering affection and regret into her slack mouth, and then I sat her up and hit her across the face with the back of my hand, just hard enough to leave a nasty bruise that her body contained barely enough blood to produce. I angled her head forward between her knees to hasten the bruising, then, when her heartbeat ceased entirely, I laid her back onto the sofa and closed her eyes.

I checked the time on the little clock with a porcelain hound chasing a porcelain rabbit around the base. Five minutes until the coming of Klaus. My timing was impeccable. Or, rather, Daniel's timing was impeccable. He had seen Klaus at the market the day before, and casually asked after Liesl; Klaus thoughtlessly told Daniel about the engagement, and their date set up for the next night at ten.

When Klaus arrived two minutes later, I let him in while I hid behind the door; he walked in holding a spray of flowers before him, his mustache stretched over his grinning teeth. "Lisel, my buttercup, where are you?"

His blood tasted of nothing more toxic than love itself.

I rode in a taxicab back to my flat, so as to spare the expenditure of the blood I had just taken. I fingered my beads, nervous suddenly, when I had been so certain before; did I have the knowledge and capability to perform Daniel's transformation? Maria and Georgina had slaughtered two servants between them, but I had not witnessed this; how much blood had been taken from each one? And they might have also consumed all of the rabbits, hens, and doves that Maria kept. Was that significant? Was that essential?

Still, still so much I did not know! Why had I not spent some of my years in Les Batignolles quizzing M. Chicot about the fundamentals of vampire reproduction? I could only conclude that I had no desire to revisit the unpleasantness, the pain and terror, of my own rebirth. I did not want to know, and I had no idea that I would ever have need of this knowledge.

I took some comfort, by the time the taxi drove up to the end of Bellevue Strasse and my boardinghouse, that instinct would have to do, as in all reproduction for the first time. If it went wrong, it was God's will. I didn't imagine any negative consequences for myself, and if I accidentally rid the world of Daniel Blum, the lack would, no doubt, be swiftly remedied.

Yes, this is what I had become. This was the color of my love—a dark, muddy admixture. I had become more like Daniel than I had thought possible.

Daniel's pale face peered from my sitting-room window, watching for me, waiting for me to return. His childlike joy at my homecoming flowed out and into me, filling me with warmth and light. Even in my darkest moments, I never doubted his love; it was as pure, and clear, and cutting as a diamond, omnipresent and direct in a way I had never experienced. I found myself humbled and astonished. I went inside, and he fell into my arms.

"You were perfect," he whispered to me. "I saw the whole thing through your eyes. You couldn't have timed it more precisely if you were a stopwatch. You amaze me. That look on Klaus's face . . ." He kissed me avidly on the mouth, then drew away, his face somber.

"What must I do?" he asked.

I took a deep breath and felt the fresh blood inside me flutter and surge in response. *Prepare for death and the loss of all that you know, fear more absolute and unavoidable than your worst nightmare, and pain worthy of the most zealous of martyrs* ran through my mind, but all I said aloud was "Take off your clothes and come with me."

He followed me into the bathroom, beloved by us both, and I sighed at the sight of it, wondering if I should have to leave this place that I enjoyed so, borne on a tidal wave of blood and offal. I resolved that I would not leave my flat, no matter what I had to do.

"Run the tub half-full of warm water; not hot, but blood-warm." While he fiddled with the taps, I returned to my bedroom and shed my clothes as well, draping them over the chair where Daniel had thrown his paint-stained trousers, women's silk undershirt, and the blue sweater with appliquéd letter *D* he'd talked out of a visiting American student. I almost put on different clothes and walked out of the apartment, away from the building, away from Berlin, but I could not decide where I would go. I balled my fists until my fingernails cut into my palms. I would not give in to cowardice; I had come this far; I would not let down the man I loved.

The water stopped running with a faint shriek of the turning of the tap.

I returned, and told Daniel to get into the bath. He did, watching me with open, fearless curiosity. I squatted next to the tub, took up my straight razor, and held it up till I saw the blade glitter.

"I love you," I said softly.

Before he could answer, I plunged the glittering edge into the right side of his neck.

I held him in my arms and drank until all the tension in his limbs had gone, and his eyes fluttered with the effort to hold them open. I let him go to slash my wrist, and he sank into the cooling water, still moving his lipstick-stained lips in silent prayer. *I will not die*, his lips formed as I lifted him up by his left arm. The trickling gash in his neck had red-on-pink lips of its own. *I will not die*.

"You *will* die," I said, hissing at the razor's edge, slicing into myself between the two big straining tendons of my wrist. Pain, yes; we are all born in pain, with pain, through pain. "But that is the way it must be."

I kept my eyes on his dilating pupils while my dark-bloodied, throbbing wrist was in his mouth. One pulse. I felt that I could jump into those black pools of nothingness and swim away into his death. Two pulses. Daniel's face twisted into a grimace, and he quaked but did not let go. Three pulses. His mouth full, he swallowed, and then swallowed again, and the feathery grip of his fingers on my arm suddenly gained a strength born of panic.

That's four, Georgina had thought. "Enough," Maria had said.

I yanked my wrist back.

Daniel fell back again, the warm water sloshing, gasping for breath. The wound in his neck still sent tiny spurting trickles down his chest, staining the water. He felt for the wound. "No," I said, stilling his wet, chilly hand. "Don't touch it, please, I beg you, you'll only make it worse."

"I trust you," he whispered. His flesh had gone stark white with shock, and sweat poured from every pore on his body, soaking his hair wet in seconds. My blood dried like smeared chocolate around his mouth. "Oh God!" He squinted and convulsed. "It burns, it feels like . . ."

"It feels like you're dying," I said. I looked down at my wrist. The razor cut had sealed itself into a writhing pink scar, feeding on itself.

I shall never forget the look of horror on Daniel's face as the blood burned its way through his belly and into his guts, like a vicious acid, twisting its way through the complex and grotesque spirals of the miles of his intestine, destroying everything it touched. He let out half a scream. The other half was fluid, sound made flesh, the contents of his belly spewing out of him and down over his bare abdomen and genitals.

Where this poisoned vomit touched, it ate away the skin.

I stood back, forcing myself to witness this atrocity, this appalling destruction of a man, bit by bit, faster and faster all the time. The vomit and blood in the water swiftly blistered all the skin it touched, until only the top half of his face and his hair remained intact.

The worst part was that he remained conscious, unable to scream, throughout all of this.

He wept copious tears, the clear salt-water pinkening, and then running red over his ravaged chin. The tears bored tunnels into his face. He put his fingers to his eyes to wipe the tears, and the fingers sunk with grotesque ease into his eyeballs.

He struggled; oh, how how he struggled. Perhaps he was wiser than I had thought; his exertions just made everything happen faster. Clumps of hair filled the tub; the slightest touch of his fingertips sheared off thick sections of skin, down to the fat, down to the muscle, the pale tissues between his ribs. His magnificent voice had been reduced to a faint, desperate wheezing, then even that ceased.

He was dead.

I sat upon the toilet and looked upon my works. He had been whittled down to a motionless carcass in the space of a few minutes. I went back into my bedroom, flung myself out on my bed, and gave in to the tears I had been too shocked to release before him. This was all wrong; that process should have taken much longer. I must have indeed forgotten something, done something wrong. I was too cocky. I had betrayed him and myself.

I clutched my beads and prayed with all my might for forgiveness for all my sins, particularly the pride and lust that had brought me to the point of murdering my lover and an innocent young couple on the verge of matrimony, imagining that I could "get away with it." Daniel's words. He had set up the whole thing, lured me into his trap, and tricked me into believing that I could reinvent myself as God, the Father, the Creator, shaping a new man out of human dust.

Once I had performed ten decades upon the rosary, however, my curiosity got the better of me, and I tiptoed back to the bathroom to see how extensive the damage had gotten and determine the difficulty of cleaning it up. When I saw the bathtub, filled nearly to the brim with an undifferentiated soup of gore, I turned around and walked out again, wishing I could vomit.

I got dressed, grabbed my coat, and sped, on foot, to midnight Mass at St. Hedwig's. It felt odd to be back here after so long; I had not gone to Mass, or to confession, in almost a year. The only others there were the exceedingly pious old ladies who are at every midnight Mass, and a few straggling younger people, their pale, haggard faces bespeaking night service jobs on the Unter der Linden.

When it came time for me to confess, I found that I could only say, "I have killed a man for what I thought was his own good, but was for nothing but pride and selfishness. . . . I know that with God's help and the guidance of the Blessed Virgin Mother, I shall never do it again."

The priest assigned one hundred recitations of the rosary, a promise that I would begin giving confession regularly, a heavy tithing of my income, and a vow to make right that which I had wronged.

I am still trying to perform the last penance, for I know of no other way than to give my life for theirs—for all of the lives I had stolen, lost in the midst of love, including my own.

"Only the Lord can tell you what to do," said Father Christopher.

I received Communion, prayed, and lit candles for Klaus, Liesl, and Daniel, and shoved four hundred marks, all I had with me, into the donation box.

* * *

I returned to the apartment with a lead anchor in place of a heart, my thoughts calmed but not cheered by the clicking of beads and the flashing cadence of Hail Marys. The apartment lay dark and silent, but smelled like an abattoir. I did not look forward to the cleaning job that awaited me, but I had promised myself on the way home (walking slowly through the festive nighttime streets, like a mortal, unwilling to lift my spirits by leaping along the densely packed rooftops as I usually did) that I would stop being such a coward, and face the unpleasant and gruesome as squarely as I faced the delightful and trivial. Besides, it was just a body; I had dealt with scores of bodies before. (Or *was* it a body? I shuddered. I imagined having to remove Daniel in buckets.)

It was indeed a body, ripped and skeletal, half-sunk in the tub full of blood. Yet it seemed more intact than I had left it. I switched on the electric light overhead, not trusting even my eyes, and saw Daniel's body, hairless, skinless, with the sealed black-opal eyelids of a newborn puppy. But moving! The body moved! No, the water moved—the blood, the dissolved tissue, swirled and trembled around the bizarre carcass.

The flash of understanding was so sudden and total that it gave me a headache. "Oh," I said, "I see," and using both hands, I scooped up the cold, bloody mixture and poured it on the exposed areas of flesh above the water. Most of it ran off, but that which remained, pooled in the channels of the ribs and clavicles, jellied and set and thickened the tissue upon which it settled.

I ran to my kitchen and grasped Daniel's large stein, still perfumed with beer, and brought it back with me, using it to ladle and pour the bloody water back onto him. "Praise be to the Almighty Father in His generosity; praise be to the Holy Virgin Mary in all Her gentleness; praise be to the only Son of God, Jesus Christ, in

His forgiveness; praise be to Saint Jude, for assisting me in my hour of need," I whispered hastily, pouring, building, as though washing away stone in reverse. "Be with me now, my Lord! Hail Mary, full of Grace!"

I wept in my happiness, and let my tears fall from my eyes into the bath. I poured them over Daniel's reconstituting body, in hopes that my joy and relief would become a part of him. "Give him faith and charity," I prayed, "give him compassion and reflection; help him to be a better person. . . ."

I prayed and poured as night succumbed to day, and darkness settled once again.

Potential and Kinetic Energy

I could not have been happier, or more astonished, at Daniel's first breath if I had given birth to him myself.

He lay, whole and beautiful again, his scalp hair a thatch of wet-spiky short bristles, his face patched with an irregular black beard and quite astonishingly thick eyebrows that grew together in the middle. Eyes still closed, his chest gathered itself and pushed his mouth open, exhaling a breath that stank of putrefaction. He had been holding it all the way back from Hell. Once the foul air had been expelled and he filled his lungs again, he began to incandesce from within, drawing his lips back from clean, bright, strong teeth, the eyeteeth vaguely pointed at the ends.

One of us, now. One of me. My child.

His skin was perfect. All of his jagged scars and pockmarks had vanished, and even his moles were gone, including one I particularly liked on the side of his lower belly. "Sometimes sacrifices must be made," I said aloud, smiling down at him. "Daniel? Can you hear me?"

He opened his eyes and stared at me blankly. The

variegated color of his irises had been altered to a deep, luminous viridian, like a mosaic of green glass shards, pulling the sphincter of his pupils tight. "Daniel?" I called again.

He sat up abruptly and took in the details of his surroundings in a glance. With a great crashing of water, he tensed his muscles and flew upward out of the bath, his foot barely grazing the edge as he launched himself through the door to my bedroom. When I heard the front door of my apartment being torn open, I leapt up to follow. He had nearly ripped the door from its hinges; certainly the doorknob would need to be replaced, as he had warped the brass construction as though it were taffy.

Chicot, I thought desperately, scanning the street until I caught Daniel's trail, *if you can hear me, please help*.

Daniel had gone, not toward the Tiergarten's lawns and woods, but toward the shops, the cabarets, the residences. Of course; like any good predator, he would go where there was prey. I had done it. And now the thing I had forgotten, in our immaculate plan, occurred to me. Of course, newly transformed, with a great deal of his blood left behind in the bath, he would need to feed immediately, and would not know sense until he had.

"I still need you, St. Jude," I muttered.

I could only guess that it was near midnight; I had left my pocket watch in my coat. A Sunday night in Berlin was just like every other night, with streets packed and pulsing with action. Daniel's trajectory took him southeast, up a tree and onto the roofs, almost as though he were backtracking the path that I had last taken, to Liesl's apartment. But then he diverged, and I concentrated on his mind, trying to determine exactly where he was going.

The Potsdamer-Platz . . . !

I stood still and called through the ether to him. *Where are you? I am trying to find you.*

I could not get his attention, but I ascertained his location, kinetic images overlapping, the thrumming of heartbeats reaching his hypersensitive ears, the immediacy of scent (petrol, piss, ozone, cologne, meat and alcohol and humans everywhere), and the seemingly infinite strength surging through his body. I let out a groan of remorse. What had I done?

Suddenly, blood. A short savage spring and tear and then blood, so keenly experienced, so primal and immediate, that my own mouth watered. I tasted his victim's panic and terror, the profoundest ecstasy for our kind, as gratifying and as fleeting as an orgasm. Daniel let the victim drop from his hands without looking at her, but I had felt the young boot-girl's throat tear away from her neck and her head flop back like a half-empty sack.

Another minor exertion, and then another, separate, fresh gout of blood shot into Daniel's mouth and directly into his bloodstream without the necessity of swallowing. The prostitute's partner, her elder cousin, who had watched the vampire appear out of the shadows of an alley and consume the young girl with the surgical savagery of a viper, met her own fate, too shocked even to scream. I hurried along the streets, dodging pedestrians and car drivers who may or may not have seen my passage.

Enough, Daniel, I sent. *Enough.*

No—not enough.

His first words; how appropriate.

He stood luminously naked in the alley, arms still around the elder boot-girl as he drank her life away. In fact, she was dead already, her thoughts entirely absent and heart stilled, and still he drank of the blood, still hot and, for the moment, still plentiful. I stood at the alley's portal to the Platz, blocking any view from outside, and watched him; there was nothing I could do but conceal him and wait.

At last he let her drop to a fur-coated heap at his feet, next to her cousin, who had been nearly decapitated by Daniel's attack. His hair had grown several inches since I had last seen him, five minutes ago, and his muscles were full and taut, his penis standing at thick, hard attention. He stared at me, wiping the blood from his bearded mouth with the back of his wrist. I had never seen him look so masculine.

"Not enough," he repeated to me.

His resonant voice could hypnotize a hummingbird into lying still, his eyes wring jealous tears from Apollo. He was mine. I had created this resplendent creature.

"You're naked," I pointed out, my eyes involuntarily fixated on his erection.

Daniel squinted at me. "I am a god," he stated, "what difference does it make?"

I laughed nervously. "No, no, not a god; just Danny. That's good enough, right? Please, my love, home, some trousers, please. Then we'll go out. I'll show you how to . . ."

"How to what? I think I *know* how." He wiped some of the spilled blood onto his penis and rubbed it in. "I think I know exactly how." His undisciplined mind flooded mine with all the magical spectrum of sensation, utilizing senses that he had never had before, his glowing hand stroking the stronger glow of his penis. His sacred halo was brightest surrounding his cock, not his head.

I bit my lip and forced myself to look away. "Need I remind you that you are not immortal?"

He laughed, licking his fingers. "Really?" he said lazily. "I'd love to find out."

I bristled. Already I could hear the sounds of traffic

on the street behind me increasing in volume. This alley was a very popular location for end-of-the-night hand jobs, and already I was tired of convincing horny Berliners to try another alley while trying to have a rational conversation with Temptation made manifest, an activity analogous to spinning plates while riding a unicycle. Focusing my thoughts, staring into Daniel's eyes, I clenched my fists, streamlining my anger into power.

"Now, Daniel," I said firmly, wrapping a bond of control around Daniel's mind, like a slightly translucent veil, pulling tighter until I knew he could make no expansive move by his own will, but only by mine. I consolidated his hurricane of thoughts, physiology, and desires into simplicity. He knew it wise to follow. His body would move as I directed. He would want to come with me.

His face twisted with fury for a moment, then softened and blanked. "You won't do this to me," he said, his voice reasonable and quiet. The will, strongest, would not bend to my control; he was not human anymore.

"Yes, I will," I said. "Come home with me this instant. Please do as I say; I only mean the best for you."

"I have heard that one before," Daniel replied calmly.

"Come," I said, holding out my hand. "Let's get out of this disgusting byway. Let me show you how to fly."

"I already *know* how," he said. But he accepted my hand. He had no choice but to do so. I was the stronger, plain and simple, and would always be so, no matter what he did; I had a hundred years and more of accumulated, increasing power, not to mention the blood of elders generations older than myself.

I scrambled up the brickwork wall of the alley, still holding his hand. He followed, barefoot, as nimble as a spider, until we stood on the roof of the building that overlooked the Platz and the station. He stared, openmouthed, across the street, at the rolling automobiles and clustering hats and overcoats, the brilliant lights and spectacle of Haus Vaterland. Daniel's knees buckled and he clapped an astonished hand to his mouth. "It is even more devastating than it was twenty minutes ago," he breathed reverently. "It's like looking through a stream at a thousand electric minnows. . . . I can see into all of their minds. . . !" He turned his stare to me. "Is this what it's like for you?"

"Once upon a time it was," I admitted. "But then, the lights were not quite so bright, nor so many."

I gazed out over the street, searching for any familiar preternatural glow dotting the city of Berlin; surely we were not the only vampires in the city? But I saw no one shine but myself and this new one. Chicot had not answered my summons, and now I was glad of it; I would not have relished explaining my rationale to him. *What were you thinking, again if you please, Monsieur Ricari?* But I heard nothing; my relief mingled with sadness. Had Chicot gone into the fire as well? I shook off the thought. "Come, Daniel. Follow me. Don't think too much about what you do; instinct will guide you, and I shall protect you. Just jump." I let go of his hand, spread my arms for balance, and made the great standing leap over the fifteen-meter space between buildings.

He made his own leap, his arms crookedly akimbo and his phallus bobbing in the wind. He gave a whoop and a laugh as he alit on the balls of his bare feet, enjoying the action even without his own conscious desire to act. "It's so *fun*," he gasped. "I can't believe I can actually do this! When I was coming here, I wasn't thinking . . . I wasn't aware of what I was doing. . . ." I had to smile, even as I turned away and continued home; he was so beautiful, so ridiculous, my clown-spider child, with his own distinct, asymmetrical way of moving, as though he created jazz with his body.

I thought to myself that children must have been designed to remind one of what it was like to be very young, as well as a way to make amends, correct mistakes, enact revenge. I wondered what my mothers would think of the transformed Danny Blum, what they would think of me for having brought him to that state. *What were you thinking, little greyhound?*

Safely inside my apartment, I released his kinetic will. Unprepared for freedom, his legs collapsed when I let him go and he hit the floor with a grunt. He glowered at me as he returned to his feet. I shrugged, but failed to apologize; I still wanted him to get dressed. I told him so without speaking, glancing at the messy pile of hastily shed clothes. He slowly, resentfully pulled on his trousers. "Clothing hurts," he muttered.

"You'll get used to it," I said mildly, handing him a clean silk undershirt from my own drawer.

His lower lip stuck out like a sulky child's. "I don't *want* to get used to it." He was so pretty it hurt to look at him, even as he pulled on the delicate silk garment as though it were a hair shirt.

"You know . . ." I laughed a little and gently helped him into his coat. "I actually went to Mass and prayed for you to survive; for some reason, I was certain that I'd killed you by accident. It's a very delicate process, you know . . . a few drops one way or the other, and you'd have just flowed down the plug hole . . ." I laughed more, helplessly, at my own absurdity, swept away with relief.

"You *prayed* for me?" His brow was black as thunder. The black beard gave his angular face startling, intense outlines. "Don't ever do that again, do you hear me?"

I rocked back, staring at him. "What? Daniel, it worked. My prayer was answered."

"Bullshit," he said. "I lived because I was determined to live no matter what. It was my act as much as yours.

Keep your God-shit away from me. I don't need it, and I don't want it. It's just a wad of idiotic superstition."

He might have punched me and hurt me less. "So is vampirism," I reminded him. "And yet here we are."

He snarl-grinned at me, showing his glittering white teeth. "Spoken like a true sinner," he drawled. "We are all just man-made chemical processes, like walking cups of coffee. . . . Wait a minute. You went to Mass? When? While I was in the tub?" My contrite silence affirmed him. "You left me alone?"

"Well . . . yes . . ."

He let out his breath in a dismissive, offended huff. "I see." I held out my hands helplessly. There was nothing I could say. He shrugged the coat more firmly onto his back, grimacing as the fabric chafed his skin. "Well, let's go out, then, shall we, and you can show me how it's done, O Socrates. Go on; age before beauty."

I took a deep breath and affixed a smile onto my face. He was young, he was blood-hungry; of course he would be unpleasant. He still loved me. I felt it in every cell of my body, every shred of my brain; my heart and body belonged utterly to him, and his to me, whether he behaved himself or not. He was my offspring, and it was my duty to nurture him as I had been nurtured, teach him as I had been taught.

And I could kill him anytime, because I was stronger.

His contagious hunger tugged me out the door and back onto the dark streets.

He returned immediately to the alley. Policemen had arrived and blocked off the area with their cars, waving away the gathering crowds eager to see the latest murders. Daniel walked past it without sparing more than a curious glance, his steps leading with determination to the service entrance in the rear of Haus Vaterland.

"Subtlety," I said.

"Yes, yes," he answered impatiently.

A gaggle of waiters and coat-check girls chatted and laughed and gestured with their cigarettes, coats on, unwilling, for the time being, to leave the comfortable, splendid aura of their workplace. Daniel approached the group stealthily, stalking them on tiptoes, silent, and undoubtedly invisible to their eyes, though he still shone in mine. One of the girls broke away from the group and waved, walking directly toward Daniel. "Come to me," he whispered, as faint as a dream of a breeze. "Come to me, Margot . . ."

"Good night!" beamed the girl. "Good night!"

He turned down toward where the S-Bahn train looped overhead, and the girl followed him into the shadows underneath. I left him to it, approaching the smokers visibly, and asking, clumsy and affable, thickly laying on the Italian accent, "Could you be sparing a match?"

I did not even have a cigarette, but it didn't seem to matter. A cigarette was produced, a lit match was offered to me, and I bent my head in the usual manner. The stylishly coiffed young staff, chosen more for their looks than their skills, continued their gossipy conversation. I did not outwardly react to the shared and transmitted sensation of the attack in the shadows, the oddly libidinous gasp, the red velvet liquid pouring, but inside I trembled and wavered with my own hunger. The smokers dispersed, never thinking of their cohort, heading for late-night clubs, late-night beds. They lived in a world without vampires, never knowing the true nature of the murderers in their midst. Or perhaps they did know. This was Berlin, land of eight-year-old whores, morphine needles, and armies of violent thugs in uniform; a fanged and cloaked superman with a ravenous hunger for blood was hardly out of place.

In the shadows I could hear Daniel suckling.

I walked up, puffing on my cigarette and blowing smoke rings into the dimness. "You really shouldn't keep drinking after they die," I said casually.

The coat-check girl's body hit the ground with a wet thud. Daniel glared at me, then rolled his eyes in shivering pleasure, his blood-rimed fingers steepling and clawing at nothing. His beard glistened like black oil and my silk undershirt bore a vivid stain. "But why? It's still hot; it's still good," he moaned. "I can feel it going into me. Oh . . . so glorious . . . She's been drinking peppered vodka and eating black toast with honey and jam. . . . She's in love."

"She's dead," I reminded him.

Daniel stroked his beard, then sucked his fingers. "How do you resist killing them? How can you restrain yourself?" He seized the cigarette from me and drew on it avidly, his face falling in disappointment when his body refused to react to the smoke. Poor thing.

"It comes with time and willpower. You will learn it. You will learn it all." I snatched the cigarette back and tossed it away. His eyes drank in my movements. I slid neatly into his outstretched arms and kissed the last traces of blood from his neck. I could taste the pepper, the drugs and hormones and pleasure of the girl; he had not hurt her at all. Instinct guided him indeed.

"I could keep killing all night," he whispered, locking his arms around me, kissing me on the lips. How wonderful he felt, the previous potential blossomed into absolute perfection. Waves of energy flowed between us, measured through our heartbeats, our breaths swirling in a loop. Hours ago he did not even exist; now he was fantasy made flesh.

His eyelashes fluttered like moths against my forehead, his spine arching and shoulders rolling with autonomic ecstasy. "Oh, Orfeo, let's keep going! Let's drink our way through Berlin; let's go places we've never been; let's challenge the sunrise; let's fly!"

And in my heart I sang songs of praise. I was no longer alone.

So Much Darker Nearing Dawn

Now I was the tutor.

Our life together did not rapidly change, in outward appearance, after that September weekend, except that Daniel had grown inexplicably even more beautiful, attractive, dynamic, seductive; also, he was no longer seen during daylight hours at all, conducting all his "business" at night. In artistic Berlin, this was not particularly unusual; even wholesome Haus Vaterland stayed open until three. His intense pallor (even more pronounced than my own) was the height of underground fashion, without need of paint or powder. And Daniel had never been a sun-worshiper; there was no abrupt transition from browned to pale. It simply appeared that he had reached the zenith of the ideal nightlife complexion and the midnight lifestyle, as he had no need to work, with me and my bottomless wallet at his beck and call. "Lucky bastard!"

None of his massive circle of acquaintances and half-enemies could specify what had changed within old

Danny Blum; he just looked *better*, somehow. Most of the girls assumed that it was the florescence of true love. Danny had never been seen with anyone for as long as he had been with me. I was happy to accept the credit for improving his looks.

In a way, it had been a transformation born of true love. But true love did not mean what I had always thought it meant.

I did not give up my apartment; neither did Daniel relinquish the Dummschwallen, which I happily paid for. I was glad for him to have somewhere else to go besides the café down the street and my bathtub. I heartily and sincerely encouraged his enthusiasm for the little theater. I made sure that he always had something to do, remembering my long stretches of Parisian boredom, broken only by hideous self-reflection, savage acts, and needless emotional involvements.

The Dummschwallen venue, after several months of inactivity, began booking musicians, poets, dancers, amateur films, and experimental theatricals. Daniel launched himself back into the cause of creative expression with a vengeance I had not seen but had been typical of his life before. If one could not get a booking elsewhere in Berlin, the Dummschwallen would eagerly provide; the place was crawling with a massive variety of nontalent. The awfulness of the performers became part of its appeal, and it was typical to have the audience hissing and shouting abuse, often degenerating into destructive brawls that spilled onto the street.

Compared to them, Daniel's poetry recitals, singing, and piano improvisations were exquisite, and of course his charisma could not be denied. He developed a cadre of regulars who always showed up with alcohol and opium pipes and watched him in silent devotion. He was mad poet and showgirl in one body, a creature of extraordinary magnetism, and best of all, it didn't cost anything. I know that if he had charged admission, these regulars would gladly have paid anything he asked.

I was hopelessly ensnared myself. I felt almost as if I were leashed, or rather, that I held the leash of a rampaging lion, with no choice but to keep holding on, though I was dragged to and fro. Even when I attempted to create time for myself, to work on a painting of the view of the Tiergarten from my front window, I felt an inexorable pull to rush to Daniel's side, even if only to be in his presence. When I was without him, I was consumed with crippling melancholy and guilt that could be eased by a visit to St. Hedwig's, but never dispersed until I was near Daniel. He sometimes scowled at me when he saw me appear after making a huge fuss earlier in the evening, with my insistence on getting away from him for a while, but I felt his relief at beholding me again, and I took a tiny comfort in the fact that he shared my affliction.

But the comfort grew less and less, the melancholy more profound, his scowls blacker and blacker.

What, again, were you thinking, Monsieur Ricari?

As the Dummschwallen transformed and grew in infamy, and Daniel gathered the adulation to which he had always felt entitled, his true nature at last began to assert itself.

"I will not be your pet," Daniel told me. "I learned how pointless that can be from you yourself, my darling. From now on, we are equals."

"We are *not* equals," I informed him. "We shall never be. That's all there is to it. There is still much that you can learn from me, if you can set aside your pride for a moment."

"I am not like you, Ricari. You were a clueless shrinking violet when you were made, whereas I already know how to set aside soft, irrelevant feelings for the lesser beings I must consume. I mean, really; how can you eat a steak if you keep falling in love with the cow? How can you have kid gloves without killing soft, sweet, tiny baby goats? And I know you don't want to give up your precious gloves. It seems that you could learn a few things from me if you'd just set aside your own . . . sinful, damnable pride."

I hated when he said these things, because I found it difficult to answer him. It is hard to use faith and compassion as an argument against an opponent to whom these virtues are strangers. He simply had no conception of the true nature of kindness, and mistook standards of moral self-discipline as a form of punishment. And he saw in himself no misdeeds worthy of punishment.

"I give the poor little mundanes ecstasy," he explained, "if they are willing to embrace it. Isn't that better than a gray life filled with meaningless symbols?"

If I tried to press the point, he would silence me with his mouth and his body, reinforced by his lustful thoughts, a weakness to which I was particularly susceptible. For our lovemaking was undeniably magnificent. I had almost forgotten the power of sex with another one of my kind; added to the pure sensuality of flesh and fluid was a higher consciousness of self and other, a combining of wavelengths, of frequencies, to form a sublime harmony of souls. Even the struggle for eminent power brought us to greater heights of passion; try as he might, he could not physically overcome me if I did not wish to be overcome, and many pleasant hours of sport ensued as he attempted, again and again.

But as soon as our clothes were on, the struggle continued in a way that caused me no pleasure whatsoever.

He was no longer true to me.

He couched it in the context of scientific study, the hunger for experience, for the novel and extreme. At first, he tried to incorporate me.

"Don't you ever miss pussy?" He said the profanity in Italian. He must have plucked it from my mind.

"Oh, honestly, Daniel, must you be so crude?" I always laughed whenever he was obscene. It was not so much that I found it funny (which I did, somewhere in my darkest corners), but it was my instinct to laugh whenever I felt embarrassed around him. It felt safer than a merely shocked or appalled expression. "I . . . well, I never thought about it."

"Oh, come now, don't bother lying to me. I know you miss it. *I* miss it. It's only natural. Men and women are designed for one another." We lay in bed, already soaked and sweaty though the sun had barely set, his clean-shaven face tucked into my armpit, his fingers tapping out a delicate rhythm on the drum of my belly. "You were just thinking about it. It's been decades since you last tasted a woman's snatch. Don't you prefer that to my ass?"

"No," I said, lightly pinching the back of his neck. "I don't prefer anything in the world to that."

"But how would you know?" he asked, sitting up. His black hair hung in a shiny curtain around his face, pouring down to his shoulders like liquid. "It's not the same. Just because I put on silk stockings, it doesn't give me a pussy. Or tits, real tits! How long has it been since you squeezed a real tit? We have to go get a woman tonight and give her the business, so that we know for sure. I know *I'd* like to find out for sure."

The business. I grimaced. "I tell you that you are enough for me." *More than enough.*

He scoffed, one eye twitching. *Exactly, boyfriend; I'm too much for you.* "Well, I'm bored. I want to go get some kicks. Are you coming, or are you going to stay in bed all night, getting moldy?"

We barely had to go four blocks before we happened upon a "five o'clock lady," lovely, young, blond, still dressed in her pleasant and modest dress from the office, but with her stockings rolled down, a lot of freshly applied lipstick, and a certain uncomfortable air of expectation. I recognized this girl, and between my smooth introduction "Haven't I seen you before, perhaps at the cinema?" and Daniel's brash, direct "Twenty marks sound all right for the both of us?," we quickly found entrance to her room.

Yet I stood, staring out the window, fully clothed, while Daniel gave the girl "the business" on her small, neatly made bed. "C'mon, Ricari," Daniel grunted, still situated between the prostitute's thighs, "get in here, would you?"

"I don't really feel like it," I said. Yet, of course, my body was aroused, with its own involuntary reaction to the stimulation of the sounds, the scents, the peripheral view of Daniel's hips rutting, and the sensations flooding to me from Daniel's overheated mind. My penis was so hard it ached, and my mouth watered. But I did not want to join them.

"Are you just going to jerk off, or what?" Daniel demanded, flinging his damp hair over his shoulder.

"I don't *want* to."

"Do I still get twenty marks?" asked the girl breathlessly. Daniel changed her words into cries with a frenzy of thrusting.

"Careful; don't hurt her," I said.

"I'm paying her twenty marks," Daniel replied. "I can hurt her if I want to; can't I, baby?" He pinched her nipples with his fingernails.

"Just don't leave any marks," she said, shutting her eyes tightly. Daniel laughed and kissed her quite gently on the mouth and neck, brushing her breasts with his hair. The girl relaxed and smiled her pretty typing-pool smile.

Then he stood up and walked to me. "What's the matter?" he asked.

It was an effort to turn around and meet his eyes, and I kept my mouth closed; to speak would be to compromise myself. *I have to stand here and watch you, my only, my precious, my beloved, fuck someone else, that's what's the matter.*

Daniel smiled smugly and mocked me by speaking aloud. "If you were truly in control of me, you wouldn't let me, would you?" He chuckled, sat on the edge of the bed, and lit the three cigarettes in his mouth at once. He handed one to me and another to the girl, who dabbed at her vulva with a handkerchief. "You just can't stand that you're not enough for me, can you?"

The handkerchief came away dotted with blood. My eyes locked onto the tiny red smudges, and a moment's accumulated saliva ran from the corner of my mouth before I could stop it. My prick writhed against my silk drawers.

Involuntary reaction to stimulation; I didn't want her, I didn't want to be there, I did not feel lustful, and yet my sex responded in a way that my consciousness could not. But the moral, or perhaps only the emotional, part of my mind instantaneously lost control. Carnal hunger will do what lewdness alone cannot accomplish.

The girl cursed. "Oh, no, you made me sick," she said, complaining without anger. She stood up to wring out the handkerchief in her washbasin, and I closed the space between us in a single step.

"Allow me," I said.

She gazed into me, and I stroked her temples and slowly backed her toward the now-mussed bed, taking the lit cigarette from her hand and stubbing it out into a little porcelain tray shaped like a clamshell. The girl fell into a trance instantly, still wearing the same gentle half-smile, and delicately lay back onto the bed surface, bending her knees and opening her thighs. I did not need to look at Daniel to see the smirk on his face.

I drew my tongue along her damp, scented channel. Her being blossomed into my mind. Such a sweet girl, intelligent and humorous, selling herself to earn money for her boyfriend (standing right downstairs, watching for trouble from other pimps or police) so he could buy a suit, so they could marry at Christmastime. Her hips arched toward me and a quiet moan fluttered from her lips. The blood had just begun, forced from her womb.

"Do you still like the taste?" Daniel said.

"This is . . . different," I replied, faint with poorly re-strained desire, "this is . . ."

"Heaven?" he said, speaking the word I could not say.

If anything could have broken me away from my act, that was undeniably effective. I stood up and broke my glamor over the girl, wiping my mouth, rubbing my damp hands down the sides of my coat. She sat up and stared at me wild-eyed, struck with the knowledge of my true and uncanny nature, only to have Daniel enfold her thighs in his arms and, murmuring sweet nothings, drain her lifeblood through her sex.

I lost my senses. Half-convulsed with horror, I fled from the apartment and rushed to St. Hedwig. I was just in time for the Compline service, into which I threw myself with the vigor of the condemned. After the recitation of opening prayers, before confession, I found enough calm to look around myself. The usual old ladies were there, and I felt a weird kinship with them; the majority of them were there to get away from their drunk, nihilistic, mistreating husbands and have a few moments of peace, quiet, and order.

"The Lord be with you."

"And with your spirit."

It was a different universe, but with echoes of the other; all throughout the service, throughout my long, painful confession and the singing of a hymn, I could feel the paroxysms of lust and the slippery, curious inner contours of a woman, and the flashing, ecstatic release of her consciousness at the moment of death. *Heaven*, Daniel kept transmitting to me. I could hear his laughter. *Heaven up here, between a young Christian girl's legs. You haven't far to go. Will loving Jesus get you here? If not, he can go screw himself.*

I bowed my head until my neck bones cracked. How could I devote myself entire when I had no privacy, even in my own mind?

That was only the beginning.

When the Great Crash came and the streets filled with penniless men and women, a great many of them attended entertainments at the Dummschwallen, retaining its policy of free admission, as long as one brought one's own chair, as the old ones had long been smashed in brawls. The fights continued, becoming their own show in many ways; now they were not simply between the audience and the performers but among the audience themselves, and not merely over aesthetic revulsion but money, grudges, random explosions of frustrated rage.

(There were never any fights during Daniel's performances; the audience sat in attentive silence, hypnotized by him.)

At the end of each night, three or four people would stay behind, eager to meet their hero, some destitute and looking for a place to sleep for the night. "These are the chosen ones," he would say to me, and upon them he would practice bloodletting with restraint. Again, I had to encourage him; if I wanted him to stop slaughtering innocents, I had to train him in the alternative. At first, he had the same difficulties that I had, and we made many deposits in the already corpse-ridden Landswehr Canal, but by spring he could finally take a mouthful without letting his control slip away.

Once he accomplished this, he kissed each of the night's five survivors deeply on the mouth and sent him home. The next sunset, all five of them were there when Daniel and I arrived, hours before the time of the performance, milling around and speaking muted syllables to one another. "Will he be here?" "Of course he'll be here. I can tell." "So can I." "It won't be long." Daniel stepped out of the taxi and stared at them with pleased incomprehension, and the five young men surrounded him and began talking to him, all at once.

I took Daniel's arm and dragged him into the collaged coal chute. "What's that all about?" he asked me.

"They're attached to you," I explained with a sigh. "It's one of the annoyances you'll face."

"Like Liesl?" he asked.

I did not enjoy his habit of stealing my memories and then repeating them to me at the most uncomfortable moments. "Yes, like Liesl. And more so because you kissed them; I never kissed Liesl for that reason."

"And others, like the fact that she looked like a dog's dinner," he added cheerfully.

"Daniel, please." I crossed myself. "Don't kiss anyone unless you mean it. And by no means should you screw anyone unless you want them following you everywhere."

"So I could make them into my slaves?" His eyes widened.

"No—! No, Daniel. Please, don't."

"In other words, yes," he said with a grin. "Thank you, *sensei*. I do learn things from you after all." He kissed me quick on the mouth, then whisked back outside to the urgent chatter of the five young men.

By the end of the night, all five were dead, their blood inside Daniel, and Prenzlauer rubbish heaps stacked with corpses. "I didn't want them following me around" was Daniel's excuse. "I don't want anyone who's not useful. Or at least very beautiful; beauty is utility, as Keats says." He laid his ruddy hand on my cheek and fluttered his thick eyelashes at me.

"It's *truth*, you vicious, illiterate bastard!" I spluttered, knocking his hand aside, too angry to appreciate that I was being deliberately provoked. His response was breezy.

"My parents were quite married, thank you very much. And I hope you know that I wouldn't keep you around if you weren't useful."

"You couldn't be rid of me if you tried."

"And oh, how I've tried!" he snapped.

"Yes, you have," I said, suddenly exhausted, tired of carrying stinking dead bodies, worn out from the strain of trying to remain calm in Daniel's presence. "You try and try. And I try, too. But you should know as well as I that we are together and we must remain that way."

"I refuse to accept that," he said. He stepped away from me, a haloed silhouette against the rising indigo dawn, and held his hand, palm out, toward me. "We can do as we please. Sleep on your own today, God-shit-whore Mary. Go home and jerk off to that ugly naked man on your cross. It is Sunday, after all."

"You—blasphemous monster!" I screamed at him. "Go to Hell!" I threw my cigarette case at him, flipping and flashing in the streetlight, and one of the corners struck him squarely in the chest, next to his heart, so deeply that it lodged in the flesh.

He stared down at it and pulled the case free; dark

blood rimed its smooth gold-plated edge and ran down the front of his dirty white vest. The pain staggered him, and nearly staggered me with the sudden force of its profound truth. It returned me to my senses.

But before I could apologize, he had launched himself at me with a roar of fury, his fingers outstretched. His claws tore at the skin of my face but did only superficial, stinging damage; but the force of his attack knocked me to the street and crushed the breath from my lungs. Once I was on the ground, he punched me in the mouth, breaking my front teeth onto my soft palate.

I threw him away from me and turned over, coughing the loose teeth out. I picked up the teeth, holding my overbite in my hand, staring with dizzy eyes as the teeth disintegrated into foul-smelling, colorless slime. Daniel lay quite still, ten or so meters away, his body on the sidewalk and his face in the gutter. I walked over to him, shaking with shock, trying not to suck the bare space in my mouth, applying pressure with my tongue. My mouth filled with blood again and again. I turned him over; his forehead had a deep purpling welt where he had hit the lamppost, his eyes glazed, his arms and neck flopping limply. His mind stuttered and could not balance itself.

I kissed him and pushed my blood into his mouth.

I half-carried him inside the Dummschwallen and settled him on his side on the stage. He blinked and stared into the darkness, so much darker nearing dawn than in the dead of night. Slowly, his thoughts regained their form and his pain ebbed, the relief soothing my own pain.

"May God forgive you," I whispered, brushing his hair from the fading bruise on his temple.

I left the theater and went home, tearing over the

rooftops as I tried, in vain, to leave my distress behind me.

When I woke up, Daniel lay next to me, unconscious and cadaverous still, his cold bones tucked around me and his lips pressed against my arm.

Simple Justice

The turmoil of my emotions was echoed in the nightlife of Berlin.

Clubs and dance halls closed left and right, choked out of existence by lack of available money for either the owners or the patrons. At first I paid little attention, as my stable Swiss income was not tied to American interests, but it became more than academic as I witnessed the growing misery and desperation of the common man, embodied in the battles at the Dummschwallen. Though the talent booked was of a much higher caliber, as the opportunities at pleasanter, paying venues diminished, no performer got so much as five minutes of uninterrupted time before a fight would break out in the audience. Through my mental control, none of these fights would grow to lethal intensity inside the theater itself, but on more than one occasion the fight would take itself out onto the street and end in a savage beating or a stabbing. One night a pugnacious, loudmouthed anarchist was baited into taking a swing at a young thug in a homemade SA uniform, whereupon the thug and his Nazi companions escorted the anarchist outside and kicked his head in.

Daniel, in an orange satin gown and straw sombrero, watched the whole proceedings with a laugh and good cheer. "Let loose your animal natures!" he bellowed over the screams of the scattering, panicky audience. "It is the only thing that will save you as Berlin is razed to the ground!"

"You disgust me," I said to him, rushing over to the anarchist. The SA thugs had run away, laughing and shouting allegiance to the Fatherland. "Are you going to allow that kind of trash in your theater?"

"Why not? I let any other old trash in. Transvestites, dogcatchers, whores, Jews, addicts . . ."

"How can you say that?" I turned the anarchist over gently, but the man was dead, and his mouth spurted fresh scarlet over my bare hands. "How can you say things like that when you yourself are a Jew?" *And a whore, and an addict . . .*

Daniel glared as though I had just spit on his dress. "Shut your hole, Ricari! You don't know anything about it!"

"I know what I got from your own mind," I said grimly, licking my hands clean before I knew what I was doing. "You are a Jew, your father is a Jew, and you can't change that by squawking about it, any more than putting on a dress changes you into a woman."

His face contorted with fury. "I am *not* a Jew!" he hissed.

I raised my eyebrows. "I don't see what difference it makes, since you don't believe in it anyway."

"It makes a difference because it isn't the truth. I am not a Jew, I was never circumcized, and you can't make me into a Jew just by saying that I am or that my father was."

"Was?" I repeated, looking up at him. Though he

tried to look away and shut me out, I saw it all in his mind clearly, like a hopelessly complicated photograph, partially rubbed out but with the details intact. His staunchly capitalist and resourceful progenitors, the Jewish cobbler and the Lutheran schoolteacher, too dull and preoccupied to bother with anything so abstract and unproductive as religion, and their only son, their brilliant, beautiful, talented, difficult son, who would not be raised as a Jew, as a Christian, would not be raised to worship anything but innovation, Berlin, and himself. Certainly, he did not worship either of them, nor honor them; rather, he despised them, for their lack of passion, their lack of vision, their commitment to an increasingly irrelevant artisan-class status quo. Their desire for him to be a shoemaker, or an upholsterer, or a tailor, or a professor or a shop owner, or anything that would make him and his family a solid living, were slaps on the bottom of his ingenuity. Though he had never been beaten as I had been, he still saw himself as viciously persecuted, misunderstood, abused, a pariah!

"You *are* a Jew, you know. . . . The blood of Judah runs through your veins whether or not you've ever read the Torah. You don't have a choice in the matter," I said, smirking nastily. "Now, what would you do if your Nazi friends found out?"

"They won't find out," he said, glancing at the dead anarchist with distaste. "And if they did, I'd hand them their dicks. You think I'm afraid of those ass-lickers?" Daniel threw his hat to the ground. "You think I'm afraid of anything? I'm in a dress and heels, my love; I have gone way past fear."

He was still able to wring a grudging smile from me.

His painted lips twisted with disgust. "They are terrified of *me;* you know they hate queers even more than they hate Jews, and it doesn't take a blood test to see that I'm not like the other boys. I'll show you a thing or two. Let's go find those hypocritical little balls of shit and I'll show you how afraid I am."

We were only able to find one of the SA thugs, standing alone at the Bahnhof, waiting for a streetcar going south; separated from his comrades, I could see that he was just a youngster, maybe seventeen at most, his fresh, beardless face and furzy brown hair naked and vulnerable in the night air. I lost my stomach for vengeance, but Daniel slinked up to him on the platform, the little spangled heels of his shoes tapping with a woman's delicate uncertainty. Daniel turned him around with a light touch on his arm, "Excuse me," then thrust his hand into the boy's abdomen.

"Are you afraid?" said Daniel softly to the boy, twisting his arm. The boy gurgled helplessly, his eyes wide. "I have a secret. I'm a Jew. Bet you couldn't tell." Daniel took back his hand, letting the gutted boy fall to the concrete. He held up his glistening arm toward me. "Are you hungry, darling?"

In a moment Daniel was beside me, his unbloodied arm around me. "Darling, darling, don't cry. It is simple justice, is it not?" He gazed at me with concern, sucking his claws clean and tracing the contours of my face with his damp fingertips.

"I hate you." My voice came out muffled by Daniel's shirt, but I knew he heard me; his heart gave a jerk inside him and his mind read as vertigo. I had never said that to him before, a statement as powerful and profound as its opposite. "Get away from me."

But he pretended that he hadn't heard. "What's that, my love? I hate so much to see you in distress. Don't let those stupid bullies get to you. I know what you need. You need to get laid. Immediately. Come on, let's go; the night is still so young." He held me, shunting away my repulsion, leaving me resigned and pliable.

In the back room of a beer garden, closed for the

night, four women and two men tangled themselves in difficult, laughing configurations upon a giant pile of odd-shaped, mismatched cushions. The air was perfumed lightly with jasmine and rose water, but I could not wash the images of violence from my mind, no matter how hard I thrust my cock into Daniel's ass. I muttered thoughtlessly, "Bloody Jew. Bloody Jew."

"Oh yes," Daniel purred in reply. "That's right."

I rolled my eyes in an ecstasy indistinguishable from pain, my eyes streaming, flooding my cheeks, biting back my moans. I had no right to make any sound of pleasure, for I felt none.

One of the women broke away from the tangled group and draped her warm, sleek, round body against my back, wiping away my tears with the back of her hand. "Don't be sad," she whispered, nibbling my ear. "Don't think about tomorrow."

"It is tomorrow," I said, seizing her soft little hand and kissing it, pressing her body between mine and Daniel's, "it is already tomorrow."

I could see the glow of buildings burning from my bedroom window, but I watched for only a few moments before I drew my curtains closed. I stood alone in my flat, holding myself, cold and shuddering all over, listening to the shouting and clamor of men, some fighting the fire, some standing aside and watching with grim satisfaction. This was no accident; this was arson. Someone had torched the Reichstag. Some Communist; some madman with an agenda, with encouragement, with assistance. I tasted the aroma of the truth from the disordered minds of the men standing before the fire, their thoughts tangling and shouting in the void, with no one hearing them but me and similar savage, sensitive beasts.

I desperately needed to taste blood. It had been

months since I'd had so much as a swallow, and my body functioned perfectly well, but I had more and more difficulty each day keeping my mind where I was and not letting it disperse over the city, settling where there was the greatest suffering and turmoil, as though distress created a vortex that drew me there. And though I had not seen him for days, I wanted to lock Daniel out of my mind, but I hadn't the strength. I would need strange blood for that, new fresh blood, human blood.

I hungered for the taste of terror as though it were salt.

I sank down onto the floor beside my bed, contemplating crawling under it, with my hands over my ears, over my temples, trying to shut out the madness, but it permeated me utterly. The rancor and spite and uncertainty soaked me like water into a sponge.

And Daniel approached, as swiftly as the wind.

I held myself tighter. *Go away*, I thought but his distress swamped the distress of strangers and unfurled me from myself. Something was terribly wrong with my child, and I could not ignore it.

He crashed into my flat, his face stark, the door swinging from its warped hinges.

"What is it?" I said in a dull voice. The door hinges had long since been hopelessly damaged.

"Come with me to the Dummschwallen," he said. His eyes examined my face. "God-shit, look at you; you look like a wraith. No matter. Come on. It will be remedied soon."

Prenzlauerberg glowed on the horizon, a smaller blossom loosed from the brilliant orange bouquet of the Reichstag, still burning; bureaucracy burns slow and hot. But as we left it behind, I recognized the location of the smaller fire: the block of warehouses and crumbling buildings that contained the Dummschwallen.

Only the theater burned for the time being; the fire

was quite fresh, and unaccelerated, but quickly and easily consuming the friable wood of the furnishings and the trunks of costumes stacked against the side walls. It had taken Daniel and me less than five minutes to arrive here. No firefighters had come, all of their attention being absorbed by the government building; left on its own, the entire block would soon burn.

"Nazis," said Daniel. "Stupid damn Nazis." At first I thought he was merely assigning responsibility for the arson, but then I saw, trembling with fear and yet immobile, three of the young bullies who had made the Dummschwallen a battleground for the last few years, standing so close to the door to the coal chute and the fire that sweat poured down their faces, mingling with their terrified tears.

"Drink up," Daniel said to me, his voice tight. "I saved them for you. I already had my three." He turned away then and ran for the telephone booth at the end of the street.

I moved the one with the smoothest face and the clearest eyes a few feet away from the building, and plunged my will into his mind. *Explain.* He shrieked in pain, but it could barely be heard over the roar of the fire. He babbled desperately, "We had to get back at the decadent pervert Danny Blum . . . he's a monster who rapes little girls and boys . . . the Reichstag has everyone occupied across town . . . we knew we could eliminate this infestation of depravity and clean up this part of town . . . this is part of the Fatherland and needs cleaning up . . ."

I silenced him with a single swipe of my claws across his throat.

I lost myself so completely in draining the young man's blood to the depths of his veins that the other two men perished, their clothing catching fire from sooty sparks from the roof. Daniel had frozen them in place, and they had to stand there, screaming, burning, their clothes searing their skins. I threw the dead man against his comrades until they lay in a broiling heap, the stench of their cooking flesh overwhelming the scent of burning varnish, wool, photographs of Theda Bara, tubes of melting lipstick, the memories, the jism spilled, the exhalations of fulfillment. All of it burned, as hot as a furnace, catching the coal dust still in the ceiling beams and swept behind the walls.

Daniel stood across the street, the wind whipping his long hair and the tails of his frock coat, his mouth working spasmodically, chewing his lower lip with one of his fangs, his eyes dry and hard. I approached but did not touch him, and he did not look at me. "This is a terrible tragedy," I said quietly. "I am very sorry for your loss. It is everyone's loss; it is the end of an era."

He merely nodded, and his expression did not change; but despite the strength and vitality of three young men coursing through his veins, his spirit struggled to remain intact and not follow the dead men down to oblivion and into God's hands.

"The whole city will burn," he murmured. "Every brick, every stick of furniture, every toy, every ball gown, every factory, every idea. Berlin will be razed and the ground sown with salt. I will it."

"Daniel, no," I reproached gently. He turned his eyes to me, the flames' reflection leaping on the gleam of his eyeballs, and stared into me, wrenching something out of my soul as he had disemboweled the young SA thug on the Bahnhof platform. I wrapped my arms around myself again, sinking almost to my knees on the sidewalk. The fire crews had arrived at last, and they ran right past us as though we weren't there. And Daniel turned away with a twitch of his coat and walked toward the city, in the general direction of my apartment.

As soon as I could collect myself, I followed him, flit-

ting over the rooftops to avoid the roadblocks and police on the route home. When I came in, Daniel had just
finished drawing a bath. He and I undressed and
stepped into the warm water together.

I had not clearly determined what Daniel had accessed inside me; it just felt like pain, like dull nails digging into my heart without puncturing it. In the
bathtub he was silent and unsmiling, but he washed my
sooty hair and neck gently with a soapy cloth, then
pulled my back against his chest and held me. "It is I
who should be holding you," I protested without conviction, enjoying too much the sensation of being enfolded in his arms and the blood-fed warmth of his
body next to mine. It had been a long time since he had
been so tender; it felt like an eternity of despising him,
despairing of ever being free of him, searching my
heart for the last scraps of tolerance.

We lay in the water until it had gone quite cold. He
kissed my temple, next to my ear, and squeezed me a little. "I almost walked in," he confessed softly. "I almost
walked in, but I couldn't; I realized that I couldn't do
that to you."

At once I felt the rusty nails in my heart again, digging deeper, seeking the center; I almost wished my
heart would be pierced at last, to relieve the pressure.

"I saw it too," he said, kissing me again. "I saw her . . .
walk into the fire." He had pulled the pure pain out of
me, comparing it with his own. And now I witnessed it
again myself, Maria's skull outlined in flames, the smell
of her blood burning, magnified and distorted through
the lens of Daniel's own rage and loss. I felt again the
dull stretching trauma of Georgie pulling away, leaving
a thread so tenuous between us that it was all but invisible. How did she do it? For she was only half my
mother; and the other half flared and disintegrated with
a scream of gases escaping charring flesh.

I shook so hard I splashed the water, and Daniel held me tighter until I stopped trembling. "I knew it would be the only way I could ever leave you, love; I should have to walk into the fire myself. I can't get away otherwise."

The nails in my heart reached their goal, but rather than relief, it released poison, flowing throughout my body, inundating my tattered shreds of tolerance, my compassion, my purity. My soul was stained as black as the smoke rising from the city. *You'd walk into a burning building to get away from me?* It was a startling shock to realize that he despised me, and longed for escape from me as much as I did from him.

"But I didn't do it," he added. "I didn't do it because I love you, not because I felt any fear or any connection to this world. I thought of you, and I thought of your Maria, and I decided that I couldn't do it. I held the young men there and went away, and came and fetched you so I wouldn't do it, and I'm not sorry." He crushed his lips to my ear and went on in a painful whisper. "I won't leave you, my love. I'll never leave you. You know that. Wherever you go, I will be with you. Forever. You made sure of it, didn't you? I will always be with you." He kissed me again and again.

"Yes," I answered, wet and cold, "and I will be with you."

There followed a paroxysm of something resembling compassion from Daniel. Now that he had finally experienced profound loss, for more or less the first time in his short life, he became extremely interested in the injustices of the world around him, and attentive to the dangerous new face of Germany.

He began by tracking down anyone who he knew was a Communist and, if they had not already been arrested, taking their lives before any of them could be discovered, as they no longer had any safe place in Berlin, or a way to escape it. And, of course, he shared his roomfuls of huddled, fear-paralyzed victims with me so I could feed without killing.

This is Daniel Blum's version of compassion.

As could have been anticipated, the authorities did nothing about the burning of the Dummschwallen. It had operated on the fringes of legitimate nightlife for so long, and the trauma of the burning of the Reichstag was so overwhelming, that it might not have ever existed at all, let alone burned to the foundations. There were no reports in the newspapers, and the police never even questioned anyone, despite the deaths of six promising young German soldiers. Only the local residents of that Prenzlauer district, and Daniel's surviving regulars, had any idea that anything had happened. I allowed myself a single night of curiosity, standing on the street corner where Daniel had dragged the corpse of the Sträubenhund gangster, and watching a bedraggled, chastened handful of young men and women approach the Dummschwallen, wanting their fix of secondhand opium smoke and Thursday-night transvestite splendor, only to find water-soaked charcoal, rope barricades, and crude racist graffiti. After that, I could not bear to return to the area; I absorbed too much of the confusion and heartbreak, and found it difficult to stop weeping for the rest of the night.

Berlin had had the wind knocked out of it, and only the puerile, superstitious Chancellor Hitler seemed to know how to react. I saw the people turning toward him, seeking something definite, a last chance to restore devastated pride, someone who would do something. Anything. But the violence did not stop; it was merely redirected, and that was good enough for the man on the street.

I struggled to fight off a sensation of creeping dread, and prayed daily that the world would come to its senses. This madness could not last—could it?

One evening, as I lay in bed observing Daniel awakening in my arms, contemplating the freshening, ivory contours of his face, he opened his brilliant eyes wide, tearing away from me and seizing his clothes from where he had flung them that morning. "Orfeo, come with me. We have to go to my mother and father," he said.

His agitation was palpable, and I swiftly dressed myself, asking in a calming tone, "Why now? Are they Communists?"

Daniel snarled at me. "Of course they're not Communists, stupid. They're in danger and I can feel it—it's as if they are calling to me—we have to go to them now."

"But you hate your parents!"

"Not now, Ricari. Don't you understand? No, of course you don't; you deserted your parents and never looked back, didn't you? At least I disliked my parents; you ran off while you still loved them." His voice broke. I felt it myself, too, now, through him; their estranged son was central in their thoughts in the manner of the last panicked thoughts of one who looks into certain doom. I had never felt such a thing from my own family, nothing so definite; perhaps they had never given me a second thought. Daniel took my hand before I could pursue further self-pity. "Come with me, please. I cannot be alone right now, as much as I'd love to leave you here. I need you with me."

Out and out we went, to the unfamiliar outlying area of Weissensee, where I had never even thought to go. In the spreading darkness of the evening, the streets were oddly quiet, waiting for something, recovering from something. The sounds of police sirens echoed, their sources hidden, following us, surrounding us. The city had been slapped, and was still reeling from the shock, everyone terrified and mistrustful of everyone else.

I recognized the pleasant neighborhood street with its trees and connected row-houses from Daniel's memories of his childhood. It seemed a continent away, a mere four miles across Berlin. In the darkness (Daniel's memories always involved sunlight, as if the skies had never dared rain on his superlative head) I could see that the windows at the front of the entire row of houses had been smashed, the doors swinging from fractured hinges. All the windows of the automobiles on the street had also been smashed, the broken bricks perched atop masses of shattered glass on the seats like a perverse jewelry display.

"We're too late," Daniel said, kicking over an empty cigar-box in the road. "They're gone. Why couldn't we have gotten here sooner? I'd have . . . I'd have . . ."

"They're not dead," I concluded hopefully. His distress looped my innards into knots.

"No; worse. They are in prison. They are being taken to the camp. In the water tower. I can barely feel them . . . I haven't thought about them in so long. I'm not sure it *is* them. It could just as well be someone else from this street. They were all Jews. This entire block has always been Jewish. Everybody knows that this is where the Jews live. My papa, my uncle Alphonse and his hideous, barren dog-faced wife, Kaspar the greengrocer . . ."

The smell of panicked sweat and truck exhaust still hung in the damp, cold air, but faintly. "It wasn't long ago. But it was before you awoke. We couldn't have gotten here in time. . . ."

"Couldn't we?" Daniel asked, his voice distant. I saw him as a child, standing in this same spot, experiencing a new thing called remorse. *Papa, I would have killed for you. They don't know you. I know you're the best papa in the world, and they don't know anything.*

The wail of the police sirens grew in pitch. "Let's please leave," I said nervously, "there's nothing we can do here . . . let's just . . ." I went to him and took his glacial hand and slipped it into my shirt, next to my heart, but I, too, was cold. Abruptly, the only logical course of action suggested itself, in the space between his cold flesh and mine. "Let's go warm up," I suggested. He met my eyes, and the corner of his mouth twitched up for only a second. "Yes. There's plenty to do out there. It is a matter of simple justice."

Knives Out

It was difficult to pinpoint in the midst of the experience, with so much other appalling chaos occurring, but
now I am able to see that it was at this time that things
began to go irrevocably wrong.

Partly, it had to be that I simply wasn't resting correctly, unable to gain that sweet, regular thoughtlessness, the precious daily escape from care, that is
essential for rational thought, the separation between
the inner experience and that without. I fell asleep with
my head crowded with ideas and memories, both innate
and foreign, every morning—that is, when I was able to
fall asleep at all. I spent whole days awake, seated at the
window, listening to the city and the minds of the people passing by on the street outside. I had always done
this idly, in those quiet hours spent painting while
Daniel engaged in one of his constant baths, but now I
could hardly control my compulsive and exhausting sur-
veillance. I did not want to be privy to the thoughts of
anyone living in Berlin, let alone the officers, bankers,
and merchants who occupied the luxury apartments

bordering the Tiergarten. The ones that weren't secretly thrilled that Germany was at last being put onto the right track hid their apprehension and fear behind gray tweed suits and briefcases lined with numbers and secrets. The rest of Berlin was no better: petty, craven, spiteful, sorrowful, from the smallest schoolchild to the very few surviving elderly, and even the tender feelings of filial devotion and young romance only reinforced my alienation from those emotions.

I grew weary of communicating in the brutal German language—hearing it, reading it, thinking it—that tongue which I had once savored as the most erotic sound in the world. I sought some small refuge in reading Italian, Latin, and French texts, whatever I could find in bookshops. But I had grown all too familiar with much of it in my time lurking in the library at the Villa Diodati, and I could not reread these same books without losing myself in reminiscence and being paralyzed with nostalgia, or with regret.

Perhaps because of this, combined with the attempted denial of the German tongue, I could not pay as much attention to what Daniel did. I slumped silently in a chair, curled around a book, while a parade of beautiful girls invaded my home with their giggles and perfume and furs. Daniel brought around woman after woman, so many that I lost track of them all, sometimes feeding on them, sometimes having intercourse with them, sometimes merely conversing and exchanging notes and information. I recognized some of them as chorus girls and dance-hall girls from the times before the troubles; no doubt they had fallen upon hard, hard times. But before they could fall too far, Daniel came around to pick them up.

He was trafficking these women, selling their sexuality and beauty to those few men who could afford the kind of girls who resembled film stars. They were the most elite of the elite, the lovely and vivacious ladies that any lonely railroad millionaire or visiting American gangster could proudly display on his arm in public, and later take home and ravish.

Of course, Daniel's whores did not merely sell their bodies for him; they adored him with the unnatural attachment that our kind produces without effort. He treated them with respect, sensitivity, and gentleness, buying them lavish dresses and diamonds, paying rent for their rooms, calling them "darling" and "beautiful," never striking or depriving them of any need. He had no need for such crude methods; any displeasure he experienced would be painfully transmitted to them without a single touch. And they had to be the most well-protected call girls in Berlin, but for those times when Daniel's own hunger or short temper overcame him. The girls knew his true nature as well as their own, accepting the risk gladly; it was preferable to the alternative. At least with Daniel, they had silk stockings and peppermint creams and the rent infallibly paid.

I sat in my chair and stared out the window and did not speak. I had become invisible once more. Even Daniel rarely said anything to me, usually without speaking aloud. But though he would spare a gentle caress or a kiss before he went out into the night, he had to keep himself busy, give himself things to do, so that he would not be tempted to brood.

His father was dead of injuries, his mother shipped off to no one knew where. I didn't know which was worse—the fact that it had happened, or the fact that it was so commonplace. The same had happened to one of Daniel's girls' father, a bookseller with a half-forgotten criminal record who had stubbornly refused to remove *The Communist Manifesto* from his window display. But they kept going. The humans, and Daniel, kept laughing and talking and screwing and dancing. It made me sick.

After a hellish three consecutive days, in summer, without being able to sleep, I took a cold bath in the late afternoon and slid into my empty bed, still mussed and fragrant from the lovemaking lesson that had lately taken place in it. I closed my eyes and visualized my mind folding itself closed, like a vast sheet of paper, one corner at a time. As my own mind folded itself away, smaller and smaller, the other minds appeared behind it.

Daniel was at the Hotel Adlon, on the roof, watching as two of his girls serviced a British diplomat in the backseat of a limousine. In one hand he held a stopwatch, at which he glanced periodically. His concentration was focused on his mother, trying to locate her, contact her, vowing to save her and slaughter anyone in his path. I could not discern any reply.

That was not what I sought, so I returned to myself. I sank into the soft feathers of the mattress, my limbs heavy, my head a lead weight cleaving the pillow. I chilled the enfolding bedclothes with my body, the grain of the fabric as soft as freshly turned soil.

Where was my own mother? Maria my mother, who had borne me? She of the crystal-blue Roman glass eyes? In the earth, no doubt, becoming a part of the earth, as I shall do.

Daniel stood immobile over me, towering like a cypress, his hair fluttering in the breeze and his trunk shielding me from the sun as I lay at his feet. I stared at the golden horizon, certain that at any moment Mamma would appear as a female silhouette on the horizon, wearing a smile, but I did not know if her hair would be dark or blond.

I lay at Daniel's feet until he took root inside me. I felt it distinctly throughout my body—shoots poking me, penetrating me, splitting me apart—and I felt that I had, at last, accessed the mind of my own mother, lying in her grave, with a tree planted over it. The tree consumed her heedlessly, waving its arms in the wind, flowering and fruiting, fed by flesh, making a mockery of the brief concerns of humanity.

This was eternity; a beauty born of brutality.

I woke parched with thirst, half blind, flailing out with my arms in an attempt to claw my way out of the dream of decay. I had had this fever for what seemed like years, and no matter how much water I drank or how often I was bled, I had not improved. Every glint of light, no matter how tiny, and every half-perceptible sound scraped across my senses.

"I am thirsty," I mumbled through numb lips, clutching the doctor's shirt. "Give me a drink of water . . . please . . ." Then louder, shouting, demanding: "Please!"

It was not the doctor's blouse I held in my fingertips, but a finer, softer fabric, enclosing a dark, thin young man with high cheekbones and red lips, who stared at me strangely, speaking to me in a garbled nonsense. He drew back his lips to reveal sparkling white pointed teeth. I gasped in terror. Some unholy creature had come to finish me off!

I leapt from the bed and backed against the wall, naked, my hands held out before me in striking position. The room lay in disarray, with unfamiliar clothes strewn across the chairs and the writing desk, and a dozen empty green glass wine bottles lined up against the wall. On the wall, opposite the bed, hung a crucifix with a small gray-furred animal nailed to it. Dried ichor ran out of the animal, down the cross and the wall, into and a paper cup nailed under it, onto which was scrawled in thick black ink. *Hic est sanguinus mei.* I stared at this blasphemy, astonished and sickened.

"Where have you taken me?" I demanded. "Where is this?"

The young man did not move to attack, or even pursue me from the bed, but rather blinked at me with a mixture of confusion and annoyance. He said something else that I could not understand, and held up his hand as if to reassure me, but the sight of his long, thin, spidery fingers, tipped with animal claws, struck panicky terror into my heart. I ran to the door but collapsed before I could get there; the consuming fear, combined with fever, had taken its toll on my strength.

As I prepared to give myself up for lost, the man at last said something to me in French. "Don't you know where you are?"

"No," I begged, "take pity on me, don't hurt me."

"I won't . . . *hurt* you," he replied gently and slowly, somewhat indignantly. "Don't you know me, my love?"

Closing my eyes, I shook my head. "For all I know, you are just a fancy—a hallucination! A demon, sent to torment me, to punish me—" I gave a little gasp, gulping air.

The man looked at me with confusion and pity. "You have lost your mind, *monsieur*. Look at your hands; you are the same as me, and if I am a demon sent to torment you, then you are a demon sent to torment me."

I did not look at my hands. "Forgive me. I am not from here. I have a fever," I said, trying to speak rationally, "and I am dying of thirst; can you not give me a cup of water?"

He came and knelt beside me, rolling up his sleeve and then, before my astonished eyes, deeply puncturing the vein at the inside of his elbow with a tiny penknife. I gaped as dark fluid beaded thickly on the surface of the skin, and my thirst mounted till I was nearly delirious. "To drink," he said. "It is not water that you need."

He placed one hand gently on the back of my head, guiding me toward him.

I put my mouth to him, shuddering with revulsion, and at once returned to myself, returned to my Berlin apartment, returned to Daniel in his silk "business" shirt, shuddering with sensual pleasure at the pricking of my teeth. "*Liebschen*," he purred, "you are cuckoo."

I licked my lips, still shuddering, and looked at him. "You *are* a demon," I told him in his native tongue. "I know one when I see one."

"That isn't very nice," Daniel replied mildly, his voice concealing his inner flare of irritation. "A demon wouldn't keep checking on you while you decided to sleep for eleven days."

"Eleven days?" I echoed. "To me it was a moment. I dreamt."

"I know; you can't hide them from me." He grinned at me, and I felt sickened. "But I figured you'd be hungry when you woke up, not amnesiac. You were speaking French! Extraordinary . . . Hey, don't scowl at me like that. I just saved your sanity; is that any way to look upon your savior?"

"My savior?" I laughed at him bleakly, pulling on the same clothing that I had worn for days previous, and stuffing my feet with their hideously elongated and clawed toes into shoes. I was a demon after all. I pointed at the crucifix. "Is this a message from my savior? A crucified sewer-rat?"

Daniel shrugged. "You weren't using it," he said.

I grabbed my coat and snatched the crucifix from the wall. The reek of the decomposing flesh on the rat filled my nostrils, and the dry, gutted contours of its body smeared my hands with foul liquid. "May the Lord forgive you," I whispered, and ran out into the street, ripping the rat from the cross and flinging its body into the gutter. I wrapped the slimy cross in a handkerchief and, shuddering with revulsion, slipped it into my coat.

I went by taxi to St. Hedwig's and searched the between-service quiet darkness of the church until I found a priest. I begged to confess, and the man of God obliged me, but when I was seated in the confessional, I could only say, "I have been having these dreams about my mother. She has been dead for over a hundred years. And I woke up today and didn't know where I was, only that . . . I only knew that I needed to escape."

"What is pursuing you, my son?"

I wanted to spit out "I am not your son; I am the son of succubi, I am the product of damnation," but that was Daniel's voice, coming from inside my head, his contempt infecting me. I could still smell his contempt seeping out from my coat.

Instead I told the priest, "My past. And I fear that it is stronger than I am."

The priest paused for a moment. "The important question to ask yourself is, is it stronger than you *and* the Heavenly Spirit together?"

I broke into a smile. "Thank you, Father."

"Ask Him for the strength. It will come."

"Thank you, Father, thank you. . . . I pray that my faith may never waver."

"It must not," the priest insisted. "Not in these times. Hold fast to your faith. Though youth and material possessions and even peace may pass away, as long as you have faith, you are never helpless, you are never alone, you are never powerless. And do not grieve for your mother; she is in God. . . . Did you say over a hundred years?"

"Yes, Father. It is true."

He made the funniest little noise, as if saying "Well, well!" and my smile felt as if it went around my head twice. "Indeed! Most unusual. The Lord be with you."

I left the confessional with a heavy sigh of relief, then went to the lavatory and held the crucifix under running water until the wood was clean again. It bore an indelible stain, though, as if the twisted, wooden Christ figure had indeed lost blood. I still felt triumphant, and I smiled as I slid the cross into my inside coat pocket.

I emerged from the lavatory and looked upon the two or three attendees of the last evening office, filing into the cathedral, their figures tiny and bent under the massive grandeur of the place. My blood craving had receded from a conflagration to a tolerable dull warmth, and I felt confident that I could stay for a while without making a victim, no matter how painlessly, of any of the churchgoers. And yet my heart sank when I realized that, of course, I would have to find someone else, somewhere else, to violate.

From nowhere I perceived an odd stab of pleasure, not at all the sort of sensation common to the little old ladies of St. Hedwig's "insomnia service," and I stared around the cathedral in search of the source of the sensation.

I did not have to search for long. Behind the altar, at the gorgeous marble crucifix, Daniel Blum stood, his trousers around his ankles, rubbing himself against the marble base of the statue.

As I watched with horror, he climbed onto the sculpture itself, lacing his legs around the base, craning his neck so that he could lick the pierced feet of the Christ. "Oh, Jesus, most holy," Daniel drawled in a lust-drunk mumble, "fuck me. . . . I know you're the greatest . . . the only Jew they'll tolerate in this old folks' home—"

I cried aloud, "Stop!"

The priests and the penitents all stared at me in astonishment, for I had not muted my voice, and the shout resounded throughout the church. Daniel turned and looked at me over his shoulder, teasingly, tossing his long, loose hair aside. "Don't you see what he's doing?" I demanded.

"Young man," said the priest who had taken my confession, "you will have to lower your voice; the service is due to begin."

"You don't see that?" I flung out my pointing finger at Daniel's quivering moon. The priest frowned at me a little. I blinked at them. Perhaps I was still mad; perhaps I had not recovered my senses at all. "I see him as clear as day! As clearly as I see you before me!" Daniel laughed and thrust his hips against the marble, then slid down and took his sex into his hand, stroking it furiously.

"The cross? Indeed, we all do." The priest put a comforting hand on my upper arm, but I flinched away from him.

"No," I said through gritted teeth, "that *man. On* the cross."

"My son, are you feeling all right? You look very pale." The priest took a closer look at me, doubting his spectacles, then staggered back, crossed himself, clutched his rosary, and kissed the cross. He had unmistakably seen my fangs.

But he had not seen Daniel. "Forget it," I said, staring into the priest's eyes until I knew that the moment had been erased. His mouth opened and closed silently. "Stay here. I will manage this alone."

"Ach, Jesus! Jesus!" Daniel half-laughed, half-moaned, spurting his copious semen onto the base of the statue, flinging loose droplets onto the altar. "It's the best I've ever had!"

Without bothering to conceal myself, I leapt toward him, and had collared him before he had a chance to recover from his orgasm or his blinding sense of ego. With another swift movement, I snatched him up and pulled him out of the church, soaring over the heads of the priests and old ladies, who gasped and screamed at the sight.

Daniel laughed even harder, disoriented, his trousers hanging from one ankle, outside on the brightly lit boulevard with dozens of motorcars going by. "This is the most fun I've had with you in years!" he declared. "Something to put a little color in your cheeks, right, Herr Ricari?"

It is very easy to break a man's jaw when one is shorter by a few inches. My fist, with the middle knuckle extended, contacted the cleft end of Daniel's chin, knocking him at least five meters down the sidewalk. A woman going by in a taxi stuck out her head and gaped, and I stared back at her, and without malice or intent, with only a focused spike of nervous energy, overloaded her optic nerves and struck her blind. Her shriek swooped and dove as she sped away into the city.

In the meantime, Daniel had picked himself up, kicking off his now-ruined wool gabardine trousers, hideous abrasions covering the side of one leg. "Is this what you want to do?" he asked me coldly, his voice crumbly through his distorted, hideously swollen jaw and lip. "Because I am more than happy to do this."

"You. Are. Trying. To provoke me. You have committed the most . . . heinous blasphemy . . . a truly foul and despicable act . . . the actions of an amoral monster. The world must be rid of you." My voice sounded strange to my ears.

He raised his bruised head in a gesture of clear-eyed defiance. "It will be, soon enough," Daniel replied, "but not as soon as it's rid of you." He approached carefully, one sidelong step at a time, arms hanging loosely at his sides. "You can't escape me."

I shot back, "And you can't defeat me."

More gawkers had slowed to stare at the man without

trousers, arguing in front of the Catholic church, and catcalls and whistles rang out from autombile chambers. I turned and walked away, keeping my fists clenched, until I reached a quieter side street, whereupon I leapt onto a rooftop and skimmed away, knowing that he would follow me, north, toward Prenzlauerberg, taunting Daniel with my thoughts. *Isn't the Dummschwallen over here? I heard that's the best show in town.*

That night, I would never make it; I had not gone more than a handful of blocks before Daniel appeared suddenly ahead of me at the edge of a roof, naked now, as luminescent as the moon on this starless, chilly night. His face had already healed completely. How much blood had he gorged upon while I had slept? Even he had lost track. "How does your God feel about you striking blindness whenever you feel like it? How does He feel about you deceiving your Father Confessor? Why are you running away? Shouldn't you believe that He will protect you no matter what, as long as you're honest? Perhaps that's your problem. Your God *knows* you're a hypocrite."

"At least I believe in God," I snapped back.

"I believe in God too. Me. I am God. I am the only God I'll ever need, the only one in who I need to believe, the only one I need answer to."

I sighed. "Fine. Worship yourself, but I demand that you stay out of St. Hedwig's. I will not tolerate your desecration of that place just to annoy me. I wonder why I do not see you desecrating synagogues; why not, Daniel? Could it be that underneath your professed autotheism, you are actually . . . a . . . ?" I shrugged and smiled a little. His face twisted in a bitter sneer. "Like your perfect papa, whom you despised and whom you betrayed? Betrayal comes naturally to you, does it not? Maybe because you're a . . . you know."

"You don't know anything."

"I only know what I get from your leaky mind. . . . My God, Daniel, you have no self-discipline; will you toilet-train yourself at last, or will you go on throwing your mental feces about? I am sick of smelling it. You shit in my mind, Daniel Blum. Your mind is a cesspool, a sewer, full of rotting half-chewed nonsense. I wish you had gone into the fire; I'd have been rid of you then."

All traces of his smug self-assurance had evaporated, and his proud stance had sunken a little, his eyes no longer completely meeting mine. I smiled to myself, enjoying the taste of his pain, and turned away, back toward home, hoping that our connection had been broken at last.

It was not.

From behind, Daniel locked his hands around my throat, and would have crushed my windpipe had I not put my foot against his shin to push him up and away. Instead, I more or less walked up his leg, his groin, and his stomach, simultaneously kicking him in the freshly healed jaw, pushing him away and twisting out of his grasp, landing on my hands and the balls of my feet. When he dove for me, I rolled away; he rolled the opposite direction and came to a crouch, paws down, head lowered, like a wolf.

"You bloody queer," he hissed, "that *hurt*."

"Just leave me alone," I said, enunciating clearly. "Go away."

"I'll see you dead first," he replied.

He hurled me from the roof of the building, dashing me to the pavement. I rolled into the impact, but my shoulder blade broke just the same and my shoulder separated with a clack. I could not swallow the pitiful howl that tore itself free from me and bounced through the concrete corridors of the alley. I slowly found my feet, then lost them again, the streetlamps a brilliant whirlpool sucking me down onto my knees.

Daniel landed beside me, almost silently, on his bare feet. The mottled bruises on his chin stood out in welts. He held out his hand to me, the palm glistening with fresh blood. "Let me help you," he said. I could not resist the lure of the blood, between the violent cravings of my own body and his psychic urgings taking advantage of my pain-weakened state. I clasped his arm and drank from the wound. I drank until his own legs failed and he collapsed beside me, eyelids fluttering and his body twitching as he lost his senses.

Then I walked away, leaving him where he lay and wiping my mouth with the back of my hand. The streets called to me; I held Daniel's ravenous, thoughtless hunger combined with the needs of my own depleted, injured body, and the first man I saw, a policeman sent to investigate the disturbance, fell to this appetite.

That same fate befell the next five people that I met on my way back to my apartment. By the time I arrived home, I was whole, and rational, and had even regained the capacity to hold my thoughts separate from those of the world, and more important, from Daniel's.

I rehung my crucifix upon the wall in its place, throwing the paper cup out the window and wiping the dried blood off the wall. As soon as I had given a prayer to Christ and St. Jude, I cleared my writing desk and began, in this rare and precious privacy, the serious consideration of my escape.

Battle

Where could I go to be able to escape Daniel?

I did not want to kill him. I could not commit to the idea of erasing the existence of my only offspring, the closest thing to a child I would ever have, and the love of my life besides. Besides, I had no real idea of how to accomplish this destruction of a nearly indestructible being, short of setting him afire or leaving him in the sun. He thought of killing me all the time, of course, filling my head with a constant display of morbid images; but in life, he seemed content to simply hurt and humiliate me as often as possible.

I considered returning to Geneva, with its serene rivers and sublime Alps; but I could not bear the idea of returning yet again to the setting of such bittersweet idleness and heartbreak. A great deal of my money was still housed there, but with the telegraph, I had access to it wherever I traveled. Paris was similarly discarded. I could not go back there; even seeing photographs of it, or reading about it, made me weep.

Wherever I chose, I would have to keep the location

secret, away from Daniel's prying mind. I developed methods for keeping my thoughts from straying to one or another particular destination when I knew that Daniel had the capacity to listen in; walking around reciting the rosary over and over again was a sure-fire way to drive his attention elsewhere, at least temporarily. As it was, I found that the only way I could keep my thoughts private was to have a great quantity of fresh human blood in my veins. I provided the Canal and the bushes of the Tiergarten with a fresh body almost every day. This horrid activity made Daniel proud of me, of course; as long as I was a fellow killer of humans, he was very pleasant to me. Daniel still slept beside me almost every day, and woke me up with a breakfast of sensuality. The surreal confusion of being kissed and suckled with a tender mouth one hour, and the next hour struggling to preserve life and limb against the same being, became the parameters of my daily existence.

He cruelly mocked me every time I went undercover to St. Hedwig's. "You can't even show your face in there anymore; why do you go? You can't go to confession if the priest doesn't know you're there. And the dried-up old women are afraid of you. You don't need any of the symbolic blood of Christ; you can drink the real thing."

I retaliated by decimating his harem of chorus girls, one at a time, and assigning the blame to him, whispering the accusations into the surviving call girls' perfumed ears. Unfortunately, this gesture did not have its intended effect; he simply coolly finished off the last three girls in a single night and stacked their corpses in my bathtub. "I am interested in your powers of interment," he said. "May I observe?"

In the meantime, I wrote letters, studied timetables, and kept my eyes on the newspapers.

* * *

The infamous Haus Vaterland reached the end of its life span, and of course Daniel and I had to attend its last hoorah. I was overwhelmed with sadness at the demise of the gaudy old place, but its time had come. With the Olympic Games consuming all of Berlin's attention and resources, a playground like Vaterland seemed a decadent relic of the past. Germany's finest was now the Sports-Palast filled with wholesome Aryan athletes and nubile girls performing dazzling synchronized callisthenics, not sleek Jewish sommeliers bearing trays of brimming glasses of champagne and nubile girls on a stage performing dazzling synchronized high-kicks.

The jazz bands played melancholy-drunk tunes, and the beer-garden tubas' notes deflated in the tasteless air. I stood and looked out over the beer garden, with only a handful of its tables occupied, and crossed myself and kissed my beads. "Don't do that in public," Daniel said testily. He had sat quietly, lost in his own reminiscences.

"I was thinking of Liesl," I said. "I used to meet her here all the time."

Daniel smirked without conviction. "Too bad your God cannot turn back time, isn't it?"

"I try not to spend my time thinking about what God cannot do, and concentrate on what He can do."

"Which is nothing," he spat. "Absolutely nothing."

I sighed, too weary for this tired debate. "I'm going for a walk," I said. "Alone, please."

As difficult as it was, I rose and walked away from him, leaving Haus Vaterland for the last time, irritation lightening my heavy heart. Daniel did not mourn Liesl; she had served her purpose as far as he was concerned, and had gotten what she had deserved. I had always toyed with the idea of writing a letter to Freddy in Geneva, explaining to him what had happened to her, but discarded the thought when I realized that I would have to explain everything and yet he probably still wouldn't understand. The past was past, and best forgotten by those able to do so.

I went for a long walk through Mitte, revisiting the official buildings and boulevards that I had once wandered in an attempt to acclimatize myself to a new city; now I saw it through new eyes, and more than anything I wished to erase it from my memories. I told myself as I passed each landmark, *I have finished here. I shall not see this again. I am going away.*

I did not return to my flat until nearly dawn, but I was not in the least bit tired; rather, I was worried that I would miss a day of sleep again if I was unable to cleanse my mind of concerns. My flat was candlelit, which I always enjoy, but my pleasure evaporated at the sight of Daniel, seated cross-legged in the center of my floor, shirtless, with my crucifix on the ground in front of him. He hummed a popular song to himself as he painstakingly pinned the bloody, tattered wings of a dead pigeon to the upright bar of the cross. The pigeon's gullet had been stuffed with bread, its twisted little feet bound together with black thread.

Daniel looked over his shoulder and raised his hand in a friendly wave. "Hello, darling, did you have a nice time?" I heard the last nail pierce the damp meat of the wing. "Heil Hitler," he added.

Some moments passed before I could speak. "No—! Not again, Daniel. Please. Haven't you learned anything? Why must you do this?"

I reached for my crucifix, but he snatched it away from me, spattering blood on the rug and the trailing bedclothes, laughing. "Mine! It's mine now. I changed it. It's now a piece of art, and you no longer have any ownership of it."

"A piece of art?" I repeated numbly.

"I rework the outdated, irrelevant symbols of the old

world. Now this meaningless object is meaningful and concrete." He smiled indulgently at the dead, oozing dove. "The world has changed," he said. "It would befit you to change with it."

I might not be able to kill him, but at that moment, I had to try.

My foot lashed out at his face, but he ducked and only the toe of my shoe grazed his forehead. He swept his arm under my bed, shoving the crucifix into the shadows. I used my active foot to pin his leg down to the floor, pressing down on his knee joint until he yelled in pain and the joint cracked. I laughed at him. "You can't hide under there," I said. "Give my cross back and I will let you go. And then you will leave here and not come back. I am finished with you. This experiment is a failure."

He glanced at me over his shoulder, and I have never, before or since, seen such infernal evil in a creature's eyes. I rocked back a fraction of an inch, blinking, astonished by the gaze, and he yanked his leg loose from under my foot.

He flung himself at me and punched me in the chest. But it was no ordinary blow. He had held a long spike of wood in his fist, grabbed from its hiding place under my bed.

He, too, had kept a secret.

The wood penetrated my chest, puncturing my heart, and emerged through my back. He stood back and stared at me, eager to witness the results, spittle glistening at the corner of his mouth.

I stared down at the stake—whittled from a stick of furniture, no doubt—with the lathe marks still on the end sticking out of my chest. It had been a fast, dirty whittling job; I could feel the sting of splinters inside me each time I drew breath. The whole of existence had gone very calm and quiet; I could clearly hear Daniel's excited heartbeat vibrating the air of the room, a clock ticking in the next apartment, the song of birds in the Tiergarten. My heart, of course, had stopped.

But what he did not understand was that my heart did not animate my blood; my blood was in command of all. My human physiology was a mere shell for the true sentience and indestructibility of the blood, and the energy, the will, the spirit, that the blood contained.

"No," I said to Daniel patiently, "that doesn't work."

I pulled the stake from my chest and flung it away, holding my hand to the wound that had cored me. I expected a gush, but my fingers caught a mere trickling ooze. The lack of excessive blood was more sickening to me than a flood would have been; indeed, the wound was already regulating, tightening itself. I gasped from the stinging of the splinters left inside, but I remained upright and mastered my pain.

Daniel's eyes were now wide and scared. Yet he did not (or could not) avoid the slicing kick that drove my foot into his testicles and drove his testicles into his guts, crumpling the fine bone shelf of his pelvis like a paper cup.

He crumpled like a doll made of tissue paper.

While he lay prone on the ground, I stamped my heel into the base of his spine, then again at his kidneys, and again at his neck, until I heard the backbones snap; and while he lay, paralyzed and choking on his breath, I brought my heel down on the back of his head, on his wrists, on his ankles, till he lay utterly shattered and senseless.

Breathing shallow, measured breaths, I seized the briefcase with which I had come to Berlin and threw a change of clothing, my notes, and my Bible into it. Tears ran freely from my eyes, washing some of the pain away from me, maintaining my control over my body, but barely; Daniel sent me all his pain, and then some. But I was the stronger, always. I checked the contents of my wallet; I had marks in plenty. Daniel lay twitching on the ground, keening faintly, his body a twisted mass of broken bones. Yet somehow—perhaps fired by the will in his own blood—he still managed to speak.

"I'll kill you," he gasped. "I'll kill you . . ."

"No, you won't," I said, wiping my wet face on my sleeve. "I am going. I don't want to see you, I don't want to hear you, I don't want to hear *from* you. Good-bye."

I dashed outside and hailed a taxicab driving slowly down Bellevue Strasse, dawdling on its way to one of the hotels nearby. I jumped in as soon as it halted and tossed a fifty-mark bill at the sleepy, astonished driver. "Potsdamer-Platz," I said, "as fast as you can go."

I quaked in the backseat of the automobile, glancing anxiously at the salmon skies to the east; the sun was due very shortly. But I had been studying the timetables for all the trains leaving Berlin, and I knew I could just catch the industrial train out of town, a few minutes after sunrise.

He would recover soon, and I wanted to make sure I was outside the city, in daylight, when he did. I clung to my rosary and prayed, *If I escape this, I will be devout, I will be pious, I will praise God with every breath.*

The changing station hummed with activity even at this early hour, with workmen attaching the massive engines to the freight cars, inspecting the contents of the cars, and changing work shifts. I looked quite out of place, staggering in my camel-hair coat and felt hat, with my hand clasped to my chest, but no one apprehended me. I struggled to stay calm and think clearly, to access the concrete thoughts of these workmen, and to keep them relaxed as well, even as the splinters wriggled in the heart that had recovered enough to pulse, however weakly and irregularly.

In my apartment, at the edges of my ethereal perception, Daniel sobbed and writhed in helpless agony. He struggled so violently to keep transmitting his pain to me that he could not heal. *Save your strength*, I said to him, *and release me*.

The freight train before me was destined for Hamburg. The last car of the train was empty, as the expected shipment of furniture had been delayed; the other cars were filled with cheap textiles, dyes, and machine parts for shipbuilding. The train would arrive at six in the evening, just in time for supper and a pretty sunset, before they would have to go back again on the same route.

I envied the workmen their suppers and their sunsets as I convinced one of them to open the door of the empty car and admit me inside. He grumbled but complied, sleepily squinting at the golden rim of the sun peeking over the horizon. Without so much as a thank-you, I scrambled inside and huddled in the dusty gloom, my light-burned eyes streaming with painful tears.

"Please come with me," I said.

The workman, a rangy fellow of middle age, regarded me curiously, then climbed into the train car, closing the door behind him, and sat next to me on the floor. "You need something else?" he asked.

I sighed, and listened to the smooth, regular swish and thud of his heart. I envied him that, as well. "Yes," I said, "and I'm sorry."

Receive My Spirit

"From there," I said, "from Hamburg, I sailed for Liverpool. The separation of the sea, or my isolation on an island, gave me a great deal of comfort; and with the help of the train lineman, I was able to conceal my whereabouts from Daniel. My fear did not subside, however, and I only stayed in Liverpool for three nights before I sailed again, this time here, to Portsmouth." I sat back, and closed my eyes. My throat was tired from speaking.

Father Christopher blinked at me. "Can you still hear him?"

"Daniel? Yes, of course." I opened my eyes and gazed at the young vicar. He did not seem reassured. "It is only a whisper. But I can hear him, and I know that at times he can hear me. But he doesn't know where I am. That is what is most important."

"I should think so," Father Christopher said emphatically. "I shouldn't want him coming here."

"No," I said, "you mustn't worry about that."

"When the church received the letter from Father

Lichtenberg, seeking asylum on your behalf, we all had assumed . . ."

"You were told that I was a dissident, and an exile, due to my strong political and religious beliefs. This is true, is it not?"

"Just not in the way that I had assumed."

"You did a very compassionate thing, nonetheless. But if I had been a Jew, I would have been refused. I know that it's nothing to do with you; it is Britain who would prefer not to provide refuge for hundreds of thousands of dirty, godless Continentals. Yes, I know. I look into your heart and I see that if you had your way, every lost soul could find a home here in your parish."

"I think you may be judging Old Blighty too harshly," said Father Christopher, smiling at me.

"Ah, of course I am. I am one of those dirty Continentals; I have my own coarse ideals of human behavior." I sighed. "Don't listen to me; I am old and very tired, and my soul has been wrung out until it is dry." I shifted until I could bow my head and clasp my hands together, the rosary beads smoothly spilling over the tops of my fists. "Now. Ahem. For all of these sins and for those that have escaped my memory, I beg the pardon of God with my heart entire, and penance and absolution of you, my spiritual Father."

The priest sat silently for a long time, his mind in a turmoil as he considered what to say. "I hesitate to agree with your ideal penitence," he murmured at last.

"Have you another solution?" I asked. "I cannot change what I am. This is a transformation that cannot be undone, no matter how I pray. If there is to be a resolution, or another transformation, a cleansing, uplifting transformation, it must come from beyond the grave. There is no sufficient price for life but life. I am offering it, with your holy assistance, with the assistance of consecrated ground, with the fullness of love and faith in my heart . . . please. Father. I beg you— accept my contrition. Accept my confession and help me satisfy my obligations to God and to the world of the living."

He held his clasped hand to his mouth, his eyes searching the distances inside himself. "It could be done," he decided at last. "There is space in our crypt, where we . . . mean to inter the most prominent holy men . . ."

"The consecrated nature ought to insulate you and redeem me, don't you think? Now . . ." I stood up shakily, and Father Christopher rushed to steady me. "I want to take a last look at the lilies, and then I shall take to my bed. When you call for me again, I shall be . . . I shall be ready."

"May the Lord be with you," he said softly, squeezing my arm so gently I could barely feel it.

I leaned against him, eyes closing, a bitter smile threatening my face.

"And with your spirit," I replied.

It is all behind me now.

I am rocked, like an infant, in the arms of the Indivisible One, a knocking upon a great door audible in my mind.

Is it salvation? At last, has the Lord come to collect me, look upon me, judge me with His infinite knowledge, forgive me with His infinite love? At last!

The rocking becomes shaking, the shaking more violent. Yes, Lord, shake me to pieces, and remake me in Your true form.

And light pours in, and I am lifted, flying, with a pure purpose, moving with an intention so focused it could only be a product of Divinity.

I am in God at last.

Breath animates me as the Lord blew into the clay shell of Adam. And light—and light—

And details, creeping outward from the center, matter and objects becoming clearer, more solid. Doubt stabs me in the belly. Am I . . . ? Did I? What's happened?

I stand in the midst of rubbled bricks and splintered wood, dust swirling thickly about me. I wear the shroud in which I was buried. What light there is, is dim, coming from dusty, groaning immensity above.

My feet—and yes, my hands—are still the extremities of a monster. And I stand in the antechamber to the crypt. And the cathedral has been crushed and broken overhead, bringing the odor of death, smoke, and charcoal from above.

The enemy has unearthed me.

And I hold Father Christopher, still alive. The broken priest flops limply in my arms, like a hatchling squab fallen from its nest. I curve his rubbery arm across his chest, neatening his posture, apologetic and gentle too late. He raises one livid finger and points it at me. "Ricari," he whispers, his lips blue, "how can it be?"

His loose-boned neck bears a seeping wound, the size and shape of my consuming mouth.

"Oh, my Lord, no," I begged. "Please let me not have done this . . . oh God, please . . ."

I have destroyed him without even thinking—this man of God, this quiet and gentle young man, without even enough experience of smiles to have left lines in his face. I broke him like a toy and swallowed him like a bowl of wine. This individual, this human. My confessor. My friend. He is gone for all time.

Yet my eyes are dry.

I am still curious, my senses sharpened by hunger, still dumbstruck, still doubting the reality of what had happened.

Soft throbs of blood soak into my sleeve, filling my head with its Dead Sea odor. His blood smells like a distilled composite of all humankind, all its sweat and brine and minerals, alcohol and tallow. He dined on Yorkshire puddings one hour before coming here tonight, washed his neck without soap, had a nip of apple brandy.

He has tended me faithfully, and in secret, for three years, each night coming down to pray for me. This time, the bombers have come at nightfall, and the wing of the cathedral that housed the crypt has fallen victim.

"Father," I say, resting my forehead against his chilly hand, "please . . . I did everything I could, but the blood is stronger than I am . . . forgive me . . ."

"Ricari," he gasps again. "I forgive you." His eyes wane to thin white slivers between his eyelids. His lungs are filling with blood, then exhaling the blood into his mouth. His next words are only bubbles. Then he diminishes, as the soul drifts away, leaving his corpse an empty shell in my arms.

And now he is gone. With one last faint expiring sigh, Father Christopher Benedict leaves me, leaves everything, forever.

I long for tears to wash my eyes clean of the remorse, but to no avail. My body is not fooled. It knows, with an atomic knowledge, that I am damned, and there is no real point in weeping about that. I have burned my final bridge. I have demolished my last connection to this world.

There is nothing left now, my Lord, except me and thee. I commend my soul to your care.

Except—

There he is. I feel him far away, listening for me, always listening, never despairing, searching for his heart's desire. And I feel his pleasure and his triumph now, filtering through me, filling my mouth with the taste of his, filled with the scarlet sustenance without which I cannot survive.

Portsmouth, is it? I'll be right there. Wait for me.

And my mouth waters.